THE DUSTY ATTIC

Where The Future Meets The Past

Nancy and Frank,

May this story
capture your hearts!

Susan Elaine Pfeiffer

Susan Elaine Pfeiffer

ISBN: 9798542031583

Library of Congress Control Number: 2021915025

DEDICATED TO

My Husband and soul mate, Kenneth Pfeiffer,
who continues to inspire my writing!

My mother, Geraldine Johnson, for her support
and help in editing by book.

INTRODUCTION

They say that time waits for no man. Sometimes I wonder about that. Can two lonely, desperate hearts cry out and be heard hundreds of years apart? Can someone from the future who is used to all the modern conveniences and luxuries live in the past when the frontier of Tennessee was wild and untamed? This is the question that Sara Mathews and Nathan Chambers must answer when Sara wanders into an old dusty attic in an abandoned house and the unimaginable happens.

Chapter 1

Sara Mathews sat limp and motionless at her desk staring out her apartment window at nothing particular for over an hour. The sky was a washed out grey, and the steady drizzling rain tapped on the windowpanes and slowly dripped from the late summer leaves to the ground below. Void of any emotion or thought she rested her hands lifelessly on her computer's keyboard.

Meanwhile, Natalie Worth sat behind her desk dreading the thought of having to call Sara that morning. She knew that Sara was going through the worst possible thing a person could go through – the loss of a loved one. She stared out her office window now speckled with raindrops as she finished the last few drops of coffee in her cup trying to find the right words to say before picking up the phone.

Moments later Sara's phone suddenly rang, jolting her back to what she perceived to be the miserable existence she found herself consumed in: one of unbearable pain and loneliness. The phone rang multiple times before she found the motivation to answer it.

"Hello," she answered in a lifeless tone.

"Hello, Sara. This is Natalie Worth, your consultant with Whitney Publishing. Remember me? I know this is a difficult time for you, but we need to talk. As you well know, you owe Whitney Publishing at least one chapter in your new book by the end of this month or you will be in breach of contract," she stated, then wished she hadn't been so blunt. She knew instantly her statement must have sounded cold and uncaring.

At this point Sara completely tuned her out. She thought Natalie had no idea what she was going through and to be honest, she didn't really believe she cared. How could she possibly know how she felt losing her husband, Richard, after only two years of marriage to an IED along a roadside in Afghanistan? Sara's heart was so crushed within her that she was unable, or unwilling, at this time to entertain any thought about starting a new book, or want any interaction with anyone. She just wanted to be left alone.

"Hello, Sara. Are you there? Have you heard a word I've said?" Natalie hesitantly questioned.

"Yes, Natalie, I'm here. When would you like to meet?" she replied despondently. She resented her intrusion into her life. It seemed like it was all for the sake of money and a few written pages that she called.

"Well, since the weather today is horrid outside, why don't we meet tomorrow at that little Italian restaurant down the street from my office, around noon time? I'll treat for lunch while we talk about how we can help you to start writing again. I have a few ideas that I think you will like. How does that sound?" she asked trying to sound more friendly and upbeat.

"Fine. I'll see you tomorrow at noon," she said dryly and hung up the phone.

Sara went back to staring out the window as a sudden gust of wind made an eerie howling sound as it passed by only adding to her depression. She dreaded leaving her solitude even if it was supposed to be for her good. She picked up the photo of Richard that was sitting on her desk and ran her finger along his face and across his square jaw. As she gazed upon it she thought about all the plans they had made together for when he returned from Afghanistan. Their life together was just beginning she thought.

Now, in what seemed like a blink of the eye, it was over, and the hole it left seemed insurmountable.

There was no use in even trying to write right now. She didn't have a single thought that felt worthy of writing down. Her stomach was letting her know that whether she felt like it or not, she needed to eat since her last meal had been twenty-four hours ago. She stood gazing into a sparsely stocked refrigerator wondering what in the world she could fix without having to go to the store. Finally, Sara decided her only option was a fried egg sandwich with some potato chips she found stuffed towards the back of her pantry.

When she finished eating, she placed her dirty dishes in the sink to be washed later and started the dishwasher that was already filled to capacity, then turned on the TV and flopped on the sofa. It was all mindless chatter to her; just something to get her through the next part of the day that seemed to drag on endlessly. She didn't have to worry about how to get through the night, her doctor had prescribed sleeping pills strong enough to knock her out until morning.

It was mid-morning the next day when Sara crawled out of bed and realized she desperately needed to shower and wash her hair before meeting with Natalie - it had been a couple of days since she had even gotten out of her pajamas. She rummaged through the closet for something comfortable to wear after she showered, thinking she would probably be in them for a while if the last few days were any indication of how frequently she changed her clothing.

It was just minutes before noon when Sara saw the little Italian restaurant up ahead, and Natalie already sitting at a small patio table outside waiting for her. She let out a heavy sigh, and marched on towards her meeting knowing that she did not have much choice in the matter.

Sara was not the only one dreading this meeting. Natalie saw her walking towards her and also let out a heavy sigh. There was no way around it; this meeting was going to be awkward, but it was necessary.

"Well, I wasn't sure whether you would show up or not, but I'm glad to see you," Natalie said and stood and gave Sara a polite hug and then took her seat again.

"It's good to see you too, Natalie," Sara said, willing herself to be polite.

"Why don't we have lunch first, and then we can get down to business. Is that alright with you?" Natalie asked still feeling uneasy.

Sara just nodded. Conversation between the two of them was practically nonexistent except for a few polite comments about the weather. Both of them chose not to make eye contact until they had finished their lunch, but now it was time to get down to business. "Sara, I am so sorry for your loss, and I know that this is a very difficult time for you. I've spoken to the president of our company about your situation, and I think we have a proposal that might be acceptable to you. First of all, he has agreed for the time being, to give you an extension on your draft of the first chapter to your new book. I've also made a few phone calls and have confirmed that the cabin we own in Tennessee is available. It's located outside the small town of Madisonville in a beautiful, secluded but safe, forest with lush valleys and rolling hills, and plenty of fresh air."

Sara sat there listening, but did not say a word.

Natalie continued after an awkward moment of silence. "Don't worry, you will have a few neighbors not too far away should you need them. They own beautiful, expensive cabins in that area and frequent them on vacations and just to get away from the rat race. We normally send some of our writers there for a couple of months if they have writer's block and that usually seems to get them started again. But, we're willing to let you use it for longer, if needed, to help you through this difficult time, and hopefully help you find that spark to start writing again. The president has only agreed to do this because your first two books have been on the best seller list for quite a while. So what do you think?" she asked gently tapping her fingernails nervously on the table.

"I don't know what to say, Natalie. This is a lot to take in at one time. Will I have to move all my things, and what about my apartment?" she asked a little overwhelmed.

"No, you won't have to move any of your things, other than your clothing. The cabin is fully furnished and paid for. It won't cost you a penny to live there, but you will need to buy your own food which is something you would have to do here anyway."

"I need a little time to think about your offer. May I give you my answer tomorrow?" Sara asked still feeling like her mind was in a thick fog.

"Sure, take your time and think it over. Oh, did I mention that you would only be about an hour's drive away from your parents? I'm sure they would appreciate being closer to you, and you might find it a comfort to be closer to them," Natalie added as an afterthought.

Sara slowly nodded her head while thinking over what Natalie had just presented to her. It would be nice to have her parents closer; they were the only family she had now. It had been nearly six months since she had seen them after Richards's funeral, and she missed them.

Sara had moved to an apartment in Indiana after Richard was deployed, to be closer to her publisher. But, now it seemed more advantageous to be closer once again to family, and yet far enough away to pull her life together in a way that seemed right to her.

She said "good-bye" to Natalie and thanked her for everything she had done for her. Maybe she did care, but she couldn't possibly understand what she was going through, Sara thought to herself.

A deepening sadness and feeling of loneliness swept over her as she was driving back to her apartment and the thought of being there alone right now was more than she could bear. It felt like her whole world was spinning out of control. Her eyes drifted from the road to some children playing ball at the city park and decided to pull over and just sit for a while and watch. As she watched the children play she thought of the children she and Richard had talked about having - now that dream was gone.

The sun shone brightly as a cluster of clouds passed by and Sara noticed there was a path covered with a canopy of maple, ash, and dogwood trees beyond where the children were playing and she felt compelled to take a walk. The fresh air would be good for her after months of sitting in her apartment alone. She knew that shutting herself off from the world was not what Richard would want for her. He would want her to be happy and move on with her life. She was young, beautiful, intelligent, talented, and normally full of life, and she needed to make a decision on what direction she wanted her life to go. She was confused and troubled about how she was supposed to hold on to Richard in her heart, yet let him go.

As she walked along the beautiful nature path with its lush variety of green foliage and a sweet fresh aroma, she felt the tension and sadness being drained from her body and mind. She seemed at peace for the first time in months and her spirit started to soar once again within her, and then she suddenly felt guilty about feeling so happy. Sara wondered if she was going crazy; her emotions were all over the place and she broke down and wept inconsolably. Finding a park bench close by she sat down and gave way to the feelings that were tearing her apart. As time passed Sara struggled to regain her composure. If only she knew what was the right thing to do, the proper balance to strive for, because this was no way to live.

She was unaware that hours had passed as she sat there struggling with the conflicts within her. The sun was beginning to set and she knew she needed to start for home and quickly picked up her pace to get back to her car. When she arrived at her apartment building the outdoor lights abruptly came on and she was relieved to have made it back before it was totally dark outside. One thing Sara had always feared since childhood and that was the dark - it always unnerved her not knowing what might be lurking in the dark recesses around her.

She quickly went up the elevator to her apartment and when she touched the doorknob she stopped as if a force was keeping her from going inside. She stood there and thought, *"This is a turning point for me. I can either enter my room and go back to sitting by the window, or I can choose to move on and be strong once again. It's my choice, not my publisher's, nor my parent's, it's mine."*

Her hand finally turned the doorknob. She smiled for the first time in a long time as she entered the apartment. She had chosen to begin the healing process of mending her broken heart.

Chapter 2

Sara slept soundly for the first time since Richard had died. She awoke not dreading the day and that was a pleasant change for her. She laid there thinking about Natalie's proposal of using the company's cabin for several months and the more she thought about it the more she liked the idea. She stepped into her slippers and started for the kitchen; it had been some time since she made a fresh pot of coffee and a real breakfast. While eating scrambled eggs and a couple of slices of toast with guava jelly she decided to call Natalie and tell her that she would like to accept their offer to use the cabin.

Sara looked down at her pajamas and thought that this was just one more habit she needed to break and quickly dressed and washed the few dishes while keeping an eye on the clock. She waited until ten after eight to give Natalie a chance to settle in, then finally picked up the phone. "Good morning, Natalie. This is Sara Mathews. I've called to let you know that I would like to accept Whitney Publishing's offer to use the cabin."

"Good morning to you, too, and that is wonderful news. I'm so glad you decided to take us up on the offer," Natalie replied feeling a sense of relief.

"When would I be able to move in?" Sara asked excitedly.

"The cabin is ready and waiting for you. You can stop by today and pick up the keys if you wish," Natalie cheerfully responded.

"Really? That would be wonderful! I'll be down later this morning to pick them up. I will need to pack and give my parents a call and let them know I will be headed their way. Thank you so much, Natalie. I really appreciate all that you are doing for me," Sara replied joyfully.

"It was our pleasure. I'll leave the keys with the receptionist just in case I am out of the office. But, please give me a call when you get there and let me know everything is alright, okay?"

"Yes, I will. I'll probably stay with my parents a couple of days before going out to the cabin, but I will give you a call when I get there. I promise," she said.

Sara was excited about the possibilities that lay before her, and couldn't wait to start packing her clothes in suitcases and boxes. When she was satisfied that she had clothing packed for the fall and winter months she loaded them in the trunk and backseat of her car, then slid behind the wheel eager to get on with her life. It felt strange to be so happy, and when she caught herself, she automatically shut that feeling down as if it were somehow wrong to feel that way so soon after losing Richard.

She wasted no time picking up the keys to the cabin from the receptionist, and proceeded to the closest fast-food Mexican establishment she could find to grab a burrito to eat on the road for lunch while driving.

It would be a long five plus hour drive from Bloomington, Indiana to Knoxville, Tennessee where her parents lived. She could make it there in time for supper if she didn't make too many stops along the way. Setting the cruise control to where she wouldn't get any tickets, and plugging in her MP3 player with all her favorite rock-n-roll music downloaded, she was on her way.

Sara was singing "*Crying*" by Roy Orbison at the top of her voice when she pulled into her parent's driveway a little after five o'clock. She quickly wiped the tears from her eyes, like she always did every time she sang that song, and put a smile on her face. She didn't want her parents to think she had been crying over Richard, but he had been on her mind while singing that song – he was always on her mind.

Don and Becky had been looking out their front window watching for Sara when she pulled in, and hurried outside to greet her.

"We're so glad you made it here safely; we've missed you so much," her mother excitedly expressed as she wrapped her arms around her.

"Okay, honey, you can let her go now. Dinner is ready and I'm sure she's hungry and tired from the long drive. Besides, it's my turn to give our girl a hug," he said with a big smile.

"Hi, Dad," she joyfully responded and opened her arms wide to accept the warm, tight, hug she knew was on the way.

"Come on you two. I still have to put the garlic bread in the oven, and Don, I need you to put the food and drinks on the table," her mom asserted.

By the time Sara had finished her plate of spaghetti with fresh, homemade garlic bread, the fatigue from her long trip had set in.

"Mom, I'll help you clean up the kitchen, but first I need to take a shower or I'm afraid I'll fall asleep. Is that okay with you?" Sara asked, then yawned.

"I'll help your mom clean up. You go take your shower, and then if you're not too tired maybe you can tell us about this cabin you're going to," her dad said.

Sara lingered under the hot water pouring over her body; it felt so good and relaxing. It was too relaxing if she had any plans of spending time with her parents. She slowly turned the knob until the water was cold enough to almost take her breath away. When she had dried off and changed into her pajamas her parents were already seated in the living room with the TV on the nightly news. Her dad quickly turned it off and asked, "So, what do you know about this cabin you are going to?"

Sara sat in her favorite chair next to their fireplace and confessed, "Not much. I just heard about it a couple of days ago. I googled the address on the internet and it brought up a photo of the outside of it, but that was all. It looked very nice, and I hear it has all the conveniences you could want or need. I'm hoping the inside looks as nice as the outside. You'll have to come see for yourselves. After I get settled in, I'd love to have you both come over and spend the weekend with me."

"That would be great. I'd love to see the place for myself and make sure you'll be okay there all alone," her dad replied.

"How long did you plan on visiting with us," her mom asked.

"Well…I planned on staying with you all day tomorrow, but I am anxious to see the cabin, and where I can go in the area to buy food and supplies."

Sara could tell by their expressions that they were hoping she would stay longer; after all, they hadn't seen her in almost six months.

"I promise we'll see each other more often. I'm only about an hour away," she said hoping that would appease their disappointment.

Sara had spent nearly the last six months totally alone, and it was difficult to switch gears and interact with anyone for any period of time; even her parents. She still preferred to be alone while trying to sort out her feelings and get her life back on track.

"Sara, we understand your desire to get there and check things out, so don't worry about us. But right now your eyes are looking a little heavy to me, and I think you ought to get some sleep," her dad said.

"We'll have pancakes and bacon in the morning; and your dad's right, you can barely keep your eyes open," her mother said with a sympathetic smile.

"I am rather tired. I guess I will call it a night," she replied and gave them both a kiss before retiring to her room. Nothing had changed - it was exactly the way she left it the day she was married.

Sara woke to the smell of bacon cooking in the kitchen, and went to join her parents still wearing her pajamas.

"There she is!" her dad said with a big smile while pouring water into the coffee maker.

"How did you sleep?" her mom quizzed.

"Like a baby! I forgot just how comfortable my old bed was," Sara exclaimed.

"Have a seat. The first stack of pancakes will be ready in just a minute. You still use the powdered sugar instead of syrup, don't you?" her mother asked.

"Yes, I still prefer it," Sara replied and took a deep breath inhaling the delicious aromas of the bacon and coffee, and tried to decide which she enjoyed most.

"Everything smells so good. I haven't had a breakfast like this in a long time," she declared and took her seat at their small kitchen table.

As her dad poured her coffee he asked, "You did remember to bring your .380 handgun, didn't you? You'll most likely be isolated out there and all alone."

"Yes, Dad, of course I've brought my handgun," she said confidently, and then she thought for a few seconds and then rolled her eyes in disgust.

"You forgot to pack your ammo didn't you," he laughed. "The gun won't do you much good without the ammo unless you plan on throwing it at someone," he said with a playful grin.

"Hey, I was doing well to remember to bring my head!" she retorted a little on the touchy side.

"I know, dear. I was just teasing," he replied lovingly.

"I'm sorry, Dad. I know you were. It's just…"

"It's okay, honey. Don't give it another thought," he said and took his seat next to her.

Becky cut in on the conversation. "Why don't you both finish your breakfast before it gets cold? We can all go shopping later and get whatever she still needs."

"Leave it to your mom to be the practical one!" Don chuckled, and Sara winked at her mom as she tried to hide the grin on her face.

The distractions of a busy day of shopping and being with her parents were a welcome change from sitting in her apartment staring out the window. It was the first day that she hadn't cried since the death of her husband, and the love and comfort she received from her parents was like a healing balm.

The afternoon brought a sudden change in the weather that caught them off guard. It was getting colder by the second and the chill of the wind made them long for the comfort of their home as an early cold front settled in with drizzling rain.

Don was quick to start a fire going in the fireplace while Sara hurried and packed the items she just bought in the trunk of her vehicle. She rushed back inside chilled by the cold rain that coated her bare arms and found her mother in the kitchen with the pantry door open.

"What are you looking for, mom?" she inquired as she looked over her shoulder.

"For starters I'm looking for the hot chocolate, and then something I can fix for dinner," she replied.

Don quickly spoke up. "Honey, why don't we just order some Chinese food and have it delivered; that way you won't have to cook."

Sara smiled at her mother and nodded her head in approval.

"Are you sure you don't want me to cook one of your favorite dinners for you?" her mother asked.

"I'm sure, mom. I'd rather spend our last night together curled up by the fire and just enjoying our time together. However, we will take you up on your offer to make some hot chocolate while we wait."

It was very late when they decided to retire for the night. Sara laid in bed and thought about the wonderful time she spent with her family today. It occurred to her that for the first time since Richard's death her thoughts had not been focused on him alone throughout the day; she had her family around her to distract her. She pondered whether this was normal to be happy at times during her grieving process without feeling guilty about it. Now that everything was quiet and she was once again alone, her mind was free to think of Richard and how much she missed him lying next to her in bed. She reached for the extra pillow on the bed and wrapped her arms around its cool, soft pillowcase and closed her eyes. Sara tried hard to imagine that it was Richard in her arms. But, there was no warmth or tender response to her embrace and she buried her face in the pillow and cried. It seemed like an eternity since she had been held close to a man's warm body, and felt the passion of making love. She missed the smell of a man, his touch, and the look in his eyes before he kissed her, and wondered if she would ever find again the kind of love she had with Richard.

Sara was up early the next morning and quickly dressed and packed her suitcase. She was anxious to get going, but could tell that her parents weren't up yet; it was too quiet. Sara found herself drawn to the bedroom window. It was an all too familiar place to her back at her apartment, and once again she was just staring thoughtlessly out the window. After several minutes she realized what she was doing, and told herself this was not a healthy habit to continue. She had to move on and start living; not just existing. Sara felt in her heart that moving to the cabin for a few months was just what she needed to jumpstart a new life.

The sound of a squeaky bedroom door hinge let her know that her parents were finally up and on their way to the kitchen. She gave them a couple of minutes, then hurried down the stairs and stopped short of the kitchen and took a deep breath. She did not want to give the impression that she was anxious to get on the road and wanted to avoid any hurt feelings about her not wanting to stay with them for a couple more days. Sara loved her parents deeply and considered inviting them to drive out to the cabin and spend the day with her there. That idea was something she decided to think over during breakfast.

She entered the kitchen with a smile on her face and approached her dad and gave him a big hug and whispered, "I love you, Dad. You're the greatest."

"I love you more," he smiled back at her.

Sara crossed the kitchen where her mom was already busy pulling eggs, milk, butter and bread from the refrigerator. When her mom stood up straight, Sara smiled at her lovingly and opened her arms wide letting her know she needed a hug.

"Oh, let me put these things down. I could sure use a hug too," Becky said and wrapped her arms around Sara.

"I love you so much, Mom. I don't know what I would do without you," she whispered in her ear as she held the embrace a few seconds longer.

"I love you too! I wish you didn't have to leave so soon, but I understand why you're anxious to get started," she sighed.

As her mother continued to prepare French toast Sara realized that her pondering on the idea to invite her parents to drive out to the cabin today was over before she had a chance to even start thinking about it. Her mother's melancholy mood gave her no choice but to ask them.

With everyone now seated at the table and ready to eat, Sara hesitantly asked, "How would you guys like to follow me out to the cabin today? You could check it out with me and maybe help me stock the kitchen with some food to last me awhile."

"Are you sure you would like us to join you? I kind of thought getting settled into your new accommodations was something you wanted to do on your own. We don't want to get in the way," he said.

"That's what I thought when I first got here, but now I think I would feel more secure if you were both with me to help check things out and get your opinions."

"Then we would be more than happy to join you," her dad stated enthusiastically.

When breakfast was finished and the dishes were done, Sara loaded her suitcase into the back of her car and waited for her parents to finish getting ready for the day's journey.

The hour's drive to Madisonville went by quickly for Sara. Only the audible directions from her cell phone interrupted her many tumultuous thoughts. She spotted a grocery store just ahead and pulled up to the front of the building and waited for her mom and dad to pull up alongside of her.

It took a full hour to buy everything they thought she would need to keep her supplied for at least a couple of weeks. Once the groceries were loaded into her parents' car they continued their short drive out to the cabin.

The paved road turned into a dirt road as they wound their way through the rolling hills and forest, past beautiful, expensive cabin style homes. They came to a fork in the road and the GPS directions told them to turn to the left and follow the little dirt road to the end.

Sara caught a glimpse of the cabin up ahead and slowed down on the slightly bumpy road until she reached the parking area in front of it. She sat there staring in amazement at the magnificent cabin that was being loaned to her free of charge by her publishing company for the next couple of months.

Don and Becky quickly got out of their car and just stood there staring at the cabin in disbelief.

Sara joined them giggling and said, "Can you believe it? I never could have imagined in a million years that the cabin would be this spectacular!"

"It is that," her dad said still shaking his head in disbelief. "Well, let's get the groceries inside and take a look around."

They each grabbed several bags as Sara fumbled for the keys on their way to the front door. Once they entered, all they could keep saying was "WOW".

The inside of the cabin was just as beautiful as it was on the outside. Everything went together: the color scheme, the cozy plush furniture, the photographs beautifully matted and framed on the walls, and tasteful accent pieces placed around the room. Sara was amazed that the cabin was ever unoccupied; it must have been a well-guarded secret or every author would be wanting to use it.

After the groceries were put away and Sara's clothing was unpacked and either hung up in the walk-in closet or placed in the large dresser, they all took a seat in the living room to talk.

"Sara, this is a beautiful place you're staying in, but I have great concerns about you being all alone out here. What happens if you get sick or hurt? Do you even get cell phone reception out here? You know, there could be wild animals, or even worse, dangerous people looking for an easy target," he said with a scowl of concern.

Sara was a little peeved by her dad's negative comments and picked up her cell phone and said, "Well, let's see if I get reception out here. I'll call your house and see if I get the answering machine."

She called their number and was relieved when she heard it ringing and quickly put the phone up to her dad's ear just in time for him to hear the answering machine come on. "See, I get reception out here. Now you don't have to worry," she gloated.

"I'm serious, Sara. I want you to keep your handgun with you at ALL times, and remember if you draw your weapon, be mentally prepared to use it. One more thing, make sure you set the alarm system every night and every time you leave the cabin," he firmly stated.

"I promise, Dad. I'll be careful. Besides, I'm supposed to be inside writing a book, remember? How much trouble can I get into doing that?" she replied sharply, not liking being treated like a child.

"Okay you two that's enough. Honey, she has been living by herself in the city for some time now, and she has always been a cautious person since childhood. She'll be just fine," her mother said putting an end to their contentious conversation.

"I guess we've been told," Sara said jokingly, and flashed her mom a quick smile.

She watched as her dad tightened his jaw and looked away; for he commonly sulked when he felt he was not being taken seriously or his opinion fell on deaf ears. He just clammed up and said nothing for hours at a time, and Sara knew this. The only thing she could think of to nip his mood in the bud was to appeal to his stomach.

Glancing at her watch she announced, "Yikes! Mom, if you're planning on driving back to Knoxville before it gets too late, we had better get started on making some lunch."

"How about some of that corned beef for sandwiches and potato salad? That should hold us over until dinner, shouldn't it, honey?" he asked.

"It should," she replied. "Why don't you go wash up? It will only take us a few minutes to get lunch ready."

Sara was pleased that her tactics had worked. She hated to see her dad upset, but she just didn't want to add any more drama to her already confused world.

After lunch and a lot of safety warnings reiterated, she finally hugged and kissed her parents good-bye. She was alone once again, and the silence was enjoyable for the moment. She stood by the front door and scanned the large room for the perfect place to set up her laptop. She chose the seating area in the back part of the cabin that had large picture windows with a beautiful view of the valley. She determined that spot would be the most peaceful and inspirational for writing; at least that was her plan. She wasn't quite ready to start writing yet and closed the top to her computer and told it, "Don't give up on me. I promise I'll be back. I just need a little more time."

Sara heeded her dad's directives to keep her handgun with her at all times. She slipped her holstered handgun onto her belt and went out the back door to sit under the covered porch and decompress. She sank into a plush lounge chair and let out a heavy sigh. It felt good to sit in the sun on a cool day and enjoy the birds singing and observe the early subtle change in color of the leaves. It was so peaceful and relaxing that Sara fell asleep.

The sun had already set when an owl hooting in a nearby tree roused Sara from her sleep, and she was panic stricken when she found herself alone in the dark. Fear consumed her as she hurried into the cabin and locked the door and set the alarm. Her heart was pounding as she went and turned on the lights in the kitchen and living room, and told herself that she was alright and had nothing to fear. She was now safe and sound in her new home away from home.

But, she could not rest comfortably until she had checked out the entire cabin. Sara could hear her father's words to always carry her handgun reverberate in her mind and pulled her handgun from the holster and carefully turned on the lights before she entered each room. Once she was sure no one had slipped by her and was hiding in one of the rooms, she placed her gun back in the holster and breathed a sigh of relief as she proceeded to the kitchen. See rolled her eyes and shook her head when she realized that she had allowed her father over the years to turn her into a paranoid woman who pulled out a handgun at the first hint of danger. A cup of chamomile tea would help her relax she told herself as she prepared another sandwich for dinner. An hour had passed since her frightful event and she found herself wishing that her parents had spent the first night in the cabin with her.

Sara quickly dismissed the thought and got ready for bed; she was a grown woman for heaven's sake and she had better get used to the thought of being alone in the cabin.

Chapter 3

The sound of wood cracking outside awakened Sara before the sun peaked over the rolling hills. She wondered what had made the noise so close to her bedroom window and grabbed her robe and put it on. She pulled back the bedroom curtains just a crack to see if she could determine what had made the noise that woke her. There was a cluster of trees just to the east of the cabin and she strained to see if there was anything moving around, but it was still too dark outside to see much of anything.

Sara picked up her handgun out of habit and took it with her to the sitting room with the large picture windows. She continued to stare at the small grove of trees and was happy to see that the sky now had a pale tint of pink and orange to it. She knew it wouldn't be long before the sun's rays gave off enough light for her to see what was moving around; if anything. She stood close to the edge of the window hoping she wouldn't be seen if there was someone out there, and scanned the valley until her eyes rested once again on the small cluster of trees.

A smile came to her face. There in the shadows was a family of deer grazing at the edge of the tree line. She let out a sigh of relief when she heard another stick of wood crack under the feet of the buck and felt a little silly being so jumpy over nothing, and decided it was safe to make some coffee and started towards the kitchen. Sara could see through the windows that the morning sky was intensifying in color and quickly fixed a bowl of cereal and hurried back to the sitting room to watch her first sunrise at the cabin. It was spectacular and she wished that Richard had been there to enjoy it with her.

She decided to take an early morning walk and explore her new beautiful surroundings. As a writer she knew that her best ideas came to her when she was busy doing something totally unrelated to writing. Her inspiration could come from anywhere and she was eager for fresh ideas; maybe something totally different in the type of books she had written before. She dressed in layered clothing knowing that she could peel off the different layers if it warmed up, and of course she had her handgun close by her side. She packed her small backpack with her cell phone, some water and protein bars in case she got hungry after such a light breakfast, a snake bite kit and a tactical flashlight that her dad had also taught her to carry on hiking trips, then set the alarm system and closed the door.

Sara stood in the front yard looking in every direction trying to decide which way she wanted to start walking. She would be less likely to encounter any people if she walked to the east since her cabin was at the end of the road and turned her head as if she was getting ready to speak to someone.

"Richard, are you ready to go on a walk with me? I'm in need of a little adventure," she said out loud and then smiled as if she could actually hear Richard respond to her.

Sara started walking and soon passed through the small cluster of trees where the deer had been grazing in the early morning hours. When she was through to the other side all that lay before her was a green grassy meadow with patches of pink, white, and yellow wildflowers for the next half mile or so, and she thought about picking some on her way back to the cabin. They would look beautiful in a vase on the living room's coffee table. After she crossed the meadow, ahead of her was a rolling fairly steep hill covered in trees that had faint hues of autumn color starting to show. As she continued her walk she could tell that she was walking on a steady incline as her leg muscles began to feel the burn. It had been months since she had any kind of exercise at all since she had mostly been inside her apartment staring out the bedroom window.

Sara was now breathing heavily as she slowly made her way up the hill and decided to take a break long enough to drink some water as she gazed around in the direction in which she came. It was alive with color and beauty from where she stood. The air was cool and refreshing as she caught her second wind to continue on. The trees and underbrush were a little thicker than what was close to her cabin and she wound her way through them pushing the brush aside since there were no paths to follow.

After stopping several times to catch her breath and unhook her clothing that was caught on the brush, Sara was just on the other side of the ridge. She paused to see where she wanted to go next, and in the valley below she caught a glimpse of a building of some kind in a large grove of trees. She started again down the side of the hill and kept her eyes open for any sign of cars or people and saw neither; not even a sign that a road might have once led to the structure.

At the base of the hill she found a mound of rocks that she could climb up on and sit while catching her breath and check out the structure she had seen coming down the hill. It appeared to be a very old house that looked like it had been built hundreds of years ago, and hadn't been lived in for a very long time, and wondered how it was still standing. It should have rotted and collapsed years ago.

Her fascination with historical sites and especially the changing architectural styles over the past couple hundred years confirmed in her mind that this house must have been built in the mid to late 1700s by a fairly wealthy family, for most homes on the frontier were log cabins.

From where she sat it looked like it had a stone foundation and beautiful stone steps leading up to the front porch and a door that now seemed to be coming off its hinges. The large covered porch that stretched across the front of the house must have been beautiful when it was built, but now she could see warped floor boards and the ornate railing around it had broken apart in many places. The roof that covered the porch was missing shingles and had holes through it. She noticed the wood on the first and second floors were badly weathered and more than a few of the boards had pulled free of the nails that had once held them in place. You could see gaps in the wall. Sara loved the dormer style windows on the second floor and attic; they had always been her favorite, and had hoped to one day live in a home that had them even though they were no longer in style. The glass in most of the windows was either broken or missing altogether, and she wondered how the house had withstood the rain and snow this area received. There were also chimneys of brick on either side of the house and one along the back wall that were in need of repair. They were partially crumbling around the top and she wondered how they had managed to stand at all after all this time had passed.

Sara removed her light jacket as it was warming up nicely as she sat admiring the grand old house and pondered what it must have been like to live in the time period when the house was built. What were the people like that first lived there? What did they do for a living? Were there Indians in this area that they had to deal with? Did they have to grow all of their own food or was there once a town close enough to buy food? How did they obtain the materials, such as the cut lumber and glass windows, way out here in the wilderness? Most houses would have been just rustic log cabins. Why wasn't this old house bought many years ago and restored? These were all questions that ran through Sara's mind as she sat there studying every feature of the old weathered house.

She was hesitant to go any closer to the house. She was leery of what kind of creatures might be living inside, and whether it was structurally sound enough to walk around inside. Being alone on her hike she was afraid that she might fall through a floorboard and injure herself and there would be no one around to help her. She decided that it was time to return to her cabin.

She had had enough adventure for one day. Besides, she had a long walk back to the cabin and her legs were already tired and a little sore. She stood and looked up the hill and it seemed insurmountable at the moment, but knew she must get started no matter how she felt if she wanted to make it back before dark.

When she finally reached the summit she took out a protein bar and a bottle of water and stood there until she had finished them both, and was relieved that there was still plenty of time for her to make it back to the cabin while it was daylight. She spoke to Richard once again and asked him what he thought about her discovery of the old house as she slowly made her way back. She carried on her discussion with him until she reached the end of the grassy field, even though she knew that it was all in her mind, but still it gave her a sense of peace. She was almost home now and began to think about what she was going to fix for dinner, but being so tired the only thing she really wanted was a hot shower and to change into something comfortable and to put her feet up.

Sara stomped her black leather hiking boots on the doormat to get the dirt off as she fumbled through her pants' pocket to find the key to the cabin's front door. Stomping her feet one last time she stepped inside and quickly turned off the alarm system and then just as quickly turned it back on and flopped her backpack on the kitchen countertop. It was a little early for dinner but Sara was hungry after such a long walk especially after only having a protein bar and a bottle of water. She opened the pantry door and stood there searching for something for dinner that would be filling but quick to make. After moving a few things around, Sara found a can of chunky beef soup that could be easily microwaved and knew that she had bread and butter in the refrigerator that would help fill her up if the soup was not enough.

Feeling much better after eating, her sore muscles were calling out to her for a hot shower and wouldn't take "no" for an answer. The hot water felt wonderful running down over her sore aching muscles and she lingered there until the room was fogged with steam then quickly dried off and slipped into her soft flannel pajamas. She took her towel and dried the bathroom mirror then stood there staring at her reflection as she brushed her hair and suddenly felt lonely being all by herself in the cabin. It had been nice talking to Richard on her walk, but she knew that she had only imagined his part of the conversation to keep from sinking back into the depression she had fought so hard to overcome.

The air felt chilly after taking a hot shower and she quickly passed through the living room to the kitchen to make some hot chocolate to help warm her as she curled up in the soft leather chair by the fireplace. While sipping her hot chocolate her thoughts wandered back to the old house she had seen earlier today. She was disappointed in herself for not going inside; she had let fear keep her from entering and looking around. Now she was consumed with curiosity, and decided she would go back tomorrow and explore the inside of the old house that time had forgotten. She felt strangely drawn to the old place and remembered how it seemed to call to her in a deep, desperate, and hauntingly saddened voice to go inside as she sat there on the outcrop of rocks studying it. It was an eerie feeling that made her uncomfortable, and yet it felt so compelling.

It was late now and Sara winced as she stood up, painfully aware of every muscle in her legs and hoped that a good night's sleep would cure what was ailing her. She crawled between the cool sheets and looked at the photo of Richard, then turned off the light and could have sworn she heard that deep, desperate, voice whisper to her again. She quickly dismissed it, thinking it was just her overactive imagination after a long and strenuous day and pulled her comforter over her.

She slept soundly that night and when she rolled over on her side to look at the clock it was already 8:00 AM.

"Good heavens, I should have been up an hour ago," she said and quickly jumped out of bed and dressed for her second trip to the old house. She was extremely pleased that her legs were not as sore as when she went to bed last night and hoped that today's walk would be easier for her.

Breakfast would be a hearty one: scrambled eggs, with bacon and raisin toast and a large cup of coffee. When she was finished she hurried and refilled the supplies in her backpack and headed for the garage in the hopes of finding a good walking stick. Quickly scanning the garage she found a good sized one standing up in one of the corners that had been left behind by one of the previous writers using the cabin and placed it with the other items she was taking with her.

Her father had taught her well on how to prepare for a hike in the wilderness, especially when you were alone. She went through her mental checklist and made sure that her cell phone was fully charged, her handgun was loaded and in its holster on her belt. The backpack was stocked with her flashlight, food and water, and her snake bite kit, and now all she had to do was set the alarm.

As she started walking in the direction of the old house she realized there was one thing she had forgotten to do, and that was to let someone know where she was hiking to and when she would return. Sara hesitantly called her dad, hoping he would not give her a hard time about hiking alone and was relieved when it went to voice mail and left him a detailed message promising to call him when she returned.

In a hurry now to return to the old house she walked much faster than she had the day before. It wasn't long before she reached the summit of the hill overlooking the house and took several moments to look around to make sure she was alone and then slowly started down the hill watching her footing.

Arriving at the stone steps she surveyed the wood planks of the porch to make sure they were sturdy enough for her to walk across before she stepped onto them. Feeling fairly sure they would support her weight she approached the front door that was partially unhinged and pushed hard with her shoulder several times as it scraped across the weathered floorboards.

Sara took a deep breath and silently said to herself, *"Well, here goes nothing,"* and stepped inside. She stood cautiously just inside the doorway as she gazed around the large room looking for any four-legged creatures who might have made the old place their home. Everything was layered in thick dust, and cobwebs hung in all the corners of the room which had a musty odor. There was no furniture in the room, and Sara tried to imagine what the room would have looked like a couple of hundred years ago. There was a very large hearth on the left side of the room with a beautifully carved wood mantle above it. Sara realized that this room was probably the kitchen, dining room, and living room all wrapped up in one, and was thankful for all the modern conveniences she enjoyed, especially in the kitchen.

There was a staircase to the right that led to the second floor and attic, but before she ventured up there she wanted to check out the room on the far right side of the house. The door was no longer there, but she could tell where the hinges had been hung. She carefully entered the room and assumed it was the master bedroom because it once had a beautiful fireplace with smooth river stones that now had some of the mortar and stones missing, and once again a beautifully carved mantle. Sara ran her hand along the mantle and admired the workmanship of the carvings and wondered if the owner had carved it himself. She was surprised at how well the wood had held up after all these many years. Once again there was nothing sitting on the weathered floor except dust and a few wooden pegs that had obviously fallen out of the wall, and had been used for hanging clothes or hats she presumed. The windows on two sides of the room had either missing or cracked panes of glass that had a slight distortion to them as she looked out at the view they might have enjoyed.

Sara was now determined to check the upstairs, and as she approached the staircase she noticed a small room behind it and took a quick look inside. There were cobwebs hanging everywhere and she noticed that there had once been shelves along the three sides of the walls for there were rotted pieces of wood lying on the heavily dusty floor. This must have been some sort of pantry she thought as she made her way back to the foot of the staircase. She was uncertain about attempting to climb the old wooden steps, especially after she had seen what had happened to the shelving in the pantry. Sara place her foot on the first step, took a deep breath and let out a sigh as she put her full weight on the step. It held, so she carefully proceeded up the staircase testing each step. The last thing that she wanted was to go crashing through the steps injuring herself with no one around to help her.

When she reached the top of the stairs she noticed how low the ceiling appeared. She estimated it couldn't be more than inches over seven feet tall. There were two small bedrooms off each side of the hallway, and once again there were no furnishings in the room, just dust and cobwebs. She did notice that there was some rotting of the wood ceilings and in places on the floor and decided not to enter any of the rooms. On her way back to the top of the staircase she noticed what looked like a piece of cloth cord hanging from the ceiling. She was curious and went to take a closer look. There was indeed a cord that was hanging from the weathered boards and she could tell that it had been much longer at one time. Sara suddenly noticed that the wood ceiling had boards that seemed out of place. There was more of a gap around them and they were shorter than the rest of the wooden boards.

She stood there thinking about what all of this meant. It was a mystery to her. As she decided to go ahead and start carefully down the staircase a thought popped into her mind. Could that cord once have pulled down a staircase that led to the attic? Sara was now excited and determined to see what might possibly still be tucked away in the attic. She told herself that it would probably be just like all the other rooms in the house – empty, but she had to know for sure!

Sara returned to where the short cord was hanging from the ceiling, and studied the boards to see how the staircase would have been lowered. *"Come on, think,"* she said to herself. As she continued to study the boards she noticed a small hook inserted into the wood at what would be the end of the staircase. She surmised that the cord was once long enough to pass through this hook and long enough to grab hold of and pull it down. So how was she going to lower the staircase? She was afraid to jump up and down on the old floorboards in hopes of grabbing the cord, but she saw no other way since there was nothing in the house to stand upon.

She walked back to where the cord was hanging down and held her breath as she stomped her foot really hard several times to make sure the boards would support her weight. Sara stood there and questioned herself; was she brave enough, or possibly stupid enough, to risk jumping up to grab the cord? She reasoned that the ceiling was no more than a couple of feet above her and having played volleyball all through high school and college, she should be able to jump high enough to reach the cord even though it was very short.

"Come on, where is the adventure in you?" she said to herself and continued, *"okay, on the count of three, jump!"* She took a

deep breath, counted to three, then jumped. Sara missed the cord on her first attempt and was determined to try once again. She jumped and grabbed the cord which quickly broke off in her hand. "Damn!" she said out loud and quickly put her hand over her mouth, as if someone might have heard her, for she rarely swore. *"Now what am I going to do?"* she asked herself.

Frustrated and hungry Sara decided to take a break and sit on the stone steps to the porch and eat her protein bar and drink her bottled water. It was a beautiful late summer day and the sun's rays felt good after being inside the cold, damp house.

She now had a decision to make. Did she find a way to lower the staircase to the attic or did she call it a day and return to the house when she had figured out how to do it. Sara looked at her backpack to see if there was any way to use the straps to latch on to the hook and pull it down, but determined that the straps were too wide; they would never fit inside the hook. *"What else can I use,"* she thought and looked at her belt with the holster on it.

"Maybe, just maybe, I can get the buckle to slide onto the hook. It looks like it's thin enough to work, so what am I waiting for?" she thought with great anticipation of it working. She unfastened the buckle and pulled the belt through the loops on her jeans and put her handgun in her backpack for the time being. She carefully walked across the porch as the boards squeaked with every step she took and cautiously made her way up the staircase to the second floor. Staring up at the hook her enthusiasm waned as she considered the odds of being able to jump up and slip the buckle unto the hook. *"Well, it's worth a try,"* she said to herself and positioned the buckle in her hand so that the narrowest part would have the best chance of actually latching onto the hook. Her first jump was a near miss, and with great resolve she jumped once again and this time the buckle latched onto the hook. As she landed on the floor the staircase came part way down with her. "Yes," she yelled out, and began to pull on the belt until the staircase touched

the floor and removed her belt from the hook and pulled it through the loops of her jeans.

The steps were covered with a mixture of dust and sand, and a few shingles from the roof as she started her slow ascent up the stairs. Suddenly the hairs on the back of her neck stood on end, and a slight breeze coming through the missing shingles on the roof seemed to whisper to her. Sara took a deep breath and shook those thoughts and feelings from her mind. With every step she took the sand started to diminish which seemed odd to her, and as she neared the last step she froze. The surreal sensation that gripped Sara's body and mind was like nothing she had ever experienced and she suddenly felt lightheaded and gripped the handrail. What she was seeing was impossible. She wouldn't be able to explain what was happening before her eyes in a million years. Sara stood there in fear and disbelief, and hardly able to take a breath as she watched mystified as the wooden steps changed before her very eyes. Not only did the steps look like they had just been built with fresh cut wood, the musky odor that had once filled the house now had the scent of pine. Sara's curiosity outweighed her fear as she slowly took the next step until she could see into the attic itself. She froze once again leaning up against the now firm railing of the staircase and wondered if she was losing her mind, or whether there was something in the air that was causing her to hallucinate. Her brain was trying hard to catch up with what she was seeing. She struggled to assure herself that she was not in any danger, and that she had to get to the bottom of what was happening.

Standing in the entrance to the attic, the sun coming through the window behind her illuminated the objects that lay before her. *"Why are these things here? There is nothing in the entire house, and why do they look as if they are new?"* she asked herself still bewildered and confused. Her first thought was to run as fast as she could out of the house and back to the safety of her cabin, but she might never find out what caused this phenomenon if she did that. She must stay.

Something told Sara to turn around and look out the attic window. What was just a grove of trees around the house, now had crops planted as far as she could see out the window, and there were two small wooden crosses under a small grove of trees fifty feet from the back of the house. She questioned herself - had this been there before and she just didn't notice it? Was she so consumed with the house itself that she failed to look at the land around it? She was sure of nothing at this point so she turned her attention to those things which had first caught her eye.

Sara slowly moved through the attic and studied each object with great curiosity. Along the side of the attic was a small, wooden, handmade rocking horse, obviously made for a very young child, and next to it was a good sized wooden chest. Sara opened it and inside were beautiful dresses in silk and lace neatly packed away. As she dug deeper into the chest there were also dresses of linen and cotton with aprons and some with little capes across the shoulders, and some with lace around sleeves that came to the elbow. When she finally reached the bottom of the chest she found stockings and shoes – these were all clothes that would have been worn hundreds of years ago she thought. Sara closed the chest and moved on to find a wooden crate of hand carved toys of different animals, and a beautiful rag doll made out of the prettiest material.

Suddenly Sara stopped what she was doing and remained quiet as she strained to listen, for she was sure she heard voices on the porch of the house. She found the courage to stand up and moved quietly to the attic window and looked to see if she saw anyone moving around outside. As she peered out the window the oddest thing happened. Suddenly the fresh pine scent was gone and the attic had that musky smell. Sara glanced down at the floor and it was covered with dust and sand. Once again her heart seemed to stop beating and she was terrified, too frightened to turn around and look behind her.

"Come on, you can do it! On the count of three turn around," she said to herself. *"One, two, three,"* and Sara quickly turned around and everything was gone; the attic was empty!

This time, Sara ran down the now weathered steps giving no thought to the fact that she could have fallen through them. At the bottom of the staircase she grabbed her backpack on the run and slung it over her shoulder and continued running until she made her way out the front door and across the rigidity porch.

Sara continued running until she reached the bottom of the hill and stopped for just a moment to catch her breath in the warm humid air. She eagerly made her way halfway up the hill until she felt safe enough to turn and look behind her. Sara was stunned. There were no crops in the ground only a grove of trees surrounding the house. Why had she seen the crops so vividly?

Sara's bewilderment and confusion drove her on. She must get back to her cabin; possibly whatever was causing these hallucinations would go away and she would be in her right mind again.

She was exhausted when she reached the bottom of the hill and stopped just long enough to take a drink of water and catch her breath as the sun beat down upon her. She trudged through the grassy field willing herself to take one step after another. The thought of picking the colorful wildflowers did not even enter her mind. All she could think about was getting back home.

Chapter 4

Sara had been so exhausted when she reached the cabin that she dropped her backpack just inside the front door and went straight to her bedroom and crawled into bed; shoes and all. She slept soundly until it was dark and when she looked at the clock on the nightstand she wondered if it was seven in the morning or seven in the evening. Her mind was still in a fog and that greatly disturbed her. She laid there wondering if everything she was remembering was just a dream she had, or if it had really happened; she really didn't know. She looked on the nightstand for her phone for it would tell her if it were AM or PM but it wasn't there, and she tried to remember where she left it.

When she sat up, suddenly she realized that she was dressed in her hiking clothes and shoes. She wondered why she would be dressed this way if she had gone to bed for the night. It made no sense…unless it was 7:00 PM and what she remembered had actually happened. She flopped back on the bed and covered her face and cried – she had lost her mind! The things she was remembering were impossible, and yet, they seemed so real.

Sara was jolted from her disturbed thoughts by the ringing of her cell phone. She pondered whether or not to answer it or let it go to voicemail, and then remembered she had not called her father to let him know that she was back home safely from her hike. She sat up and dried her eyes and took a deep breath. Her father must never know about what she had experienced today; he would have come immediately and taken her back home with him.

By the time Sara reached her cell phone it had gone to voicemail and hesitated a moment before calling him back. She needed to rehearse what part of the truth she was willing to tell him.

Sara finally tapped her dad's number on her phone and he immediately answered. "Sara, I thought you were going to call me when you got back from your hike. Is everything okay?" he questioned.

"I'm sorry, Dad. I meant to call you right away, but I was so tired that I thought I would just sit for a few minutes and then I fell asleep. But don't worry, everything is okay. It was just so beautiful outside today that I kept walking; a little too far I'm afraid," she replied hoping her answer would satisfy him.

"As long as you're okay, that's all that matters. Before I let you go, I was wondering if you've found any inspiration on these hikes you've been taking?" he curiously asked.

"I believe I have. As a matter of fact I'm tossing around an idea I came up with today. I hope to be writing again real soon," Sara declared.

"I'm happy to hear that. Well, I'll let you go get something for dinner, and we'll talk again real soon," Don replied.

Sara was glad her dad had called when he did. It enabled her to get some kind of control over her thoughts. She went to the kitchen to find something to fix for dinner. Finding a microwaveable dinner in the freezer, she decided that was the quickest way to go and popped it in the microwave. She lit a fire in the fireplace while her dinner was cooking, and when the microwave beeped she went and brought her dinner back to her favorite chair and the warmth of the fire. As she ate she tried not to think about the events of the day, but to no avail. How do you forget about things changing right before your eyes and then disappearing? When she was finished she set her food tray on the small table next to her, and rested her head back against the chair and closed her eyes in an effort to clear her mind of any thought.

What occurred at the old house today was not something she wanted to think about; she found it unnerving to not be able to come up with any reasonable explanation for what she had seen and experienced. She no longer felt like she had lost her mind, but did not rule out the theory that it was a hallucination caused by…caused by what, she thoughtfully pondered. She had to figure this out or it would torment her day and night. There would be no rest for her until she confronted her fears and the unanswered questions in her mind. No matter how insane it seemed, she had to return to the old house and search for answers.

Still stressed out and tired, Sara decided to turn in early that night. She found that in the quiet solitude of her bed was the best time to talk to Richard. He was always good to turn to when she needed advice, and she desperately needed it now.

"Oh Richard, I wish you were here. I miss you so much," she sighed. "You're the only one I can trust to talk to about this nightmare I'm going through. I don't know what to do," she sighed even louder. "What would you do, Richard? Would you go back to the old house in search of answers, or would you have nothing further to do with the place?" she desperately asked and waited for his answer. "I knew you would say that! I knew you would go back, but I'm not brave and strong like you are. I'm scared, Richard, really scared. You know I've always been afraid of what goes bump in the night, and afraid of situations where I feel I have no control at all. Oh Richard, I wish you were here to go back to that old house with me. I know you would protect me with your life," she uttered mournfully, and turned off the light on her nightstand; still confused as to what she should do.

Sara finally fell asleep only to find herself repeatedly waking wide-eyed and terrified from the same recurring nightmare. She was trapped in the old house attic that kept quickly changing back and forth from dusty and empty to new and filled with discarded objects and memories, and no way out. She screamed for help, and stomped on the floor, and banged on the window hoping someone would see or hear her and let her out. The only way out was to wake up.

When she could not take it anymore, she got up around 2:00 AM and went and made some hot chocolate and sat in her comfortable chair by the fireplace. Her mind was so troubled and depression now consumed her to the point where she alternated between praying and crying. She had no idea what time it was when she finally fell asleep in the chair, but she woke with the empty hot chocolate cup still in her hand on her lap.

She groaned from the pain in her back and neck from slumping over in the chair for so many hours. She wiggled back and forth trying to loosen up her aching muscles wishing she could find the strength or will to get up and make some coffee.

There was no way she was going back to the old house today she told herself. She needed time to recover from the terrifying ordeal of yesterday, and lack of sleep last night. Besides, she wanted to do some research on the computer to see if she could find any articles on the abandoned house. When was it built, who owned it originally, who owned it now, and were there any odd events reported involving the old house that was now falling apart?

Sitting alone with so many unanswered questions only added to her already troubled mind. The desire for her morning coffee finally kicked in, and motivated her to get up and get going.

Taking her coffee and a light weight blanket she went out on the back porch in hopes of enjoying the sunrise and eventually the warming rays of the sun. The cool morning air felt refreshing against her face, which was the only part of her body not covered by the blanket. Though she was tired, her mind felt free for the moment and she prayed it would last long enough to get her back on her feet to do the things she needed to do.

With the beautiful hues of the sunrise gone, it was time to get another cup of coffee and some breakfast to go with it. It was a start; at least she was moving and not just sitting around.

When Sara was finished with breakfast she took her seat behind her laptop where she had a beautiful view of the valley, and was happy to see that it was going to be a bright sunny day. She pondered where to start looking for information on the long forgotten house, and decided to start on "Google Maps". She typed in the address to the cabin she was staying in and brought up a satellite image of the area surrounding her cabin to see if any other properties were mapped out. Sara traced the path she had taken to the old house and found a large surveyed area, but there was no address or owners name on the property. A dead end for the time being. Next she searched sites on the history of Madisonville and the surrounding areas to see if they mentioned anything about the first settlers in that part of Tennessee. She read every article she could find and researched every name that was listed in those articles. It was like trying to find a needle in a haystack.

Frustrated over finding nothing useful in all her searching, Sara took a break and stretched her legs. Standing on the back porch with the sun shining brightly and the birds singing in the trees close by was like medicine to her. She inhaled deeply and unexpectedly an idea came to her. Why not take a trip to the county clerk's office and continue her search there. Maybe someone working there could help her find out who owned the house, and if she were real lucky maybe they had heard some old tales about the place. It was worth a try; she could always continue her search on the computer later.

She drove the twenty miles to the clerk's office with great expectations for she desperately needed some answers to what happened to her. When she arrived she found the records clerk in the back room filing documents.

"Hello, I'm Sara Matthews. I was hoping you could help me," she called out loudly.

The woman closed the file cabinet and returned to the front counter. "I'll certainly try. My name is Donna Lewis. How may I help you?" she inquired.

"I was hoping you could tell me who owns a piece of property close to the cabin where I'm staying. I can show you on a map the area I'm interested in."

"I have a map of the whole county here on the wall. Why don't you tell me the address of your cabin and well take it from there," she replied.

Sara gave Donna her address and she was able to quickly locate it on the large wall map. "Okay, where is the property you're interested in?" Donna asked with her finger still pointing to Sara's cabin.

Sara looked closely at the map and found it a little confusing judging distances on such a large map. She ran her finger east of her cabin and found the ridge she had hiked over and the valley below.

"This is the spot!" she said excitedly.

Donna went to a drawer and pulled out a property map of the area and laid it on a table and quickly located the area Sara had pointed to.

"I'm afraid this area belongs to the BLM," she said and looked up at Sara who had an inquiring look on her face.

"The BLM is the Bureau of Land Management, and it looks like this property was turned over to them for non-payment of taxes and abandonment," she said matter-of-factly.

Sara let out a sigh of disappointment. "Is that all you can tell me?" she asked disheartened.

Donna could see how disappointed she was and stopped to think of where she might find more information on the property. A smile came to her face and she looked at the map once again and wrote down the property number and went to a filing cabinet and started thumbing through the files.

"If we have any other information on the property it will be in this file," she said and asked Sara to join her at the table. Opening the file she started turning the pages and Sara sat there anxiously watching her hoping she would find some bit of information that would help her.

"Here, take a look at this," Donna said and leaned closer where Sara could look at it with her.

"I'm afraid the document is faded and it is very hard to read the handwriting, but from what I can tell the original owner died in 1786. The document never gives the name of the original owner; he probably settled there after the Revolutionary War. The property remained unsold until 1803, and a Mr. Thomas Lancaster bought it and abandoned it only two years later," Donna said with a scowl as she tuned some more pages. "There's a Xerox copy of the original handwritten statement from the county authorities of that time who stated that the man who bought the property and house was from New York. He brought his family out after he had made repairs to the house and they lived there for only two years then abandoned it and went back to New York. They claimed it was too isolated, and society in Knoxville too unsophisticated for them. The General Land Office took possession until the BLM eventually took over the property in 1946," she said and closed the file. "Was that of any help to you Miss Mathews?" she continued.

"I don't suppose there was anything mentioned in the file about strange things that took place in the old house?" Sara asked hesitantly.

Donna looked at her perplexed by her question and asked, "Like what kind of strange things?"

"Oh, just strange things. Well, you've been a great help. Thank you so much for taking your time to help me," Sara replied with a smile, though she was disappointed that there was no mention of any strange occurrences at the old house.

On the drive back to her cabin, Sara's mind was running wild with thoughts about what she had just learned. She pondered why there was no mention anywhere of people either appearing or disappearing from that house; surely they went up into the attic. There wasn't even any mention of unexplained changes or events involved with the attic. Why did it change when she entered the attic she questioned? She wondered as she continued her drive home what had changed over time that would have caused this strange phenomenon.

When Sara arrived home she went out on the back porch to sit and think. There was a lot to consider before returning to the old house, and she questioned whether she should even do it. She wondered if there was a chance that she might never return if whatever was causing this phenomenon suddenly stopped while she was looking for answers, or whether there was something different in her present time that would always allow her to return safely.

It was time for lunch and as Sara prepared something to eat she deliberated whether she could use this unexplained mystical event to write about in her new book that she owed Whitney Publishing. It was very different from the first two novels that she had written, and it would definitely be an exciting change.

By evening time her decision was made to test her theory about being able to return to her time if in fact she had entered some kind of a time portal to the past. It was dangerous, but she thought it necessary if she was going to write about it as strictly a science fiction novel.

Her thoughts continued well into the night. As she lay in bed she realized this was the first time she had even thought about writing again since Richard had died. He loved adventure and would have definitely supported her idea for her new book, but only if he could come along to protect her. She speculated whether he would approve of her going alone. She also had to think about her parents. What would it do to them if she never returned? She knew they would never under any circumstances want her to return to that house. It was too dangerous. Being a grown woman now twenty-six years old, she was capable of making her own decisions she reasoned, but she would have to somehow let them know what she was up to.

While drinking her coffee the next morning out on the back porch she decided to write her parents a letter explaining what she had discovered on her hikes and the possibilities of what could happen to her if she returned to the house. She would leave the letter there in the cabin in plain sight so that they could easily find it and have closure should something happen to her. Sara's mind was now firmly set on returning to the old house tomorrow, even if the very thought of it terrified her. She was hoping that her theory about being able to return was correct and that it would just be something exciting that she would be able to write about; maybe even throw a little romance into it to keep her publisher happy.

Chapter 5

The sun was not up yet when Sara climbed out of bed anxious and yet excited about her trip out to the old homestead. Once she was through with breakfast and dressing she went through her checklist of things to do and things to take with her as she explored the old house for answers. The last thing she needed to do was to leave the letter for her parents on the entryway table in case something did happen and she couldn't return. Once that was done she set the alarm system and closed the door.

The sun was just peeking over the hill she was about to climb. It was going to be another beautiful sunny day and with her walking stick in hand she started her journey. With every step she took she wondered if she was doing the right thing. The unknown had always unnerved her and today was no different. She forgot about the potential trouble that might lay ahead as she passed through the patches of wild flowers still in bloom, and hoped she would have the chance to pick them this time on her way home.

Sara was across the large grassy field and now at the bottom of the steep hill when the feeling of impending doom swept over her. She doubted her decision to return to the house and now thought it was a foolish and dangerous idea. She stopped and looked back at the cabin and tried to make up her mind whether to return to it or whether to press on in search of her answers.

After several minutes of debate with herself, her anxiety subsided and she decided to press on. As she climbed the hill, she saw this excursion to the old house as a way to recapture her passion for writing and a chance at moving on with her life instead of just staring out of bedroom windows.

At the top of the hill Sara looked down through the trees at the old weathered house and contemplated why it seemed to keep drawing her back to it. She saw nothing different about the place since her last visit a couple of days ago so she pressed on with new determination to deal with whatever she might encounter.

She walked carefully across the front porch and entered the house through the partially unhinged door and stared at the staircase and took a deep breath trying to keep her nerves in check, then slowly made her way to the second floor as each step on the stairs seemed to squeak out a warning to her. Once again she found herself staring at the staircase that led to the attic. The staircase was still down from the last time she was there, and the steps were still covered in dust and sand, and still had a musty odor to them. She remembered how terrified she was running down those steps and out of the house the last time she was there, but was determined not to let that happen again. Closing her eyes and taking several deep breaths to calm her nerves for it was now time for the hard part – actually going up the stairs. Her heart started to pound within her chest and she felt lightheaded as she stood there looking up at the dusty steps that stood before her. Sara's hand shook as she placed it on the railing and put her first foot on the step. She took several more deep breaths and fought for the resolve she once had, and closed her eyes once again as she slowly climbed up each step waiting for the scent of pine to once again fill the air. Her hand told her that she was at the top of the stairs and she winced as she opened her eyes; afraid and yet hopeful of what she might see.

The attic was empty and she was deeply disappointed. Then suddenly she detected the smell of pine and watched as the attic changed before her very eyes. She was elated and terrified at the same time, and the urge to run was present, but the urge to see what the rest of the house looked like was even stronger. She listened carefully to see if she heard any voices like she thought she heard the last time the attic changed, but all was quiet, relieving her fears.

She turned and went back down the stairs that were now sturdy and new and could see a hand-woven rug in the hallway below her. She slowly looked around and the bedroom doors were all closed and she slowly opened each one and quickly looked around, but only one of them was sparsely furnished, so she decided to venture down the stairs to the first floor. She was curious to see how people lived in the late 1700s and took her first couple of steps into the living area. She was impressed by how every furnishing was beautifully crafted and every object had a practical use. Sara felt that it was a man's room because there were no frivolous items laying around and only a few feminine touches here and there.

As she ran her hand along the smooth wood of one of the rocking chairs that was placed next to the fireplace, all of a sudden, without warning, the front door abruptly opened and in walked two very different looking men.

Sara froze like a deer in the headlights. She was terrified and oblivious as to what to do, and yet she was intrigued by the men's stature and appearance. The English gentleman, who looked to be about 30 years old, was the most handsome man she had ever seen, and if she hadn't been so terrified, she was sure she would have blushed. He was very tall for that period in time, about 6'4" she thought, and had jet black hair that was neatly pulled back in a ponytail and tied with a blue ribbon with bangs that hung partially across his forehead. His eyes were almond shape, penetrating, and an amazing blue, and he had a masculine square jaw with a small dimple at the bottom. His cheekbones were rather high on his well-proportioned face, and his nose had a long, straight ridge to it, and lips that were perfect; rather thin on top and bottom. He wore tight, camel color, wool breeches that ended just beneath his knees, which showed off his muscular long legs, and he wore white stockings that came up just over the knee, and black leather boots that almost covered the stockings. His white linen, long sleeve shirt had a white linen cravat tied around his neck and the shirt was partially covered by a dark brown, sleeveless, waist coat with a "V" opening at the bottom. This accentuated his extremely broad shoulders that tapered down to his waist that was trim and fit.

The man standing by his side was an impressive, fierce looking Cherokee who had pierced ears and two large feathers tied at the crown of his head. He wore a cotton trade shirt, a loincloth, deerskin leggings, and a red blanket over one shoulder that was held in place by a beaded belt tied around his waist.

Meanwhile, both men were looking bewildered and suspiciously at the unknown woman standing in their home. They had never seen a woman as tall as she, and certainly had never seen one wearing a tight fitting lavender sweater that clung to her every curve with tight fitted blue jeans and black knee-high boots. Her long blonde hair was in a ponytail that hung several inches down her back with bangs hanging partially over one side of her beautiful face with sparkling hazel eyes and lips the color of ripe strawberries. She wore long, multi-looped, silver pierced earrings and a gold locket necklace, but more importantly to them, she wore a pistol of some sort on her belt.

Both parties were equally surprised by the encounter and stood staring at each other for what seemed like the longest time, but actually only a few seconds had passed.

"What are you doing in my house?" asked the English gentleman with a furrowed brow and piercing gaze.

Sara was too startled to speak; she just stood there trembling and wishing she had never returned to the old house.

"I ask you again, what are you doing in my house and where did you come from?" he sternly asked in a calm, deep rich voice as smooth as whipped butter. The Englishman, Nathan Chambers, was angry to find someone in his home. Neither man nor woman had any reason to be there uninvited.

Sara stood there silent and perplexed. She wanted to answer, but knew that he would never believe her even if she told him the truth.

The Cherokee, whose name was Inola, which meant black fox, spoke in broken English to Nathan. "She evil spirit. I take her to forest; kill her for you," as he drew his long bladed knife from its sheath.

Sara, without thought, instinctively drew her weapon and fired a warning shot hitting the door frame next to where they stood. Holding her weapon with both hands she kept it aimed at them and commandingly said, "Stand down; the next bullet won't miss. I mean you no harm. I just want to go back to where I came from."

Nathan reached over and grabbed Inola's hand which held the knife. "Put your knife away Inola," Nathan cautiously said without taking his eyes off Sara. He was stunned to see a woman who knew how to handle a weapon the way this woman had just done.

"I don't believe she is an evil spirit. Though I will admit her appearance is very strange," he said still holding his gaze upon her.

Sara was breathing heavily as she watched Inola slip his knife back into its sheath, but she could tell by the fire in his eyes that he still would have preferred to kill her.

"Where is it you come from?" Nathan questioned in a direct manner.

Sara did not want to tell him she came from a different time in the future, so she replied, "Look, I never meant any harm in coming here. I was just curious how people in your time lived.

Please, just let me leave the way I came in and you will never see me again. I promise," she said still aiming her weapon directly at them.

Nathan was startled! What odd things to say – how people in your time lived, and let me leave the way I came in and you will never see me again. How did she even find his place, where was her horse, and where would she possibly go in the middle of nowhere?

"I'm leaving now, so just stay where you are and don't move" she said as she slowly backed up then turned and ran up the stairs into the attic and closed the staircase behind her. Nothing. She just stood there looking around with a puzzled look on her face.

"Why is everything still here? Why didn't it change back to dust and cobwebs?" she asked herself shaking so violently that she had to sit down. Her heart was pounding so hard she feared it would burst and she was scared out of her mind. She had never in her life ever pointed a gun at anyone, and now she did not know how they would respond now that she was trapped in the attic.

"Dear God, please get me back to my time and I promise I will never do anything this foolish again." Once more she questioned herself, *"Why am I still here? What did I do differently last time? I was able to leave last time, why not this time?"*

Sara remembered that the last time she just ran down the stairs and out of the house. But, now she was too frightened to go back down the stairs – the Cherokee had wanted to kill her! Sara just broke down and sobbed. She was frightened and alone and didn't know what to do.

Nathan could hear her crying and hung his head, sighing heavily. He was still in a state of shock over what had just occurred and his mind could not comprehend how any of this was even possible. None of it made any sense whatsoever to him. Why in the world would she say that she just wanted to leave the way she came in and then head for the attic? How does someone just appear out of nowhere, and especially one dressed as strangely as she was and carrying a weapon that was inconceivable to him? He was frustrated and confused, and still angry about having to deal with such an unexpected and unbelievable situation.

"What you do now, Nathan?" Inola asked having no patience for women who cried.

"Well, I'm not going to kill her; that much I know," he answered in an annoyed tone.

"You figure out; let me know. I go hunting now," he replied and started for the door.

Nathan sat down in his rocking chair to think about what to do, but his thoughts kept coming back to how beautiful she was, and how much she reminded him of his wife. But with further reflection, he realized she was nothing like his wife. What troubled him the most was that he wanted her more than anything he had ever wanted before, but knew that she did not belong there and that would only lead to heartache and he wanted no part of that.

He was frustrated, annoyed, and hungry, and that was always a bad combination. The crying had now stopped, but the silence bothered him just as much, but he had no intention of lowering the staircase. She could just sit up there until he came up with a plan to get her back to wherever she came from, or at least figure out a way they could co-exist without possibly killing each other.

Nathan's hunger now overpowered his disturbed thoughts and he went to the hearth and rekindled the fire under the pot of stew leftover from the morning. There were still chores that needed to be done so he stepped out on the porch to carry in more firewood and figured his unwanted guest would still be there when he got back.

Sara heard the front door open and close and knew that she was now alone in the house, but what should she do? She still had no idea what the trigger was for returning to her own time. She paced around in the attic looking out the window now and then, and wondering what was going to happen to her. She was now out of food and water, and there was a Cherokee roaming around somewhere that wanted to kill her, and a man that she knew nothing about. He didn't appear to be a ruthless man that would harm her, or one that would take advantage of her, but that was just the problem; she knew nothing about him other than the fact that he was ruggedly handsome and had an English accent that she loved.

Still confused and frightened, she went and sat down in the corner of the attic where she could easily see who was coming up the staircase should they lower it. After her long hike and the subsiding adrenaline rush from confronting the two unexpected men, Sara fell asleep. What seemed like hours later, the sound of the door opening and closing stirred her from her sleep and she stared at the staircase wondering what was going to happen next. Would he just leave her there to starve or should she get up the nerve to go downstairs. Downstairs to do what – point a gun at him and demand something to eat? *"Oh why did I ever return to this house? Why do I have to be so darn curious all the time?"* she asked herself; for it got her into nothing but trouble this time.

Meanwhile, Nathan had just finished stirring the stew and was cutting some leftover bread to go along with it. He was expecting Inola to show up at any minute so he placed two plates and forks on the table and then thought about the woman hiding out in his attic. She had to be hungry now, and went ahead and set another plate and fork on the long wooden table.

Nathan was not looking forward to another encounter with this peculiar woman, but knew that it was the Christian thing to at least check on her and offer her some food. The fact that she was wearing a firearm crossed his mind, but figured she wasn't the type to use it unless she really needed to, or she would have already shot them.

He lowered the staircase and loudly announced, "I'm coming up, and I mean you no harm."

He still climbed the staircase cautiously, not knowing for sure how she would react in her current state of mind. Even before reaching the top he could see the stranger sitting in the corner of the attic with her arms wrapped around her legs and her head resting on the top of her knees. He looked closely to see if she was still holding her weapon or whether she had put it back in its holster.

Nathan thought about what to say and then simply asked, "Are you hungry?"

Sara raised her head and looked suspiciously at him and just nodded.

"When you're ready you can come downstairs and get a plate of food," he stated plainly, and turned and went back down the steps.

Sara continued to sit where she was and wondered whether she could trust him or not and whether he held a grudge over having a handgun pointed and fired at him. Well, not right at him, but close enough to keep from being killed by the Cherokee who was with him.

Sara heard the door open and close again and knew that Inola had returned, and would be seated with Nathan at the table. Her hunger was more powerful than her fear right now, and besides, she still had her weapon at her side should she need it. She cautiously climbed down the stairs and stood at a distance looking at the two men; trying to size up the situation before going any further. They both looked up and noticed immediately that she was still carrying her weapon, and went back to eating.

Sara thought that under the current situation, this was as good a reaction as she could expect to get. Trembling, she approached the table and slowly reached for her plate. Nathan looked up and saw the fear in her eyes and felt pity for her. No woman should ever be that fearful because of him.

"Please, help yourself to whatever is in the pot," he calmly said and went back to eating; trying to be as non-threatening as possible.

"Thank you," she replied as the plate shook in her hands.

She took a deep breath and moved swiftly to the cast iron pot hanging inside the hearth and scraped the bottom for the remaining stew and carried it back to the table and sat across from Nathan. She still did not want to be in arms reach of the fierce looking Cherokee that was watching her closely with hatred in his eyes.

Nathan noticed that she had nothing to drink so he took a cup and went to a wooden bucket filled with water and scooped out a cup full and placed it in front of her.

Sara was horrified. Did he actually expect her to drink water from a wood bucket sitting on the floor?

As he placed it in front of her he guessed what she was thinking by the look on her face and smirked. "I have some whiskey if you prefer that over this tasty water."

Sara glanced at Inola; he was not amused. In fact, if looks could kill she would be dead. He had been greatly insulted that a woman had forced him to sheath his knife. His eyes seemed to pierce right through her and it made her very uncomfortable and she rested her hand on top of her handgun. That only infuriated him even more and Nathan intervened and turned quickly to Inola and told him to just eat his food.

Inola took a bite of the stew and looked belligerently towards Sara and started to stand up with the plate in his hand when Nathan grabbed his arm and spoke to him in Cherokee very forcefully. Inola just looked at him and made what Sara believed was a snide comment by the look on his face, and sat back down and broodingly ate the remainder of his stew.

She lowered her eyes and took a bite of the stew and chewed it for a long time for she found it hard to swallow with her stomach feeling as hard as a rock. She ate in silence not wanting to provoke Inola any further, and took a small sip of her water and was pleasantly surprised and drank until her cup was empty, but was afraid to ask for more.

Finishing his stew and bread Inola looked at Sara with contempt and left the table abruptly and started for the front door. When he opened it he turned to Nathan and said something to him in his native language and quickly closed the door behind him.

Nathan scowled and abruptly left the table and went and opened the front door and just stood there looking out over the hills at the dark clouds that lit up with every strike of the lightning.

"I'm afraid a storm might be headed our way. I'm going to check on the animals…and please don't leave the house for any reason," he said in a tone that had her concerned, but not as much as the look in his eyes.

For what reason did he not want her to leave the house she wondered. She thought he wanted her out of his house as quickly as possible. Would she be in danger from Inola, the coming storm, or was he just being protective of a complete stranger in his home that had taken a shot at him?

She went and looked out the front window and even though it was starting to get dark she could see the storm clouds rolling in, and could hear the soft rumbling of thunder off in the distance and wished she was back at her cabin sitting by the fire with a cup of hot chocolate. She closed her eyes and gently shook her head finding it hard to believe the mess she had gotten herself into, and couldn't for the life of her figure out how to get out of it.

Chapter 6

Since she was now in the house alone, Sara quickly cleared off the table and washed the few dishes and put them away knowing that Nathan had his hands full getting things ready outside before the storm hit. She hoped that he would take what she had done as a sign that she could be reasonable, and her only objective was to return home as quickly as possible. She noticed that the fire was down to embers in the fireplace and because she was cold in the light-weight sweater she was wearing, she promptly went and put more logs on the fire and then sat down and waited anxiously for Nathan to return.

An ominous, eerie sounding wind started to howl and she could hear heavy raindrops hitting the windows and wondered if Nathan was going to lock her in the attic for the night. She had given him no reason to trust her, but that seemed unnecessarily cruel to her. She felt like she was holding on to her sanity by her finger tips when Nathan suddenly stepped through the door and she felt the sudden chill from the wind reach her all the way over to the fireplace.

"I'm glad to see you started the fire. It could get real nasty before this storm blows over and it could bring with it some really cold weather," Nathan said while taking off his wet coat and hanging it on a peg in the wall. His eyes darted quickly to the dining table and noticed that it had been cleared, but did not say a word.

He took his seat by the fire to get warm and glanced at Sara and instantly took note that she was still wearing her weapon and figured she had not yet been given a reason to remove it. He couldn't help but notice how beautiful Sara looked in the glow of the firelight. He found it hard not to stare at the curves of her body made more prominent by the sweater she wore and the tight fitting jeans that showed off her long well-toned legs. It had been over a year since he sat with a woman by his fireplace, and never with one as beautiful as she, and for a moment he wished she would stay.

He finally diverted his eyes to the roaring flames of the fire and asked, "I suppose those are the only clothes you have with you. You don't happen to have anything warmer packed away in your bag do you?"

"No, I didn't know when I left home this morning that I wouldn't be returning," she softly replied.

Nathan looked at her and without saying a word went upstairs and shortly returned with a colorful handmade quilt that his wife had made and handed it to her.

"Thank you, it's beautiful" she said glancing up at him with a subtle smile and quickly wrapped the quilt around her for she noticed how he looked at her and it made her uneasy.

"What's your name?"

"Sara, Sara Mathews," she replied softly.

"I'm Nathan Chambers" he said looking right at her, and hoped that she would raise her head and look at him. "Your name suits you," he continued.

They sat in total silence for several minutes while the lightning cracked loudly overhead only adding to her stress and uneasy feelings. Sara glanced at Nathan who was staring off into the crackling fire and could almost see the wheels turning in his head. She wondered what he was thinking about, and she was about to find out.

"Sara, we need to talk if we are going to be in the same house together."

She knew this conversation was inevitable and necessary so she asked him, "What would you like to know Mr. Chambers?"

"Can you explain to me how you came to be in my house?" he asked in a very direct manner.

Sara sighed as she looked directly at him and then lowered her eyes and tried to figure out where to begin to explain this unexplainable event to him in such a way that he would believe her.

"I'm a writer who recently lost my husband in a war and moved to a cabin just a little way over the hill in front of your cabin…"

"There isn't any cabin within fifty miles from here that I know of," he interrupted looking at her quizzically.

"Well, there will be in a couple hundred years from now," she replied hesitantly and closed her eyes tightly; dreading to see the look on his face.

Nathan was taken aback by her answer and his brow furrowed as he asked her to continue; already suspicious of her story.

She could tell that she was off to a rocky start when she opened her eyes, but continued on with her story. "Anyway, I decided one day to take a hike and came upon your place quite by accident. Even though it was badly weathered and unfortunately past the point of repairing, I found the architecture to be quite beautiful. I didn't enter your house the first day because I was afraid there might be some kind of animals inside or it might be too dangerous to walk on the floor boards that might give way. My curiosity got the better of me and I returned the next day and decided to check out the inside of your house to get a glimpse of how people lived in your time. The first two floors were completely empty and filled with only dust and cobwebs. Then I saw what I was pretty sure was your attic and figured I might as well check it out while I was there. The draw ropes leading to your attic were gone so I used my belt buckle to slide onto the hook and pulled down the staircase. Then the strangest thing occurred," Sara said visibly upset and her lips started to quiver and she bit her lower lip, as her eyes teared almost to overflowing and she turned her face away from him.

"Go on, please finish your story," Nathan said gently, curious about what she was going to say that had her so upset.

"But you won't believe me. I can tell by the look on your face you think this is just a story I'm making up. But it isn't; it is an actual account of what happened. I can't understand what happened, nor can I explain it," she replied on the verge of hysteria.

Leaning forward towards her he said very calmly, "Take a deep breath and try to regain your composure. You've got to tell me everything whether it sounds crazy to you, or me. Don't you want my help in figuring all this out? I know you want out of here as quickly as possible, and I aim to help you."

Sara nodded and wiped her eyes dry before continuing. "I started to climb the stairs and they were very dusty and badly deteriorated, and then all of a sudden the wood started to change before my very eyes. There was a sudden scent of pine in the air and the wood looked and felt like it had been recently cut. When I got up my nerve to enter the attic it was full of things: a large chest with a woman's clothing inside, crates of hand carved toys, and a wooden rocking horse. I thought I heard someone outside on the porch and looked out the attic window, but did not see anyone and then all of sudden everything had changed back to dust and rotting wood. I ran as fast as I could out of the house and was determined to never return or tell anyone about my experience...You don't believe me...do you?" she asked desperately and gasping for air.

Nathan took a deep breath and let it out heavily, and looked at her with confusion and thoughtfulness. "I don't believe you to be crazy or to have made this story up, but…" he hesitated.

"But…it is the truth no matter how crazy it sounds," Sara replied emphatically, searching for some sign in his countenance that he believed her.

"But, since you're here, I can only assume that you returned once again to my house," he said trying to get her to continue her story no matter how crazy it sounded to him.

"A couple of days after that harrowing experience I knew that it would drive me crazy if I didn't try to get to the bottom of what happened. So, yes, I returned and the same thing happened – everything changed before my eyes. When I didn't hear any noise outside I decided to take a look downstairs to see if things had also changed down here, and they had. A few minutes later you and your Indian friend walked in through the front door," she exclaimed then burst into tears. She quickly tried to wipe them away and asked with a shaky voice, "This has never happened before? No one has ever shown up out of nowhere and then found their way back home?"

"Never. You're the first, and you say it all happened just because you entered my attic?" he questioned while looking at her with piercing blue eyes.

"Well, your house is secluded on BLM land, that's government land, and miles away from any development. Maybe no one has come upon it like I did. There aren't any roads or trails leading here. Or, if they did find it they weren't interested enough to enter your attic. It is badly weathered in my time," she explained.

Nathan just looked at her intently for just a minute and wondered what she meant by "in my time". It seemed like he really did not want to ask her his next question; perhaps he did not want to hear her answer. Finally he asked, "What year is it, Sara?"

"In my time it is two thousand-twenty," Sara responded and asked, "What year is it here?"

"It's seventeen hundred eighty-six. Don't you think it curious that no one else in over two hundred years has mysteriously shown up in my house?" he replied with a troubled look.

The only sound that now broke the silence was the continued cracking of lighting over their heads, the thunder rumbling off into the distance, and the heavy rain beating against the house.

"I know all this sounds like a bunch of nonsense to you, but I swear it is the truth. I can't explain why your attic only seems to change when I'm in it, but it does," she said soulfully wanting so much for him to believe her.

Nathan turned his head away from Sara and stared at the leaping flames in the fireplace. He did not like the confused state his mind was in. He didn't know what to believe or how to explain away her strange clothing, or weapon, or how she suddenly appeared in his house. One thing he did know, and that was Sara believed every word of what she had told him. So, either she was just plain crazy, or she was telling the truth.

What was he supposed to do with her? There was no one around for at least fifty miles in any direction that he knew of, except for a few Cherokee, perhaps. So turning her out of his house was not an option, and taking her to town dressed the way she was, was also not an option. Nathan found himself between a rock and a hard place – he would have to let her remain with him for the time being at least. This realization both tormented and angered him at the same time. Any man would want her in his bed. But to look and know he could not touch was almost unbearable, and the sooner she returned to where she belonged the better off he would be.

Sara took a deep breath and breaking the silence hesitantly asked, "Mr. Chambers, would you mind stepping outside on the porch for just a moment. I know it is raining, but I was able to leave your house the last time I was here when you were not inside. Maybe it would work again," she said hopefully.

Nathan turned and looked at her and did not say a word for several seconds. "You can try," he said, and stood and started for the door hoping for his sake her plan worked.

Once the door had closed behind him, Sara ran and pulled the staircase down and ran up the stairs into the attic. Nothing. It was still filled with his unused or unwanted items, and she hung her head in despair. She couldn't bear the thought of having to go downstairs and face Nathan, but what choice did she have? She slowly descended just in time to see Nathan carrying in an armload full of firewood he picked up on the front porch.

"Welcome back," he said with a bit of a grin and sarcasm. "I didn't think it was going to work, but I guess it was worth a try," he continued.

"I'm sorry. I know you don't want me here. But I honestly don't know what is keeping me from leaving," she said softly in a defeated tone as she walked back to her chair by the fireplace.

"Don't worry; we'll figure it out sooner or later," he said as he stocked the wood in a pile beside the fireplace.

Sara was sympathetic to the predicament that Nathan found himself in. She had a hard time believing what had happened to her, and she at least was familiar with the concepts of time travel, portals, and worm holes in time. These were things he had never even heard of, and yet she was asking him to believe in them.

Sara wanted desperately to break the silence; it made her uncomfortable. She hesitated to be the one to do it, but it must be done.

"Mr. Chambers," she said and waited for him to look at her.

"Mr. Chambers, where am I to sleep tonight?" she asked fearful of his answer.

Nathan looked at her and Sara thought for a fleeting moment she detected pain in his glance as he quickly turned his face towards the fire. He thought for a moment then replied, "Let me light an oil lamp and I'll show you."

He soon returned with a lamp and started towards the stairs and Sara followed him until he stood in front of one of the small upstairs bedrooms. As he opened the door and let her in he stated, "This was my daughter's room. The bed is a little small, but it will have to do. There are blankets in the chest at the foot of the bed."

Nathan hesitated before leaving the room. This was the first time he had actually stood close to Sara, and was surprised at the athletic build to her curvaceous body, and noticed that she was almost as tall as he. He guessed she was pretty close to six feet tall and this was unheard of, and gave him something else to ponder. He glanced once more at her weapon and firmly stated, "Sara, I would prefer not to have to sleep with one eye opened all night. I would sleep much sounder if you would surrender your weapon to me."

Sara's eyes immediately widened and she took a couple of steps back into the room while placing her hand on her gun. "I can't do that. If you stay in your room and I stay in mine there shouldn't be any problems. I'm sorry, but I'm afraid your "friend" might return and try to kill me. You know he detests me," she declared fearfully and passionately.

Seeing the fear in her eyes he could hardly fault her for her decision, and not wanting to make matters worse he simply said, "Good night then," and closed the door.

Sara let out a sigh of relief and listened carefully at the door to make sure Nathan was indeed heading back to his room. Her room was dark, as Nathan had taken the oil lamp with him, and her backpack with her flashlight was still up in the attic. The only light in the room was when the lightning lit up the sky, and Sara quickly made her way to the small bed and curled up with the quilt Nathan had given her earlier. Even though the pillow was small and the mattress was thin and lumpy Sara fell asleep quickly in the dark room as the sound of thunder could be heard rumbling off in the distance.

Chapter 7

Sara was awake before dawn and pulled the quilt up to her chin. She looked around the darkened room disoriented at first and then realized where she was and wished that it had all been a bad dream. All the events of yesterday ran through her mind and she wondered what this new day would hold for her. She laid there shivering and contemplated getting a blanket from the chest at the foot of the bed. She listened carefully to see if she could detect whether anyone was moving around downstairs, but heard no one, and finally decided to get up.

Her feet were numb from the cold and she quickly put her boots back on and went to the window wrapped in the quilt Nathan had given her, and looked out over the valley and could see a dusting of snow on the ground in the early morning light. She thought how strange it was to have snowed so early in the year, but was happy that the storm had passed and had great hopes that the sun would come out and warm things up. All she could think about at that moment was her nice warm jacket back at her cabin, a hot cup of coffee with her favorite creamer, and sitting by the fireplace in her favorite chair.

Her thoughts were interrupted by the sound of the front door closing. She moved closer to the window and strained to see where Nathan was going, but only caught a glimpse of him walking in the direction of the barn in his heavy overcoat. Sara immediately thought about his Cherokee friend and wondered where he was. He was unpredictable and she trusted him about as far as she could throw him.

She decided to venture downstairs to see if Nathan had built a fire before leaving the house, for she was still freezing and felt reasonably safe since she still had her handgun by her side in case Inola showed up unexpectedly. She wondered where he had slept last night during the thunder storm with its pouring rain and high wind gusts, and was surprised that Nathan hadn't invited him to stay inside. She was glad that he hadn't stayed because she wouldn't have been able to sleep while listening for footsteps on the staircase or the unlatching of her door.

The heat from the fireplace greeted her as she reached the bottom of the stairs and was thankful that Nathan had started a fire before leaving. After pulling a chair closer, she sat stretching out her hands towards the fire and soaked in its warmth while she tried to figure out why she wasn't able to return to her time. She could smell the strong scent of coffee coming from the hearth and wrapped the quilt tightly around her and went to pour a cup and noticed a plate with bread and cheese and a coffee cup set out on the table. Finally some coffee; that was just the thing to help her warm up. She took the coffee pot off a little shelf inside the hearth and poured its rich, dark coffee into her cup and looked around for some sugar or cream and realized she would have to drink it black. Any coffee was better than having none she told herself and took a slice of bread and cheese with her back to the rocking chair to eat by the fire.

The coffee was horrid, bitter and strong, but the bread and cheese helped mask the awful taste and made it bearable to drink. She prayed that this was not a typical morning breakfast, and if it was, she hoped that she would find a way home soon, back to the comforts she was used to.

As she sat by the fireplace eating, Sara continued to try to figure out why her attempt yesterday to return to her time had not worked. She went over in her mind each step she had taken the first two times she crossed over to see what step she might have left out.

"Well, I tried just going back into the attic and that didn't work, and I tried going into the attic with Nathan outside the house on the porch and that didn't work. So, what haven't I tried," she thought to herself.

There was one thing that came to Sara's mind. *"I've always come over the hill and through the forest to enter the house. Maybe that's the missing step!"* she thought.

Sara went to the front door and unlatched it and peeked outside to see if she saw either Nathan or Inola, but saw neither and walked to the edge of the porch and still did not see either man. She looked at the hill in front of the house and the tree line ended close to the bottom of the hill and snow still clung to the branches and in patches on the ground. It was really frigid outside and she debated whether it was worth the risk to test out her new theory with only the lightweight clothing she was wearing. She stepped back inside and warmed herself by the fire to think things through. *"If I don't test my theory I'll be stuck here for who knows how long, because my first two ideas sure didn't work,"* she thought.

Sara went to the window and looked out at the hill and figured it was only about one-hundred yards to the base of the hill and about another hundred yards to the top of the hill, and wondered if she would have to go all the way to the bottom of the hill and then start her way back over it for her plan to work. That meant that Sara would be gone for possibly half an hour to test her theory. All she had on to keep her warm was a light sweater and a thin pair of jeans as it was still on the warm side when she left her cabin yesterday. She couldn't think of another option and held her hands over the fire one more time to warm them and then headed for the door.

She unlatched it and looked both ways and when she didn't see anyone she took off running as fast as she could towards the hill. Her heart was pounding by the time she reached the base of it and stopped for just a minute to catch her breath as a cloud of moist vapors escaped into the cold morning air before starting to make her way through the brush and trees to the top of the hill. As she started to run again Inola spotted her and called to Nathan and pointed towards Sara.

"Damn!" Nathan yelled and took off running to the barn. He quickly mounted his horse and took off with a "yeah" galloping towards Sara well on her way up the hill. He grew angrier having to weave his way through the brush and when he finally caught up to her, he jumped down off his horse and grabbed her tightly around her waist.

"What's wrong with you woman? Are you trying to kill yourself, or just make my life more miserable?" he asked angrily.

"Let me go!" she yelled and tried to fight her way out of his arms, but he held her all the tighter.

"We can do this the easy way or the hard way, now calm down," he said forcefully.

Sara stopped her fighting and started to cry out of pure frustration.

"Just like a woman, try to cry your way out of this. Well it won't work. Would you kindly tell me what you were hoping to accomplish besides freezing to death?" he asked slightly loosening his hold on her.

She pulled herself away from him with a hard jerk and went to grab her gun but he caught her hand and looked at her so piercingly that she stopped her fighting.

"I was trying to return to my own time! What do you think I was trying to do? I know you don't want me here, you've made that quite clear," she stated boldly wiping her tears of anger and frustration away.

Nathan was breathing heavily as he stared at her intently. As angry as he was he had to admire her tenacity and spirit.

"Okay, tell me, how is running over this hill going to return you to your time?" he asked in a more civil tone.

"I don't know if it will or not. But it is something I haven't tried. I thought if I made it over the hill and then came back over it and saw trees all the way up to your house then I would be able to enter your attic and cross back over to my time. Then you would be rid of me forever," she answered brazenly.

Nathan stood there silently looking at her and then suddenly mounted his horse and reached out his hand to her. "Give me your hand. You'll freeze to death dressed the way you are if you don't do this quickly," he said roughly; still annoyed with her.

Sara took hold on his arm and when he had her arm securely he swung her up behind him and urged his horse to the top of the hill and paused. "Well, has anything changed?" he asked.

"No. Maybe I have to go to the bottom of the hill and climb back up by myself before things will change," she said with her arms still wrapped tightly around him; enjoying the warmth of his body.

Nathan didn't think her plan stood a chance, but he had come this far and he figured he might as well go the rest of the way. He lowered her to the ground and took off his heavy overcoat and tossed it down to her.

"Put that on or you'll freeze before you ever make it to the bottom and back up. Where do you figure I need to be for this plan of yours to work?" he asked gruffly.

"I don't know, anywhere but inside your house, I guess," she said in a confused state of mind for he befuddled her.

"I'll watch for you to reach the top of the hill and if I see you then I'll know your plan didn't work and I'll come get you," he said and turned his horse sharply and rode away.

Sara put his heavy coat on and descended the hill as quickly as she could and caught her breath. Her legs were already tired and she dreaded having to make her way back through the brush and trees to the top of hill, but she had no other choice. She looked across the valley to see if she saw anything familiar, but saw no sign of anything as far as she could see and started back up the hill.

Meanwhile Nathan rode back to his house and put on his only remaining overcoat and went back outside to watch for Sara. He was annoyed that this silly plan of hers was costing him time and keeping him from his work that was crucial if he was going to save any of his crops.

Sara was breathing heavily as she climbed the hill in his heavy overcoat and had to stop frequently as her legs were cramping from the strain, but the crest of the hill was only a few minutes away now and she prayed desperately that there would be a forest in front of her when she made it to the top.

She pressed on with new resolve and made it to the top and when she stood on the threshold to the downward slope, she covered her face and cried. Nathan spotted her at the top and sighed heavily; she would be back under his roof once again, and who knew what she would try next time. He quickly rode to meet her coming down the hill and she was still crying uncontrollably and he felt sorry for her. He realized she was not trying to make his life more difficult, she was only trying to get back home.

"Give me your hand and step up on the stirrup," he said patiently.

Sara did as he asked and he pulled her up and seated her in front of him and put his arms around her and grabbed the reins and started down the hill with her face now red from the cold and sobbing all the way. He didn't know what to say to comfort her so he remained silent until he reached the house and lowered her once again to the ground.

"Please stay inside. I don't have time to come running after you again," he said plainly and rode back to where Inola was working.

Sara went back inside shivering and laid Nathan's coat on the floor in front of the fire and laid down afraid that she would never be able to return to her cabin, and cried herself to sleep.

Nathan worked through lunch time with just a few pieces of jerky to keep him going until it was time to fix supper. Inola had been fortunate and caught a couple more rabbits and cleaned them before taking them inside the house. He saw Sara sleeping on the floor and went and stood over her and placed his hand around the handle of his knife. He knew that his friendship with Nathan would be over if he harmed her, so he quietly went to the hearth and added some wood to the fire and skewed the rabbits and started them cooking. He glanced at Sara on his way out and when he found Nathan in the field he asked him why he had bothered to go after her. Nathan gave him no answer but went back to work, pondering Inola's question.

When Nathan was finished with his work for the day he returned to the house and found Sara still asleep on the floor and went to check on the rabbits and turned them before sitting by the fire. As he sat there looking at Sara he had compassion for her. She had not intentionally intruded into his life, but she was there just the same. She looked beautiful lying there, and his eyes ran over every curve of her body and she reminded him just how much he missed having a woman around, even one who threw his life into turmoil.

He could tell by the aroma in the air that the rabbits were ready to take off the skewer and quietly returned to the hearth to do so and set the table for three, and when he was finished putting the bread, apples and roasted corn on the table he went to awaken Sara.

He bent over to gently shake her shoulder, but drew his hand back and looked at her long blonde ponytail lying on his overcoat and reached down and ran his fingers through her hair feeling the soft, silky texture. It had been about a year since he had touched a woman's hair and he missed it especially at night when his wife would let her hair down. He sighed lightly and touched Sara's shoulder and shook it ever so gently as he called her name.

"Sara, it's time to wake up. It's time to eat," he said softly.

Sara was roused from her deep sleep and jerked away, startled when she saw Nathan hovering over her.

"It's okay. It's time for supper and I know you must be hungry," he said as he stood up.

"I'm sorry for all the trouble I caused you today. I thought that there was a small possibility that my plan would work, and you wouldn't have to put up with me any longer," she said disappointedly as she stood up and pulled her sweater down over her hips. "I guess you're still pretty angry with me," she continued and glanced up at his face, but did not see the clinched jaw or the piercing eyes, but instead it looked more like a look of regret for the rough way he had treated her.

"Come, supper is getting cold and I don't like cold rabbit," he stated and started walking over to the table.

Inola came through the door just as Sara was taking her seat and looked at her and said nothing as he sat at the far end of the table, grabbing what food he wanted and quietly ate while glancing up often at her. He did not understand why Nathan put up with her foolishness. In his tribe the women worked hard, and were respected for it. This woman, in his opinion, was lazy and seemed incapable of doing anything helpful, and thought that Nathan should send her on her way and have nothing further to do with her. But he knew that the white men were soft and doting with their women and it was useless trying to talk any sense to Nathan especially after the way he caught him looking at her.

Sara sat quietly until both men had helped themselves to their food and then took a small portion of what was left. She glanced at Nathan often, for only a moment at a time trying to get a feel for what kind of a man he was. She had seen him very angry today, which she found very alarming, and she had seen him kind and gentle at times. It was obvious to her that it would take a bit more time around him before she knew for sure what his true character was like. She wondered what he really thought about her. He seemed so guarded and distant most of the time and questioned what had caused him to be that way.

"I'll clean up," she offered and stood to wrap the bread and cheese but hadn't seen where Nathan kept them, and was too embarrassed to ask.

He watched as Sara looked around trying to discover on her own where things would logically be kept, and then he spoke up and told her where each food was properly stored and why they were stored there.

When Sara had finished washing the plates and utensils and putting them away she joined Nathan by the fireplace just long enough to tell him that she would turn in for the night and handed Nathan his coat from off the floor.

"Sara, wait, it is too cold for you to sleep up there. Please, won't you remain here while I light the fireplace in your room?" he asked.

"You don't have to trouble yourself, I'm capable of starting a fire," she said and picked up an armload of wood and turned to walk upstairs.

Nathan really wished that she would stay and talk. It was lonely sitting by the fire every night with no one to talk to, but he said nothing to stop her.

Chapter 8

Once again Nathan and Inola were outside working by the time Sara got up. She brushed her hair and pulled it back into a ponytail and wished she had clean clothes to change into, but did not see that happening any time soon. She went downstairs and found both fires going and food set out on the table again and gladly added being considerate as one of the things she admired about Nathan. She dreaded pouring a cup of coffee to go with her breakfast, and determined that if she could only bring one thing back from her time it would be her coffee creamer.

When Sara had finished eating, and drinking what she could of her coffee, she cleaned up after herself and walked around inside thinking about how she could keep herself busy and wished she had her music to listen to. She thought about what happened yesterday when she attempted to return to her own time, and how angry Nathan reacted and was not anxious for another repeat performance. However, she was going stir crazy with nothing to do and tried not to think about how worried her parents would be and angry that she had not stayed in touch with them like she had promised.

She went and sat by the fire and stared into the mesmerizing flames and thought about home and all the things she missed and longed to return to, but could not for the life of her think of what step she was missing in the process to allow her to return. What was that all important trigger?

She gave up thinking about it, for her thoughts kept drifting back to Nathan. She wondered what it was about him that so captivated her to him; other than his rugged good looks and gentle and quiet spirit most of the time. It was almost like a force within her drawing her to him in a way she never thought possible after losing Richard, and it troubled her.

Restless, she began pacing back and forth across the room and thoughtfully considered going outside just to look around if only for a few minutes even though it was still very cold. Her pacing took her by Nathan's bedroom door several times and she stopped and contemplated going inside to see if she could find his extra overcoat even though she knew it would be swimming on her. She needed something to wear and figured she would return to the house before he ever knew that she was gone. For some time now, Sara had her eye on the grove of trees behind the house where the two crosses had been placed and was curious to see what was written on them.

Against her better judgment she entered Nathan's room and found his overcoat hanging on a peg and put it on. She felt ridiculous. The sleeves were way too long and the coat came almost to her knees and was so heavy she thought about it making her lose her balance like it had several times yesterday, but she was determined to take a short walk before anyone returned to the house. Besides, she might not be able to return to her time yet, but she certainly wasn't a prisoner in this time. Walking had always been a good way for her to release stress, and under her current situation she thought walking was just what she needed.

She unlatched the back door and stepped just outside and looked around to see if she could locate Nathan or Inola, but they were nowhere to be found. But what she did see was that the ground was soaking wet and muddy, and figured the snow had melted, or it must have rained during the night and she had slept too soundly to hear it. Her boots were going to be a mess when she returned, but she was not going to let a little, or lot, of mud stop her; so she carefully started weaving her way around the larger puddles towards the small grove of trees. It felt good to be outside in the fresh air and she pulled Nathan's coat collar up over her neck and ears and stuffed her hands deep inside his coat pockets. The sky was such a pretty blue with only a few light gray clouds remaining in the distance, and she felt free from her immediate worries and chose her footing carefully.

It didn't take long to reach the red oak trees behind the house and Sara now found herself in front of the two wooden crosses. Bending down to read what had been carved into them, she discovered that Nathan's wife's name was Elizabeth and she was born in 1759 and died in 1785. That made her Sara's age, and she immediately knew what Nathan must be going through. Richard came to her mind and she clutched the gold necklace with the heart pendant with both their pictures inside that he had given her before he left on his tour of duty to Afghanistan. She quickly developed a real sympathy for Nathan that was not there before and moved over to the second cross. It bore the name of his daughter Katheryn; she was only two years old when she passed away and Sara's heart broke for him as she wondered what had caused their deaths. She thought she understood now why Nathan was so guarded and gruff at times – he had had enough pain in his life and he wasn't looking for any more.

She stood up and considered returning to the house before it was discovered that she was gone, but then a cluster of wildflowers with a dusting of snow on them caught her eye and she decided to go and at least see them. When she reached the spot where they were growing she bent over to pick some, and then stopped short of doing it. She wondered how it would be perceived by Nathan if she placed flowers in his house, and decided it would be best to just enjoy them there.

Looking around for the least muddy way of returning to the house she proceeded to pass a group of rocks near the end of the grove of oak trees and noticed that there was a sudden drop off where the rain water had run down into a large ravine. Before she could change direction the ground gave way beneath her. She went tumbling down the slope with rocks breaking loose from the wet ground and falling against her at the bottom of the wet, muddy ravine. Sara lay there shocked for several moments, then realized the rocks had pinned her down bruising her ribs and her ankle hurt something awful.

Panic quickly took hold of her. No one knew where she was, and what if Inola found her first? She was afraid to scream for help and just laid there, muddy, cold and hurt not knowing what to do, for she was unable to move the rocks that had pinned her to the ground. "Oh Richard, I thought you would always be here to protect me," she whispered.

Meanwhile, Nathan had returned to the house and quickly looked around for Sara and noticed that she had eaten some of the food he had left behind for her. He thought he would have found her sitting by the fireplace to stay warm and then wondered if she had returned to her room or to the attic where she might have been looking for a way to return to her time. Nathan quickly climbed the stairs and stood by her bedroom door and called her name, and when he received no response he opened the door to find that she was not inside. He was starting to get annoyed and went to the attic staircase and called out sternly, "Sara, if you're up there please come down."

When she didn't answer he quickly ran down the stairs to look for her. He asked himself where she could be this time. Was she able to return to where she came from, or had she once again wandered off somewhere? He was now angry. He had enough problems to deal with because of the storm and now he was forced to deal with a woman who showed up uninvited and heaven only knew where she ran off to this time.

He went out the back door and saw her footprints in the mud and loudly called her name.

"Sara…Sara…if you can hear me answer," he yelled as his eyes scanned the countryside behind his house.

Sara was relieved that it was Nathan calling her name, yet she thought he would be angry with her for running off again after what happened yesterday, but she had no choice but to call out for help.

"Help…Please help me," she loudly cried out and then anxiously waited for him to appear; though dreading it at the same time.

Nathan heard her cries for help and pin pointed the direction they had come from and quickly ran towards it splashing through the mud. It didn't take him long to reach the spot where she lay at the bottom of the ravine.

His anger quickly vanished and all he could see was a woman that was, cold, muddy, hurt, and in need of his help. Sara looked up with pleading eyes at Nathan towering over her, but words failed her for she feared he saw her as nothing but trouble, especially since she was wearing his only extra overcoat.

Nathan saw the remorse in her eyes and spoke gently to her, "Sara, just lay still while I look for the safest way to get to you." He stepped back from the edge that was starting to give way under his feet and looked further down the ridge to see where it would gently slope down to her position. He identified the route he would take about thirty feet away and took off in a run. He hurriedly made is way to her and knelt down beside her and tossed the rocks that were pinning her down off to the side.

"You'll be alright. Just put your arms around my neck and hold on," he said assuredly.

Sara reached up and wrapped her arms around his neck, and for the first time she was unafraid of this man who once was so suspicious and cold towards her. She was mortified that the overcoat she had taken from his room was now wet and muddy as he easily scooped her up in his arms and wondered what he thought about his coat now caked in mud.

"Thank you," she softly said and then buried her face into his chest, embarrassed to look at him as he slowly and carefully carried her safely out of the ravine and into the house; setting her down on one of the dining room chairs.

He squatted down in front of her and looked at his muddy overcoat and her muddy clothing and boots. "You just can't stay out of trouble, can you?" And looking directly into her eyes he frankly stated, "I guess you'll be needing some dry, clean clothes, but first, I'd like to check out your ankle and side if you will let me."

Sara felt flush and hoped that her face had not turned red. He was so ruggedly handsome that it was hard to look directly at him, and the thought of him touching her, if only to check out her injuries, sent tingling sensations all through her body that she had not felt since being with Richard.

Sara lowered her head in an attempt to hide the blush in her cheeks and replied, "Okay." She noticed him scowling as he looked at her boots and softly said, "You just pull down on that little metal tab at the top of my boots to remove them."

Nathan unzipped them and carefully pulled them off, then gently ran his strong hands over her ankles and turning each one slowly to see if it was sprained.

She tried hard to mask her excitement as his hands ran along her ankles, and winced in pain when he moved the left one. Nathan glanced up at her and grabbed another chair and rested her foot on it.

"You'll need to keep that elevated for a while," he said. Then looking down at his muddy overcoat he pulled it off her and placed it on the back porch steps to be washed, and quickly knocked the mud from the coat he was wearing off onto the ground.

When he returned, he knelt by her chair and placed his hands on the bottom of her soiled sweater and looked up to see her reaction before he gently raised it up over her side that was scraped and bruised.

Sara gasped and held her breath; feeling extremely stimulated and anxious at the same time. Nathan was a bit surprised by the effect he seemed to have on her, or was it just her pain that he was sensing – he wasn't sure. She suddenly realized his hand was close to her handgun and yet he did not reach for it. She saw him look at it and then up at her, and sensing her anxiousness and his own lack of concern about his safety, looked back down at her bruised side.

"That must hurt…let me get a clean cloth and clean that up for you," he said calmly and left to get some fresh cool water and a cloth.

Sara wondered if he felt what she was feeling, or if he just wished she would return to wherever she came from. She closed her eyes and took several deep breaths and winced from the pain as she tried to suppress the feelings that had so stimulated her. She doubted that he had felt anything because he seemed so calm and unaffected by anything he had done. Once again she was embarrassed and felt guilty about the feelings that stirred within her every time he touched her, as if she had betrayed Richard.

When Nathan returned with a basin of water and a clean cloth, he gently washed the mud from her bruised side and then handed her the cloth and said, "You might want to wash up with this while I go look for something for you to wear."

Sara took the cloth from him and began to wash her face, neck and hands. While doing so, she wondered how and where she was going to change her dirty clothes. She glanced at her handgun and holster and they were also caked in mud, and she wished she had never taken a step outside.

Meanwhile, Nathan had gone to the attic to look through the chest that held Elizabeth's clothing. It brought back painful memories of his wife as he searched for something that would fit Sara comfortably. He came across a blouse and skirt that he thought might fit, but the skirt would definitely be short on her for Elizabeth was at most only 5'4". He dug a little deeper and found a pair of stockings that he hoped would fit her long legs, but he would have to clean up her boots because none of his wife's shoes would fit within a mile. Once he had gathered up everything he found he took it to his daughter's room and laid them out on the bed.

As he came down the stairs he watched as Sara pulled her hair out of the ponytail. She combed her hands through her long, lightly curled blonde hair that now hung below her shoulders trying to loosen some of the mud from it. He couldn't help but think how beautiful she was, and didn't continue towards her until she happened to look his way.

Nathan was asking himself the same question Sara had just a few moments ago asked herself; how is she going to get out of her dirty clothes and dress herself? He did not know how to even begin to ask her about dressing herself. He certainly was not going to have any part in it.

He now stood before Sara with a bewildered look, so Sara helped him out by asking, "Did you find something for me to wear?"

He looked relieved and replied, "I've placed some of my wife's clothing on the bed upstairs. I hope you can manage to..."

"Oh, I can manage," she interrupted and then continued, "Would you mind terribly giving me a lift upstairs?" she asked coyly.

He lifted her up in his arms and as she wrapped her arms around his neck their eyes met for several seconds, and Sara was flummoxed, and wondered if Nathan had felt anything. If he did, he certainly didn't show it.

Nathan climbed the stairs effortlessly with her in his arms and carried her into the bedroom and set her down on the bed. Before he left the room he turned to her and said, "Your room is still pretty cold. When you're finished dressing give me a holler and I'll come get you so you can sit by the fireplace," and then turned and closed the door. He asked himself why he was so drawn to this woman that he knew nothing about, other than she had a knack for causing trouble. All that he did know was that he loved holding her in his arms.

It was quite a struggle for Sara to pull off her dirty sweater and jeans, but when they were finally laying on the floor along with her handgun she slipped his wife's blouse over her head then pushed her arms through the long sleeves that only covered three-quarters of her arms and was happy that they had lace around the bottom of the sleeve. She was a little embarrassed by the way she filled out the top of its swooped neckline and tugged it up as high as she could, but was still showing more of her breast than she wanted to. Taking a couple of deep breaths she bent over and pulled the stockings up with great effort and pain as far as they would go, and then put her legs through the skirt's opening and stood putting her weight on one leg as she pulled it up around her waist. She looked down at her legs once she had fastened the skirt and laughed; it only came down to just below her knees. She thought she looked ridiculous in clothes that were obviously too small for her, but what choice did she have. Sara hesitated to call Nathan for fear of humiliation, and his reaction at seeing his wife's clothes on her. Her side was really aching now so she sat back down and debated whether to call Nathan or just stay in her room with an extra blanket to keep her warm. But, even with an extra blanket she decided her room was far too cold to remain in and reluctantly called for him.

When he entered the room his eyes immediately went to the clothes he had given her to wear that belonged to his wife. As hard as he tried not to laugh, he broke into a hearty laugh that sent Sara into tears and she turned her back to him. He didn't mean to make her cry, but it was the funniest thing he had seen in a long time. Nathan felt badly that he had hurt her feelings so deeply, but it felt good to laugh again.

"Go away," Sara said tearfully.

"I'm sorry I hurt your feelings. You look beautiful in whatever you wear, even my floppy overcoat. Now please let me take you downstairs where you can get warm and have some lunch."

Sara turned around slowly, but could not bring herself to look directly at him and thought that his apology was very patronizing. What she didn't realize was Nathan had meant every word of what he had said about her looking beautiful in whatever she wore. As she stared down at the floor she noticed her weapon lying there, and when she saw him looking at it she became uncomfortable and wondered if she had misjudged him. It was too late for her to reach for it. The pain in her side wouldn't have let her do it anyway. Sara took a deep breath and held it as he approached, and gradually let it out when he passed by her handgun and picked her up in his arms.

Neither of them said a word as he carried her down the stairs then set her in a chair by the fireplace and elevated her leg onto another chair.

The warmth of the fire felt wonderful after being so cold, but she still reached for the quilt she had left there from this morning and covered herself; still humiliated by his laughter. After a few moments of reflection, she felt that perhaps she had been too vain, and should have just laughed along with him. She had to admit to herself that she did look quite odd, or maybe comical would be a better word. Besides, he did walk past her gun, and that should count for something.

She finally turned her head away from the fire and watched as Nathan was busy preparing something for them to eat. Out of the blue, Inola walked through the front door carrying a rather large groundhog and handed it to Nathan.

"This will make a fine supper, Inola," he said as he took it and placed it on the table to prepare for roasting it over the fire. Inola gave Sara a disdainful look and turned his back to her and quickly took his knife from the sheath and grabbed the groundhog to clean it.

When Sara saw the knife in his hand, goose bumps ran up and down her body and she wished she had her handgun. But she remembered how kind and gentle Nathan had been to her today and reasoned that he would never let Inola harm her, and so she relaxed just a bit and rested back in her chair.

She heard them speaking to each other in Cherokee and it seemed to start off friendly enough, but it soon grew louder and more contentious. Inola frequently motioned in her direction so she knew he was talking about her.

She looked away, back at the flames in the fireplace as her anxiety grew by the seconds. Suddenly, in the middle of their quarrelsome conversation she heard Inola's first English words - women's work - then cleaned off his knife, gave her a look that could kill, and stormed out of the house.

She could tell that Nathan was fuming and frustrated and knew that she was at the center of what was bothering him. Sara moved her left ankle and whereas it was still very tender and sore, she felt that she could walk, and unwrapped the quilt from around her and stood up tugging at the top of her blouse trying to cover a little more of her breast.

Nathan was in the middle of placing the groundhog onto a skewer when he looked up and saw Sara walking his way. He did not look happy and gruffly asked, "What do you think you're doing? Are you trying to cause more trouble for me?"

She stopped abruptly in the middle of the room, surprised by his harsh sounding remarks.

"No, but what your friend said is true. What you are doing is considered to be 'women's work' and I can help. I know you must have a hundred things you need to be doing besides preparing meals" she sharply replied, and continued to walk gingerly over to him.

He was surprised at her directness and was silent as he placed the skewer onto the hooks in the hearth. When he stood up Sara was standing next to him in her stocking feet, but it was her neckline that caused him to sigh heavily as he looked directly at her, confused as to how to handle this strong-headed woman. This time Sara did not blush as she held his gaze.

"My friend's name is Inola, and I was going to cook some potatoes and corn in that pot of water."

"I can do that," Sara replied with a raised eyebrow, still humiliated by the way she looked.

"Do you know how to make biscuits? There isn't enough time to make bread," he said.

Sara thought to herself, "*Sure, you just pop open a can of them, place them on a cookie sheet and stick them in the oven until they're golden brown.*"

Nathan could tell by her hesitation that she had never made biscuits from scratch, and a very small grin came to his face.

"Go ahead and laugh. We just do things quite differently in my time," she replied defensively.

"Fair enough. If I put out the ingredients and give you a few quick instructions, would you be willing to try?" he asked having a hard time keeping his eyes from wandering down to her neckline.

She looked away thoughtfully and then replied, "Yes, I would be willing to try, but will you be brave enough to eat them?"

"Woman, I can eat just about anything if I'm hungry enough," he said and started to bring her the ingredients that she would need. After giving her instructions he started towards the front door and when he reached it he turned to Sara and said, "Good luck, and thank you for your help," and closed the door before Sara was even able to answer him.

She stood there baffled. One minute she is shooting at two strangers in their own home and the next minute she is offering to help bake biscuits for supper. She shook those thoughts from her mind and hurriedly ate her lunch then busied herself even though her ankle and side were now throbbing in pain, and wished that she had packed something for pain in her backpack. Once she got started she was sure that the vegetables she was cooking would be fine; not even she could ruin them. But, the biscuits she was about to fix was a whole different matter.

She could see through the window that the sun was beginning to set and Nathan would be coming in soon after being away for hours, and she wondered if Inola would be with him. She set the table as quickly as she was able, but could see that her ankle was badly swollen now and her side was aching from bending over the fire to turn the roasting groundhog, stir the vegetables, and now to take the biscuits off the shelf where they had been baking. As she removed them something didn't look or feel quite right as she set them on the table. She tapped one of them and her heart sank. They seemed a little on the hard side to her, not soft and flakey like she had hoped; but maybe that was just the way they were made back then she told herself.

Sara was limping when Nathan entered the house and hung his black tricorne hat on its peg. Aware of her condition he immediately went to her and kindly ordered, "You need to sit down. I can finish putting supper on the table."

Sara did not argue. She hobbled to her chair at the table and sat down with a groan, and at this point she didn't even care if

Inola showed up for supper. Nathan removed the groundhog from the hearth and pulled it off onto a platter that Sara had set on the table and emptied the potatoes and corn into a large bowl. When he was sure that everything was on the table that was needed, he went to Sara and asked to see her ankle.

As he gently held her ankle in his hand he could tell that it was badly swollen and quickly pulled another chair over for her to rest her foot on. "That looks bad," he said and quickly went and got a cloth and soaked it in cold water and wrapped it around her ankle.

The cold cloth made Sara gasp at first, but then it felt so good she let out a sigh of relief as Nathan fixed a plate for the both of them and sat down next to her.

"I never should have let you stand on that ankle so long. I hope you're not too tired to eat." Nathan said.

"And I hope it's all fit to eat," Sara replied with a look of doubt on her face. After he had laughed at the way she was dressed, she didn't need him laughing at her lack of cooking skills. Her confidence had already taken a beating that day.

Nathan wasted no time digging into his food as Sara watched out of the corner of her eye. So far, so good, she thought; at least he hadn't made any faces. Then he picked up one of the biscuits and she noticed a bit of hesitation and a bit of a scowl. To his credit he took a bite without saying a word. But, with the second bite she watched him try to soak up some of the juices from the meat and vegetables, and she couldn't help but laugh.

"I'm sorry they're so bad; I really did try to follow your instructions," she said with an embarrassed smile.

He looked at her with a grin and replied, "I told you I could eat just about anything if I was hungry enough," and they both laughed.

About that time Inola walked in and saw them both sitting at the table laughing. Nathan looked over at him and acknowledged his presence with a slight nod of his head.

"Grab yourself a plate, there's plenty to eat. Just watch out for the biscuits," he joked and Sara and he laughed again.

Inola seemed to ignore them both, and piled his plate full of food and sat at the opposite end of the table. He couldn't help but notice Sara's low neckline to the blouse Nathan had given her, but more importantly he noticed that Sara was not wearing her weapon. He ate without speaking to either of them, for he did not appreciate Nathan making light of his opinions when it came to "women's work". When he was finished eating he stopped in front of Nathan on his way out and said something to him in Cherokee.

Nathan looked petulantly at him and roughly said, "That's enough, Inola."

Inola made some kind of gesture with his hand and peevishly left the house.

Sara didn't question Nathan about the incident, but wondered what Inola had said that made him so angry.

When they had finished their supper in silence, Nathan stood and turned to Sara and commented, "I don't want you standing on that foot any more tonight. You wait here and I'll come and get you in a few minutes."

She watched as Nathan moved the rocking chair she had been sitting in and replaced it with a beautifully upholstered couch close to the fireplace. Sara was stunned. This couch was considered an extravagant piece of furniture for that time and would have only been used when company came to visit; not that Nathan would be receiving any visitors this far away from any settlements. It certainly would never have been placed that close to a fireplace for fear that an ember might spark and damage the expensive material on the seating area. She questioned why he would do this for her, when all he really wanted was for her to return to where she came from. She was bewildered and thought him to be a man of inconsistencies.

When he was finished moving the furniture he returned to Sara and asked, "Are you ready?"

Sara raised her arms in the air and welcomed the opportunity to once again be held in his strong muscular arms, but still felt uncomfortable about him carrying her from room to room. Nathan gently picked her up and seated her where she would be able to elevate her foot and went to get another cold cloth to wrap around her ankle. She couldn't figure out why it upset her that he seldom ever made any eye contact with her, but kept his eyes fixed on where he was taking her. She was supposed to be in mourning, and yet she now welcomed the chance to be close to this man she barely knew who seemed to be full of contradictions. She loved Richard; he would always have a special place in her heart. But she had to admit that she also missed the security of Richard's embrace and protection. Was this why she now wanted to be in Nathan's arms? Was it only because of the sense of security that she felt, or was it his good looks? She did not understand herself at all and felt like crying, but held it in.

Nathan wrapped the ice cold cloth around her ankle and took his seat in the rocking chair by the fire. Sara thanked him in the hopes that he would look at her or speak to her, but all he said was, "you're welcome", and then stared at the roaring fire. There were many things that Nathan had wanted to say to Sara, but didn't know where to start, and it just didn't seem like the right time to bare what was on his mind. They were important things due to the early winter storm they had just gone through, and now he would not have enough food to get him through the winter months. On top of everything else, he had a woman in his home that he knew would have to be left alone and unprotected while he went to the settlement in Knoxville. It weighed heavily on his mind that it was at least a two days' drive by wagon and a two day return which meant that Sara would be left alone in a time she knew nothing about.

Sara could tell he was troubled about a multitude of things, so she remained quiet and returned to her own troubled thoughts.

About an hour passed and Nathan got up and grabbed an armful of firewood off the front porch and placed it next to the fireplace for easy access.

"It has been a long day and I have a lot to do tomorrow, so I'm going to turn in now. If you need anything just holler. I hope you won't be too uncomfortable on that couch, but you should be warm enough."

"Thank you, Mr. Chambers, for all you have done for me. Good night."

Sara's mind was overactive now, vexed by her feelings for two men and she knew she would never be able to fall asleep anytime soon. She made herself as comfortable as possible and laid there staring into the fire.

Chapter 9

Sara was still asleep on the couch with the quilt wrapped tightly around her when Nathan got up in the morning and walked quietly to the fireplace putting several logs on top of the smoldering ashes then blew gently on them trying to reignite the fire. He glanced behind him and Sara was still sleeping, and he thought about how desirable she was and quickly pushed that thought from his mind. She would be leaving as soon as she found a way to do it, and he didn't need his heart broken once again.

He tried to be quiet as he went to start a fire in the hearth and put a pot of coffee on to brew. Sara heard him moving around and waited until he had left to get something from the cellar before she sat up and smoothed out her hair and rearranged her clothing, then put the quilt across her lap.

When he returned he was carrying a plate of smoked ham and noticed immediately that Sara was awake.

"Good morning," Sara said.

"Good morning. I hope you weren't too uncomfortable last night," he said as he watched her put her hair in a ponytail.

"Not at all. May I give you a hand fixing breakfast?" she asked cheerfully.

Nathan placed the ham on the table and went to Sara and knelt down beside her. "I'd like to check your ankle, if I may," he asked.

Sara raised the quilt above her ankle and replied, "You may."

"Would you mind removing your stocking so I can see if it is badly bruised?" he asked looking a little uncomfortable. Touching her was almost unbearable for him. It had been a long time since he had touched or held a woman, and the problem was, he wanted all of her.

Sara reached over and winced from the soreness in her ribs and took hold of her stocking and pulled it off.

Her wincing did not escape Nathan's attention as he lifted her leg and gently held her ankle and slowly moved it around. The swelling had gone down during the night, but the bruising was now more obvious.

"How does it feel?" he asked looking up at her.

"Not too bad right now," she replied.

"Do you think you will be able to put your boots back on? I cleaned them off yesterday and left them on the porch," he replied soulfully, for he was not yet prepared to tell her that he would be leaving her tomorrow.

"If I do, will you allow me to help you fix breakfast?" she asked with a questioning look.

Nathan looked at her and sighed as he thought about it. "I guess you may, but I want you to stay off it as much as you can today. I need it to heal as quickly as possible so I don't want to catch you dancing around," he said as he stood back up and started for the door to retrieve her boots.

Sara quickly pulled her stocking back on with a groan and waited for Nathan to hand her back her boots. He returned them without saying a word and swiftly returned to the hearth – he had a lot to do today and the sun would soon be rising over the hill.

With some effort Sara slipped her feet into her boots and zipped them up. When she stood and looked down at her feet she was pleasantly surprised that Elizabeth's skirt didn't look half bad with the addition of her boots. She concealed the pain she was in and joined Nathan in the dining area and asked, "What may I do to help?"

"I'm afraid there isn't much for breakfast this morning. I just haven't had the time to bake any fresh bread. Do you think if I give you Elizabeth's recipe that you could bake some bread today, at least three or four loaves?" he asked having some doubts after her attempt to make biscuits.

"I believe with a written recipe I'll be quite able to bake some bread," she replied, guessing that he was questioning her abilities in the kitchen.

He nodded with a grin as he sliced some ham and placed it in a frying pan over the fire to heat it up. He turned to Sara and said, "If you wish you may slice what is left of the bread to go with the ham, but remember that knife is for the bread and not for me."

"Just as long as you behave yourself it will be just for the bread...Will your friend be joining us for breakfast?" she asked while she got out a couple of plates and forks, then cups for their coffee.

"No. He'll most likely be gone for several days trapping," he replied.

Sara was relieved. She still didn't trust him and doubted that she ever would.

"Please sit," he said as he placed some fried ham on her plate and turned to grab the coffee pot.

Sara cringed at the thought of the horrid coffee that was about to be poured into her cup. "I don't suppose you have any sugar close by?" she asked afraid to seem ungrateful for what he had provided.

With a perplexed look he asked, "For what?"

"For my coffee," she replied hesitantly.

With a puzzled look he went and got a small covered bowl of sugar off the shelf and watched as she put a couple of spoonful into her coffee and stirred it.

"Ah, at least it is drinkable," she said to herself and looked at Nathan who still had a puzzled look on his face as he watched her take a sip.

"Haven't you ever seen anyone put sugar and cream in their coffee?" she asked baffled by the look on his face.

"Not for a long time. We always drink it black. Sugar and cream are a luxury we usually don't have much of," he replied.

She felt bad now having asked for it, and if she ever had to drink coffee here again she wouldn't do it again.

Nathan quickly ate his ham and drank his coffee and got ready to head outside. He set Elizabeth's recipe on the table next to Sara before he placed his hat on his head and grabbed his rifle that was standing next to the door.

He turned and said, "I'll be back around dinner time, and by the way, that skirt looks nice with your boots," and quickly stepped outside and closed the door.

A big smile appeared on Sara's face. She no longer felt humiliated about the way she looked in Elizabeth's skirt. She happily finished her ham and coffee while she pondered all the comments he had made this morning without any explanations. Why so many loaves of bread, and why was he so anxious for her ankle to heal so quickly? Was he planning on taking her somewhere, or was he going somewhere and leaving her behind to fend for herself? She continued to think about these things while she cleaned off the table and prepared the bread for baking.

While the first couple of loaves were baking, she found the wash tub and washboard outside and filled it with water from the well. Unable to find any soap she went ahead and added the water that was heating in the hearth to the ice cold water and washed her sweater and jeans and Nathan's overcoat the best she could and hung them on a crude clothesline to dry; wishing all the time that she had her washing machine and dryer.

Heeding Nathan's orders to stay off her feet as much as possible she went inside and sat by the fire wrapping the quilt around her. Her hands were numb and red for the heated water had turned icy cold by the time she was finished washing the clothes and wished she was back at her cabin where she could get nice and warm and have a decent cup of hot coffee. Here she felt like a misfit; not only the way she dressed and her physical attributes, but also unable to do the simplest of things that were so common place for this period in time. It wasn't long before the aroma from the baking bread reached her by the fireplace and she had to abandon her little pity party. She unwrapped the quilt from around her and limped to the hearth and removed the pans of bread that were baking and placed the loaves on a towel to cool and put the last two loaves in to bake. The warmth from the hearth felt wonderful but she needed to get off her ankle and returned to her seat by the fireplace where she could elevate her foot and rest her black and blue ribs.

Quiet times like these always brought thoughts of Richard to mind. She lamented over the things they never were able to do, and how much she missed him. She hadn't known him for very long before she married him, but felt that he was her soulmate and wondered if she would ever have again what she had with him. The hours seemed to pass by quickly, and Sara finally heard Nathan's footsteps on the front porch, or at least she hoped it was his. She turned anxiously and watched until Nathan finally entered and hung his hat on the peg.

He stood there and inhaled the aroma of bread that filled the air and turned and smiled at Sara. "I think you might just be better at baking bread than making biscuits," he said and took a seat by the fireplace to warm himself.

After several minutes, Nathan looked directly at Sara and reluctantly said, "Sara, there's something that I've been meaning to talk to you about," then paused finding it hard to tell her he would be leaving her soon for Knoxville.

Sara's mind instantly went wild trying to imagine what he had been keeping from her for she was at his mercy whatever he had planned. What had he found so difficult that he couldn't or wouldn't tell her, and her heart pounded waiting for him to speak.

He looked at her once again and said, "The storm we had did a lot more damage to my crops than what I had expected. The hard freeze destroyed a lot of food that I was counting on to get me through the winter. I'm forced to go to Knoxville and buy supplies that I will need to make it until spring. It will be a two day journey there by wagon, a day to buy the supplies and a two day journey back if nothing goes wrong. I'm sorry…but I can't take you with me, and I don't want to leave you here alone in the house. I honestly can't think of any other way to do it. I don't suppose your family or anyone else from your time will come looking for you?" he asked and looked away with a heavy heart.

"They wouldn't know where to start. I haven't told anyone, not even my family about this house and where it's located. They would have just thought that I was crazy if I told them what happened whenever I entered your attic," she replied in a distressed state of mind.

Sara sat quietly. She was in no position to make any kind of demands; he owed her nothing. Her heart was beating wildly and it was more than her mind could handle thinking about being alone in the house with no protection. And what about his friend, Inola, that couldn't stand the sight of her; what if he returned before Nathan did? Fear had driven out any ideas or suggestions she might have come up with, and then Nathan spoke.

"I will leave you well stocked with firewood and food enough until I return. I know you are worried about Inola, but he will be away trapping for some time. I'm not expecting any of his friends to pay a visit, but should they come, just go to the attic and keep quiet until they leave. I don't believe them to be violent or destructive, but they might be hungry and take some of the food they find."

"When do you plan on leaving?" Sara asked.

"Tomorrow morning before the weather turns bad again," he replied.

Sara turned her face away; she didn't want him to see her tearful. He had enough problems and she hated being one of them. Nathan could see the distress she was in and moved over next to her and put his arms around her intentionally for the first time.

"Sara please don't cry. I would prefer to take you with me, but under the circumstances I don't see how that would be possible," he said regretfully.

Sara hung on tightly to Nathan, she trusted him and counted on him to protect her until she found a way to return home. Suddenly she remembered her gun upstairs; it was caked in mud and needed to be cleaned but at least she would have a way to protect herself.

"Mr. Chambers, would you be willing to bring my belt, handgun, and holster down to me so that I can clean them? I would feel much safer if I had them. I usually don't miss what I aim at," she said releasing him from her grip and looking pleadingly into his eyes.

"Sure, we'll do it right after supper and I will help you," he said assuredly and held her briefly once again in his arms. At that moment there was no other place on earth that Sara would rather be than in his strong powerful arms. Her fears melted away and all was right in the world as long as he was there with her.

The aroma from the last loaves of bread baking finally reached Sara, but she did not want to be free from Nathan's embrace; not yet. She would have gladly gone hungry than give up the serenity she felt, but knew that Nathan was hungry and reluctantly let go.

"Come on, let's go get some supper and we can figure all of this out later," he said and gave her a hand up. When he saw her limping he reached down and picked her up in his arms and carried her to the table; chastising himself for getting so attached to Sara when he knew she would be leaving him.

They sat in silence as they ate their supper. Both were deeply troubled about what awaited them over the next several days, and neither could think of another way to alter what seemed inevitable. When they were finished eating, Nathan suggested that Sara go sit by the fire while he cleared the table and finished packing for his early morning trip to Knoxville.

A simple, "okay" was all she said and tried to walk without limping back to her seat by the fire. She was lost in a trance staring at the sparks flying up from the fireplace and was unaware that Nathan had gone upstairs to get her handgun. Unexpectedly Nathan called her name and she jumped. "You looked like you were a thousand miles away," he stated.

"No. Just over the next hill," she replied thinking about the things she had left in her time, and then noticed her gun in his hand.

"I'm afraid you're going to have to show me how to take this apart if I'm going to clean it for you. I'm fascinated by its design, and eager to figure out the workings of it," he said and handed it to her.

"Why don't you come sit next to me and I'll take it apart for you," she said forcing herself to smile.

He laid a cloth across her lap and watched as she quickly disassembled the weapon and smiled as she looked over at him. He had never seen anything like it and examined each piece in amazement.

"After you clean it, do you think you can put it back together again?" she asked, amused by the way he studied each piece, especially the magazine clip that held the bullets.

Nathan gave her a confident look that let her know there wasn't too many things he was incapable of doing especially when it came to firearms. She watched as he thoroughly cleaned her weapon and holster and put it all back together and handed it to her with a satisfied look.

"I've got to get an early start tomorrow so I'd better turn in. Is there anything you need before I do?" he asked in such a way that it made Sara wonder how he really felt about her. She knew that they had only known each other for a couple of days under very difficult circumstances, but something had definitely changed about him.

"No, I believe I have everything I need. Good night Nathan," she said tenderly.

"That's the first time you've called me Nathan. I like it. Good night," he said and closed his door.

While Nathan laid in bed, his troubled thoughts would not allow him to fall asleep. His mind was in turmoil. Just four days ago he was angered by the intrusion into his home and life by this most peculiar woman. He had been grieving the loss of his wife and daughter, and now he welcomed the presence of this woman in his life, and the thought of her returning to where she came from greatly disturbed him. He was not a man accustomed to sudden changes; he was a simple, pragmatic man, used to working hard. Nathan now felt like he had lost his ability to be sensible, logical, and practical – Sara had totally thrown him off his stride.

Meanwhile, Sara was fidgeting on her make-shift bed, unable to sleep. Her thoughts were also troubled. The angry man she once could not wait to get away from, she now dreaded his leaving. She was also bewildered by the fact that the loss of Richard in her life no longer occupied her mind like it had just a couple of days ago. She wondered how she could long for all the conveniences she enjoyed in her time period and yet not mind the hardships she was now going through with this man by her side. She questioned whether the feelings she thought she now had for him would fade once the reality of a life filled with washing clothes by hand, cooking meals in only a pot over a hot hearth, or sewing clothes by hand instead of shopping at a store occurred on a daily basis for the rest of her life. She needed to consider these things seriously, because there was always the possibility that she might not ever be able to return to her time; the portal could close.

They both longed to sleep, but it would be hours before either would be able to do so.

Chapter 10

It was still dark when Nathan quietly left his bedroom. He was determined to get an early start, and hopefully put a lot of the thoughts that had kept him awake last night behind him. He needed this time to clear his head and put things back into proper perspective.

Sara heard him open his bedroom door and yawned hard and long after her restless night. She sat up and greeted Nathan with a smile. "If you would like, I'll get breakfast going so you can finish packing the wagon for your trip," she said cheerfully trying not to let her disappointment about his leaving show.

"That would be most helpful...thank you," he said and quickly made his way out the front door. Sara was still bewildered by him. One minute he seemed guarded when he was around her and then the next minute he seemed to open up and be vulnerable – it was most confusing.

It was cold in the house, and the first thing Sara did was start the fires in both the hearth and in the fireplace, and then quickly went to make the coffee. Since Nathan was in a hurry to leave, breakfast would have to be kept simple: sliced ham, bread, and some apples which she would also slice for easy eating. Knowing that he would probably eat jerky for lunch as he drove along she decided to surprise him with some ham sandwiches to take along since the ham and bread were already out.

As she was waiting for the coffee to finish brewing, she went out on the front porch happy that it was finally warming up and watched as Nathan was loading his bedroll, food, and blankets into the back of the wagon, then covered the back portion with a tarp. As he climbed up into the seat he saw Sara standing on the porch and lowered his head. It pained him to leave her behind. For as hard as he had tried to tell himself not to get attached to this woman who could leave him at any moment, his heart wanted her more than anything in the world. He slowly drove the wagon from in front of the barn up to the front porch and sighed heavily as he tied the reins to the post.

Sara had turned and gone back into the house before Nathan had reached the porch. She dreaded his going, but did not want to make things harder than they had to be by letting her emotions show. She was pouring his coffee as he came through the door, and then took her seat.

Nathan removed his hat and hung it on the peg, and made a beeline to the hearth to warm his hands before sitting down. As he rubbed them together over the fire he turned to Sara and thanked her for making breakfast.

They glanced at each other as he took his seat, but neither one wanted to be the first to speak, and even if they had, they wouldn't have known what to say. They both had a lot on their mind and in their hearts that would be hard to express, and maybe best if they did not express them.

Nathan relished the hot coffee and poured himself another cup while he hurriedly ate his breakfast. Sara on the other hand just nibbled at the food on her plate, and hadn't bothered to pour herself a cup of coffee but drank a cup of water instead. Her stomach and heart were tied in knots and food was the last thing on her mind.

When Nathan was through with breakfast he sat there quietly for a few moments and then turned to Sara and said in a soft and reluctant voice, "Well...I best be going. Thanks again for breakfast." Sara quickly handed him the basket of sandwiches and meekly stated, "I thought you might like something other than jerky for lunch." He was deeply touched by her thoughtfulness and fought back the emotions that were fighting to be expressed and quickly retrieved his hat and rifle that were by the front door and quickly stepped outside. Unprepared for him leaving so abruptly she followed him out to the wagon, restraining the tears her heart wanted to pour out.

Untying the reins he started to mount the wagon when he suddenly stopped and turned towards Sara. They both stood their looking longingly into each other's eyes, both wanting to say what was in their hearts. But, both were afraid that what they were feeling would only lead to heartache, and both had had enough heartache; it was too soon to go through it again.

Nathan took a deep breath and heavily exhaled as he looked at her more deeply than his heart could bear. He wanted more than anything to take her in his arms and kiss her goodbye, but couldn't bring himself to do it and quickly climbed into the wagon before he gave way to his desires.

Sara looked up at him and willed her tears not to run down her cheeks as Nathan with one last look at her, said, "Take care of yourself, Sara Mathews," and quickly urged his team on. He never looked back as Sara stood there crying, watching him until he was no longer in sight. She wished that he had looked back at her; that would have at least given her some indication of how he really felt about her.

What Sara did not know was that as Nathan drove away from his house he wanted more than anything to look back to see if Sara was still standing there watching him as he drove away. He tried to tell himself that he was doing the right thing in not looking back. He was only being practical. Why pursue a relationship that you believe might not have a future; you only open yourself up to more heartache.

Sara quickly ran to the attic hoping that she could catch one more glimpse of him, and then out of the blue, she was instantly covered in goosebumps and turned and looked around the attic. It was old and weathered, and she quickly looked back out the attic window and the land that was just a few moments ago a cleared field was now covered in trees, and she stood there breathless and bewildered. *"What just happened? Why did everything suddenly change?"* she asked herself. She thought for a moment and then said, "Nathan left his property. That's it! Nathan is the missing puzzle piece to the time portal!" Sara's fears about being left alone instantly left and she was free to return to her own time.

She realized that she was still in the clothes that Nathan had given her and was happy that she had remembered to put her own clothes in the attic when they had dried after washing them. Sara hurriedly changed and found where the chest once stood and left Elizabeth's clothes neatly folded on the dusty floor close by for Nathan to find.

She quickly limped down the stairs and out of the house with her backpack and gun at her side when she suddenly stopped dead in her tracks only feet away from the front porch. She was leaving Nathan. The thought that she might never see him again hit her like a ton of bricks. Sara was overwhelmed with feelings that she never thought possible after losing Richard, and turned and looked back at the house. The thought of Nathan never taking her in his arms and kissing her deeply and passionately was tearing her apart. But she needed to go home, and she turned and started up the hill with a heavy heart and burning tears.

When she reached her cabin she was emotionally and physically drained. She turned off the alarm system and reset it after closing the door and leaned back against it and the cabin seemed empty, just like the old house when Nathan was not there, and she was once again all alone. She could see from where she was standing that there were messages on the answering machine and knew that her parents must be out of their minds with worry.

She plugged in her cell phone to be charged and noticed that there were at least a dozen messages left on it, and as much as she did not want to talk to anyone yet, she knew she had to call her parents. She dialed her dad's number and as it rang she tried to think of an explanation of why she was not answering her phone over the past several days. She didn't want to lie, but she also wasn't ready to tell anyone what had really happened to her.

Her dad recognized her number right away and answered. "Sara, where have you been? Why didn't you return any of our calls? Are you okay? We have been out of our minds worrying about you, now start talking, and I want the truth!"

"Hi, Dad. I'm fine. I'm sorry I made you and mom worry. I got so caught up in writing my new book that I turned everything off. You know how I get when I get a breakthrough; I write day and night and only stop for a quick bite to eat and a short nap when I can no longer keep my eyes open. Please forgive me. I promise I won't let that happen again."

"Well you had better not," he fumed. "That must be one hell of a book! What's it about?" he asked.

"Dad, I don't want to ruin it by telling you just bits and pieces. I promise, you will be the first person to read it."

"Well, now that we know you're alright, your mom wants to know if we can come over and stay with you this weekend?" he asked.

"Tell mom I would love to have you both come and stay with me," she said trying to sound enthusiastic. But the truth was, she didn't know if she would be able to hide her troubled thoughts and feelings from them, and there was much to think about.

"Okay, we'll see you in a few days, and you had better give your editor a call. She has been calling us asking if we had heard from you," he stated sounding a little annoyed.

"Okay, Dad, I will. See you this weekend. I love you. Bye," she said eager to hang up the phone. Her editor would have to wait a while longer. Sara went straight to her room and threw herself on the bed and cried herself to sleep.

It was already four in the afternoon when she finally woke with a long yawn and deep stretch, and hungry after only taking a few bites of her breakfast. She forced herself to get up and make something to eat and called Natalie.

Now that that was done, she went outside on the back porch with an icepack for her ankle and sat alone with her thoughts waiting for the sun to set. Sara couldn't shake the feeling deep inside of her that she had made a mistake leaving Nathan, for there was a definite chemistry between them that she couldn't deny. She wasn't ready to choose between the two worlds, but it was wrong to let him worry about what had happened to her. She hadn't even left a note explaining that she was now able to return to her own time, or to tell him how she really felt about him. She had only been with him for a little more than three days and yet it seemed like her world revolved around him and her soul grieved being away from him. She wondered if his soul would grieve for her when he returned and found that she was gone. The million "what ifs" running through her mind were more than she could bear. She had to try to find a way to drive him from her mind if that were even possible. What she felt for him couldn't be put into words at this time, or could it?

Sara got up immediately and went to her laptop and turned it on. The words started pouring out of her like a mighty raging river flowing downstream. She started at the very beginning; a young woman who had lost her husband and her ability to write books. The words kept pouring out so Sara kept writing. Day and night she wrote and only stopped to blow her nose or when her hands could no longer stay on the keyboard from crying so hard. The deeper the pain grew in her heart, the faster she wrote pouring those feelings out for all the world to read.

While Sara was busy writing at night, Nathan was lying on his bedroll with a fire burning close by. He stared up at the stars and thought of Sara. She was so very different from his wife Elizabeth. He wondered what his life would look like with Sara by his side, for she had awakened a passion in him that he had never felt before; not even with his wife. Once he had gotten past his anger of her abrupt appearance, he was drawn to her like a moth to the flame and he pondered what it was about her that he found so captivating, almost intoxicating. In the short time he knew her she had been both strong and confident and fearful and vulnerable. He could see her face clearly in the night sky and the way she would look at him, and the way she would sometimes blush, and a smile would come to his face. She was beautiful, no doubt about it, but it was more than her beauty that attracted him to her. The small glimpses of her zest for life, her playfulness, and her genuine character of being loving, kind, and always willing to help and work hard, these were the things he also cherished about her. He tried desperately to drive these thoughts from his mind; he needed his sleep, he had a long drive ahead of him tomorrow.

Sara had been writing for three days now, practically nonstop, and it was only the sound of the doorbell that forced her to stop now. She closed down the top to her laptop and went to the door to let her parents in. She turned the alarm off, took a deep breath, and put a smile on her face before she opened the door.

"Hi Mom, hi Dad, come on in," she said with a smile.

Once inside her mother gave her a good hard squeeze of a hug and said, "It's so good to see you. You had us so worried there for a while when you didn't answer your phone for days."

"I know, Mom. I promise not to do that again. I will give you a heads-up next time I feel the need to turn my phone off," she said.

"Oh no you don't. There will be no more turning your phone off. You can answer and say – I can't talk now; I'll call you later," Don said in a serious tone.

Her mom, trying to change the subject, asked, "We heard of a really good restaurant in the next town over and would love to take you there for lunch; would you like to go?"

"Sure, whatever you would like to do is fine with me," Sara replied.

It was harder than she imagined to hide her feelings and the turmoil she was going through from her parents. Though she had a smile on her face, words kept pouring from her heart and they longed to be written down while they were fresh in her mind.

During lunch her father urged her to tell them about the book she was writing. She tried hard to convince them to wait until it was finished, but her dad would not relent. Sara grudgingly gave in and decided to just give them the basic outline of her story.

"That sounds so exciting! How do you ever come up with such ideas?" her mother questioned.

"This time it just came to me on one of my hikes, and I thought it would be a good change of pace from the books I have written," she replied, never letting them know that what she was writing was not a fictitious story, but an unbelievable reality that she still didn't know how it would end.

Sara had hoped that this weekend with her parents would be a good diversion from her tormented mind, but her thoughts of Nathan kept fighting their way through and the weekend seemed to drag on. If this was to be her final decision to remain in her own time, then she wanted to be free from the feelings and thoughts that were haunting her. She wanted to enjoy the visits from her parents and move on with her life and find happiness once again, but doubted whether she would ever be free from the memories of Nathan.

Chapter 11

It was now Sunday afternoon and Sara was waving good-bye to her parents as they drove away. It was a beautiful sunny day and Sara looked in the direction of the old house. She wondered if Nathan was on his way home from Knoxville, and what he would do when he discovered that she wasn't there. She felt sorry for him. If he felt the way she felt about him, then he would leave no rock unturned looking for her. Oh, how she wished she had left him a note; it was cruel not to have.

Sara went back inside feeling distressed for what she was about to put Nathan through, and her urge to write a happy ending to her story grew ever stronger. She decided to sit on the back porch for a while and just think. The battle to decide which world she wanted to live in raged on, and just when she thought she had figured it out, the other side would gain momentum; it was a battle that she couldn't seem to win.

Nathan was indeed on his way home with his wagon full of supplies to get him through the winter. He urged his horses on faster than he normally would drive them for he was eager to see Sara again. He would not fail this time to let her know how he felt about her and beg, if necessary, for her to stay with him. *"For if I lose her now I fear I would die,"* he thought to himself.

He could now see his house off in the distance and drove his horses even faster as his anticipation of seeing Sara grew stronger by the minute. It wasn't long before he pulled the wagon up in front of the house and quickly tied the reins to the post. Nathan called out Sara's name as he ran up the steps to the front porch, and quickly stepped through the front door. He stood just inside looking around and called her name out once again in the silent and darkened room. There was no answer and no sign of her being there; the fireplace had not been used in days. He took a deep breath and thought about what his next move should be. He willed himself to remain calm as he climbed the stairs and checked out the bedroom where she had slept and then went to the attic to look. *"Where next?"* he thought as his heart started to race. He went out back and looked for tracks to see if there was any sign that someone had been there and taken her away but found none, and decided to go look through the grove of trees where Sara had gone once before. He walked from one end to the other, even looking in the ravine where she had lain – wet, muddy, and hurt.

He told himself not to panic; he would find her. He had seen the way she looked at him and the way she blushed; surely she would not have left on her own freewill. But first, he needed to put away his supplies and feed and wipe down his horses; he had pushed them a little too hard in his eagerness to get home.

It was now too dark to go out searching for Sara and he made himself fix something to eat though his stomach felt hard as a rock. He would start looking again for the woman he loved at first light.

Meanwhile, Sara was in her bed staring up at the ceiling trying to keep her mind as blank as an unwritten page in a book. She casually reached for the locket around her neck and was surprised to find that it was not there. *"That's strange"*, she thought; *"I always wear it."* She tried to remember where she was the last time she saw it and couldn't remember. Sara decided she must have put it in her backpack for some reason, maybe while she was changing clothes and got up and went through her backpack - nothing.

She wondered if it had fallen off her somewhere in the attic, or possibly she had lost it when she fell into the ravine and did not realize that it had come off. She was perplexed about what to do. Richard had given that to her and she would always cherish it. She was tired now and decided to search the rest of the house tomorrow when there would be more light to help her find it and went and crawled back into bed.

Nathan rose early and went back upstairs to the attic to look for possible clues. He found the clothes he had given Sara to wear neatly folded and lying on the floor and told himself that she changed just because she felt more comfortable in her own clothes that fit her. He refused to believe it was a sign that she had found a way to return to her own time. As he was about to leave the attic a ray of light burst through the attic window and reflected off of something in the corner. He briskly walked over to it and when he bent down to pick it up he discovered it was Sara's locket. She would never have left that behind he told himself unless she was forced to leave the house in a hurry; that was the only explanation his mind would accept.

He put the locket safely away and went out to the barn and saddled his horse; he was going to find Inola. Even though it made no sense to him why Inola would come and take Sara with him, he was determined to make sure that Inola had nothing to do with her disappearance, and rode out to where they normally went trapping.

Later that afternoon he found Inola's campsite and looked for signs that Sara had been there. He found nothing and swore at himself for not telling her how he felt about her before he left for Knoxville. He was tired after his long ride and decided he would wait for Inola to return for the night and hear what he had to say. Nathan made a large fire and put a pot of coffee on for it was starting to get cold and Inola should be back soon.

As he was eating a strip of deer jerky Inola came walking into camp with an armload full of skins and dropped them on the ground on the outskirts of his camp. He was happy to see Nathan and greeted him warmly, but was surprised when Nathan seemed worried and out of sorts about something. Nathan got right to the point, "Inola, is Sara with you?"

Inola was bewildered by his question and looked at him strangely and asked, "Why would Sara be with me? I've been trapping here since I left your place."

Nathan tilted his head back looking up into the sky and sighed heavily; he was out of ideas as to where she could be.

"Sara is missing, Inola. When I got back from Knoxville with supplies for the winter she was gone," he sighed regretfully.

"I told you, she evil spirit," he roughly declared.

Nathan's anger boiled up within him, but Inola was about the only friend he had, and so he bit his tongue and let his comment go. "I'm turning in now. I've got to get an early start tomorrow," he said and grabbed his bedroll and blanket from off his horse and found a spot close to the fire to lay down.

His anger and frustration would keep him awake for hours. His hopes of finding Sara were fading quickly and he feared that she had indeed found a way to return to where she came from. What was troubling him was why she chose to leave, unless what he thought he saw when he looked into her eyes was something different than what she actually felt. Was her world really that much better than the life she could have had with him? Now it was too late to tell her how he felt. She had been standing in front of him and he said nothing. If he had, maybe she would have decided to stay, but now he would never know; for he seriously doubted whether he would ever get a second chance to tell her how he felt about her.

Sara woke around eight o'clock and fixed a pot of coffee and toasted a couple of waffles for breakfast. As she ate she couldn't help but think about the awful coffee she drank black with Nathan. It brought back memories that were now precious to her as she remembered the different sensations that swept over her whenever he was near. The phone rang and interrupted her daydreams and she glanced at the number and ignored it; it was a telemarketer. Good timing she thought; I'm supposed to look for my locket before I start writing again. She searched the entire house including the back and front porches and found nothing. Her frustration killed any desire to write; she wanted her necklace back and knew that it had to be somewhere in the old house.

She lit a fire and sat in her favorite chair to think. She reasoned that she had entered the old house a couple of times when there was only dust and cobwebs. If she were lucky enough she might be able to do it again and find her necklace without Nathan ever finding out. Nathan was a problem. She knew that if she ever saw him again she might not have the will to leave, and once again imagined being held in his arms and what it would feel like to be kissed, and she meant KISSED by him. Goosebumps surfaced from head to toe at the very thought of it.

This was insane. She only knew the man for several days for heaven's sake, and she was acting as if he was the love of her life; her soul mate. She decided she would never go back. She would just have to learn to get along without Richard's locket and without a man she barely knew, even if he did drive her wild.

Nathan was up early the next morning and had breakfast with Inola before starting for home. He did not push his horse hard this time, but went along at a steady pace; he needed time to think. It was easy for him to know what his heart wanted: it wanted Sara to be there waiting for him, but his head told him that he would probably never see her again. He tried to imagine what it would have been like to take her in his arms and kiss her, really kiss her, but quickly drove that thought from his mind because he knew it was never going to happen now that she was gone.

As he approached his land he had decided to do what he had always done before Sara showed up, and that was to work hard.

His workload was almost double now that his wife had died, and there were no other settlers around to give him a hand with the harvest.

He knew instantly that Sara was not there when he climbed down from his horse, or she would have been there to greet him. His heart was crushed within him and he feared it was beyond repair and hung his head and sighed deeply. He was on his own once again and the reality of that was unbearable.

Knowing that her book was only half completed she went back to her laptop and read the last chapter to get back into the flow of her writing. She remembered all too well the part she had written for it was real and powerful; it had really happened. But now she had to write about things that were fictional and she pondered how she wanted her book to end. Would it end: happily ever after, or would the heroine decide to return to her own time and learn to live without the man she loved?

Sara's last thought stuck in her mind – to live without the man she loved. Did she really love him, or was it lust she felt? She sat back in her chair and folded her arms across her lap and pondered that question. Yes, she usually blushed when he looked directly at her with that ruggedly handsome face and body of his, and yes she was extremely stimulated whenever he was close to her. But what else about him did she admire? She forced herself to think past those physical things and think about the man himself. He was protective, hardworking, tender at times, thoughtful, a gentleman, trustworthy, and dependable; what else could you ask for in a man?

Suddenly her mind was flooded with thoughts of Richard. He had all of the same qualities she thought she saw in Nathan. Had she only wanted Richard so much that she imagined those feelings she had for Nathan so she could remember what it felt like to be loved by a man; to be held in his arms and no longer feel lost and alone? These were questions she needed to answer before she could write another word. Sara spent days sitting on the back porch staring off into space trying to sort through her feelings; what was real and what was imagined. Was there really a specified time that one should grieve for their partner? Who determines how quickly you can fall in love again?

So, how would her book end? Sara had not yet been able to answer all the questions she felt needed to be answered, but she knew she needed to submit something soon in writing to her publisher. She finally decided to straddle that issue and write about how she would imagine living with Nathan in 1786 would be like, then decide whether she would choose love, or life in 2020.

Sara wrote with passion once again, but writing about Nathan only kept him at the forefront of her mind. As long as she was writing she was fine, but when she stopped for the evening she was miserable and found herself crying more times than not.

The phone rang and Sara saw that it was her mother that was calling. "Hi, Sara," her mother said cheerfully.

Sara replied with a melancholy, "Hi, Mom."

"Okay, what is going on? You've been out of sorts ever since you started writing that book. You know, you really shouldn't get so involved with your characters," she said emphatically.

"I know, Mom," she said and started to cry; she just couldn't stop herself this time.

"That's it. You're coming home for a visit. You need a break from that book," her mom seriously stated.

"I think you're right, Mom. A week with you and dad would do wonders for me," Sara replied in a deeply depressed state.

"Well then, pack your bag and we'll see you tonight and we'll all go out for dinner," her mom stated trying to lift her spirits.

"That sounds great. I'll see you in a couple of hours," Sara replied hoping that her visit with her parents would distract her from all the confusion she was going through.

Sara packed her bag and sent Natalie the next several chapters of her book and let her know that she would be at her parent's home for the next week. Once she was on the road she turned up the volume to her rock-n-roll music and sang along, hoping to drive Nathan from her mind. But, every love song just reminded her of him.

The week with her parents went by quickly, and she soon found herself waving good-bye to them. Her stay had turned out to be a pleasant diversion, but now she was headed back to the cabin and back to her book, and she was no closer to deciding how her book should end.

By the time she entered her cabin, her resolve to never return to the old house was weakening. She was approximately two miles away from the old house, and that meant that she was also only about two miles away from Nathan. She tried to tell herself that if she decided to return, it would only be to find her locket that Richard had given her, but her heart knew differently. These few weeks away from him had seemed like an eternity and she decided to just go look at the house, but not enter it. Maybe that would help her answer some of the questions that still lingered in her mind and decide which world she wanted to live in.

Chapter 12

Sara stood holding her coffee cup staring out the large picture windows leading to her back porch. It was overcast and breezy and she hoped that the weather would change before she prepared for her hike back to Nathan's house. She was fully prepared in her mind, at least, to just sit at a distance and look at the house and think, for she was not ready to take a chance that Nathan might be there.

A short time later she started on her two mile hike and when Sara reached the base of the hill, she turned and looked back towards her cabin and wondered if that would be the last time she saw it. That was nonsense she told herself; she was only going back to the house to look and think! Besides, she hadn't left any note this time for her parents explaining her decision should she decide to stay.

She continued her climb to the top of the hill and stared down at the once grand house that was partially obscured by the trees and brush and hesitated going any closer. The closer she got to the house the more she felt the connection between them was so strong that time itself could not keep them apart. She wondered if it was possible for the laws of nature to have been suspended for a short period of time just to bring the two of them together.

She continued to stand there at a distance pondering whether she would be strong enough to resist the urge to once again go inside. It took almost a half-hour for her to decide to continue down the hill and sit at the base where she sat the first time she came upon the old weathered house.

Sara climbed up on the outcrop of rocks and sat and stared across the field and wondered if Nathan was inside, or out working in the fields harvesting what he could of his damaged crops.

Her breaths were short and shallow as her mind and heart waged their war inside her. Her heart longed and ached for a love that burned like fire, but her mind told her that her responsibilities and life were here in 2020. Did she really want to give up all the luxuries she was accustomed to? She questioned whether she was now ready to let go of Richard and open a new chapter in her life.

Sara sat there for over an hour and let her mind and heart fight it out. She finally had to step in and take control and reasoned that maybe it was possible to live in both worlds. Maybe the portal through time would always be there and she could cross over from time to time to see her parents, or get things she wanted, or take care of things she needed to do.

She was now willing to take the risk. She psyched herself up as she crossed the field of trees and took her first step up on the porch. She took a deep breath as her hand rested on the door handle of the partially unhinged door then finally pushed it open. When she stepped inside all she saw was dust and cobwebs, and felt a sudden gusty chill sweep through the front door that sent goosebumps over her body. Her heart pounded as she wondered where he was right now. She assumed he was out in the fields working to finish harvesting what he could from the damaged crops before the next cold front moved through, and quickly rushed up the stairs and then into the attic to look for her locket.

She looked in every nook and cranny but could not find it, and decided to go check around where the couch would have stood in the past. She might have time if she hurried, but there was no way she could leave undetected if Nathan was to suddenly show up.

Sara managed to get down the first two steps and then the scent of pine filled the air, and she watched the steps change once again before her eyes. She gasped in apprehension and froze where she stood, for now she was bound to meet him and tried to prepare herself for the inevitable. She was nervous and unsure how he would react after what she had put him through over the past several weeks and took a deep breath and exhaled deeply.

Sara slowly descended the stairs, and as she turned the corner there stood Nathan. Just the sight of him took her breath away as she watched him slowly reach into his pocket never taking his eyes off of her.

"Looking for this?" he asked as he held up her locket.

Sara just nodded unable to speak.

He unfastened the necklace and held it apart in his hands and just looked at her begging her with his eyes to come closer.

She knew at that moment the war was over. She surrendered and walked slowly over to him never breaking eye contact.

Nathan looked at her tenderly and clasped the necklace around her neck and softly said in a tender voice, "I'm so glad you came back."

"I didn't think I would miss you so much," she replied as she longingly looked into his eyes. "Are you ever going to kiss me?" she asked glancing at his lips and then back up into his eyes.

Nathan cradled her head in his hand, and pulled her body tightly up against him and looked into her eyes as he leaned in and kissed her with the full force of his love behind it.

It was everything and more than she had ever dreamed of. A fire blazed within her and her body throbbed and tingled as she craved more of his love.

Nathan continued to kiss her passionately as they both embraced each other; their hands never ceasing to caress each other's body.

Sara was sure that he would sweep her up in his arms and carry her to his bedroom, but she should have known better. Nathan was a gentleman, honorable and disciplined. While still holding Sara tightly in his arms he looked at her and begged, "Please stay. Choose me and my world, I couldn't bear to let you go again. I love you Sara."

These were words Sara never dreamed she would hear so soon after both of them had lost their partners; people that they had deeply loved and had planned on spending the rest of their lives with.

Tears ran down her cheeks as she buried her face against his broad chest and shoulders. She knew she had found her soul mate, and she would allow nothing in her world to tear them apart; not her parents, her job, or memories of Richard.

She looked at him with a tear streaked face and lovingly said, "I chose you Nathan Chambers for as long as I shall live…but, I need to be able to travel between both worlds, for the time being at least."

He looked bewildered. "Why must you go back, Sara?" he asked knowing that this couldn't be good.

It was best to just get it over with. Tell him the reasons she must leave him, and certainly being a reasonable man he would understand; at least that is what she was counting on.

"Nathan, please sit and I will explain," she said as she pulled the other rocking chair close to his and sat on the edge of her chair looking at him with a most troubled gaze.

"Nathan, there are things left undone that I need to take care of at some point. When I returned to your house today I never dreamed that things would turn out the way they have. I had fully expected to quickly search for my locket and return home today still torn between which world and time I belonged in. I wasn't sure how you really felt about me the way we left each other without saying a word about how we both felt. You never even looked behind you once you pulled away. Then there's my parents. I've never told them about you or this house being real. They think it is something I made up to write a book about, and I fear they will think that I have lost my mind when I tell them that everything I wrote about is true. I have money and possessions that I need to put in my parents name since I have no one else to leave it to. Plus, I want to submit my book about us to my publisher for printing now that I have the perfect ending to it, and then I promise I will return and stay with you forever if you still want me," she stated with a pleading look; afraid that he would be angry and hurt.

Nathan stood up and walked over to the fireplace and leaned against the mantle without saying a word. He stood there silent for several minutes thinking, and then turned and looked at her sitting there begging with just a look to understand the importance of what she was asking.

"It would only be for a short time that I would need to travel between our two times," she said. Oh, how she wished he would say something; get angry, yell, it didn't matter as long as he decided to welcome her back when she was finished with what she needed to do.

"A week, I'll give you a week, but I need you here with me. It will soon be too dangerous for you to travel back here; winter will have set in and I fear for your safety crossing the open country," he said with a furrowed brow.

Sara knew that would not be enough time. She was thinking that it would take at least a month or more to accomplish all she needed to do. But how could she convince him that she would be able to cross over to his time safely; he was totally unaware of all the innovations that had been invented over the past couple hundred years.

"I'm afraid that won't be enough time. Nathan, I'm not traveling to another place, I'm traveling to another time. In my time we have motorized vehicles with their own heating systems where I can drive right up to your front door safely. Even though it was cloudy and breezy when I left this morning, there were no signs of a cold front moving through. I know you must think that I have lost my mind, but I haven't. I can't explain how all this happens, but we both know that it does happen; my being here is proof of that," she said and watched him turn his face away and stare into the fire.

He needed time to process everything she just told him. It was a lot to ask anyone to believe such unimaginable things, and she feared that she might have pushed him away forever. But then she remembered: love was supposed to conquer all, and that perfect love drives out fear, and she knew in her heart that their love was true and that it would stand the test of time.

An idea came to her out of the blue, and she quickly went to her backpack and pulled out her cell phone and went and stood next to him.

"Nathan, please look at this," she said and waited for him to look at her. When he did, she saw how troubled and confused he truly was, and feared what she was about to show him would only add to that confusion. But, she needed to drive home her point that they were from different times, not places.

Holding her phone she turned it on, and brought up the photos she had taken over the past year and held the phone in front of him. His eyes widened and he quickly glanced at her in disbelief and then back at the pictures she was thumbing through.

"Now do you believe me?" she asked with hopefulness.

He looked at her with a confused gaze trying to take it all in. She waited patiently never breaking her gaze into his eyes. He finally looked back down at her phone, and then at the clothes she was wearing, and even at the zippers on her boots and backpack, and then nodded his head ever so slightly.

"I can't make sense of any of it, but I'm compelled to believe it," he said in a troubled tone and looked back down into the fire.

Sara returned her cell phone to her backpack and stood a short distance away, giving him time to think things through. It seemed like an eternity to her, but he finally turned and held out his hand to her.

She smiled and ran to his arms. He was reluctant at first, but soon wrapped his arms tightly around her, but the joy he had once felt while kissing her was gone; uncertainty had replaced it.

Nathan took her by the hand and led her to his rocking chair by the fire and gently pulled her down to sit on his lap. They were both content to sit there together by the fire when suddenly the sound of thunder rolling over the hills could be heard in the distance and gusts of wind started beating against the house.

"I should return home, no one knows that I left," she said looking up at him.

"You can't possibly go anywhere today, that storm is headed our way and I fear it will be much worse than the last one," he stated with great concern.

"Remember, in my time this storm is not headed my way. But okay, I'll stay the night," she said lovingly and leaned back against his chest.

Nathan smiled and pulled her close, not wanting the tears welling in his eyes to be seen; for he was grateful he was given a second chance to tell Sara that he loved her, and was willing to do anything to get her to choose him and his time. His heart felt like it was about to burst with happiness – he could deal with anything as long as Sara was by his side, but he wondered how he would deal with her leaving him in the morning.

The storm raged on throughout the afternoon and the rain turned to heavy snow which piled up with the gusting winds, but the house was warm and filled with their love and laughter.

After supper Nathan put some more logs on the fire and extra blankets on top of the rug that lay close to the fireplace and Sara laid there in his arms as they talked; for each knew very little about each other. They stopped often to kiss and gaze contentedly into each other's eyes until one of them came up with another question.

"Nathan, why did you and your wife and daughter move to such an isolated place? Weren't you afraid of the Indians, or getting hurt or sick without a doctor within a hard day's drive?" she asked.

"I served in the War of Independence for five long cold years. I saw more death and destruction than any person should ever have to see. I was sick of killing and people in general so I sold my house in Boston and headed south and west until I found a place where I could find peace, and I had hoped happiness again. My wife was pregnant with my daughter and stayed with my parents until I built this place with the help of some of the men in my regiment who moved to Knoxville. It took me more than a year to build it and then I sent for my wife and baby in the early spring. They both died of influenza that first winter. I've been alone ever since, except for Inola who showed up at my place sick and hungry. He does most of the hunting and trapping while I do the farming and help him whenever I can," he replied to her question.

Sara looked over at him with compassion and laid her hand against his cheek and softly said, "I'm so sorry for your loss. I know firsthand the agonizing pain you've been through. I pray to God that I never bring more pain into your life, but only love, happiness, and the peace of mind and soul that you have been searching for. And, if I can make you laugh every now and then that would be great, for I dearly love to laugh."

He smiled and brushed a lock of hair away from her eyes and said tenderly to her, "You already have. I just wish you didn't have to leave in the morning. Can't you stay for just a little while longer?"

"Oh Nathan, I would if I could. Believe me it pains me to have to leave you, but the sooner I leave the sooner I can return to you. I promise to take care of things as quickly as I can. Besides, I plan on buying a four-wheel drive ATV so I can be here in a matter of minutes instead of hours, and each time I come I'll bring more of my personal things out here with me," Sara replied with excitement.

Nathan grinned, "I haven't a clue what a four-wheel drive ATV is, but you had better be careful on it. I don't need you getting hurt, there's a lot of work to do around here," he teased.

"Oh, I see now; you only want me around for the work I can do," she said with a raised eyebrow and a hint of a smile.

"That's not all I want you around for," he said with a look that brought a flush to Sara's face and she lowered her eyes.

"Why Sara Mathews, I believe you're blushing," he said and rolled over, wrapped both arms around her and kissed her playfully at first, then fervently, wanting much more than a kiss.

Nathan slowly released his hold on Sara and rolled back over on his back before he reached the point of no return, and pulled Sara up close to him again and could feel and hear her breathing rapidly.

"I know what you're up to Nathan Chambers. You think you can overwhelm me with your charm, good looks, and masculine sexuality so I would be unwilling to leave you in the morning."

"So is it working? Will you stay with me, or should I try a little harder this time?" he teased.

"I think you need to go roll around in the snow and cool off," she said.

"I could always take my vest and shirt off if that would help," he smirked.

"No, you leave your vest and shirt right where they are! You're like kryptonite to me," she said most emphatically!

Nathan laughed. He had no idea what kryptonite was, but he loved the effect he had on Sara, and wondered if she knew she had the same effect on him. There was a definite bonding that was taking place between the two of them and he was sure that she would return to him after she had taken care of what needed to be done in her time.

"It's getting late and we both need our sleep. I'm going to light the fireplace in my bedroom if you want to grab the blankets."

Sara looked at him a little surprised – *"Didn't he hear a word I said, and now he wants me go sleep in the same bed with him?"*

Nathan picked up some logs in his arms and looked at the surprised look on her face and assured her, "You have nothing to fear. I promise I will be the perfect gentleman and your honor will be intact in the morning. Now bring the blankets," he said and led the way.

Chapter 13

The sun had not yet peeked through the bedroom window when Nathan rolled over in bed with just enough light to see Sara lying there next to him. Though the fire had died in the fireplace, all but a few glowing embers, the fire that burned within him for Sara was still blazing. As he watched her sleep he couldn't help but think about her leaving today, and wondered how in the world he would get along without her. He had longed for another love in his life since his wife had died, but had almost given up hope living so far away from any settlement. Then Sara showed up seemingly out of thin air; beautiful, desirable, gentle, loving, and with a sense of humor that he found delightful.

As much as he wanted to just lay there beside her, he could hear the rooster crowing and knew the house would be cold after the heavy snow they had last night, and he needed to get up and light not only the hearth, but the fireplace. He quietly and slowly pulled back his blanket and stood up making his way to the bedroom door. Looking back at Sara, she appeared to still be sleeping so he unlatched the door ever so quietly and squeezed through the gap before its hinges could squeak.

Leaving the door slightly ajar, he went about his business of lighting the fires and putting on a pot of coffee, then went and stood at the front window to see how deep the snow was piled across the field and up to the base of the hill when Sara emerged from the bedroom wrapped in one of the blankets.

"Good morning," he said with a smile and motioned to her to join him by the window.

"Good morning," she replied and snuggled up close to his side.

"How did you sleep last night?" he asked looking into her brilliant hazel green eyes.

"Surprisingly well," she answered, but chose not to tell him that she always slept well when she was in the arms of the man she loved.

Nathan looked out the window again and asked, "Are you sure the weather will be different when you leave to return home? If your weather is as bad as it is here, it won't be safe for you to return," he said in that deep, smooth, masculine voice she loved so much.

"It was beautiful yesterday," she assuredly replied smiling up at him.

"Tell me again how all of this works on you returning to your time," he asked.

"Well, at some point this morning I will go to the attic and watch from the window and you are going to have to cross that snowy field and possibly part way up the side of that hill. When everything changes back to dust and cobwebs, I'll know that I can return. If it doesn't change, then I will wave to you and let you know that you need to move further away. I believe you need to be out of your house and off your porches for me to return," she said watching all the time for his reaction.

"You mean to tell me that if I don't leave my house, you can't return home?" he asked with a raised eyebrow and then a big grin on his face.

Sara quickly sobered up. "Nathan...don't you even think about it!"

Nathan wrapped his arms around Sara and pulled her close, determined not to let this opportunity to tease her pass him by. Smiling mischievously he remarked, "Well now, this is a very interesting situation," he said nodding his head like he was thinking.

"Nathan, I mean it!" Sara suddenly realized, "You're playing games with me, aren't you?" she asked suspiciously.

Nathan laughed heartily and said, "Yes, I'm just playing with you. Come on, let's go get some coffee and something to eat."

Sara removed the blanket she was wrapped in and carefully folded it and laid it on the couch as she watched Nathan pouring the coffee and noticed that he remembered the sugar bowl and was touched by his thoughtfulness. It was such a simple thing to do, but to her it meant the world.

The sun had not risen over the rolling hills when Nathan and Sara had finished their breakfast. He glanced through the window and noticed that the sky was partly cloudy and snatched the blanket off the couch and turned toward Sara.

"Come with me," he said and held out his hand for her to take and led her out the front door and stood at the edge of the porch.

Nathan wrapped the blanket around Sara and then wrapped his arms around her.

"What are we looking for?" Sara asked.

"Be patient, my dear. It'll be any minute now," he said as he held his face close to the side of hers, then kissed her several times down the side of her neck causing goose bumps which pleased him greatly.

"Oh, look! It is beautiful!" Sara exclaimed.

Nathan just smiled as he held Sara in his arms and watched the sun rise in magnificent shades of pink, orange and purple.

When the once brilliant colors had faded, Nathan whispered to Sara, "Let's go back inside and get you warmed up."

He tossed the blanket over the back of the couch and he and Sara sat together in his rocking chair by the fire.

"Do you really have to leave today? Can't you stay for just one more day," he pleaded.

Sara sighed heavily as she looked at him. It broke her heart to see him so downcast, but how could she worry her parents again? Once again her mind and heart couldn't agree on what to do. She placed her hands on both sides of his face and kissed him tenderly.

"I can only stay for an hour or two," she said regretfully and laid her head against his shoulder.

He held her snug against himself and slowly rocked the chair in silence, content for the moment that she was with him.

Nathan could tell by the position of the sun that it was time for Sara to leave.

"How long do you figure it will be before you return?" he asked.

"I'll do my best to get as much as I need to get done in two weeks, but I might have to return for shorter periods of time before I'm able to stay with you permanently," she replied looking up into his troubled eyes.

"How will I know when you're ready to return?" he questioned.

"I'm not 100% sure how this works. But I think all I need to do is enter your attic and if all I see is dust and cobwebs then I'll know that you are away hunting or working in the fields and I'll sit tight for as long as I can and see if you return. If when I come down the attic stairs and everything is like it is now I'll know you're home and believe me I'll come find you."

Nathan just nodded with a somber look.

"I'll miss you Sara."

"And I'll miss you Nathan."

"Well this won't get any easier, so why don't you grab your backpack and head up to the attic and I'll step far enough back off the porch and wait to see you in the window," he stated with a heavy sigh.

"I need one more kiss to carry me through these next two weeks, and remind me of what I am missing out on," Sara said with a forced smile, for her heart was breaking.

Nathan took her in is arms and kissed her several times then stated, "You better leave now before I change my mind about letting you go, so scat," he said with a forced smile of his own.

Sara picked up her backpack and when she reached the staircase leading to the attic she stopped and looked back one last time, and then quickly climbed the stairs before she burst into tears. She made her way quickly to the attic window and watched as Nathan trudged through the snow until he was far enough away to look for her in the window.

The strangest thing happened. Sara could have sworn that for a split second everything went blurry, like it flashed back and forth between the two times. That had never happened before and she decided that her eyes were just blurry and irritated from crying and she imagined the things she saw.

Sara dismissed the uneasy feeling and waved at him as she continued to weep bitterly and Nathan took several more steps then turned and looked, and Sara was gone.

Chapter 14

Sara hurried from the old house crying as she went, eager to get things done as quickly as possible so she could return to Nathan. When she reached her cabin the first thing she needed to do was call her parents.

"I thought we had an agreement that you would answer your phone day or night, and if you couldn't talk to just tell us you would call back. What happened to that agreement?" her dad asked highly annoyed.

"Dad, I'm sorry..." she replied.

"I'm tired of hearing 'I'm sorry.' I want you to be responsible..."

Sara interrupted; she was in no mood to be lectured by her dad. "Dad, I'm 26 years old, and don't need to call you every few hours to tell you I'm okay. If this place was so unsafe do you think Whitney Publishing would have sent me here? I am sorry for worrying you and mom, but I have a lot of things to get done and I can't do them if I'm calling or answering the phone every few minutes," she irritably replied.

Sara's mom took the phone from Don who was so upset that he couldn't speak without saying something that he knew he would regret, and asked, "Sara, how could you speak to you father like that? I've never known you in all your life to speak so disrespectful to anyone. What in the world is going on?" she petulantly asked.

Sara took a deep breath and sighed, "Mom, I didn't mean to be disrespectful. I just need a little space right now, and I feel pressured on all sides to do this and do that, and we need this by this time. I'll call dad after we both have had a little time to cool down. I need to go into town right now, so I'll call you a little later. I love you, Mom."

"I love you too," her mom replied wondering what was really going on that had Sara so out of sorts.

Sara was so flustered after talking to her parents that she sat down and made a list of things she wanted to get accomplished in town. She decided to start at the bank and get both her parents added to all her accounts and finish up her list of things to do at the grocery store. She needed to buy enough food to get her through the next two weeks, and start buying things she wanted to take back with her when she returned to Nathan – like creamer for her coffee, spices, baking ingredients, maple syrup, cooking utensils, and most of all toilet paper. She knew these things wouldn't last long, but she would enjoy them while she could.

When she returned home, she started placing items she wanted to take with her in one of the spare bedrooms. As she watched the pile grow she wondered how she was going to take all of these things back with her, and questioned whether an ATV would even be able to carry everything she wanted to take with her. That was a decision that she could figure out when the time came; there were still things she needed to get done today.

Next on her list was to call Natalie and ask her to email forms to her so that she could add her parents as beneficiaries to her royalties should anything happen to her, and then she could take a short break and get something to eat.

The cabin was getting chilly now that a mild cold front was moving through and brought rain with it, so she built a fire instead of turning the heat up a couple of degrees and took her food with her to sit in her favorite chair. Sitting by the fire only reminded her of what she was missing – she was missing Nathan and gradually found it hard to even swallow her food. She closed her eyes and imagined him holding her in his rocking chair, and kissing her with that hungry look in his eyes, and immediately she was covered in goose bumps and longed to be with him.

She finished eating what she could and thought about finishing her book. She definitely had more chapters she could write, but her thoughts right now were still too fresh and painful to write about and went in her room to lie down and rest for a bit. She slid under the covers and rolled over on her side, and when she did she was staring right at a framed photo of Richard sitting on her nightstand. It was like shock therapy. Richard had not even entered her thoughts yesterday or today, and she was now confused and troubled. She held the photo in her hands and remembered how in love she was with him, and still was. How could she possibly love two men at the same time? The desires she once had for Richard she now had for Nathan and it was his kisses she was craving right now. She laid the photo of Richard face down on her nightstand and rolled over and faced the other way – she had a lot to think about.

Even though Sara's mind was deeply troubled she fell asleep rather quickly from shear exhaustion. She awoke several hours later and figured the only way to work things out in her mind was to put words to those feelings and troubled thoughts then pour them into her book. At this point she didn't care whether some people thought she was crazy or not, for there would always be those people who fully understood and related to the issues she was dealing with. Sara wrote to well into the night, and was certain that her book would be finished by the end of the two weeks. She thought about printing a copy for her parents to read, and get their opinion before she sprang the news to them that everything they had read was real, and that she planned on marrying Nathan and living in 1786 with him.

After mulling that idea around for a while she decided that perhaps that was not the best plan of action, and she would definitely need to give it some more thought. She knew her parents well, and they would fight her tooth and nail before they would ever let her run off with a man she barely knew, and especially one that she believed was alive in the 18th century. She was sure they would think that she was having a nervous breakdown over losing Richard and made up this fictitious man in her book to fill the hole in her heart. She actually believed they would have her committed before they would let her go, never to see them again; after all she was their only child.

It was very late and she needed her sleep. There was much that still needed to be done before she could return to Nathan and she didn't want to keep him waiting.

When Sara finally crawled out of bed, coffee was her first objective. Without coffee her brain would not get the jumpstart it needed to once again pour out her heart into her book. She knew the book had to be completed soon or she would have to keep returning to work on it and Nathan would not be a happy camper.

After another three days of only writing, eating, and sleeping Sara needed a well-earned break. She submitted her newly written chapters to Natalie for editing and treated herself to a day of shopping in town. She was able to buy some of the simple items she wanted to take with her, like over the counter medical supplies and a cookbook with simple recipes, but was not happy with the lingerie selection in the little town of Madisonville so she drove to Knoxville to buy something sexy, yet classy.

Sara was finally finished with all her shopping and had it packed away in the trunk, and decided to go visit her parents and try to smooth things out with them. She knew that her leaving would be hard on them, but she hoped that her future happiness would ease some of their anguish when, and if, she would no longer be able to return. It seemed almost unfair to her that she had to choose between her happiness and a life with Nathan, or her parents' happiness, but that was the choice she was forced to make. She gave them a quick call to let them know she was on her way, and prayed for God's help in finding a way to tell her parents of her decision to leave. She would not do it today, but it would have to be done eventually.

Sara stayed with them through dinner and dessert, but left soon after. She still did not like being alone in the dark and looked forward to being with Nathan where she would never have to fear what goes bump in the night. She played her rock-n-roll music and sang along to ease the tension of driving home alone, and suddenly an idea popped into her head. If I take enough batteries with me I can take my old MP3 player and play my music for quite some time. She wondered what Nathan would think about rock-n-roll. She was pretty sure he wouldn't mind listening to her sing and watch her dance swaying to the music while doing her chores.

It was back to writing the next couple of days as time was drawing near to when she had promised Nathan that she would return. All that was left to write was the part where she told her parents she was leaving to marry a man in the 1700s and the happily ever after ending which she was sure she would have.

Two days had passed and she would be finished by nightfall and submit it to Whitney Publishing, and they could do with it whatever they wished; she wouldn't be there to make any changes. Little did she know when she finally submitted her book what lay ahead in her future.

Sara now had all of the things she wanted to take back with her. The last thing she needed to find was a truck that could take everything she wanted to take with her out to the old house in one trip and put it all in the attic. Her father had a truck she could use, but she knew there was no way of borrowing it without him asking a lot of questions. So, she phoned several rental agencies and finally found one that would rent her a four-wheel drive truck for the day, because she was not yet ready to tell her parents that she was planning on starting a new life with Nathan.

Chapter 15

Sara faced one problem. How was she going to get over the steep hill in front of Nathan's property in a truck? She found her map and searched for a way around the hill instead of trying to go over the hill. She thought she finally found one, but it would take her miles out of her way. There were also no roads that she could find on the map, and prayed that she would at least pick up a dirt road along the way. It was risky, but she didn't see where she had any other choices; she intended to take everything she had bought with her.

Sara made arrangements with the rental agency to pick her up at the cabin in the morning and drive her back into town to pick up the truck. She wanted to get it packed, then drive to the old house and leave her things in the attic and then return to her cabin and have the rental agency come pick up the truck. That way, when she left in her car to tell her parents good-bye and where she was going she could make a quick get-away before they could stop her. She knew that they would try, and feared to what extremes they might go.

Sara had worked herself up into a frenzy. This was going to be much harder than she anticipated and the stress of it was making her physically ill. She would eat no supper that night, take a long hot shower and go straight to bed; sleep might be the only escape she had from her anxiety.

She was dressed and ready to go when the rental agency knocked at her door in the morning. Sara's stomach was still tied in knots and she didn't feel like fixing breakfast, not even coffee. She rode to their lot in silence, looking out the window trying to find the right words to tell her parents that she was leaving; at least for the time being. She loved them dearly, but she couldn't let that keep her from living her own life and marrying the man she loved.

Within the hour she was back at her cabin and started right away to load the back of the truck with all the things she wanted to take with her. Brunch was in order because she had chosen not to eat breakfast, and would be gone during lunch time and did not know when she would be returning. She made a quick sandwich and grabbed a small bag of chips and some tea to drink and sat out on the back porch to eat. She had a good view of the valley and the terrain she would shortly be crossing and took a deep breath to suppress the nerves that were starting to build up. She tried to finish her brunch before she thought any more about how she was going to drive to Nathan's place.

Hurriedly she cleaned up the kitchen and grabbed her purse and truck keys, and set the alarm on her way out. As she climbed up into the cab of the truck she forcefully exhaled as she envisioned what she was about to do and wondered if she was crazy to try such a foolhardy thing. She turned the key and the engine started with a roar, and she slowly pulled out of the driveway. Turning to the right she drove in the direction of town. She had seen a little clearing several miles up the road where she thought it would be safe to cut over to the valley and maybe find some kind of tire tracks that she could follow through the valley.

After several minutes she found the spot she was looking for and stopped in the road to catch her breath and calm her nerves since no one was behind her. It was now or never she told herself and drove off the road and onto the rocky dirt clearing. It was bumpier than she thought it would be and the sound of fallen branches being crushed under the tires only added to the anxiety she was already struggling with. She drove slowly at first until she got the feel for what the truck was capable of and the differences in the terrain she was driving over.

She drove along for miles, keeping her eyes on the ridge running alongside of her and looked for a spot that was not too steep to drive over. Sara spotted an outcrop of rocks ahead and drove to the base and stopped the truck. She wasn't going to take the chance that the rocks that were tightly fit together at the base would become individual boulders further up the slope forcing her to have to back down. She slowly climbed her way to the top of the outcrop where she could see clear to the other side of the ridge. Ecstatic she yelled with pure delight as she hurried back down the hill; she had indeed found a way over the ridge. It wasn't going to be easy, but it could be done if she took her time and chose her path carefully.

Sara climbed back into her truck and put it in four-wheel drive and gave it the gas to climb up on to the initial rocks and sat as far forward as possible on the seat where she could see more clearly where she needed to drive. She wound her way through the mounding boulders and around stray trees until she had cleared the ridge and was safely in the valley on the other side. She had to force the thought of having to do this again to get back to her cabin out of her mind as she drove through the valley looking for Nathan's house. She knew she had miles to go and turned on the radio in hopes that it would keep her from thinking about the crazy thing she was doing.

About a half hour later she recognized Nathan's house up ahead and drove a little faster until she reached the tree line around the house and wove her way through them until she finally parked by his front porch. Pushing open the front door she carefully made her way to the stairs leading to the attic and pulled them down and quickly climbed them to see if Nathan was on his property. When she reached the top there was only dust and cobwebs, nothing was changing and she knew she had to unload the truck as quickly as possible before Nathan returned or the truck would disappear. A terrifying thought crossed her mind; what if the time portal had closed and she was unable to return? She took a deep breath and forced that thought from her mind; Nathan must just be away hunting or trapping with Inola she told herself. After all, it was a day earlier than what she had told him to expect her.

Sara carefully emptied the back of the truck and carried everything up to the attic and set the boxes down in places that she remembered were empty of things Nathan had stored there. When she was done she waited for him with great anticipation at the top of the attic stairs hoping that he would return before she was forced to leave.

She waited for hours pacing the floor and looking out the attic's windows and finally gave up hope that Nathan would return in time for her to see him. She was desperately hoping for a few minutes in his arms to help her get through the ordeal she would be facing with her parents. She picked up her purse and took one last look around then turned and grabbed the weathered handrail and slowly took the first step down the stairs in utter frustration, when abruptly the steps in front of her slowly started to change before her eyes. A smile came to her face as she rushed down the stairs and onto the front porch just in time to see Nathan dismount his horse.

He noticed her standing there and gave his horse a slap on its hind quarters to get him to move out of the way and ran up the steps to the porch and swept Sara up in his arms and kissed her eager lips that clamored for more.

When he finally lowered her to the ground he said with a big grin, "I wasn't expecting you today, but I'm awful happy to see you."

He whistled for his horse, and when he came trotting back he tied him to the post and wrapped his arm around Sara's waist and led her back into the house.

"How long can you stay?" he asked after hanging his hat on the peg.

"Not long I'm afraid. I have to get the truck I rented back to the dealer before they close for the night or I'll have to pay extra."

"A truck?" Nathan asked with a puzzled look.

Sara smiled. "A horseless vehicle. I needed it to carry all my things out here. Come and see what I brought," she said excitedly.

Sara led Nathan up the stairs and into the attic and started opening the boxes. She held up item after item and explained what some of them were and what they were used for, and when she came to the toilet paper, Nathan laughed until he thought his sides would burst. Sara loved to hear him laugh and asked, "So, what do you think about the things that I brought, did I choose wisely?"

Nathan peeked over her shoulder and noticed the cookbook Sara had brought sticking up from one of the boxes she hadn't fully opened and grinned, "I'm happy to see you brought a cookbook with you," and laughed again.

"Funny, very funny…wise guy," she said and went back to opening one of the boxes she brought and pretended to be annoyed at his teasing – but in fact she loved it!

"Come on, let's go downstairs and sit for a while. I need to get some answers from you," he said and turned to go down the stairs.

Sara followed close behind and when he reached the bottom he put a couple of logs on the fire and sat in his rocking chair and held out his arms toward Sara, who quickly joined. As she leaned against him she could feel the beat of his heart within her breast and they beat as one, and she was in no hurry to leave him. As a matter of fact, she seriously considered just writing her parents a detailed letter explaining everything about her abrupt departure. She couldn't see how they would be hurt any less if she did it in person, and at least she could avoid the drama that was certain to occur.

"What's on your mind, Sara? You seem awful quiet," he asked.

"I have one more thing I need to do before I can remain with you for as long as you want me," she said still leaning against him.

"What's that, Sara?"

"I need to tell my parents that their only child will be leaving them forever for the man she loves," she stated with a sigh.

"You're not a child any longer, you're a woman and entitled to live your own life now," he said softly.

"I wish you could be there to tell them that. They would believe it coming from you, and at least they would understand why I would want to be with you. I wish I had a picture of the two of us together; maybe then they would believe you were not just a figment of my imagination, someone I conjured up in my mind to fill the hole in my heart that Richard left."

Sara suddenly sat up, "Wait a minute. I think I have an idea."

Sara went to her purse and pulled out her cell phone and returned to Nathan and sat on his lap once again and aimed the camera at them and took a selfie. She quickly looked at the picture and excitedly said, "Perfect! This picture will prove to them that I'm not crazy. Let's take one more together sitting in front of the fireplace."

Nathan was not thrilled posing for pictures, but if it made Sara this happy he figured he had to do it. When Sara was finished getting all the evidence she thought she would need to convince her parents that Nathan was real she put her cell phone back inside her purse.

"You live in a strange world, Sara Mathews," he said with a look of bewilderment. "I'm afraid to ask you what a truck looks like and how it works."

Sara asked Nathan if he had any writing paper, and pulled a pen from her purse. Nathan returned with a piece of paper and Sara started drawing a picture of a truck putting in as much detail as she could, and then explained vaguely how it worked.

Nathan studied the drawing and then looked at Sara with some concern. "And you drove that through the valley and over the rugged hills to get here?"

Sara nodded like it was no big deal, and left out the part where it nearly scared her to death doing it. There was nothing she wouldn't do to be with Nathan, and she didn't think he fully understood what lengths she would go through to do it.

"Nathan, I need to return the truck today. I want to get everything taken care of so all that I have to do is see my parents tomorrow morning, and then come right back to you," she said anxiously.

Sara stood up and picked up her purse and keys and Nathan wrapped his arms around her waist as they said their good-byes.

"I'll wait for you tomorrow, but I'm afraid I'll have to leave the next day. I've promised to meet Inola. I'll be taking the wagon to pick up the pelts he has ready so they can be taken to Knoxville and sold. I'll probably be gone for several days, but there will be plenty of food and firewood for you, and if you stay inside everything should be okay. You did bring your pistol with you, didn't you?" he asked with a concerned look.

"Yes, and plenty of ammunition. I'll be fine," she confidently replied.

Nathan looked dolefully at Sara and lightly brushed his fingers along the side of her face and gently brushed her bangs aside, then kissed her tenderly wishing she didn't have to go. It was hard for him to put his feelings into words, but he felt them deeply just the same.

"I hate to leave you so soon after you return, but I have no choice. I need to get those pelts before winter settles in."

"I'll be fine, Nathan. I don't expect you to stop working just because I'm here, and besides I'm used to being alone. I live alone now," Sara said with a reassuring smile.

"Oh, I almost forgot. I've got to head up to the attic if I want to leave. So, kiss me again like you mean it, and then I'll watch for you out front," she said and lifted her head slightly, waiting for one last kiss.

Nathan gave her a kiss that she would surely remember, and turned and quickly headed out the door; the longer she stayed the more their parting hurt.

Sara climbed the stairs and watched as Nathan backed away from the porch and then she suddenly vanished from his sight.

Chapter 16

Now that Sara knew the way to get back safely, she drove with more confidence and managed to return the truck before they closed for the day. After they dropped her off at the cabin she began packing her backpack for the next day. She wanted it ready in case she needed to make a hasty departure tomorrow. Sara cleaned the cabin the best she could, but most of her clothes and a few personal things would get left behind and eventually either be put into storage or given away. She was okay with that; she wouldn't be needing them where she was going.

After dinner she sat by the fire and rehearsed what she was going to say to her parents tomorrow. She dreaded this meeting with them more than she had dreaded anything else that had ever happened to her, other than losing Richard. She was sure in her mind and heart that Richard would be happy for her, and she took comfort in that. Sara turned in early that night for she needed to be at her best tomorrow if she was going to go toe-to-toe with her parents; especially her father.

She called her mom in the morning to let her know that she would be coming over to visit them in a couple of hours. Her mom sounded cheerful and Sara knew that wouldn't last long. She had her backpack with her in her car just in case she was not able to return to the cabin for some reason; she wanted to be prepared for any situation that might prevent her from returning to Nathan. Her heart was pounding during the hour long drive, and she wondered what it would do when the fireworks started.

She pulled into their driveway and just sat there for several minutes trying to catch her breath and get her emotions under control. She couldn't walk into their home in her current condition or they would know that something was wrong right away.

She finally got up the courage to knock on their door and enter calling out, "Mom, Dad, I'm here."

"We're in the kitchen," her mom responded.

Sara took a deep breath and joined them just long enough to ask them if they would join her in the living room.

"Sure, what's up?" her dad asked cheerfully on the way to take his seat.

"I just need to tell you both something," she said and took a seat as her chest tightened under the stress.

"Have you finished your book?" her mom asked eagerly.

"Yes, I submitted it to my editor yesterday."

"That's wonderful, Dear. Going to the cabin was a great idea. Look how quickly you were able to write your book, and I just know that it is going to be at the top of the best seller list. You just wait and see," her mom replied proudly.

Sara thought, *How in the world am I going to tell them that I'm leaving them for 1786 when they sound so happy? I'm about to take them from the pinnacle to the depths of hell in just a matter of moments.*

Her dad could read her like a book. "What's wrong, Sara? Something is bothering you. You might as well get it off your chest and just tell us what is going on."

Sara's face was already showing the anguish she felt and she took a deep breath as she watched the once happy look on her mother's face quickly vanish.

"I'll be leaving today to go back home, but it won't be the home in Indiana. I've met someone and we'll be getting married soon, I hope," she said reluctantly looking back and forth between her parents.

A scowl instantly came to her dad's face and he asked, "Isn't this kind of sudden after Richard's death? When and where did you have time to meet anyone when you've supposedly been out at the cabin writing?"

Sara took a deep breath and let it out long and slow before she answered. "I met him on one of my hikes. The story I wrote about isn't fictional; every word of it is true," she said and waited for the response that she knew was coming.

"Have you lost your mind? You must be insane to believe what you just told us, or think that we are both fools if you expect us to believe that!" he responded deeply befuddled.

"I haven't lost my mind, and I don't believe either of you are fools. Look, I know this is hard for you to believe, but it is the truth and I love this man. Is it so hard to believe that it's possible for two lonely hearts to call out through time and space to each other?" she asked already knowing their answer.

"He's a character in your book for heaven's sake! Look, Sara, we know you took Richard's death really hard, but to fall in love with an imaginary man is crazy and you need help. Two lonely hearts calling out to each other – do you hear yourself?" her father asked both scared and angrily.

Sara pulled out her phone and brought up the pictures of herself with Nathan. "Does he look like he is imaginary?" she asked defiantly.

Her dad took the phone from her and looked at it and handed it to her mom.

"Sara, posing with someone you don't know is both dangerous and delusional. Why are you doing this?" he asked bewildered.

"Did either of you take the time to really look at those pictures? If you had you would see that we clearly love each other.

Mom, look at him. Does he look like the type of man that would pose for pictures, and what about his clothes? Have you ever seen clothes like that in any store?" she asked hoping that surely her mother would understand. Her mom didn't say a word, but did pick up her cell phone again and looked at the pictures.

"Come on Dad, Mom, I'm not making this up. I can't explain what has happened in any way that you would believe me."

"Try us," her dad replied gruffly.

"Okay, I'll try. Scientist for a long time have believed time travel or time portals to be possible..."

"Okay, that's enough," her dad interrupted.

"Honey, let's hear her out. Go ahead, Sara," her mother said as calmly as she could under the circumstances.

"The house in my book is a real place. I've been to it numerous times, and like in my book when I enter the attic and Nathan is there I suddenly find myself back in 1786. Like I told you, everything in my book has really happened to me. That's why I didn't return your calls; I was trapped there until I discovered a way to return to my own time. I know how all of this sounds, but you've said so yourselves that it is not like me not to call you or return your phone calls. Do I sound crazy to you? Let me rephrase that. Am I acting like a crazy person right now, or someone who is truly in love? Do you really think I would put you both through this if it weren't all true? I love you both with all my heart, and I would never purposely hurt you for any reason. But, Nathan is my soul mate..."

"That's what you said about Richard. Boy, how quickly you forgot about him," her dad roughly interrupted.

Sara hung her head and fought back her tears. That last comment cut her to her very soul, and she knew that they were never going to believe her or even try to understand. It was best that she just get up and go; nothing was going to stop her from being with Nathan.

"Sara, think of what you are giving up. Are you really willing to give up your car, for instance, or your computer, microwave, TV, or air conditioning?" her mother asked pleadingly.

"I'm thinking of what I will be getting in return," she replied.

"What, hard work, feeding animals, harvesting crops, cooking in a pot over the fire? Yeah, that will get old really quick," her dad stated sarcastically.

Don turned and whispered in Becky's ear, and she excused herself and went into the kitchen. Sara immediately suspected something.

"Sara, I would like for you to stay with us for a few days and think clearly about what it is you're planning on doing. Surely you can do that for us," her dad said calmly.

Sara listened carefully and could hear her mother in the kitchen speaking quietly on the phone. This was her cue to leave immediately; they were up to something just like she had feared they would.

Sara grabbed her purse and said, "Good-bye, Dad, remember I love you both."

She ran to her car quickly, and when she was closing the door she could hear her dad yell from the doorway, "Sara, don't go. Please come back and let's talk about this."

Sara started the engine and quickly pulled out of their driveway and onto the street. She wasn't sure who her mother was speaking to, but she knew it meant trouble for her. She drove the speed limit through Knoxville, not wanting to draw any attention to herself, and when she left the city limits she set her cruise control to five miles over the speed limit. She now found herself in a race with time. Who had her parents called, and who might they call now that she was gone? Would there be someone at her cabin when she arrived? All these questions kept running through her mind and she was glad that she had thought to put her backpack in the car with her.

It was the longest hour of her life. Her father's harsh and belligerent attitude was so out of character for him, and his words would haunt her for a long time. He had always been loving and supportive; more like a best friend than a father, and she wondered how he could change so quickly and drastically.

As Sara neared the cabin she slowed down considerably to see if any cars were parked outside of it. Her heart sank as she saw an unmarked vehicle sitting in her driveway and she stopped the car in the road and looked for a safe place to pull over.

Sara grabbed her backpack and left the keys in the car; she wouldn't be needing them anymore. She cut through the wooded area until she came to the valley and started for the ridge. If she was able to reach the base of the hill without being detected she could follow it until she reached the spot on this side of Nathan's house. She wished now that she had been vague about the location of Nathan's house in the book. It would take them time to find it, but she would be with Nathan by then.

When Sara reached the base of the hill she stopped and called her parents, but it went straight to voicemail and she left them a message – "Mom, Dad, tomorrow I want you to go to the library or go online and look for books written by Sara Chambers. God willing you will find several of them there, and they will all be dedicated to both of you, and then just maybe you will believe me. You know how much I love you, and I hope that someday you will find it in your hearts to be happy for me. I truly love this man with all my heart, and who knows, someday your great, great, great, grandchildren might come knocking on your door."

Sara hung up the phone and placed it back in her backpack and started walking along the base of the hill. It didn't take her too long before she recognized the spot where she climbed the hill and started up the side. She stopped and looked back at her cabin in the distance and could see several cars were parked there now. She quickly made it over the top and started down when she realized that Nathan had to be at least on his porch before she could return and prayed that he hadn't forgotten to be close by.

Chapter 17

With renewed hope of seeing Nathan again, Sara regained her strength and ran across the field of trees and into his house and up the stairs to the attic. When she reached the top she sat down to catch her breath. Nothing had changed yet, so she continued to sit there and wait for Nathan to return.

"He said he would wait for me today. I wonder what came up that he couldn't be here to meet me," she thought and looked at her watch. It was later than she had planned on returning, but he had promised to wait. After waiting for hours, Sara got up and looked out the windows of the attic and the sun was beginning to set. She looked around the attic again and all she saw was dust, cobwebs and badly weathered boards, and not even the things she placed in the attic yesterday were there, and she was starting to get cold. She realized there were no blankets or firewood stacked outside to make a fire, and there was no food in the house for her to eat while she waited for Nathan to return.

Maybe she could find some firewood outside before it got too dark, but then she remembered she had no matches to light the fire, and she couldn't return to her cabin in the dark. Besides, there were people there waiting for her to return. Sara had no choice but to wait in the cold and dark for Nathan to return.

Her mind started playing tricks on her as she sat all alone in the empty house. Were her parent's right? Had she made all this up in her mind because she was so lonely and desperate for love? Had she imagined his kisses and the way he held her in his arms, or the way he laughed, and the way he looked into her eyes with such longing and tenderness?

Her heart was yelling, "No, don't you believe that lie!" but her tired mind could only see what was around her. She didn't know what to believe, and wondered if she really was going crazy.

Then suddenly the room became blurry again, changing back and forth faster than the mind could keep up. What was happening; she questioned fearfully. Then just as suddenly, the rapid changes stopped and the attic was full once again.

Sara rushed from the attic, and Nathan could hear the sound of her footsteps as she ran and was there waiting for her when she reached the bottom in tears and panic.

He reached out his arms and pulled her close against him. Holding her tightly he soothingly said, "It's alright Sara; I have you now. Shhh, it's alright."

"Where were you? I thought you were going to wait for me?" she asked hysterically.

"I've been here all day waiting for you. I was beginning to think you weren't going to return," he replied with a befuddled look.

"I've been upstairs waiting for you for hours," Sara stated with the same befuddled look while wiping the tears from her eyes.

"It has always changed every time you've entered the house. Why didn't it do it this time?" she asked with a troubled look.

Nathan shook his head, "I don't know. But I'm glad you're here with me now. Come, let's go sit by the fire; you're cold as ice."

Nathan snatched the blanket off the couch and handed it to Sara as she pulled her chair closer to the fire and wrapped the blanket tightly around her. Meanwhile Nathan went to the hearth and poured two cups of hot coffee and handed one to Sara.

"Here, this should help warm you up," he said and watched the look on Sara's face. "I suppose you want some of that creamer you brought for your coffee," he asked with a grin.

Sara looked up at him with her hands tightly wrapped around the cup for warmth and asked, "Would you mind getting me some?"

He immediately started towards the stairs without saying a word, for he was a quiet man by nature, and once in the attic started going through the boxes until he found the creamer.

When he handed it to her she looked up and smiled timidly, "I'll be needing a spoon."

He looked at her and let out a small sigh, but said not a word as he left and soon returned holding the spoon. "Anything else you need before I sit down and drink my coffee while it is still hot?"

"No, not a thing; just your company," she replied and took a sip of her coffee.

"So, how did it go with your parents?" he asked curiously with a raised eyebrow and a slight slant of his head as he sat down in his rocking chair.

He watched as Sara's shoulders slumped, and she took a deep breath and held it before letting it out slowly. Her reaction told him everything he needed to know.

"About how I expected," she answered and looked down at her coffee cup trying not to cry as their encounter played over again in her mind.

"I'm sorry," he said, and thought back to how his parents reacted when he left Boston for the hills of Tennessee after the war.

"I hope in time those memories will fade. Why don't you come and sit with me?" he asked softly.

Sara left the blanket behind and took her cup of coffee and sat in Nathan's lap. He placed one arm around her as he drank his coffee in silence, gazing off into the fire.

Sara wondered what he was thinking about. She actually knew very little about him to make any assumptions as to what might be on his mind.

"Are you hungry? I have some stew warming in the kettle," he said.

"That sounds good; I haven't eaten all day," she said and stood up pulling her sweater down over her tight jeans. Nathan looked her over and then lowered his eyes; he had made up his mind not to touch her in the way he wanted too until after they were married.

Sara took a seat at the table while Nathan dished out a heaping spoonful of stew onto each of their plates. After she ate several bites, she was glad she had brought a cookbook – it needed a woman's loving touch. Nathan ate his stew like he too had not eaten all day and got up and filled his plate again. She was glad he was not a picky eater, because her cooking from scratch with limited ingredients was an untested skill.

When they were finished eating, Nathan suggested they sit by the fire and poured himself another cup of coffee. He let Sara sit in the other rocker by the fire and handed her the blanket before taking his seat. It was hard enough for him to be in the same room with Sara without craving physical contact, especially dressed the way she was, but to have her sit with him was almost unbearable.

He sat there quietly staring off into the fire, not able to find the right words to tell her how he was feeling or what he was thinking about. Sara knew the look on his face all too well. She knew he was waging a battle of some kind and chose to let him tell her in his own good time; for now she was content just to be with him,

After several minutes of silence, Nathan turned to her and asked, "Sara, how long did you plan on staying?"

"For as long as you want me to stay," she replied.

Nathan looked at her with his jaw firmly set and his eyes piercingly focused on her. He wanted her more desperately then she would ever know, but tonight was not the right time to propose or to have her share his bedroom.

A soft smile came to his face and a slight nod of his head, "I guess you'll be staying then." Nathan swallowed hard and forced himself to say what he didn't want to say, "I think it best that you sleep here on the couch where you will be nice and warm." He pulled the couch closer to the fireplace and then softly kissed her as she sat in her chair.

"Good night, Sara," he said, and with great resolve he started towards the bedroom door, and before he closed it he looked back at Sara. Nathan saw the hurt look on her face, and knew that she did not understand his reasons for not wanting her beside him tonight. He sighed heavily as he stood there behind his closed door fighting the urge to open it and open his arms to her. He closed his eyes and let out another heavy sigh and then went and put several logs in the fireplace before he laid down.

Bewildered, Sara got up and fixed her bed on the couch and pulled the blanket up over her and stared at the dancing flames. She was confused by his sudden manner of conduct and wondered why his behavior had changed towards her. She questioned whether she had made a mistake in coming back. Maybe the initial excitement of having a woman around was slowly fading, and the reality of having another person around to take care of and protect was something he was unsure of especially after having lost his wife and young daughter. But she was sure that he would never want her to stay just because she was an extra pair of hands to help out around the farm. She understood that men had strong physical needs and wants just like women, and pondered whether this might be the reason he seemed so distant right now; maybe he wanted her just as much as she wanted him. The difference being that he obviously had more self-control than she had. This was an explanation that she could live with, because the thought of him not wanting her was more than she could endure.

Chapter 18

Nathan was usually up by now having at least brewed a pot of coffee, but he laid there in bed thinking about Sara and how he had hurt her, or at least confused her by his actions last night, and that was not sitting well with him. He was unsure about many things as he laid there. He would prefer to stay with Sara these next few days, but had promised Inola that he would join him today, and the money they would earn from the pelts would get them through this next year. He considered whether he should go ahead and ask Sara to marry him with the promise they would be married when they took the pelts to Knoxville to sell. At least that would put her mind at ease as to whether he truly wanted her to stay, and more importantly that he cherished her more deeply than he could ever express to her in words – she was his reason to live, and he would do anything to keep her by his side.

The problem was he considered himself to be a simple man who lived a simple life, and Sara was this vibrant woman of a sophisticated time in the future. He wondered whether the hard work and lack of all the conveniences she was used to would be enough to make her want to return to her own time. Sure, he saw the desire in her eyes now, but would that last forever? He decided there was only one way to find out; go out there and assure her of his love and ask her to marry him before he left to join Inola.

He finally got out of bed and found the ring his mother had worn securely tucked away in his dresser drawer. Looking at it he wondered if Sara would like it; it was all he had to give her, and then tucked it in his vest pocket.

When he opened his bedroom door Sara was still lying down, and he quietly walked over to her and knelt beside her. "Good morning, sleepyhead," he said tenderly and watched as her eyes opened.

"Good morning," Sara replied with a smile and sat up. She was happy to see that he was behaving more like the man she was used to being around.

Nathan debated whether he should ask her now to marry him, since he was already down on one knee, but decided this was not the right time. Instead he leaned in and kissed her, then stood and offered her his hand which she gladly accepted and stood setting aside her blanket.

"Do you have time to eat breakfast before you leave?" she asked somberly.

"Yes, I do. I don't have to leave for hours," he said.

"Good! I'd like to fix you pancakes with some maple syrup I brought with me," she said with a big smile; happy that she could spend a little more time with him and started towards the attic.

"Don't forget to bring your cookbook down with you," he teased and laughed jovially as he left to add wood to the fire and start the coffee brewing.

"Funny, very funny," she replied as she made her way up the stairs.

Sara returned with a small box full of the items she would need to make the pancakes, and yes, she brought the cookbook with her. This would be her first attempt at making pancakes from scratch instead of a ready mix box, and she didn't want them to turn out the way her biscuits had. She quickly set the table and was pleased that she had chosen to bring syrup and creamer with her and hoped that Nathan would enjoy some of the simple things she was used too.

As Sara was stirring the batter, Nathan took down a cast iron skillet and placed it on the table next to her and standing behind her wrapped his arms around her. He started just below her ear half kissing and half nibbling down the side of her neck, bringing a slight blush to Sara's face and goose bumps over her body. Nathan smiled after watching her squirm with pleasure and sat down at the table with a cup of coffee and eagerly watched to see if Sara really knew how to make pancakes.

She heated the skillet and with a wooden spoon poured four dollops of batter into it when she realized she didn't have a spatula to flip them. She glanced at Nathan with a look of panic then looked up where utensils were hung near the hearth and was overjoyed to find one hanging there. She quickly retrieved it and flipped the first four pancakes, and smiled. When they were a light golden brown she picked up his plate and had a look of satisfaction as she turned and placed his pancakes in front of him with a huge smile.

Nathan couldn't help but laugh; he had never seen anyone so pleased that they were able to make pancakes. Sara didn't know what to think at first, and then laughed along with him and went back to making more pancakes.

When their plates were finally full she poured syrup over them and stirred some creamer into her coffee. "Are you going to try some of the caramel macchiato creamer in your coffee?" she asked enthusiastically.

How could he refuse even though he enjoyed his coffee black.

"Sure, go ahead and add some. I'll give it a try," he said just to please her.

She proudly stirred a couple of spoonful into his coffee and handed it to him and waited for his reaction. Nathan looked at her and then down at his light brown coffee and took a little sip, and then another as Sara looked on smiling all the while.

"This is actually pretty good; a little sweet perhaps," he said then took a big gulp.

"Do you mean it, or are you just being polite?" she asked wanting an honest answer.

"It's different. I'm used to drinking it black, but I think I would enjoy it more as a dessert at night when we're sitting by the fire," he said, hoping his answer did not disappoint her.

Sara smiled, "That's a great idea. I hadn't thought about it like that, but it would be nice to drink it while we sit by the fire."

"The syrup you brought was a very pleasant change. I haven't had syrup with my pancakes since I left Boston," he said.

After Nathan had finished his breakfast, he took his dirty dishes and placed them in the bucket to be washed and turned to Sara and said, "Well, Sara, that was a mighty fine breakfast you fixed. I need to hitch the horses to the wagon and load my supplies for the trip, but I'll come back to the house before I leave."

Sara smiled and nodded; she knew this was hard for him and didn't want to make it any harder. She cleared the rest of the table and washed the dishes while he was gone, and then waited for him by the fire. While waiting there she thought about what she could do to busy herself while he was away and then it hit her; I'll start writing a book she said to herself. I did tell my parents to look for books I had written, so I guess this would be a good time to get started.

Nathan walked in and saw Sara sitting on the couch by the fire and went and sat next to her wrapping his one arm around her. He reached over with his other hand and turned her face towards him and looked intently into her eyes and said, "You know it is not my desire to leave you." When she acknowledged him with a slight nod and smile, he asked reluctantly, "Will you walk me to the door?"

Sara stood and Nathan immediately took her by the hand until he reached the door. He put his hat on then picked up his rifle as he opened the door and turned towards Sara. "You take care Sara Mathews," he said, then crossed the porch and put his rifle into its holder by his seat in the wagon. He placed his foot on the wagon step like he was going to step up, and stood there like that for only a few seconds. Then stepping down he tossed his hat up on the wagon's seat and returned to Sara who was still standing in the doorway.

Nathan looked into her eyes like he was searching for something, and then suddenly went down on one knee. Sara looked stunned for a second, but when he took her by the hand she smiled.

"Sara Mathews, will you marry me?" he asked.

"Yes, Nathan, with all my heart!" she exclaimed beaming enthusiastically.

Nathan reached into his vest pocket and pulled out his mother's sapphire gold filigree ring and slipped it on Sara's finger and watched for her reaction. It was all he had of value to give her, and hoped she wouldn't be disappointed. But, all he saw was love and happiness looking back at him and he was satisfied.

Nathan stood and kissed her like he had never kissed her before, and when he finally let her go, it was with a smile as big as the noonday sun.

Nathan had a spring to his step as he mounted the wagon and grabbed the reins and told the horse to "walk on". He rolled several feet and suddenly told the horse to "whoa" and turned and looked back at Sara and noticed that she was not wearing her weapon.

"Sara, I want you to go get your weapon and wear it while I'm gone, and use it if necessary. You hear me?" he stated with concern.

"Yes, dear, now go so you can hurry back to me," she said and smiled.

Sara went back inside and did as Nathan had asked and sat by the fire to get warm and plan her day. She needed to alter one of Elizabeth's skirts to make it long enough so she wouldn't look ridiculous when Nathan took her to Knoxville to buy new clothing. She also wanted to start writing again, but hadn't quite come up with a good story line so she picked up her sewing and sat back in her chair by the fire.

Meanwhile, Nathan was still beaming with happiness, and planned on marrying Sara as soon as he returned. All he could think about was that the giant hole left in his heart when his wife and daughter died was now filled with his love for Sara. He would no longer be lonely, and he had a partner that he could laugh with, work with, sleep with, and yes, make love with.

He pulled into Inola's camp late that afternoon and started loading the pelts that Inola had ready for him. It would probably be hours before Inola would return from checking their traps and in the meantime Nathan gathered wood for the fire, and sharpened his knife so he would be ready to help skin whatever Inola brought back to camp.

As Nathan sharpened his knife he thought about Sara being all alone. Even though he had not seen any trappers, settlers, or Indians moving through his area, he was still uneasy. Sara was not used to this life style; it could be hard and dangerous and he did not know Sara well enough to know if she could deal with whatever might happen. Then he recalled how she handled herself and her weapon that first night when she encountered Inola and himself, and how she managed to drive a truck across the valley and hills to get to his place; he guessed that she was indeed capable of handling most anything that came up.

Inola finally came walking into camp holding up several fox and beaver skins that still needed work. He greeted Nathan as he tossed the skins down on the edge of their camp not wanting to attract any animals to close to them that were looking for food while they slept at night.

Nathan went ahead and built a fire and started a pot of coffee so they could sit and talk while they ate some jerky for supper. Inola had much to tell Nathan about where he was trapping and what to watch out for. He spoke of a bear that had been poking around in the area and to be careful; he had set a trap for it. Their talks went well until Nathan mentioned that Sara had returned and that he had asked her to marry him. Inola still hadn't gotten over the fact that Sara pointed her weapon at him and fired a warning shot. She looked strange to him and he did not trust her, and it angered him that she might come between him and his friendship with Nathan.

Before turning in for the night, Nathan tried to assure Inola that Sara was not an evil spirit or a threat to their friendship, and asked him to try to get along with her for his sake. Inola agreed to try, but made no promises as they both pulled their blanket over themselves on their bedrolls by the fire.

Nathan spent two days helping Inola clean and trim the skins that were brought into camp, and kept a close watch for the bear that had raided their camp while they were away checking their traps. Inola was eager to trap the black bear and wanted its hide for himself and the meat to take back to his home to eat since Nathan did not particularly care for the taste of bear.

On the third day, Nathan went looking for Inola since he was finished cleaning and packing the pelts and was eager to get back to Sara. He started out in the direction that Inola took when he left early that morning and took his rifle with him in case he met up with the bear. After picking up Inola's tracks not far from camp he followed them hoping to find Inola soon; it was already later than Nathan had wanted to leave. As he passed by a tree that the bear had marked he cautiously looked around for the trap Inola had set, but couldn't find one so he proceeded a little further. He figured he was getting close to Inola and called out his name and waited to hear a response.

"Over here," Inola yelled.

Nathan looked in the direction the voice came from and quickly slid over the fallen tree in front of him, planting his left foot squarely in the jaws of the large bear trap covered in twigs and leaves with its long sharp jaws clamping into his upper ankle. He yelled out loudly in excruciating pain and fell backwards to the ground; momentarily unable to even attempt to release his ankle from the jaws of the trap. *"Damn"* he thought, *"I know better than to go over a tree without looking."* He knew that one careless and thoughtless move had put himself in great danger.

Inola came running to his aide as he knew exactly where he had placed the trap. When he reached Nathan they both exchanged a glance; there was no need for words, each one knew the seriousness of what happened and what needed to be done. Inola bent over and pulled as hard as he could prying the jaws open while watching Nathan's face tighten in pain. He held it open while Nathan pulled his ankle free then released his grip letting the trap snap shut.

Inola could see the puncture marks penetrating Nathan's leather boot and the blood oozing from it and said, "Don't move. I be back with horse," and immediately started running through the woods to get back to camp. It wasn't long before he returned to Nathan sitting back against the tree and just quaking from the pain. Inola helped him to his feet and Nathan grabbed a handful of the horse's mane as Inola helped him mount his horse.

"I meet you back at camp. Must find root of yarrow and hamanelis virginianam (witch hazel)," Inola said and took off into the forest.

Nathan's whole leg was throbbing in pain as he rode back to camp, and occasionally looked down and watched as blood dripped from his boot. He slid from his horse landing on his one good leg with a groan and hobbled to his bedroll and leaned against his saddle for support. He knew better than to remove his boot and waited for Inola to return with the roots Cherokees used for medicine to treat wounds, bleeding and fever.

Nathan closed his eyes as he thought about Sara and wanted to get back to her as quickly as possible. He figured that in two hundred years man had probably come up with some medicines that would help save his life if an infection set in, and Sara would make sure that he received the best care possible. He dreaded what his carelessness was going to put Sara through, for he would be laid up for weeks and she would have to bear the brunt of the work. This was certainly not how he wanted to start out his life with her.

Inola returned to camp carrying the roots of the two herbs he needed. He went straight to work without saying a word to Nathan building a fire and putting two small pots on the fire to start boiling, then added the cleaned and chopped roots. The roots would have to boil for hours, and while they were, Inola went to Nathan to finally pull off his boot.

"Go ahead, Inola, pull," he said as he gripped tightly the sides of his bedroll and tightly clinched his jaw expecting it to hurt like hell.

Nathan did not yell, but felt lightheaded and gasped in pain as he continued to tightly grip his bedroll until his knuckles turned white. Inola took two canteens full of water and poured them over Nathans ankle trying to wash out the wound and wash away the blood so he could see the extent of the injury.

He looked squarely at Nathan and stated, "Not good," and ripped some cloth off the bottom of Nathan's pants leg to wrap around his ankle until the potion he was making was ready. Placing Nathan's rifle and knife by his side, he left camp to refill the canteens and get a bucket of water. While away, Nathan could hear the bear huffing and clawing at a tree not too far outside of camp and readied his rifle and kept a constant watch; he couldn't afford to make another careless mistake.

No more than fifteen minutes passed when Nathan heard a shot ring out and the sound of one angry bear, and prayed that Inola would have enough time to reload. He listened intently for the second shot knowing that Inola had only wounded it; making it more dangerous than before. But when the second shot rang out he was sure he had gotten the job done, and laid his rifle by his side.

As nightfall was rapidly approaching, Inola's potions were finally ready to give to Nathan. He handed him a full cup of the yarrow tea to drink, and brought the condensed potion of witch hazel and spread it over the puncture wounds and wrapped his ankle in large leaves, as the cloth wrap was now soaked in blood. He tore another strip of cloth and wrapped it over the leaves and tied it snug around his ankle and looked up at Nathan who could only nod his head in appreciation.

After eating a little jerky and the last of the bread Nathan brought with him, Inola said, "Try to get some sleep. We leave first thing in the morning."

"Thanks, Inola, I'm indebted to you," he gratefully said and eased down onto his bedroll and pulled his blanket over him. The intense pain and throbbing kept Nathan awake most of the night, and Inola was wakened to the sound of groaning. He poured another cup of yarrow tea that was supposed to help with pain and fever and handed it to Nathan and told him, "Drink all of it my friend."

He quickly hitched Nathan's horse to the wagon and tied his horse behind it and stated, "We leave now, eat later." Helping Nathan to his feet he supported his weight as he hobbled to the back of the wagon and laid down on top of the pelts with a groan and pulled one of the skins over him for it was cold in the early morning hours. They broke camp just as the sun was shining its first rays over the rolling hills in front of them. The wagon was full and heavy on the trip back and it would take much longer over the rough terrain to reach home. Even if Inola pushed the horses hard they wouldn't make it back before dark.

Nathan drank the yarrow tea that was poured into his canteen and wished that it had been a hot cup of coffee on the bumpy ride back to his house. Although his ankle hurt something fierce, all he could think about was that he would soon be with Sara, and how he wished it was under better circumstances. He had very much wanted to start their journey to Knoxville to be married, for he couldn't wait to hold Sara in his arms and love her the way he wanted. That dream was now gone.

Chapter 19

Sara was sitting beside the fireplace sewing on her skirt when she heard the sound of a wagon rapidly approaching shortly after sundown. Before she could put her sewing down and toss her blanket on the couch, Inola stepped through the doorway and said, "Come," and motioned with his hand. Sara was shocked to see Inola and wondered why he was there instead of Nathan. She knew this couldn't be good and quickly went after Inola who had already left the room and followed him outside. The only light was from the full moon and stars as Inola led Sara to the back of the wagon.

When she saw Nathan lying there and not moving she cried out, "Oh, dear God, is he dead Inola?"

"Not dead. Help me get him inside," he said and lowered the back gate to the wagon.

"What happened, Inola?" she anxiously questioned.

"Stepped in bear trap."

He roused Nathan and he sat partially up resting on one elbow and smiled when he saw Sara's face. She burst into tears of joy that Nathan was alive, but they soon turned to tears of fear as she caught a glimpse of his bandaged ankle and saw the pain that he was in.

Inola gave him a hand getting out of the wagon and when he was standing, Inola turned to Sara, "Come," he said as Nathan put his arm around Inola's shoulders to help support his weight. Sara quickly went to his side and he put his other arm around her shoulder as he limped up the steps then into his bed.

Sara was about to leave his bedside to go to the attic to get the medical supplies she had brought with her when Nathan reached out and took hold of her hand.

"Don't I even get a kiss?" he asked with a smile looking up at her tear stained face as tears still filled her eyes.

Sara stopped and sat on the bed next to him and leaned in, placing both hands on the sides of his face and kissed him tenderly as tears rolled off her cheeks and onto his face then quickly wiped them away. The pain and fear he saw in Sara's eyes was far more painful to him than his mangled ankle and slowly sighed as he held her hand.

She forced a smiled and said, "I'll be back, my love," and stood to leave once again.

Inola had watched her carefully for he was still suspicious of her, but even he could see how much Sara loved his friend, and decided maybe she wasn't an evil spirit after all.

She quickly left the room to put a pot of water over the fire to heat, then pulled out a basin and washcloth from a cabinet in the kitchen and set them on the table. Hurriedly she climbed the stairs to the attic to bring down the box of medical supplies and set them next to Nathan's bed. Her heart was racing as she anxiously rushed around, for the only thing on her mind was the necessity to help Nathan as quickly as possible.

She poured some of the heated water into the basin on the table and took the washcloth with her when she returned to Nathan's room and called for Inola.

"Inola, would you please bring me a chair from the dining room?" she asked kindly as she set the basin at the foot of the bed and opened the box that was close by.

Inola brought the chair she asked for as Sara lit the candle on the small table by his bed. She went to remove the leaves that Inola had wrapped around Nathan's ankle when he grabbed her wrist to stop her.

"Leave alone. It good for him."

"I must look at it Inola. It needs to be cleaned and some anti-bacterial ointment put on it," she said looking up at his stern and contentious face.

Inola looked at Nathan propped up in his bed for his decision on what was to be done as he continued to hold Sara's wrist tightly. Nathan had no idea what anti-bacterial ointment was or even meant, but he trusted Sara and gave a simple nod of his head looking directly at Inola, and he roughly released Sara's wrist and left the room. Nathan could not worry about hurt feelings. He could already feel cold sweats coming on and his heart rate going up and knew that he would soon be in serious trouble if he did not receive the proper care. He had seen far too many men in his regiment during the war lose arms and legs due to infections and it crossed his mind how he would be able to work his farm with only one good leg.

Sara slowly and gently unwrapped the leaves from around Nathan's swollen ankle and gasped as she looked up at Nathan with fear written all over her face. She looked back down at the thick witch hazel salve poured into his wounds and wondered how she was ever going to get that cleaned out without hurting him. She looked up at Nathan once again with questioning eyes as her hands trembled.

"I'll be okay, Sara. You just do what you need to do," he said tenderly as beads of sweat covered his brow.

She quickly went through her box of medical supplies and found an instant ice pack, a syringe, and a bottle of ibuprofen.

Sara poured a cup of water and handed Nathan four pills to swallow and then gently wiped his brow and placed the icepack across his forehead.

She looked lovingly at him and said, "I'm afraid I'm not very good at doing this kind of thing, my love. This is going to hurt cleaning out that salve."

"I know, but you go ahead and do it," he said breathing rather rapidly.

She hastily went and got another basin to put under his ankle while she filled the syringe with warm water and squirted it into each open wound and wiped it as gently as she could. When she cleaned the wound on top of his ankle she saw clear down to the bone and felt faint and put her hand down on his bed until the spinning and lightheadedness cleared.

"Sara, are you alright," he asked looking at her pale face and her gasping softly for air.

She just nodded, still unable to speak as stars darted before her eyes. When her head cleared she smiled at him and said, "I'm fine, please don't worry about me," and went back to cleaning out the rest of the wounds. Once they were clean she gently spread the ointment into each one of them and wrapped gauze around his ankle. All she could do now was wait to see if they would become infected and keep Nathan as comfortable as possible.

He was resting somewhat comfortably now as the pain medicine took effect, and Sara pulled her chair up by the head of the bed. She laid her head down next to him and fell asleep for it was very late into the night.

Nathan began to stir in the early morning hours waking Sara. She placed her hand on his forehead; it seemed warm to her. She rummaged through the box of supplies and found the thermometer and swiped it across his forehead – 101 degrees. She poured him some water and handed him four more pain pills, and put a cool, wet cloth across his forehead. He smiled at her and took her hand and pulled her down on the bed next to him.

"Sit a little while with me, things can wait a bit," he said tenderly.

She smiled as she held his hand, but he could still see the deep concern in her eyes and knew in his heart that she would always be there for him, and his love for her grew more deeply.

Sara noticed Nathan staring at the doorway and turned to see what he was looking at. She was surprised to see Inola standing there drinking a cup of coffee.

"Coffee ready, and plenty of stew," Inola said and turned and walked back to the hearth.

"Are you ready for breakfast?" Sara asked.

"Very," he replied.

"And how would you like your coffee?" she inquired

"Black if you don't mind," he replied.

"Black it is…I'll be right back," she said with a smile and hurried off to what she considered the kitchen.

Inola was sitting at the table eating and noticed that Sara was still wearing her weapon. As Sara turned with a plate full of stew and a slice of bread for Nathan she saw that Inola was staring at it and her disdainfully. She knew she needed Inola's help and placed Nathan's food on the table and removed her weapon and placed it on the edge of the mantle over the hearth, then placed Nathan's breakfast on a tray and took it to him with his cup of black coffee. Sara needed Inola now, and was counting on him staying until she was sure Nathan would recover. Removing her weapon was the least she could do in trying to mend bridges.

Nathan practically inhaled his food which Sara took as a good sign, and relaxed a bit while she ate her breakfast and washed it down with coffee sweetened with her favorite creamer.

Inola entered the bedroom carrying logs for the fire and Sara thanked him as he quickly made his way to the fireplace.

"Inola," Sara said and waited for him to stop and look at her.

'Inola, would you please stay with us until Nathan is back on his feet? I could really use your help," she asked with humility.

"Inola will stay," he replied and left the room.

"Wow, I don't think I've ever seen him that agreeable. What happened between the two of you?" Nathan curiously asked quietly when Inola was in the other room.

"I removed my weapon and placed it on the mantle for him to see," she replied with a smile.

"I love you Sara Mathews. I do believe you now have that man wrapped around your little finger," he said and patted the bed next to him wanting Sara to join him.

Sara placed the front of her hand on Nathan's brow and then rested it on his chest all the while looking sweetly at him. He could see the worry in her face no matter how hard she tried to mask it. He knew exactly what she was doing; feeling for fever and heart rate, for he recalled doing the very same things to Elizabeth and his young daughter. He remembered the fear and worry he had felt, and that was what Sara was now going through.

Nathan took her hand in both of his and said, "Sara, please try not to worry. I survived five years in the militia, I'll be up and around before you know it."

"I'm sure you will be. Now hold still while I check your ankle and put a fresh dressing on it," she said.

She carefully unwrapped the gauze and when she looked at his ankle her eyes widened and she quickly tried to look calm for his sake. Nathan's ankle was noticeably swollen and red around each wound and she feared that infection had already set in. She tried to tell herself that Nathan had a strong constitution and his own body would fight this, then put a clean dressing around it.

Nathan watched her every move carefully and saw her eyes widen and wondered just how bad his injury was; for the only doctor was a hard two day drive both ways and doubted whether there was anything the doctor could do for him that wasn't already being done. He admired the strength and courage Sara showed in remaining calm for his sake, but knew she was worried by what she had seen.

"Am I going to live, Doc?" he asked jokingly.

"If I have anything to say about it you will. I already have a request in up above for a full and speedy recovery," she said and went back up to the top of the bed to sit with Nathan.

Inola stood in the doorway to the bedroom to speak to Nathan. "Nate, okay to put pelts upstairs until you ready to take to town?"

"Sure. Just stack them in one of the bedrooms, and feel free to put your things in the bedroom with a fireplace."

"I sleep downstairs by fire," he said and turned to go back out the front door.

"I'm going to get some more water for you to drink. You need to be drinking lots of liquids," she said and started for the door.

As Sara was approaching the kitchen Nathan called out to her, "I would prefer some more coffee if there is any left."

"Water would be better for you," she called back.

"That might be so, but I would still prefer the coffee," he called out.

"I'll bring both," she replied with a deep sigh.

When she returned she handed him the cup of coffee with a raised eyebrow and set the pitcher of water on the table by his bed, and he subtly smiled because he found a woman that could hold her own with him, and he liked that.

She sat next to him on the bed and began to sing softly to him some of the rock-n-roll love songs that she knew by heart. Nathan hadn't heard anyone sing in a long time, and listened contentedly to her beautiful soft voice until he could no longer keep his eyes open.

Sara took every opportunity she had when he was sleeping to go do some chores. She didn't expect Inola to do the cooking or baking so she prepared enough for lunch and supper and also made a couple pans of bread.

After Nathan had eaten a hearty supper and everything was cleaned up, Sara went in and laid down beside him, laying her head on his chest.

He put his arm around her and softly stroked her arm, "You must be exhausted. You're trying to do too much. Tomorrow I want you just to lay here beside me and keep me company, and you can sing to me again, if you wish."

"Okay, you talked me into it," she said sleepily, and it wasn't long before she fell asleep next to him. He looked at her for the longest time wanting to hold her in his arms while he was still able, and pondered whether he would survive if Sara had not chosen to stay with him.

During the night, Nathan started shivering with chills so hard that she could feel the bed shake and woke before it was light outside. She quickly placed her hand on his forehead and could tell right away that he had a fever, and quickly got up and lit the candle next to the bed. She poured a glass of water and hurriedly took four pills from their container and gently roused Nathan.

"Here, take these," she said and raised his head from the pillow that was now soaked and quickly turned it over and held the cup for him to drink from.

"I'll be alright, Sara. Come lie back down until it's light outside," he said softly.

Sara quickly wiped the tears from her eyes, hoping that Nathan had not seen them in the candle light, and laid back down beside him. She prayed for daybreak when she could look at his ankle again, but dreaded what she might find.

Nathan had seen her tears, and he could tell that her breathing was rapid as she lay next to him, and was clueless as to how he might comfort her. Nathan said a prayer of his own asking God to heal him because it wouldn't be right to leave Sara alone and heartbroken once again. Besides, he still longed for a lifetime spent with this most amazing and fascinating woman that would always find new ways to befuddle him.

As soon as it was light enough, Sara got up and unwrapped the gauze around Nathan's ankle. She was shocked, and Nathan could see the terror in her eyes as she glanced up at him. She looked back down at his ankle and the redness was spreading further up his leg and there was a slightly green cloudy drainage coming from the individual wounds – it was septicemia.

Sara could no longer hide her tears. "Nathan, I'm scared. I don't know what else I can do. I've tried everything I brought with me but nothing is helping," she cried.

"Sara, come sit," he said in his calming deep voice and once again patted the bed beside him.

As she sat there crying and holding his hand tightly Nathan said, "I'm in God's hands now, and I believe He's not ready for me to leave this old world or He wouldn't have sent an angel to take care of me."

Inola heard Sara crying and entered the bedroom to look at Nathan's injury. He only needed to glance at it to know that his friend was in trouble. It was plain for Nathan to see that Inola was also deeply concerned, and for the first time he felt afraid. Sara left the two of them to talk while she went and prepared breakfast and brought it back in to Nathan and encouraged him to eat.

Over the next couple of days Nathan grew worse and Sara stayed by his side while he slept and covered him with a blanket when he got the chills and placed a cool cloth across his forehead when his fever returned. Inola entered the room to place more logs on the fire while Nathan was tossing and turning in his sleep and could hear him calling Elizabeth's name and looked at Sara. Tears were running down her cheeks as she held his hand and prayed, and Inola had pity for her. He too felt his friend might die and quietly left the room.

As Sara continued to sit by his side she suddenly recalled her conversation with the City Clerk, Donna Lewis. She remembered her saying that the original owner died in 1786. Her eyes widened as she looked at him and then down at his ankle. She was instantly seized with horror, this was 1786; Nathan would die from his injury! She knew she needed to act immediately if she was going to have any chance of saving his life.

Sara looked up and saw Inola in the other room sitting by the fireplace and quickly stood and went to him.

"Inola, I want you to stay with Nathan. I'm going back to my time to get medicine for him. If I don't, he will die! Will you stay? It will take me hours before I am able to return."

"Inola stay. You hurry."

Chapter 20

Sara hurried and put her weapon in her purse and her backpack on then remembered Nathan had to be outside just off the porch, and she needed to be in the attic before she could leave. She wondered how they were going to get him outside in his condition – nothing seemed to be going right and Sara was at her wits end.

"Inola, do you think you can take Nathan outside just off the porch, and then get him back inside without my help? I don't have time to explain why we have to do this, but we do," she stated desperately.

"I find way," he replied.

Sara went and set a chair outside for Nathan to sit on and then quickly returned to help Inola bring Nathan as far as the front door. He had become delirious and they doubted that he even knew what was going on.

"Give me a minute Inola to get to the attic, and then you can take him outside. Wait a minute or two and then it will be okay if you help him back to the bedroom." When Inola nodded she ran up to the attic as quickly as she could and prayed the portal hadn't closed.

The room quickly changed before her eyes and she immediately descended the stairs and ran out of the house and through the trees to the base of the hill. She caught her breath, then as swiftly as she could she climbed to the top, and then over the hill praying that her car would still be at the cabin. A little over an hour had passed, and as she neared the cabin she slowed down and cautiously looked to see if anyone was there looking for her. She saw no one, and thanked God that her car was still parked where she had left it, and quickly opened the door and climbed in, but didn't notice an envelope with her name on it fell to the floor of the car.

She sped along the winding road leading to town where she thought she wouldn't get pulled over, but slowed down when she approached the main road through town and went straight to their only pharmacy. There were only a few cars in the parking lot and she waited impatiently for the people to come out before she entered. It was agonizing as she sat there staring at the entrance to the store knowing that every minute she waited Nathan was getting worse. She thought about how she was going to get the needed antibiotics without a prescription as she waited. She doubted whether she could convince them to just let her pay for them for fear of getting in trouble. She wondered if she could slip over the counter unnoticed and just take what she needed. She had no choice; she would do whatever it took to get them because she was not leaving without them. She took her phone out of her purse and prayed that it still had enough of a charge to google which antibiotics worked best for septicemia and saw that the battery was down to 12%, and finding two she quickly wrote them down so she would know what to look or ask for.

When all the customers had left she quickly entered the building clutching her purse close to her side and looked around at the situation and noticed only two people behind the pharmacy counter, and slowly approached it looking for any other personnel that might be working. At that time the pharmacists' backs were turned to her filling prescriptions for pickup, and she quietly slid over the counter and ducked behind the first shelves of medications. *"Now what"*, she thought, *"I don't even know which shelves stock the medicine, and I'm sure to be caught."* She unfastened her purse and pulled her handgun out, and couldn't believe herself capable of robbing a store at gunpoint. She slowly stood and began reading the names of the medications on the shelves she was standing behind, then slowly moved to the next row and started looking while glancing often at the two pharmacists.

While scanning the names of the medications in the next row she heard, "Hey, what are you doing back here? You don't belong here now get back behind the counter or I'm calling the cops," one of the pharmacists curtly ordered.

Sara froze when one of them came towards her demanding that she leave right now. Feeling threatened she instinctively raised her handgun and pointed it at him. By this time the other pharmacist was moving closer and she could tell that he meant business.

"Stand down, and you won't be hurt," Sara said loudly, trembling from adrenaline.

The two men looked at each other, and the one said to the other, "She won't shoot," and took a step towards Sara.

She was in fight or flight mode and she was determined not to take flight and fired a warning shot that came dreadfully close to hitting one of them in the shoulder.

"That was your one and only warning shot, the next one won't miss," she said with a firm two-handed grip on her handgun and the two men stood still with their hands raised in the air.

"Have either of you ever wanted something so badly that you did all the wrong things to get it? Well that's where I'm at," she said on the verge of tears.

"What is it you want?" one of them asked angrily.

"I need antibiotics for a man that will die without them."

"Do you have a prescription?" he asked belligerently.

"If I had a prescription do you think I would be here pointing a gun at you?" she asked in disbelief at such a stupid question.

Out of the corner of her eye she saw movement in the store and quickly looked to see who was there.

"You, drop your phone and come over here," she ordered and wondered if the person had already dialed 911 after hearing the shot fired.

When the stock person reached the counter she told him to slide over it and stand next to the other two men.

"I need antibiotics to treat a bad case of septicemia," Sara demanded boldly.

"You'll need to give them intravenously if it's a bad case and we don't carry that."

"That's not an option anyway," she replied. Looking down at the names she had written out she continued, "I want you to fill a bag with 'azithromycin' and 'ciprofloxacin ceftriaxone'; all of it," she demanded.

The two men just stood there daring her to shoot; that medicine would cost a small fortune. Sara turned on the laser to her gun so they could see that it was pointed at the one man's heart.

"I suggest you get moving; I'm not going to let the man I love die. Do you understand me?" she stated resolute and fuming.

"Go ahead, Sam, get her what she's asked for, she's just crazy enough to shoot."

Sam grabbed a bag and moved to the isle with the requested antibiotics and emptied them into the bag and returned to where he had been standing.

"What else will I need to save his life?" Sara asked anxiously.

"You'll need to stay alive," Sam said disdainfully. Sara knew exactly what he meant and her anger burned.

The other man, Thomas, looked at Sam angrily and turned to Sara and said, "You should try to clean the wounded area with peroxide and let it air out. That might help. You need to give him the antibiotic three times a day, and make sure he finishes the entire pack. Also, try to keep the fever down and make sure you give him plenty of fluids. Grab a canister of something with electrolytes in it on your way out."

"Thank you, and may God bless you," Sara said gratefully. "Now toss the bag over here," she continued, and once she had it and placed it in her backpack she backed away from the men and slid over the counter still training the weapon on them. She quickly found the canister as she ran from the building pushing past someone trying to enter.

She could hear Sam hollering, "Stop her, she just robbed the store!"

Sara ran to her car and tossed her backpack in the seat next to her and took off with her tires screeching as she stepped on the gas.

Just a block away she heard sirens coming her way and immediately slowed down to the speed limit to not draw attention to herself, and hoped that no one had given the police a description of her vehicle or her license plate number. After the police cars passed by, she sped up through the winding road leading to her cabin, and when she had pulled into the driveway she started to reach for her backpack then stopped. It would take her over an hour to reach Nathan and that was if she ran most of the way. There had to be a faster way to get there, she thought, and quickly decided to pull out of the drive and head towards the valley that led to the hill in front of Nathan's house. She drove the car hard not caring about the toll it would take on her vehicle; she could live without her car if it broke down, but she couldn't live without Nathan.

Sara was fortunate. Her car made it almost to the base of the hill, and in less than a half hour she would be with Nathan and prayed that she had returned in enough time. She grabbed her backpack that had fallen on the floor and when she picked it up she saw the envelope lying there and stuffed it in her purse. Nothing mattered but getting back to Nathan in time to save his life.

She climbed the hill in almost a straight line pushing her way through the brush and forest of trees and ran across the porch pushing hard on the front door as it scraped across the weathered floor boards. Once through she ran up the stairs to the attic and when she reached the top she turned around waiting for everything to change so that she could hurry to Nathan's side.

The scent of pine filled the air and she knew that everything was about to change and started quickly down the stairs to Nathan's room. Inola was by his side chanting something in Cherokee when he saw Sara, red-faced, and out of breath.

"How is he Inola," she asked still panting as she grabbed a packet of antibiotics and quickly read the instructions, and looked up for his answer.

"Hurry," was all he said and Sara quickly ripped open the packet and poured a cup of water that she had mixed with the electrolyte powder. Lifting his head she said, "Nathan, my love, you must swallow this. Come on, open your mouth," she begged and forced the pill in his mouth and put the cup of water to his lips.

"Drink, Nathan. You must drink!" she said desperately.

Nathan took a couple of gulps and she laid him back down, and put a fresh cool cloth on his forehead, and took another cloth to bathe his chest and arms. She hurriedly untied his shirt and with Inola's help, they lifted his shirt off him. Sara immediately started washing him down with cool water to help reduce his fever and gave him four more pills to swallow and went back to bathing him until she felt his fever subsiding.

As she sat on the edge of the bed looking attentively at him, her eyes drifted and studied his broad and muscular chest and arms, and lightly ran her fingers thru the hair on his chest. This was the first time she had seen him without his shirt on and had to turn her eyes away. The only thing that should be on her mind was doing what she could to save him.

A couple of hours passed and he was now resting quietly and Sara began to remove the gauze from his ankle. His wounds were troublesome to look at. She cringed inside as she poured the peroxide over them and watched it fizz over the infected areas, and let the excess run off into the basin, then propped his leg up on an extra blanket to let it air dry.

Sara stayed by his side, and covered and uncovered him as the chills came and went, and listened to him call out Elizabeth's name in his confusion and took no offense to it. She fed him when he was awake and not necessarily when it was lunch or supper time. She gave him his medications at their appointed times whether she had to wake him or not, and always encouraged him to drink more water. Sara sang softly to him not knowing whether he was aware of it or not. But it was for her good as well, because it kept her mind from worrying whether she had chosen the right antibiotic or not.

By the third day Sara began to see some improvement in his condition. He was able to sit up for short periods of time. His mind was now sharp and her fears greatly subsided for she knew he would make a full recovery within a week or two.

A smile returned to Sara's face as she sang to him while tending to his needs, and Nathan was most content just to have her by his side.

He was sitting up one afternoon when Sara entered the room after finishing some of her chores. He patted the bed next to him and with a smile on his face he said, "Come, and sit for a while."

Sara gladly joined him, and quickly took him by the hand and smiled, noticing how his beautiful blue eyes sparkled once again.

"Inola came in to talk to me while you were at the hearth cooking and asked me what you meant by returning to your time. I'm afraid I didn't do a very good job at trying to explain that to him, because he left just as confused as when he came in. He mentioned that you left to get some medicine for me and you were gone for many hours. He also mentioned that you left with your weapon. Would you mind telling me about that?" he asked giving her a questioning look.

"I had no choice but to cross over to my time. I feared you were going to die if I didn't get you the antibiotics to fight your infection. My car, or horseless carriage to you, was still at the cabin and I was fortunate to be able to drive it to the only pharmacy in town. Without a prescription from a doctor it is impossible to get any medications. So I had no other choice but to take the medicine at gunpoint."

"Do you realize how dangerous that was? You could have been caught and taken to jail – I might never have seen you again, Sara," he stated with great concern.

"I had to go! You might not have seen me again if I had stayed," she quickly rebutted.

"You didn't have to shoot anyone did you?" he asked seriously.

"No, but I did have to fire a warning shot to let them know I meant business. One of the men wasn't quite as belligerent as the other. As a matter of fact, he turned out to be most helpful and kind, and not only gave me the medicine – at gunpoint of course – but suggested things I could do to help in the healing process. I heard the police..." Nathan looked at her quizzically and Sara smiled and continued, "That would be a sheriff, or the law, to you. Anyway, they were coming after me and I managed to make a quick get-away and drove my car over the rugged terrain of the valley almost to the hill before it broke down and I had to come the rest of the way by foot. I prayed that I would get to you in time," she said while recalling the events.

At this point, Sara's eyes began to well with tears and her lips trembled as she tried to continue her story.

"It's okay Sara. Inola told me how you found me near death, and stayed by my side day and night even though I kept calling out Elizabeth's name," he said and sighed deeply, momentarily looking away from her gaze.

"Nathan, you have nothing to feel bad about. It was only natural for you to call out her name. I took no offense to it. You were delirious and said many strange things," Sara said with a smile hoping to comfort him.

"I love you, Sara. God surely sent me an angel when he sent you to me," he said and reached over pulling her close and kissed her for the first time in days.

As Sara sat back up with a huge smile on her face, Nathan watched her eyes and noticed they glanced quickly between his face and his chest that was still bare. He was feeling well enough to tease her. He took her by the hand and placed it against his chest over his heart and waited to see her response.

Sara blushed a deep red as her fingers lightly ran through the hairs on his chest, and Nathan laughed. That was just the reaction he was hoping for.

"You're so bad, Nathan Chambers," she said embarrassed, and jumped up heading towards the door.

"Where are you going?" he asked still chuckling and pleased with himself.

"I've got work to do," she said and closed the door, just to hear him still laughing.

Inola was by the fireplace when Sara came out and blurted out with a hint of a smile, "I guess he better now," and then got up to go outside and chop some more wood for the fire.

"Oh, we have another comedian in the house," she said and continued on to the kitchen.

Sara busied herself making a venison stew for supper, and then washing Nathan's vest and shirt that had been soaked with sweat during his fever and hung them outside to dry.

It had been well over an hour since Sara left Nathan's bedside. Still in a playful mood he finally called out loudly, "Hey Sara, where's my supper? I'm getting mighty hungry all alone in here."

Sara appeared in his doorway with her hands on her hips, "Are you going to behave yourself, Nathan Chambers?"

"Yes, my dear, I'll behave myself," he replied trying his best to hide a grin,

Sara shook her head and chuckled, "Oh, Nathan, you have no such intentions at all," and turned around to get his supper for him.

Chapter 21

"What are you doing," Sara asked as she walked through the bedroom door and hesitated as Nathan was pulling his shirt over his head.

"I believe it's called getting dressed. I'm through lying in bed all day. I want to sit by the fire, have my meals at the table, and start lifting a hand around here," he said boldly.

Sara smiled. She was happy to see that spark ignited in him once again, and eager to see what new adventures lay ahead for them.

"Well then, I guess your coffee will be served by the fireplace," she told him with a big smile on her face.

Nathan walked with only a slight limp to his rocking chair by the fire, and sat down with a sigh of satisfaction. It felt good to get out of bed.

Sara soon joined him with his coffee cup in hand and the last of his ten day dose of antibiotic.

"What are you smiling about," Nathan asked.

"It's good to have you sitting by the fire with me again," she stated still smiling and picked up the skirt she was piecing together and resumed her sewing.

"So how's it coming? Are you almost finished, because I hope we can get started to town by the end of next week," he questioned. "My leg should be well enough by then," he continued.

"I should have both pieces finished by then," she replied and continued sewing.

Sara looked up and noticed that Nathan was staring at her and curiously asked, "Why are you staring?"

"Does it bother you?" he asked with a grin.

"No, I was just curious what you were thinking about while you were staring," she replied with a raised eyebrow.

"Well, if you must know, I was wondering what you would look like in a dress instead of those tight fitting clothes you wear," he stated with a provocative look.

"I see," she said looking up at him for a moment, and then went back to sewing. "To tell you the truth, I've been wondering the same thing. In all the movies I've watched, or pictures I've seen of women wearing all these bulky skirts and dresses, I always thought how glad I was that I didn't have to wear such clothing. I prefer the more casual dress of my day," she said matter-of-factly.

"I do too. There's only one problem with it…a man can't keep his mind on his work or anything else when you're around him," he said with an alluring smirk, waiting to see if she would blush.

Sara kept her head lowered, and fought to keep from smiling or blushing. She finally looked up at him and just shook her head and went back to sewing.

She was finished with the skirt now. She stood up holding the skirt up to her waist and bent over slightly to see if it reached the floor.

"So, what do you think? Will I look ridiculous when we go into town?" she asked.

Nathan rubbed his chin while he thought, and finally replied, "No, you'll look quite stunning, my dear."

Sara looked pleased and sat back down and picked up the blouse with a sample of the ruffles she was going to add around the bottom of it to make it long enough for her.

"If I add this ruffle around the hem and neckline, do you think it will look alright? I don't want people staring at me because I look funny," she said feeling a little awkward.

"You'd better get used to people staring at you. They're not used to seeing someone as tall and beautiful as you. I'll be a proud man, Sara Mathews, walking next to you," he said lovingly.

Sara could no longer restrain the feelings that were building up inside her and laid her sewing aside and went and sat on Nathan's lap. She gently brushed his bangs aside and kissed him long and eagerly, knowing that one day she would give in to his irresistible, beguiling charm. It wasn't right to tempt Nathan beyond what he could bear, and she reluctantly returned to her own rocking chair and wondered if he could tell just how much she craved his touch.

Nathan looked off to the side, staring thoughtfully in the direction of the fire.

"Sara, would you mind setting your sewing aside long enough to put a pot of water on the fire to heat up? I think it's about time that I take a bath and shave," he said.

Sara just nodded and went outside to draw the water to be heated, while Nathan returned to his bedroom and set out some clean clothes on the bed. He set his soap and sponge on the stool by the fireplace and next to a wooden tub to catch the water.

A little while later Nathan emerged still limping from the bedroom with clean clothes and a shaven face. His hair was still wet and hanging loose around his shoulders as he approached the fire with a comb in his hand. Sara quickly went to her purse and pulled a hairbrush from it and returned to her rocking chair.

"Nathan, come sit here on the rug by me and I'll brush your hair for you," she said with an inviting smile.

He looked at her surprised and hesitated until she said again, "Come sit by me. It'll feel so wonderful and relaxing that you might not ever want to comb your hair again."

He nodded his head and said, "Okay," and took his seat on the rug. Sara started brushing through his long hair, and he continued to let her brush it long after it was free of tangles. She could feel him relaxing with each stroke of the brush and began to sing softly to him, then finally pulled his hair back and tied a ribbon around it.

"See, now didn't that feel wonderful?" she asked avidly.

Nathan stood up and turned towards her shaking his head, "As if you didn't already have enough work to do, now you can add brushing my hair to that list." Sara smiled; pleased that he seemed to really enjoy it.

The next several days passed by quickly as Sara worked to finish the alterations to her dress and wished with every pull of the needle that she had a sewing machine to do the work for her. Nathan was back to helping Inola with the work outside that needed to be done before winter was upon them. He only came in for meals and occasionally to just see Sara and sit and rest his leg for a while.

Two days before they were scheduled to leave, Sara finished her dress and tried it on while Nathan was outside working. She couldn't help but notice when she was changing that she hadn't shaved her legs in days and went to her dresser and took out her razor. After filling a basin with water and picking up some soap, she went and sat on the stool by the fireplace in the bedroom. Her skirt was pulled up around her upper thigh when Nathan happened to walk into the room. He looked at her with a curious look and asked, "Is everything all right?"

"Yes, I'm fine," she replied with a somewhat look of surprise on her face.

"What are you doing?" he asked.

"I'm shaving my legs! No man likes a woman with hairy legs."

Nathan just stood there with a confused look on his face; not knowing what to say.

Sara looked at him still standing in the doorway when she was finished and asked, "Haven't you ever seen a woman with shaved legs?"

"Never," he replied.

"Well, come take a look and tell me what you think," she said daringly.

Nathan slowly walked over to her and knelt down next to her and looked at her legs from the ankle all the way up to her thighs, then looked at her without saying a word.

"So, what do you think? Do you like the way it looks, or not? Go ahead and run your hand along my leg and see if you like it," she said feeling a little scandalous at the moment.

Nathan looked at her to see if she was joking and then placed his hand close to her ankle and ran it up along her leg just below where her skirt laid across her thigh, and a huge smile came to his face. Sara could have sworn that Nathan blushed but it was hard to tell for sure in the dimly lit room.

"I could easily get used to it," he said with a look that made Sara lower her skirt.

Sara stood up and twirled around in the dress she altered and asked, "Does it look good enough to go to town in?"

"You did a fine job, Sara. I can't wait to take you to town to show you off," he said and reached out and pulled her close and kissed her; leaving her wanting much more than just a kiss.

He could see the look in her eyes and let go of the hold he had around her waist. He wanted her so bad it hurt, and wondered if she knew just how hard it was for him to resist her.

"Come with me. There's something I want to show you," he said calmly and took a deep breath as he led her to the far side of the bedroom where a wooden chest sat that had gone unopened by Sara. Nathan opened it and she saw that it was full of Elizabeth's apparel and looked at him inquisitively.

"Before I can take you into town you are going to have to put a couple of these petticoats under that pretty dress of yours. You're also going to have to put your hair up," he said and stopped when Sara gave him such a surprised look.

"Why do I have to put my hair up?" she asked with an emphasis on the word "up".

"Because women, in my time, only wear their hair down when they are all alone with their husbands. You wouldn't want people to think you were a…"

Sara raised her hand stopping him from completing his sentence, and he could see that she was serious and thought it best not to tease her.

He took a deep breath and continued, "Finally, my angel, pick out a bonnet that will go with that pretty dress of yours and a pair of stockings."

Sara gave him one of those "you've got to be kidding" looks and Nathan didn't know whether to find it amusing or troubling.

"Well, I'll leave you to it and see you at supper time," he said plainly, and left the room with Sara just standing there staring into the chest.

When supper time came, Sara dished out the food for Nathan and Inola and took her plate and sat opposite of Nathan. She remained silent throughout supper and Nathan and Inola glanced at her often and at each other without saying a word as Sara seemed to just be staring off into space.

Since Nathan had recovered from his injury Inola took his bedding upstairs to one of the rooms figuring Nathan and Sara would like some time alone.

When she had finished clearing the table and washing the dishes she joined Nathan by the fireplace and remained quiet as she stared into the fire.

"What's troubling you Sara? I haven't seen you this quiet since the day you walked into my life," he asked with concern.

Sara just looked up at him without saying a word and could tell that he was befuddled as to what was troubling her.

"Everything is troubling me," she said and fought back her tears.

"Do you want to talk about it?" he asked gently and waited for her to respond.

As Sara looked at him intently she knew that she loved him more than she had ever loved anyone in her life. She craved everything about him, but the fear of not being able to fit in with all the acceptable norms troubled her greatly.

She could see the anxiety she was causing him, and finally said, "Nathan, I'm sorry to have troubled you. I'm just being a silly, foolish woman," she said on the verge of tears.

"Sara, come here," he said extending a hand towards her.

She quickly came and sat on his lap and buried her face against his chest and cried.

Nathan rubbed her back as he tried to comfort and quiet her. "Shh, it'll be all right, Sara. There's nothing that we can't face as long as we are together." He waited for her to calm down and then patiently asked, "Won't you tell me what's troubling you? Maybe I can help."

She wiped the tears from her eyes and face before sitting up and looking at him. "I feel so foolish now…I'm just so overwhelmed by the lifestyle I'm expected to fit into. All these clothes I'm expected to wear; I just don't know how women do everything they need to do wearing such restrictive clothing. How do people even make love; they would be exhausted by the time they took all their clothes off. Then I have to wear my hair up! Women pay a lot of money to have someone put their hair up for them on big occasions in my time," Sara declared overwhelmed by it all.

Nathan had to chuckle just a bit, "That's what has been bothering you? Sara, you may dress anyway you like and wear your hair any way you like when we're at home. You'll never hear me complain about your tight fitting clothes or your hair in a ponytail or flowing over your shoulders. But, I am concerned about how you might be treated if you go into town looking that way. I don't know if I'm strong enough to take on the whole town at one time, but I would certainly try if that is what you chose to wear."

Sara looked at him and tried not to grin and then threw her arms around his neck and kissed him.

"I love you, Nathan Chambers."

Chapter 22

"Wake up sleepyhead. It's time to get up," Nathan said already dressed for their journey into Knoxville.

"I'm coming; I'll have breakfast ready in no time," she said and yawned and stretched as she lay in bed.

Sara didn't know whether to be excited or scared; this was going to be her first big adventure away from his house. By the time she made her way to the kitchen Nathan and Inola were already packing the back of the wagon with pelts, bedding and supplies for the trip to town. She hurried and made breakfast and even packed a lunch for later. She was pouring the coffee when Inola and Nathan walked in through the front door.

"Good timing, breakfast is hot and ready," she said cheerfully as Nathan hung his hat on the peg.

"Good, because I'm hungry," he said and took his seat quickly by the hearth to warm himself.

Nathan was excited and eager to get started. He had not told Sara yet of his plans to marry her before they left town; it would be his only chance to find a preacher anytime soon. It didn't take long for them to finish eating and Inola went back to packing the rest of the pelts in the wagon.

"Sara, why don't you go change your clothes and I'll clean up the kitchen," he stated.

"Okay, but this might take me some time, so please try to be patient," she said anxiously.

Nathan smiled, "Take your time, we're not in that big of a hurry."

Sara started dressing, first with her stockings and then the new white lace-up boots she bought knowing that she couldn't wear her boots with zippers; at least not when she went to town. She stepped into her petticoats and slipped the pink calico skirt trimmed in a solid pink deep bordered hem over her head and fastened it around her waist and then buttoned up her blouse made out of the same material. Now for her hair. She sat in front of the mirror and just stared at herself wondering where to begin and decided to put her hair in a ponytail and then try to wind it around into a bun and use lots of Elizabeth's hair-pins to hold it in place.

"Hmm, not bad for a first try," she thought and put the solid pink bonnet on and tied a pretty bow off to the side of her cheek. *"Well, I can't hide in here forever; I might as well get this over with, and if they laugh, they laugh,"* she said to herself and picked up a warm cape that was Elizabeth's from off the bed and draped it over her arm.

Nathan and Inola had finished packing and were sitting by the fireplace when Sara finally came out of the bedroom. She nervously looked at them and fully expected them to try to muffle their laughter or at least hide their grins, but both men did neither. Sara walked out into the middle of the room and found them both speechless as they looked her over real good. Nathan stood to his feet and walked over to Sara and held both of her hands, and looking directly into her anxious hazel eyes said, "You look beautiful, my dear." She could tell that he truly meant it and no longer dreaded what the town's folks would think, for Nathan thought she looked beautiful.

Nathan turned to Inola and thanked him for looking out over his place while they would be gone, and told him if they weren't back in a week and a half to come looking for them.

Inola stood on the porch as Nathan helped Sara into the wagon and turned and gave Inola a quick nod of his head and told the horses to "walk on".

Sara was finally excited about their trip and wrapped her arm around Nathan's as he held the reins, and she smiled breathing a sigh of relief. Nathan looked over at her smiling and was so happy that he broke out singing a song in his deep, smooth voice as they drove along. Sara listened in amazement, never figuring Nathan to be a singing man; he was usually on the quiet side and spoke when necessary.

"That was lovely, Nathan. I wish you would sing more often; you have such a beautiful, soothing voice," she said smiling at him.

"I'll trade you a song for a song," he said and noticed that Sara looked cold and reached behind him and picked up her cape and helped her wrap it around her shoulders. A breeze picked up rather suddenly and Nathan glanced to the southwest and noticed that the clouds were darkening in the distance and seemed to be headed their way. He said nothing to Sara, but kept a close eye on the sky; the last thing they needed was rain for he was hoping to make close to twenty miles before nightfall.

Though the wooden seat was hard and the breeze brought a definite chill to the air, Sara was enjoying the ride and marveled at the beauty of the landscape untouched by man. After riding for four hours in the wagon Sara was feeling the effects of the hard seat and was ready to stop for lunch. Nathan found a nice patch of trees with some lush grass that had not been killed off by the recent snowstorms to stop for a break and eat their lunch. He held her hand as she raised her petticoats and skirt trying not to trip over them climbing down and when she had reached the ground she let out a long "Ahhhh" as she rubbed her backside. Nathan noticed her discomfort and grabbed a blanket from the back of the wagon and looked for a soft spot in the grass to spread it out. Meanwhile Sara took the basket with the lunch she had packed and followed Nathan to the place where he was now sitting.

"How can you sit after that long ride?" Sara asked and placed the basket down and bent over to unwrap the food.

"How else am I going to eat my lunch?" he asked looking up at Sara who was still stretching with a bit of a grimace, and smiled; not because she was sore, but because he adored her and found her reactions to life amusing.

"Standing!" Sara said and handed him a sandwich, and then unwrapped hers and took a bite and moaned as she savored it.

Nathan laughed and said, "Come sit by me. I've found you a really soft spot right here," he said and patted the ground.

Sara never was able to refuse him, and though she let out a long sigh she sat down beside him and ate her sandwich and handed Nathan another one.

When they were finished, Nathan laid back on the blanket and told Sara, "We're making good time, we can rest for a few minutes; why don't you lay down?"

Sara looked at him lying there with his hands behind his head and laid down a couple of feet away from him and it felt good to stretch out. He looked over at her and that was not quite what he had on his mind, and quickly moved over close to her. Leaning on his elbow, he placed his arm around her waist and bent over and kissed her, and then kissed her several more times before laying down beside her.

Nathan was afraid to get too comfortable, so after several minutes he stood up and said, "Sara, why don't you lay there while I give the horses something to drink? We still have several more hours to ride before we can stop for the night and I'm not sure if we'll find another spot to water them."

"Okay," Sara replied and continued to watch the clouds drifting by and thought about when Nathan was planning on marrying her. She wanted more than just his kisses, and she wanted more than feeling like a house guest. She wanted to be Mrs. Nathan Chambers!

When the horses were finished drinking, Nathan called to Sara and told her it was time to get rolling again, and Sara folded the blanket, picked up the lunch basket, and started towards the wagon. After putting the basket away, Nathan took the blanket from Sara and folded it once again and placed it on the hard wagon seat for Sara to sit on, and then helped her into the wagon.

As the wagon started to roll, Sara looked at Nathan and she was now several inches taller than he because of the blanket beneath her.

"I'd be happy to share this blanket with you," she said.

Nathan looked over at her and smiled, "That's alright; I happen to like tall women."

It was now late in the afternoon and Nathan started looking for a good spot to stop for the night. He found one on the backside of one of the rolling hills hoping that the hill would block some of the wind that was now starting to blow a little harder. Sara helped him gather some sticks for the fire and once it was going she prepared supper – sliced bread, cheese, apple and the little bit of sliced meat that was left after making the sandwiches. The coffee pot was brewing over the fire and Nathan had placed their bed rolls close to it and doubled Sara's blanket for her to lay on, but purposefully left his blanket large enough to where two could lay on it.

She sat close to Nathan while she ate as it was now starting to get cold as the sun was setting. Noticing that she was shivering he went and found another blanket to wrap around her while she held her coffee cup in both hands and sipped it even though they had not brought any of her creamer. The sound of the fire crackling was relaxing to Sara and suddenly in the not too distant stand of trees the sound of a pack of coyotes could be heard and Sara looked over at Nathan to see if he was alarmed. Nathan smiled; this gave him the chance to be seen as her brave protector and he was happy to play the part.

"I love the sound of coyotes yipping at night, don't you?" he asked looking into Sara's wide eyes and continued. "You have nothing to fear, my dear; I'll protect you from those wild animals," and wrapped an arm around her, proud of how well he played the part. Sara caught on quickly to his little act and tried not to let on as she struggled not to smile – she might have been born at night, but it wasn't last night.

When they had finished their cup of coffee Nathan put some more sticks on the fire and suggested they turn in because they needed to get an early start in the morning. Sara carefully laid down on her bedroll straightening out her skirt so as not to wrinkle it and pulled the cover up tightly under her chin.

As Nathan laid in his bedroll loosely covered he gazed at Sara through the glow of the fire light and couldn't wait to make her his wife. As he watched her he noticed that she was squirming around trying to pull the blankets tighter around her and looked at the extra space he had purposefully left on his bedroll.

"Sara, if you're still cold you could come lie next to me. I promise to be a perfect gentleman," he said and held his cover open for her to see that he had plenty of room.

Sara did not need to be asked twice; she was freezing, and quickly got up and laid down close to him shivering violently. He pulled her up close to him and pulled the covers over them and softly asked, "You don't mind if I put my arm around you, do you?"

"I don't care what you have to do to keep me warm," she said with a trembling voice and pressed her body even more tightly up next to his and could soon feel his warmth starting to penetrate through the layers of her clothing.

Nathan was content just to have her lay beside him tonight, but that would all change in just a couple of nights, and with that thought he tried to get some sleep.

In the morning Sara dreaded having to leave the warmth of the blankets that were now doubled over her. Nathan had kept her warm all through the night and now she was going to have to face another chilly day riding on a hard wagon seat for long hours, but at least she could look forward to another night in Nathan's arms, warm and snug and that brought a smile to her face.

Nathan was already up and had made a small fire to brew a pot of coffee. Reluctantly sitting up she pulled the hair-pins from her hair and ran her fingers through it to try to straighten it out before putting it back into a bun. Nathan watched her as he poured himself a cup of coffee and thought how beautiful she was, but wondered if she could truly adjust to a new life style, especially such a hard one.

After a light breakfast Nathan put the campfire out and helped Sara into the wagon. It was going to be another long day of sitting on a hard wooden seat, but she was thankful that the wind was not blowing making it colder than it already was. Nathan was quick to point out the deer grazing in the early morning hours near a stand of trees and a fox scampering off into the forest.

"Wow, far out!" Sara exclaimed.

Nathan looked at her perplexed and said, "No darling, they're right at the edge of the trees," and pointed again.

Sara then looked at him quizzically, then realized he did not understand the idiom from her time and burst out laughing.

"What's so funny?" he asked.

"I saw the fox and deer, honey. 'Far out' means 'that's wonderful', or 'how exciting' in my time," she said with a smile. He looked at her like she was joking, and then they both had a good laugh.

It wasn't long before they picked up a trail of wagon tracks leading to Knoxville. It turned out to be a lot rockier than the open valley and rolling hills Nathan had taken the day before. Sara found herself being bumped off the seat every time the wagon hit what she referred to as a pothole and grabbed onto Nathan's arm.

She looked at him suspiciously and asked, "Are you actually trying to hit every pothole you see? Because if you are, I think you missed one back there."

He turned to her and smiled. "Maybe you should just hold on to me a little tighter."

"How's that going to save my rear end? It feels like it's been beat with a meat tenderizer," she stated wearily and continued her squirming.

He pulled up on the reins and when the wagon came to a stop he asked her, "Would you like to get out and walk for a while beside the wagon?"

"Are you serious?" she asked with a straight face.

"Sure, if you fall behind I'll wait for you a couple hundred yards up the road," he replied trying not to grin. He knew that Sara would not last long in her long skirt and new high heel boots, but it would certainly convince her that riding in the wagon wasn't so bad after all. Nathan knew that their attraction to each other was strong, and that they truly loved each other, but that love had not been tested. He wanted to see under everyday circumstances how she would respond during a little hardship and frustrations.

Naively she said, "Yeah, I think I will try it; you know I love to walk. That's how I found your place."

Nathan helped her down knowing that she probably wouldn't make it to the top of the hill up ahead. He climbed back in the wagon and told the horses to 'walk on' and rode about a hundred feet up the trail and turned his head to check on her just in time to see her trip on the hem of her skirt and nearly fall, and started to chuckle. He drove on to the top of the hill and sat there and watched her struggle lifting her heavy petticoats and skirt so she wouldn't trip again, but still stumbled because she couldn't see her feet or where she was stepping. By the time she reached Nathan's wagon she was breathing heavily and fuming.

"Need a lift, pretty lady?" he asked with a smile knowing that he was probably going to catch hell for it. Sara just glared at him still breathing heavily and waited for him to climb down and help her back in the wagon. She no longer sat next to Nathan for the next hour but held on tightly to the seat to keep from bouncing around.

Nathan learned something that morning about Sara; she could be a very strong headed woman used to being independent, yet liked being pampered and he was waiting to see how long it would take her to get over being upset with him. He knew that what he did was not the kindest thing to do, but he wanted to make a point that she needed to trust his judgment; it could save her life one of these days.

"How long are you going to stay mad at me," he asked looking at her.

She glanced at him and then looked back at the trail ahead. "I don't know. That wasn't a very nice thing you did knowing full well that I could fall and get hurt," she stated still a little miffed at him.

"No, in hindsight it was not a very nice thing to do, but I was hoping that it would teach you to trust my judgement and know that I will always do what is best for you," he said honestly.

Sara looked at him intently and thought about what he said. She was used to doing things by herself in her time, but she was now living in a whole new world. She needed to be able to trust the man she had chosen to be with; and there was no finer man than Nathan. She had sulked for so long that she didn't know how to make amends. It was hard for Sara to swallow her pride, but it needed to be done and now was as good a time as any.

"Nathan, I'm sorry for the way I've behaved. It was childish and it won't happen again," Sara said and bit her bottom lip refusing to cry.

Nathan pulled up on the reins and stopped the wagon and took Sara in his arms and kissed her soft supple lips. "You're forgiven, now will you forgive me?" he asked. Sara smiled and softly replied, "I already have," and snuggled up close to him once again and never said another word about the bumpy trail.

In the end, Nathan was glad that he had done what he did; it told him a lot about this woman he wanted to marry and now his desire to do so was even stronger.

They only stopped to take short breaks and to eat lunch. Nathan wanted to reach Knoxville before noon the following day because he would need to sell the pelts before he had enough money to pay for all the things they needed.

He found a nice place to stop for the night alongside a small brook and set up camp; this time only spreading out one bedroll.

"I'll be back shortly I hope. Would you mind getting a fire started?" he asked as he picked up his rifle.

"No, I'd be happy to, but where are you going?" she asked.

"Hopefully to catch something for supper. I'm tired of bread and cheese."

As he stuck his knife under his belt he noticed Sara looking around in every direction, and wondered if she felt uncomfortable being left alone, and was looking for hostile Indians, coyotes, or perhaps strangers on their way to town.

"I won't be going far; just over to that stand of trees. If you should need me just give a holler," he said assuredly.

"Okay, be careful," she replied and started looking around for some wood.

Sara had a nice fire going when Nathan returned holding a skinned woodchuck, and Sara looked a little squeamish and he wondered why. He rigged a stand to roast the woodchuck over the fire and sat down to have a cup of coffee. Sara came and sat down beside him with a blanket wrapped around her for it was already getting cold.

"Sara, I'm curious; why did you look squeamish when I brought the woodchuck, or groundhog as we prefer to call them, back to camp?" he asked a little puzzled by her response.

"Well, in my time we go to the store and all the meat is in nice little packages all cut up, and you really don't stop and think about it actually being an animal that someone had to kill just so you could eat it. I guess seeing the groundhog that way, just made it seem all too real to me," she replied.

Nathan nodded his head. "I can understand that. Thanks for explaining it to me. I sometimes forget we come from two different times and things are done quite differently," he said and put his arm around Sara and thought about how different things were going to be for her tomorrow. He had seen pictures of big cities in Sara's time from magazines she had brought with her and remembered how strange they seemed to him. Now she was the one that was going to have to experience a time in history that seemed strange and probably backwards to her. It was important to him to be there by her side to guide her and assure her that he would always keep her safe.

The groundhog was almost done and even Sara was looking forward to something different for supper. Nathan carved off a piece of meat and put it on her plate with a piece of bread while Sara poured the coffee and placed the cups on the ground next to where they were sitting.

She took a tiny bite of the groundhog and Nathan watched to see what she thought of it. She slowly chewed it and swallowed hard.

Nathan just had to ask, "So, what do you think of groundhog?"

"I think it would be really good with a little salt and BBQ sauce," she said and smiled at Nathan and took another bite and hoped she hadn't hurt his feelings.

She thought about it and thought it best so say something nice about it; he had gone to a lot of trouble to fix it. "You know, it kind of grows on you; it is certainly better than a lot of things I've tried." *Oh dear, that didn't come out the way I wanted it to,"* she thought and tried again.

"Actually, it's quite good," she said trying to sound convincing.

Nathan chuckled to himself and took another big bite, for he actually loved roasted groundhog. Sara, it's okay if you don't care for it. It's more important that you're always honest with me, okay?"

"Okay, but wait until you've tried it with BBQ sauce; that is, if I can make BBQ sauce. I've always just bought a bottle of it from the store," she said with a thoughtful look.

Nathan laughed hard. He loved Sara's sense of humor, even when she wasn't necessarily trying to be funny.

After they had finished eating, Nathan spread out his bedroll and grabbed a couple of blankets while Sara went to the wagon and pulled her tactical flashlight from her purse and put it in her skirt pocket. Even though she knew that Nathan would always protect her, she was still afraid of the dark, and it was pitch black that night as the clouds covered the moon. She laid down snuggled up close to Nathan and fell asleep quickly with his arm wrapped around her waist.

Sara was suddenly awakened in the night and listened carefully for several minutes. "Did you hear that?" she asked quietly.

"Huh? Is something wrong?" he replied and yawned after being awakened from a deep sleep.

"I said, did you hear that?" she whispered.

"Hear what?"

"There it is again!" she stated nervously.

Nathan listened carefully and finally whispered, "It's too dark to see anything, and it was probably just some little critter rooting around. It won't come into camp with the fire burning. You'll be okay."

Sara tried to go back to sleep but heard the noise again and pulled her flashlight from her skirt pocket and turned on the spotlight feature and started scanning the woods around them. Nathan sat straight up startled by the bright light that seemed to light up the night sky and quickly looked down at Sara and noticed that the light seemed to be coming from her hand. "What is that you have?" he asked befuddled.

"It's my flashlight. I need to know what is making that noise," she stated and scanned the area close to their wagon. "Nathan, is that a bear?" she asked frightfully.

"It's just a young one," he replied then yelled, "Go on, get out of here!"

Sara immediately turned on the strobe light and the pulsating beams sent the young bear running off into the night, and Nathan asked bewildered, "What in the name of heaven is that?" When Sara was sure that the bear was gone she turned towards Nathan and stated, "It's a strobe light. Isn't it great?" Nathan looked at her speechless, unable to wrap his mind around this most peculiar invention and just nodded then laid back down and pondered the many strange things he had seen from her time. He wrapped his arm around her waist once again and closed his eyes and hoped that he could fall back to sleep.

Chapter 23

The sun had not risen when Sara stirred under the blankets that covered her on the bedroll. She glanced where there once was a roaring fire, and now there were just a few glowing embers, and snuggled a little closer to Nathan for warmth. Her mind was now too active and troubled to even think about going back to sleep. She lay there and thought how she had always considered herself to be a strong, capable woman with a good head on her shoulders. But now she questioned whether she still had those attributes in this new world of hers.

They were about to embark on the last leg of their journey, and all Sara wanted to do was to lay there with Nathan's arms around her where she felt safe and loved. Nathan stirred beside her and he could tell by the soft sighs he heard that Sara was awake. He gently brushed back her hair exposing her neck and shoulder and whispered, "Good morning." He softly kissed her bare shoulder then along her neck until she rolled over facing towards him and said, "Good morning."

"Are you ready to get up and get started? We only have about ten miles to go before we reach town," he asked blissfully.

Sara bit her bottom lip and gently shook her head.

"Sara," he said not even knowing what to say to her. He thought she would be happy and find it exciting to step back in history and explore the very things she used to study about. But now all he saw was apprehension.

"Sara, you have nothing to fear. These are just simple, hardworking folks not looking for trouble. Sure they're going to look at you. You're beautiful, and yes, you will be taller than most people in town, but they're not going to bite. Besides, I'll be right there next to you, and you know that I would die before I ever let anything happen to you," he stated deeply concerned.

"You're right; I have nothing to fear with you by my side," she said and smiled showing some enthusiasm.

They broke camp quickly after they had breakfast and Sara did fine the rest of the morning until she saw the town up ahead. It wasn't anything like she thought it would be. She told herself that she had watched too many movies where the towns where charming and quaint, but the reality was quite different. She recalled her mother's words "think about what you're giving up," and her response, "I'm thinking of what I will be getting in return," and then looked over at Nathan. It was only when she looked at him that she thought she had made the right decision, for without him her life in the 1700s would be unbearable.

Nathan saw out of the corner of his eye Sara taking a deep breath and very slowly letting it out through her mouth. She started straightening out her clothing and brushing her hair and putting it into a neat little bun. She covered it once again with her bonnet and tied the ribbon in a pretty bow by the side of her cheek.

Nathan felt bad for Sara and told the horses "whoa" as he pulled back on the reins bringing the wagon to a halt. Sara looked like she was on the verge of tears and could hardly breathe.

"Sara, look at me," he said and waited for her to turn her head.

"Sara, you look beautiful, so stand tall and be the confident woman I know you to be. For any woman who can hold up a store at gun point, this will be like putting a pot of water on to boil. Besides, I'll be right there with you," he said with confidence.

"Now, put a smile on your face and take a deep breath, and let's go have some fun. It isn't often that we'll get a chance to come into town," he said.

Sara was a bit stunned by their two different perceptions of the town before them. It was a treat for him and a place to have fun and be around people for a while, but for Sara it was drab and not quite civilized. She determined to never let him know how through her eyes she saw the town. She thought differently and acted differently than these people, and knew she would stick out like a sore thumb. All she wanted was to blend in and become invisible to their prying eyes.

Sara smiled and took a deep breath and tried to relax as he pulled up in front of the store that would buy his animal pelts. Nathan tied off the horses to the post then came around and helped her down from the wagon. She took another deep breath and smiled at him as he took her by the arm and started towards the shop. Sara could already feel eyes watching her and heads coming together to whisper. She was sure they must be talking about her and immediately held on to Nathan's arm a little tighter as the fight or flight mindset took over.

Women weren't normally seen inside this shop and would wait for their husbands at the Mercantile while their husbands conducted business, but Sara chose to stay close by Nathan. There was a seat outside the shop in front of a large window where Nathan could see her at all times, and where she would also be able to see him if she became uncomfortable.

"Sara, why don't you have a seat here and I'll try to be as quick as I can with my dealings, but I need to get a good price for these pelts. I'm counting on this money to get us through this next year. Just smile and nod your head if people pass by and you'll be fine," he said assuredly.

Sara smiled at him, "I can handle it," but inside she was less confident remembering Inola's reaction the first time he saw her.

Nathan started unloading the pelts with the help of one of the shop owners, who glanced at Sara each time he passed by her. She turned her head and lowered her gaze to the ground until they had finished unloading the wagon, and then lifted it and tried to act as if she belonged there.

Inside the store Nathan was haggling over each pelt until he felt he was getting a fair price, but was getting a little annoyed with the owner who kept looking past him at Sara.

"The woman you're with, where's she from?" he asked in a manner that irked Nathan.

"I don't see where that is any of your business. Your business is buying pelts," Nathan answered roughly.

"It was a harmless question; no need to get in a huff about it. I'd just like to know where she's from," he said in a perturbed manner.

"Well, since you're asking me, my guess is she fell from heaven," he said with a straight face.

The owner sneered at him and said, "Next pelt," and Nathan placed the next one on the counter.

An hour later Nathan was counting his handful of money to make sure it was all there. He placed it in his money belt and turned to the owner and said, "Nice doing business with you. I'll see you next year."

Nathan stepped through the doorway with a great big smile. "We did well Sara, real well," he said and took her by the arm as they walked through town to the Mercantile. He stood tall and proud with Sara on his arm and smiled at each passerby and said "morning" with a nod of his head, and Sara just smiled. Both were aware of the way people were looking at them and giving them a wide berth as they passed by; they were both somewhat of an oddity. Nathan and Sara were both a good head and shoulders taller than most people in town, and the fact that they were both good looking drew even more attention. More than one woman gave her husband a hard yank on the arm and a dirty look when they caught them checking out Sara with a smile that was only going to get them into trouble. Nathan observed this and was proud of the way Sara was handling the attention.

When they entered the Mercantile they were greeted by the owner's wife, Claire Jones, who appeared to be in her mid-forties. She was short, overweight, and wore a simple solid blue cotton dress with her hair in a tight bun close to the top of her head with a few ringlets hanging by the sides of her face. She looked Nathan up and down in a way that Sara could fully understand and held no hard feelings towards her. Then Claire got around to looking at her, and Claire's eyes opened wider than Sara even knew was possible.

"Oh dear," she said gasping and put her hand to her chest and tried not to stare.

"What can I do for you today?" she asked nervously, still a little befuddled. She had a hard time looking Sara in the face, for she had never seen a woman that tall and statuesque.

Her husband, Daniel Jones, who stood no taller than 5'7", was balding and wore plain shop clothes with his sleeves rolled up. He came from the back of the store and stopped short in amazement when he saw the two of them standing together. He caught his breath and composure and slowly joined his wife at the front of the store.

"Good morning, how may we help you folks?" he asked looking up at Nathan.

"Well, your Misses can help my soon to be wife find some dresses that will fit her, and I would appreciate being shown where you keep your boots," Nathan replied.

"Oh, I don't believe we will have any dresses that will fit your fiancé. I'm afraid they will have to be special ordered," Claire stated still befuddled by the two of them. "I would be happy to take her measurements and show her some yard goods to choose from," she said still looking Sara over from head to toe.

"That would be wonderful," Sara replied still feeling a little awkward; this woman didn't even come up to her shoulders.

"Why don't we go stand back in the corner by the side of the yard goods? We should have some privacy there," Claire said nervously.

"Sir, if you will come with me I'll show you the few boots we have in stock, but you might have to go to the cobbler across the street," he said and led Nathan towards the back of the store.

Meanwhile Sara heard the doorbells jingling at the front of the store as two ladies walked in and headed for the yard goods. When they saw Sara they looked at each other startled and casually walked to another part of the store whispering and giggling as they went.

Sara paid them no mind and stood still while Claire tried to take her measurements for the skirts and petticoats. The waist was not a problem, but when it came to the length of the skirt, the woman was not tall enough to get the measurements without Sara's help.

"If you wouldn't mind holding the tape to your waist I'll get the length measurement," she said and bent down to the floor. "Oh my, I'm not sure we have much of a selection in those lengths, but let's look and see. First let me get your blouse size, then we can see if you can find something you like," she uttered nervously.

Sara picked out several fabrics she liked and some lace and buttons to go with them and followed Claire to the front counter to wait for Nathan. While waiting, she walked around looking for some of the items on their list when two men about her age walked into the store dressed in common work clothes. Sara continued her browsing hoping the two men would just look at her as a curiosity then go about their business. She could see out of the corner of her eye that they were coming her way and let out a long, slow breath and wished that Nathan was close by.

"What do we have here? Where did you come from, darling," one of them said in a flirtatious manner.

Sara made no comment or eye contact, but continued her browsing.

"Yeah, we've never seen a filly quite like you," one said as they moved closer to her where she had no room to retreat.

"How about taking one of us for a ride?" he asked moving up close to her face and chuckling vulgarly. Sara's anger reached a boiling point as her hand tightened into a fist. She wished at that moment that she was a man. She would have decked them if it were in her power.

Nathan heard what was going on and dropped the boots in his hands and moved in like an angry grizzly bear. By the time he got to them he aggressively postured over them, and with a tightened jaw and eyes filled with anger hostilely stated, "Friend, if you want to leave with the same body parts you came in with, you'd best be going."

The two men looked up at him, and sizing him up quickly took a couple of steps back.

Nathan had fire in his eyes. He made a fist and was in the process of drawing back his arm when the two men sneered and backed their way out the door cussing profusely.

Nathan quickly turned towards Sara who looked horrified by the whole situation. She had never seen anyone as angry and aggressive as Nathan had just been, and was somewhat alarmed at what he was capable of doing.

"Sara, are you alright?" he asked anxiously, yet tenderly, and Sara was a bit surprised by how quickly he could change his demeanor.

"Yes," she replied breathing rapidly and realized that he had only done what she wished she could have done to those two men.

Nathan turned to the store owner who had kept a safe distance behind his counter from the altercation and handed him a list of supplies they needed. "Mr. Jones, will you see to it that we get the supplies on this list? I'm taking Sara with me to get the wagon and bring it up here. We can square things up when we return if that's okay with you."

"Yes sir, Mr. Chambers, that will be just fine," he said nervously after watching this man in action.

Nathan put his arm around Sara as they walked through the front door and then he offered his arm to her as he looked cautiously around. He was still furious at the audacity of the two men and was determined to see that what happened did not happen again. His greeting to people passing by that were staring at them curiously was not as warm and friendly as before. He had promised to protect Sara, and protect her he would.

When Nathan and Sara returned with the wagon they found their order neatly stacked close to the counter. Nathan asked how much he owed, then discretely pulled his money from his money belt and payed the man. Claire spoke up quickly, "I'm afraid it will take the seamstress at least a week and a half to have the two dresses and petticoats ready," she said timidly.

Nathan looked disappointed. He had told Inola that they would be back in no more than a week and a half, and was deep in thought when Sara spoke up.

"Nathan, don't worry about the dresses. I'm sure I can make patterns from the ones at home, and it will give me something I can do during the winter. Let's go over to the cobbler's store and get you a pair of boots," she said with a smile.

"I really wanted to buy you some new, pretty, store bought dresses," he said looking into her smiling eyes.

"I know you did, but it can wait until another trip to town," she said and turned to the owners and thanked them for all their help.

They loaded the wagon and Nathan drove the team over to the cobbler's shop while Sara walked across the street with a new confidence knowing that Nathan was there to protect her from any further harassment.

She could smell the scent of leather before they ever went inside the shop. She walked around looking at the different styles of women's shoes while the cobbler measured Nathan's feet and he picked out a leather that he liked.

"Your boots will be ready tomorrow afternoon," the owner stated and then glanced at Sara.

"Does the misses need a new pair of shoes?" he asked.

"What about it, Sara? Would you like a new pair of shoes?" he asked eagerly wanting to please her.

"A new pair of shoes for around the house would be nice," she said.

The shop owner looked up at her, "Wonderful, please have a seat so I can measure your feet." He watched as she removed her store bought lace-up boots and looked at them curiously. He had never seen boots quite like them and wondered where they were made, and how they were made with such precise stitching, but never questioned her.

As he measured her feet his eyes grew wider as he looked at the measurements and checked them again, then slowly raised his eyes to look up at Sara. She saw him swallow hard and was amused by his reactions. She knew that her feet were going to be larger than the other women he made shoes for, but she would look funny with tiny feet and just smiled at him.

"Ah, I can have the misses' shoes ready in a couple of days, and you can pick them both up at the same time if you like," the owner stated as he tucked his pencil behind his ear.

Sara showed him the style and leather she liked, and Nathan seemed pleased that he could buy something special for her.

Chapter 24

When they stepped outside Nathan looked up at the sun to judge the time of day. "I think we should head over to the Inn to see if they have a room available for the next couple of days and get something to eat; I'm mighty hungry. How about you?" he asked.

"Yes, I would love to get something to eat," she said and took him by the arm as they strolled down the street quite content at the moment.

The Inn was nothing like Sara had expected. The dining area was small and plainly furnished, and the bedroom was about the same, but at least she could sit at a table to eat and wouldn't have to sleep out in the cold on the hard ground.

As Sara and Nathan took their seats in the dining area she thought about all the luxury hotels she had stayed in over the years, and all the fabulous restaurants she had eaten in, but then she looked at Nathan sitting there with a smile on his face and just happy to be with her. She recalled the last two nights she had spent with him under the stars, snuggled up close with his arm around her and the goodnight kisses by a roaring fire, and she realized she wouldn't have given that up for all the five star hotels in the world.

A short thin man with a dirty apron came to their table to take their order and Nathan observed that Sara looked a little confused.

"Sara the menu is written on the blackboard over there," he said with a grin, and Sara turned her head to see that they offered three different meals.

The man stood there waiting for Sara's order, then looked at Nathan.

"I'll have the steak, medium rare, and fried potatoes, and why don't you bring the same for the lady only a half order. Oh, and I'll have a beer and bring a cider too," Nathan said.

The man turned and walked away and Nathan whispered across the table, "It's the best thing on their menu; it's pretty hard to ruin a steak."

"Will they know to bring some ketchup for the potatoes, and salt and pepper with the order," Sara asked naively.

Nathan laughed heartily and Sara quietly asked, "What's so funny?"

"I'm sorry to disappoint you angel, but no one here even knows what ketchup is. They might be able to bring a small bowl of salt if you ask nicely," he smiled still chuckling. Sara was not amused, but did not want to cause a scene. After looking around the room at the few people seated she realized no on even seemed to be aware of their conversation. She quickly chose to see the humor in the situation and decided it was always a good thing to see Nathan laugh.

After their food was brought to their table, Sara asked with a surprised look, "That's a half portion?" The steak looked enormous and there were enough potatoes on her plate for several meals.

"That's what I like about this place; they're generous with their portions," he said and immediately cut into his steak and took a huge bite.

"Eat up, it's really good," he said still chewing.

Sara was cutting her steak when two couples walked in that had just gotten off the stagecoach. They stood at the entrance to the dining area as if they were people of importance that commanded respect and prompt attention, for they were well dressed and in Sara's opinion had a pious air about them.

She turned her attention back to the food on her plate. "This is really good," she said with a surprised smile after taking a bite of her steak and potatoes.

"I told you the food here was good, nothing fancy, just good," he said taking another big bite.

Sara watched as the two couples were seated at a table close to them and noticed that the women took seats facing Nathan, and thought to herself, *"Eat your hearts out ladies, he's mine."* She could tell instantly what they were thinking, and her blood began to boil as she saw the flirtatious looks they gave when their husbands were not looking. Nathan looked up from his meal and caught one of them flirting with him and quickly looked at Sara who had fire in her eyes, and grinned as he chewed on his steak. She was jealous and angry and he had to admit that it pleased and amused him greatly. He thought about having a little fun, and proving to Sara at the same time he only had eyes for her.

Sara looked at Nathan and could tell that he was up to something. She had seen that mischievous look before and couldn't wait to see what he was up to. It somehow took the fire from her eyes and put more of a sparkle there as she continued to eat.

Nathan turned and caught the waiter's attention and called him to the table.

"Sir, would you mind bringing an extra napkin to that lady at the table. I think she has something caught in her eyes. She keeps batting them when she looks this way."

The lady's husband turned and looked at Nathan, and then looked at his wife suspiciously and gave her a disdainful look. I watched as the lady's face quickly changed to one of humiliation. Sara thought her heart would burst with satisfaction, and she could hardly chew her food for smiling; Nathan had put her in her place brilliantly. He seemed pleased with himself, and smiled at Sara letting her know that he was all hers.

Sara could eat only half of the steak they had put on her plate, while Nathan's plate was clean enough to put away.

"Are you through with your steak, dear?" he asked eyeing it.

Sara nodded and whispered, "Go ahead, take it," she said as if they were about to do something naughty. He casually looked around and when he thought no one was looking took his fork and quickly took her steak and put it on his plate. Sara smiled and marveled at his seemingly bottomless pit.

The gentleman at the table next to them stood and Sara noticed the look of irritation on the man's face as he firmly took his wife by the arm and ushered her from the dining area when they were finished with their meal. As she thought about it, she felt bad about how she felt and responded to the woman's flirting with Nathan. How could she blame her? Nathan would turn any woman's head. She watched the couple walk away and hoped that the woman's husband was not a violent man. No wife should have to fear her husband, but a sharp rebuke was probably in order.

When Nathan was through eating, he placed fifty cents on the table and gave Sara the number to their room and said, "I need to take the team and wagon to the livery stable and make sure they're taken care of. Why don't you go to the room and lie down for a bit. It has been a long day and I'm sure you would like to freshen up. I'll be back in a little bit…okay?"

"Okay," she said and gave him a little parting kiss and headed towards their room. It was small and only had the necessities: a bed, a table with an oil lamp, a wash basin and pitcher full of water, and a chair off in the corner. It wasn't fancy but it would do for a couple of nights. She sat on the bed and could hear the springs squeaking and started bouncing up and down on it. She closed her eyes and thought, *"Oh my, what are the people next door going to think?"*

Meanwhile Nathan was through at the livery stable and was headed down the dirt street to a little church at the end of town. He opened the door and stepped inside and called out to see if anyone was there. Suddenly a man walked in behind him and he quickly turned around.

"I'm the caretaker here. Who are you looking for?" he asked.

"I was hoping the preacher would be here. I was wanting to get married today if at all possible," he stated while anxiously fiddling with his hat.

"Well, the preacher is out of town at the moment, but he's supposed to be returning on the morning stage," the caretaker replied.

Nathan looked down at the wooden floor in disappointment as he thought, then finally asked, "What time does the morning stage arrive?"

"Oh, anywhere from about nine to ten o'clock if everything goes well," the caretaker replied.

"Thanks for the information, I'll be back tomorrow," Nathan said as he left the church disappointed and extremely frustrated. He did not think that he could endure one more night of being with Sara without fully loving her as he desired. It was torture lying next to her and knowing that he could only look and not touch; for a man and woman were created to be together. Her body was meant to be touched, every soft curve caressed, and now he would have to wait another day.

As he walked back across the dirt street leading to the Inn, the last thing he wanted to do now that the shops were beginning to close for the day was to be in the bedroom alone with Sara. There wasn't much they could do but to take a walk, for he did not want to expose her to what went on in the local pubs. Bringing a woman as beautiful as Sara would only lead to confrontations and fights. Even though he was discouraged and deeply depressed, that was no reason to leave Sara alone in the room wondering where he was. Nathan inhaled deeply and slowly let it out as he approached the bedroom door and gave a quick knock before opening it.

"There you are. I was beginning to think you got lost, or a hoard of lonely women jumped you in the alleyway," she said with a smile; relieved that he had returned.

"Would you like to go for a walk? It's beautiful out this evening and it's about the only thing we can do now that the shops are closing."

"I would love to go for a walk," she said and grabbed her cape.

Nathan was very quiet as they walked down the street with Sara's arm wrapped around his. The only sound you could hear was coming from the pub and a few horses nickering tied to the posts, and Sara had a pretty good idea of what was bothering him. She wondered whether he had planned on marrying her while they were in town, because he had never mentioned anything to her about it. Although, he had introduced her one time as his soon to be wife. She pondered whether she should bring the subject matter up or not. She certainly wanted to get married; that was her reason for choosing to remain in his time.

They were now at the end of the street with nowhere to go but back to the Inn. Nathan paused and pulled Sara close and looked longingly into her eyes before kissing her. She could feel his torment and the passion that was all tangled up in the kiss. She longed to tell him it was alright with her if he came back to the room and loved her the way she longed to be loved. But, she knew that he would not until they were married, even if she wanted it as much as he.

When they were back at the Inn, Nathan walked her to the room, and once inside he reluctantly said, "Sara, I think it's best for me if I stay with the wagon tonight. Just keep your door latched and you should be fine. I'll be close enough to hear you should there be any problems," and gave her a soft kiss good night and left.

He knew that she would cry, and would probably be as depressed as he was, but he saw no other option; the preacher wasn't in town.

Chapter 25

The next morning Sara sat alone in the bedroom brushing her hair and putting it up in a bun and wondered when Nathan would come knocking at her door, or if he expected her to just meet him in the dining room for breakfast. She was just finishing lacing up her boots when she heard him knock at her door and hurried to open it; excited to see him after the rough night she had.

She greeted him with a smile which he returned and said, "Good morning. I hope you slept well," he said, but the look on his face told her that he knew she hadn't.

Sara did not want to lie, but she also did not want to tell him the truth. She had a miserable night. She was either crying or tossing and turning wishing he was there with her.

"I managed to get a little sleep. I hope you weren't too cold or uncomfortable sleeping in the wagon," she replied.

"I managed as well. I see you're ready for breakfast. You look beautiful," he said and offered her his arm.

Nathan chose a table where he could see out the front window and watch for the stagecoach should it come in early. He was anxious to see whether the preacher made it back to town, or not, and wondered if he would recognize him by the way he dressed.

When the waiter showed up Nathan ordered steak and eggs, and Sara, eggs and bacon, and both ordered coffee.

"What do you have planned for the day," Sara asked.

Nathan looked at her with a raised eyebrow as he chewed on his steak and when he had swallowed replied, "Well, we finished most of our shopping yesterday, but there are a few things I'm hoping to get done today, and we still need to pick up our shoes from the cobbler before we leave."

Sara found his response to be very vague, and was hoping that he would say something like, "I was hoping to marry the woman I love today. Do you think she would be willing to do that?" But there was no mention of that in his answer, and she wondered if that was even in his plans.

"What would you like to do today," he asked out of curiosity, wondering if she would bring up the subject of marriage.

Sara gave him a look that clearly said "wouldn't you like to know" and lowered her eyes while she cut another piece of bacon. She intentionally looked over at the ring on her finger and wiggled it, and hoped that would be enough of an answer.

Nathan quickly picked up on that little gesture and smiled. Sara was as anxious as he to get married and that gave him a whole new outlook on the day as he looked out the window for the stagecoach.

After a leisurely breakfast, Nathan wanted to hang around the shops close to the Inn so that he could see who got off the coach. They were in the bakery looking around at what they would like to buy for their return trip when Nathan heard the stagecoach pull in and come to a stop in front of the Inn.

"Sara, would you mind looking around for just a minute? I'll be back before you know it," he said, and started for the door before Sara could even answer.

Nathan stood just beyond the bakery window and watched to see who disembarked from the coach and when he saw a man with a white collar get off, he hurried over to him.

"Sir, hold up for a moment. Are you the preacher in town?" he asked.

"Yes I am. What can I do for you?" he asked as he brushed the dust off his suit.

"I was hoping to get married today, the sooner the better," he replied anxiously.

The preacher replied with a smile, "Well, if you will let me get back to the church and settled in, I can get you married if you come back in let's say… an hour."

"That would be great. We'll see you in an hour," he said with a huge grin.

He tried hard to wipe that grin from his face before returning to Sara. He wanted this to be a surprise and didn't want to give it away by grinning like an idiot for the next hour as they walked through town.

He regained his composure before walking into the bakery and calmly asked Sara, "Are you finished picking out something for tomorrow morning?"

"Yes. I'm very pleased with their selection. Where are we going next?" she questioned.

"Why don't you take my arm and find out," he said plainly, not wanting to make his intentions known.

Sara wondered what had happened when he left the bakery that changed his whole countenance. Whatever it was, she was happy to see the change. Nathan knew that they needed to kill about an hour and slowly walked into several stores and browsed around until they reached the florist shop.

"Let's go inside and look around; I know how you love flowers," he calmly stated.

As they entered the shop Sara was starting to suspect something, but it was hard to be sure what he was up to since he seemed so serene at the moment.

After browsing for several minutes Nathan requested, "I want you to pick out a bouquet full of your favorite flowers," and slipped his arm around her waist and gave her one of those looks that always took her breath away.

"This is it," she thought to herself. *"He is planning on marrying me today."* She reached down and felt for the gold ring she had slipped into her skirt pocket that he knew nothing about and smiled.

After he had paid for a bouquet of flowers in her favorite colors of pink, lavender and white tied together with a white ribbon, he took her by the arm again and started walking towards the end of town and briefly entered the few remaining shops along the way. Sara looked ahead and saw the church at the end of the street and a big smile came to her face as she looked over at Nathan. He returned her look with only a satisfied grin on his face and kept walking down the street, and they both seemed oblivious to the stares of people passing by.

They had passed by all the shops in town and only the church was left in front of them and he stopped at the corner of the last building.

"Will you marry me today, Sara Mathews?" he asked tenderly after he had wrapped his arms around her waist and looked yearningly into her eyes. He knew from the first moment he saw her that he wanted her more than anything he had ever wanted in his life. The barriers he threw up and the distant, cold attitude he portrayed at first was just a way to protect himself from having his heart broken once again. He questioned why would such an amazing woman want him and a life of hardship and isolation when her world could offer her so much more?

"Yes, I'll marry you today, Nathan Chambers," she replied enthusiastically with the biggest smile; he was the only reason she remained in his time.

Nathan picked up the pace as they walked the last fifty feet, or so, to the church. When they entered, the preacher was already at the front platform holding his Bible, and his wife and the caretaker were sitting in the front pew. Sara slipped the ring Nathan had given her when he first asked her to marry him off her finger and gave it to Nathan to put in his pocket.

"You might be needing this," she said with a smile.

When they reached the front of the small church the preacher asked, "Are you ready?"

Nathan and Sara both nodded and the preacher continued, "We are gathered here today in the sight of God to join this man and this woman in holy matrimony...your names please," he asked.

"Nathan Chambers and Sara Mathews," Nathan replied.

"Nathan Chambers, do you take Sara Mathews to be your lawfully wedded wife, to have and to hold from this day forward for as long as you both shall live?"

"I do," he said looking at Sara with overwhelming love.

"And do you Sara Mathews take Nathan Chambers to be your lawfully wedded husband, to have and to hold from this day forward for as long as you both shall live?"

"I do," she said with trembling lips staring into his beautiful blue eyes that were filled with desire.

"You may exchange rings now," the preacher stated with a grin. He couldn't recall the last time he saw two people so eager to get married.

Nathan pulled the ring he had given her once before and placed it on her finger, and Sara reached into her skirt pocket and pulled out a gold band and placed it on his finger.

"By the power vested in me by the State of Franklin, I now pronounce you man and wife. You may now kiss your bride," he said, and by this time his face was lit up with a huge smile for he knew beyond a shadow of a doubt where they were headed next.

Nathan quickly grasped Sara in his powerful arms and she could feel his strong hands holding her firmly against his body, and the way he looked into her eyes started her heart pounding. She could feel her face flush with heat anticipating his lips pressed hard against hers. But she never imagined the passion in which his mouth consumed her eager lips, causing any doubts of what he had planned next to vanish.

The preacher, his wife, and the caretaker were stunned by such a display of passion, then smiled figuring this marriage would surely last if they could keep that fire burning. The preacher restrained their departure until both had signed a marriage license and paid their dollar fee then watched gleefully as Nathan quickly took Sara by the hand and hurried from the church.

Chapter 26

There was no doubt in Sara's mind where they were headed next. She was having a hard time keeping up in her full skirt as it swished back and forth against her legs as they headed back to the Inn. She couldn't help but wonder what he would be like once they were behind closed doors, for he had waited a long time to unleash his love for her. They were soon standing in front of their bedroom door at the Inn and Nathan unlatched it as quickly as he could, then swept Sara up in his arms looking intensely into her willing eyes. He carried her over the threshold slamming the door behind him with his foot.

As he gently allowed her feet to touch the floor he still held her close with his hand spread out across her back. His eyes seemed to devour her bit by bit and she could tell that he intended to take his time savoring each step of the way.

Nathan untied the ribbon by her chin and removed her bonnet and let it fall to the floor, then reached for her hair in the bun and as he removed the pins she heard them hit the floor one by one. His hands gently combed through her hair until it hung far below her shoulders as she watched his desire for her grow.

Sara's breathing was rapid and shallow as he took his time and looked down towards her breasts as they were heaving in anticipation. He unbuttoned the first several buttons but then stopped, and led her to the bed and sat beside her as he quickly pulled off his boots and stockings then slid down to the floor in front of Sara and started unlacing her boots. Sara's hands were trembling as she untied his cravat and pulled it off and tossed it aside, then untied the string to his shirt and started on the buttons to his vest.

There was a burning fire in Nathan's eyes as he looked up at her after removing her boots then reached up under her skirt and pulled her stockings off, running his powerful hands gently up along her soft quivering thighs. She gasped repeatedly trying to catch her breath as she felt her body come alive.

He paused from unbuttoning her blouse and held her tightly in his arms and kissed her repeatedly with open mouth kisses that held her lips tightly in his until she felt lightheaded. She felt his hot breath as his mouth with hot kisses slowly moved down her neck until he reached the top of her blouse. He gazed once again into Sara's eyes as he unbuttoned the rest of her blouse and pulled it back over her shoulders and off her arms exposing the last impediment to her voluptuous breasts.

Sara reached behind her back and unfastened her red silk bra and tossed it aside. Nathan was focused on her soft, full, white breasts and reached up and cupped them in his hands and momentarily looked up at her then filled his mouth, moving between each breast caressing and kissing and mouthing each one until Sara thought she would lose all control. There was no blushing this time over the way he looked at her or touched her. She was far beyond that now and everything was throbbing and pulsating within her and she craved his body.

Nathan stood, and as Sara was removing his vest and shirt he unfastened her skirt and untied her petticoats and let them drop around her ankles exposing her red silk, bikini panties. He felt like he was ready to explode looking at her near naked body; firm, skin soft as silk, curvaceous, and tantalizing beyond words.

She crawled naked onto the cold sheets of the bed and felt goose bumps as she laid her head on the pillow and watched as Nathan finished undressing and then joined her in the bed. She could feel the heat pouring off his body and there was no need of a fireplace in their room as Sara reached for his broad chest eager to run her hands through the hair and feel the firm muscles of his upper body. She continued running her hands down over his body as he took his time and kissed, mouthed, and caressed as he explored almost every square inch of her body. It was all that she dreamed it would be and more as she laid there and moaned as he seemed to devour her one morsel at a time. With every look and every touch as their bodies entwined she could hear the rhythm of the bed springs and with every thrust of his body she was taken to new heights of ecstasy, and felt her body and soul join with his to become one.

She now laid exhausted against his body with her head resting on his shoulder as steam could be seen rising from their heated bodies in the cold room. They laid contented and satisfied, but neither were in any hurry to leave the room, not for food or anything else. They both knew that this had only been the first round of their passion that needed to be satisfied that day and they had only stopped to catch their breath.

Chapter 27

When Sara opened her eyes in the morning, Nathan was lying next to her just gazing at her with a hint of a smile and then reached over and lightly ran his fingers along the side of her face brushing her hair back. "Good morning, Mrs. Chambers."

"Good morning, my love. I guess you'll be wanting breakfast soon," she said then swung her legs over the side of the bed and quickly ran her fingers through her hair and twisted it into a bun then proceeded to dress.

"What are you doing? Get back over here. I'm not finished with you yet."

Sara turned and looked at him speechless.

"I was thinking about working up a good healthy appetite first," he said with an impassioned look that brought a big smile to Sara's face.

She slid across the cold sheets and ran her fingers through his hair and looked at his lips and then up into his eyes and said, "Well, what are you waiting for? You best get started, we're burning daylight."

Nathan wasted no time and reached up and pulled her hair from the bun until it draped across her shoulders and down her back, then gently pulled her closer and zealously kissed her sensuous lips and moved on from there, releasing the passion that had been building up inside him for some time until he had indeed worked up a healthy appetite.

"Now I'm ready for breakfast Mrs. Chambers," he said and leaned in for one more kiss.

"I should think so," she said out of breath. "Why don't you wash up first then start getting dressed while I catch my breath," she said smiling at him as her body still throbbed.

Nathan washed and started dressing as Sara climbed out of bed and stood at the wash basin naked. He looked at her standing there with her long blonde hair hanging loosely down her back and continued until his eyes reached the floor and knew their love and passion would make for a marriage that would get them through the tough times.

He came up behind her and wrapped his arms around her and softly said, "I'll meet you in the dining room and get them started making breakfast," and kissed her several times along her bare slender neck as his hands caressed over her body one last time and lingered for just a moment finding it hard to pull himself away.

When Sara finally finished dressing and joined Nathan at his table, the waiter was already headed their way with the food. Her eyes grew wide when she saw all the food on his plate and looked up at him with a look of disbelief.

With an amused look Nathan stated, "I told you I was going to work up a good healthy appetite," and cut into his steak.

When they had finished eating it was already later than Nathan had planned on leaving and they still needed to pick up their shoes from the cobbler and buy food to eat on their journey back to their farm. Sara took care of the shopping while Nathan went to the livery to get his team and wagon and then pulled it up in front of the Inn to pick Sara up.

"Let's go home," Nathan said and Sara wrapped her arm around Nathan's arm and sat there on the hard wooden seat smiling as he drove the team homeward.

They rode along for hours before Nathan stopped alongside a stream to give the horses some water, and time for them to stretch their legs before continuing. He heard a branch snap in the distance and glanced around discretely through the forest of trees now in full autumn color to see what had made the noise without alarming Sara. His breathing became slow and shallow as his eyes continued to scan the horizon and heard the faint sound of a horse snorting in the distance and slowly turned his eyes in that direction while just barely moving his head.

"Sara, it's time to go. Let me give you a hand up," he said calmly, and then calmly took his seat and told the horses to walk on. He didn't mention to Sara that he had seen a small group of Shawnee, maybe four or five, off in the distance and wondered how long they may have been following them, and prayed that they were only hunting for food. It was not common to see Shawnee, and he knew that they were always fighting with the Cherokee in that part of Tennessee. He kept an eye on them and drove the team at a normal rate as not to tip his hand that he had seen them watching them from the cover of trees.

"Sara, your firearm is close by you, isn't it?" he asked calmly.

"Yes. I always travel with it in my purse," she said with a puzzled look as to why he would ask that question.

"Don't you think it is about time that you showed me how to use it?" he asked glancing over at her.

"Now?" she asked. She noticed that his countenance had changed even though he tried to hide whatever was bothering him.

"Now is as good a time as any," he said and looked past her at the ridge parallel to them, and Sara went to turn her head to see what he was looking at.

"Sara, don't turn your head!" he said insistently.

"What's wrong, Nathan?" she asked anxiously.

"Probably nothing, but I would like for you to take out your firearm and show me how to use it," he said in a more serious tone and she noticed his jaw starting to tighten.

Sara swallowed hard and found it difficult to breath; she was frightened and it showed as she looked over at Nathan. "Nathan, tell me what's wrong," she pleaded.

"Go ahead and get your firearm out. There's a small party of Shawnee following us at a distance. Nothing to worry about yet, but I want to be prepared. They could just be hunting, and if that is the case we have nothing to worry about," he stated with authority.

"And if they're not just hunting?" Sara asked as she bent over to get her purse, and pulled her handgun out and placed it on her lap.

"Okay, show me how to use it," he said and looked past her once again without answering her question.

Sara held the handgun and pointed to a little lever. "You push this little lever up and the weapon is armed, and then you pull back on this top piece and let it spring back, like this, and it chambers a bullet and it is ready to fire. The trigger is very sensitive, so be careful. It will fire as quickly as you can pull the trigger and you have up to seven shots before you need to slip in another clip of ammunition. Any questions?" she asked as her body tensed in fear.

"No. You did a fine job explaining things. Now just hold it on your lap and try not to worry," he said and looked into her eyes and then off in the distance.

The forest of trees along the ridge would be coming to an end in about 300 yards, and Nathan noticed that the Shawnee had started to angle in closer to them and took a deep breath and slowly let it out. He knew that meant they would probably attack before they came to the end of the trees as their cover. Sara watched as his jaw tightened and his eyes narrowed, and knew he was planning his strategy; the Shawnee were going to attack.

She closed her eyes and took a deep breath and tried to steady her nerves. She told herself Nathan was well acquainted with using a firearm. He had spent five years in the militia fighting the British and she just needed to stay out of his way; he would give his life protecting her if necessary.

"Sara, if they come charging I'm going to stop the wagon as quickly as possible so hold on tight. That will give me time to get in position to open fire and hopefully scare them off or kill them. How accurate is this weapon of yours?" he asked.

"Very, especially if I turn the laser on. It's a red light that will show exactly where the bullet will hit, unless it is too bright outside to see it," she stated nervously.

"Go ahead and turn it on and get out another round of ammunition just in case I need it. When I stop the wagon I want you to slide down in front of the seat and stay there until I tell you it's safe to get up. Do you understand?" he asked with a battle hardened look.

"Yes, I understand," she said and took another clip from her purse. Every muscle in her body was so tight that she found it hard to breath, and thought to herself that this was only supposed to happen in books and movies. She never dreamed she would find herself in this position and wondered if this time period was where she was really meant to be.

Nathan glanced over his shoulder and knew they would start their attack any minute as they were no longer riding in a single file as they neared the end of the tree line and got ready to pull back on the reins.

"Sara, get down!" he yelled and pulled back on the reins and the horses reared and neighed, then came to an abrupt stop as the Shawnee came racing towards them with bows drawn yelling out in high pitched cries. Nathan got in position and waited to make every shot count. He had seven bullets and there were only five of them. Sara looked up from her seat on the floor and could see his resolute steadiness and calm confidence in his ability to shoot straight and opened fire as they were closing in. She could hear their arrows whizzing by and lodging in the wood of the wagon and heard their horses loudly neighing as several of their riders fell to the ground, and the others turned and headed back towards the forest of trees.

"Sara, give me the other clip, and take the reins" he said, and quickly changed clips and was ready for another charge if it came.

"Haw," he yelled and the horses bolted as she took the reins and climbed back on the hard wooden seat. Nathan could see that the three Shawnee he shot were only wounded as the other two returned to help them, then headed back into the trees for cover. He took the reins from Sara, and drove the horses hard until he felt he was a safe distance away and then turned to Sara who was shaking and in shock.

As he slowed the team down Nathan put his arm around her and drew her close letting her bury her head against his shoulder as she continued to shake.

"It's alright now Sara. They won't come after us again," he said in a softer tone now that the danger was over.

"How do you know they won't follow us and attack us tonight while we sleep?" she fearfully asked.

"Indians don't usually attack at night. Besides, they'll be tending to their wounded. They won't soon be forgetting that weapon of yours; they were expecting a single shot firearm. They'd be fools to come charging in like that again," he said gently in his deep soothing voice.

Sara looked up at him, his jaw was no longer tight and his eyes were sparkling and kind, and her trembling subsided as she rested against him. Her mind thought about all the western movies her parents had played when she was a kid with Indians attacking wagon trains heading west and thought nothing about it, but it was quite different in person. She was terrified and feared for their lives. She wondered if this was the way it was always going to be, afraid all the time and always having to be on her guard. She was familiar with the dangers in her time and knew the proper precautions to take, but no one had prepared her for the dangers she would be facing in 1786.

Chapter 28

Nathan climbed down from the wagon and pulled the arrows from it and tossed them aside. He rested the team after pushing them hard after the attack and let them graze while they ate their lunch. Then they pushed on for the next four hours and looked for a good spot to stop for the night.

Sara was still a little jumpy as she gathered firewood from amongst the fallen autumn leaves in their rich red, orange, and yellows, and kept looking around over her shoulder while Nathan got out the bedroll and blankets. He would keep the fire smaller tonight so as to not attract attention in the hopes it would relieve some of Sara's fears. As Nathan drank his coffee after dinner he watched and listened carefully to make sure they were truly alone then stretched out on the bedroll and held out his arms for Sara to come join him.

She laid down beside him and Nathan pulled the layer of blankets over them. As she looked into his eyes they went from content to playful in only a matter of seconds and she knew she was about to find out how people made love with most of their clothes on. The first several kisses were tame enough, but soon went to a whole different level as his mouth consumed her lips and his hand started to unbutton her top. Sara was already breathing hard when Nathan pulled her top open only to find that she was not wearing her bra.

"I thought it would just get in the way," she said breathing heavily.

"I like the way you think," he said and kissed her once again then filled his mouth and hands with her breasts that were now heaving. Moments later his hand quickly found its way under her skirt and ran it up along her leg until he reached her panties then swiftly removed them. Before she knew it he slid between her legs as she moaned wanting all of him. He took his time as they were both enjoying making love under the full moon, and didn't stop until he was sure she was satisfied. He laid there next to her panting body and ran his fingers through her hair that was clinging to her face and neck waiting for her to cool off a bit before he fully pulled the blankets back over them and pulled her against his body to keep her warm for the temperature was dropping rapidly that night. Sara fell asleep watching the stars that filled the night heavens. Happy and content, she never gave the Shawnee a second thought for she felt safe in his arms and the fears that only a short time ago consumed her mind faded away.

When morning came, Sara found another blanket over her and Nathan making coffee. She quickly redressed under the blankets and joined him for some breakfast by the fire. When they were finished, it didn't take long for them to pack up and hit the trail once again for home. The skies to the north were turning grey and Nathan was hoping they would reach home before the next cold front reached them. He had been caught in these fronts before where it rained for days on end with flurries of snow mixed in usually in the late night hours.

Between keeping an eye on the weather, Nathan was also watching for any Shawnee hunting or war parties; he didn't need an encounter like he had the other day. He still had some fears that if things got too hard that Sara would start thinking about returning to her time where life seemed less dangerous and had far more luxuries. The one thing he did not doubt was that Sara truly loved him, and she seemed to thoroughly enjoy their intimate times together. But would that be enough to make her want to stay with him forever. He wondered how making love on the cold hard ground could ever compare to the luxury hotels she was used to staying in and that thought tormented him as they rode towards home.

They pressed on only stopping when necessary, and Sara sang every song she could remember the words to. Nathan even tried to teach her a couple of new ones that he enjoyed to help pass the time. By late afternoon Nathan knew the horses were spent and so were they from bouncing around on the hard wooden seat of the wagon. He was satisfied with the ground they had covered and they had managed to skirt some of the rain heading down from the north, but the temperatures were dropping. He found a spot on the edge of a cluster of trees where they would not be easily spotted by anyone who happened to be in the area, and where they could make a larger fire to help keep them warm that night.

Thunder could be heard in the distance and while Sara gathered wood for the fire, Nathan cut brush and branches from the pine trees to make a lean-to in case it rained through the night. It wouldn't keep all the rain out, but it should keep them from getting soaked.

"Sara, keep your firearm close by. I'm going to try to catch us something for supper and hopefully won't be gone for too long," he said and headed off into the woods.

Sara sat close to the fire as it was getting colder by the minute. She thought about her favorite plush chair by the fireplace at her publisher's cabin and how nice it would be to sit there with a cup of hot chocolate in her hands. She forced that thought from her mind and continued to scan the woods for any movement, for she was still frightened by the attack of yesterday. She listened to the horses as Nathan had taught her; they would alert her to any suspected danger. It was less than an hour when Sara heard a noise coming from the woods and held her breath and firearm until she saw that it was Nathan returning with supper in his hand.

It didn't take Nathan long to roast the squirrels over the fire, but Sara gave him a hard time over killing something so cute as squirrels especially since there wasn't much meat on them.

"Sara, you obviously have never tasted squirrel. It's considered a delicacy fit for a queen," he said and carved her off a piece from the hind quarters and handed it to her with a straight face.

She held it in her hand and looked at their little bodies over the fire and felt sick to her stomach.

"I just can't do it. Here you can eat both of them I'm sure. I'll just get a little jam to go with my bread," she said and handed the meat back to Nathan.

Nathan chuckled and thought that she had never in her life been truly hungry, and hoped that she would never be hungry enough to eat a cute squirrel; not if he could help it.

When they were through eating and still huddled by the fire Nathan curiously asked, "Don't most people eat some kind of meat every day in your time?"

"Yes we do, but remember, in my time meat comes already butchered and wrapped in neat little packages where it no longer resembles the animals they came from. Therefore, you forget that it's even an animal you're eating; at least I do. It's like buying vegetables, fruit, or bread, it's just another product. Am I making any sense to you?" she questioned.

"I think so, but our worlds are very different, aren't they?" he said thoughtfully.

Sara nodded and realized that she probably hurt his feelings by not appreciating the efforts he went through to provide a hearty meal for her instead of just bread and cheese again.

Sara looked at him tenderly, "Nathan, please forgive me for being so silly and thoughtless, I should have eaten the squirrel you provided and been grateful. I'm sure it was delicious, and next time I'll try it. I promise."

Nathan looked into her sincere eyes and his love for her swelled inside and he reached over and wrapped the blanket around her and pulled her a little closer.

It had lightly drizzled through the night and there was a heavy mist that hung in the air when Sara squirmed around on the bedroll stiff and sore from laying on the hard cold ground. The sun was not up yet, and she figured she wouldn't be able to see much of it when it did come up. She could tell that the fog would be heavy when they pulled away from camp and prayed that it wouldn't rain again until after they got home.

Nathan opened his eyes and gently smiled as he looked at Sara and then pulled her close against his body and wrapped his arms around her. "You're freezing," he said as he rubbed her body to warm it. "I'll try to find some dry kindling and get a fire going."

"Nathan, I just want to go home," she said, and saw the look in his eyes like she had just stabbed a knife into his heart.

"Oh Nathan, you silly man. I want to go home with you, to our house, our fireplace, and our warm bed," she said as she looked into his tense eyes.

Nathan sighed and kissed her ardently and held her close. Sara could hear his breathing, short and trembling as he held her tightly. This was the second time she had hurt him with her words unintentionally. She told herself to choose her words more carefully for it was clear to her that he was dealing with the loss of one woman he had loved, and was afraid of losing her to a time he could not enter or compete with.

"Let's go home then. We can stop a little later to get something to eat if the weather clears just a bit," he said and gave Sara a hand up.

It only took a short time to break camp and harness the horses. They headed towards home through a thick fog and Sara marveled how Nathan could navigate through such weather when you couldn't even see your hand in front of your face, and she felt anxious. It was like being in the dark and fearing what you couldn't see, and she prayed for the fog to lift as she rode along silently.

"Are you okay? You're awfully quiet," he said looking at her with some concern.

"Yes, I'm fine, but only because you're here with me. I get a little uneasy when I can't see what's around me. But you, nothing seems to bother you, except strange people showing up in your house uninvited," she said teasingly and smiled.

"Oh, there's a lot of things I'm afraid of. I just don't show it," he replied thoughtfully while he stared straight ahead.

As the hours passed by the fog for the most part had cleared and with it the anxiousness that Sara had felt. Nathan stopped the team and they ate an early lunch, hungry from having skipped breakfast and let the horses graze on the wet grass along the trail. They would be home in just a few more hours and Sara was excited to start her new life with Nathan. She eagerly asked questions about what life would be like during the cold winter months without television, or hot chocolate, or popping pizzas in the oven. Nathan painted a picture of the winter months in a way that got her to thinking about the new way of life she had chosen, and she tried hard to focus on the passionate times she would spend with Nathan by the fireplace and in the warmth of their bed.

Nathan did not mind the hard work and enjoyed the peace and quiet of farm life, for it often drove the horrid memories of war from his mind. But Sara was used to a much noisier environment: TVs playing in the background, traffic and sirens, people everywhere you went, and planes flying overhead. She pondered these things as they drew ever closer to home.

She finally recognized the rolling hill in front of them and wrapped her arm around Nathan's and smiled. They were almost home and she could get off the hard wooden seat that had jarred her body for days. Sara could already see the hint of smoke rising from their chimney and knew that Inola had started a fire and she couldn't wait to feel its warmth wrap around her like a blanket.

"Whoa," Nathan said and jumped down from the wagon and tied the reins to the post, then turned and helped Sara down with a big grin on his face. Sara rubbed her backside as she stared at the house that enticed her to enter into a whole different world, and was startled to find Inola standing behind her when she turned to help Nathan carry supplies into the house.

"Inola, it's good to see you! Any problems while we were gone?" Nathan asked happy to see him.

"No problems, she was not here to cause any," he said with a bit of a grin hoping to get a rise out of Sara.

"Inola, Sara is now my wife, and I'm hoping that you two will become best of friends just like you and I," he stated in a friendly manner.

Inola looked at her intently and stated, "You be a good wife to him, and then I will call you my friend."

Sara smiled and held out her hand to shake his. "You have a deal. I will be a good wife to him and you will always be welcome as my trusted friend."

"Now that we're all friends, what do you say we get these supplies unloaded and get in out of the cold," Nathan said and finished untying the tarp over the wagon and pulled it back.

It didn't take long for Nathan and Inola to unload the supplies, setting Inola's aside to take with him when he returned to his people at their winter camp, and Sara began preparing supper. As it was cooking she went to the attic anxious to bring down her own clothes and put them away in the bedroom's dresser. She had been wearing the same clothes for days and she was looking forward to a bath and wearing her new pajamas that she was sure Nathan would like.

After supper the men sat at the table and discussed their plans for trapping during the winter months and Sara chose to sit by the fire in her rocking chair soaking up the warmth which was something she greatly missed on the ride back from Knoxville. She sat contented with a hint of a smile as she gazed into the fire thinking about what she would like to do over the long winter months that lie ahead. She thought it would be a great time to start writing her next book, and then gazed at Nathan and knew how she wanted to spend her time with him. Nathan glanced her way often, and seeing that she seemed to be content kept talking with Inola.

As Sara's mind was focused on the things she wanted to do, slowly things that she would need to do started creeping into her thoughts. She told herself that her cooking and baking bread and making cheese would have to be done before she could write. Then she had laundry to wash by hand, and dresses to make, and feeding the chickens and gathering eggs, followed by bringing water in from the well. Slowly her countenance changed to a furrowed brow when she stopped to think that she no longer had the conveniences of an oven, dishwasher, washing machine, or even running water in the house. Nathan noticed the sudden change and wondered what she was thinking about that so disturbed her. Sara had been so caught up in the romance of her love for Nathan that she blocked every unpleasant thing from her mind. She now realized what her mom had meant about thinking about what she was giving up, and it all seemed overwhelming to her at the moment. Sure, she didn't mind these tasks so much now, but over time how would she feel about a life of hard labor with very little time to herself, and would she be too tired to even care about the affections she now craved from Nathan. She was deeply troubled by all these thoughts colliding at one time in her mind.

Nathan noticed that something was terribly wrong and told Inola that it had been a very long day, and he thought it was time for them to turn in for the night.

"Inola, you're welcome to sleep wherever you want, and we'll talk again in the morning," he said with a concerned look on his face, and Inola turned and looked at Sara.

Nathan quickly went and knelt by Sara and asked, "Sara, are you alright?"

She just looked at him and did not answer. She wondered if her love for him could be so shallow that it could be overpowered by her enjoyment of an easier life, and that thought troubled her more than any other thought she had.

"Come on, it has been a long day and you need your rest," he said baffled by what could possibly be troubling her. Taking her by the hand to help her up, he walked with her to the bedroom with his arm around her.

Sara sat on the bed and watched as Nathan poured some water into the wash basin and put some more wood on the fire before sitting down next to her on the bed.

"Sara, please tell me what's troubling you. You know that I would do anything for you," he said looking concerned.

She looked into his desperate eyes and gently replied, "I know you would. I just had a few things on my mind, but I'll be fine. I'm just going to wash up now and get into my pajamas."

"I'll join you in a few minutes. There's a few things I need to check on before coming to bed," he said and stopped at the doorway and looked back at Sara just sitting there, and was deeply troubled.

"Come on, get your act together. You're torturing that poor man. Remember what you have gained that few people ever find instead of asking yourself – What am I willing to give up if I truly love this man?" Sara thought as she sat there on the bed. She smiled and got up and went to her dresser drawers and pulled out her silky nightgown and held it up. *"It's really a little cold to be wearing this, but it should put his mind at ease that everything is*

okay," she thought and after washing up she slipped the sexy, silk nightgown over her head and pulled it down into place.

Nathan stepped through the doorway moments later and just stood there silent, wide-eyed, and wanting her so badly that it hurt.

"Do you like it?" she asked already knowing the answer.

"Very much. I just don't think it will remain on you for very long," he replied with a desire in his eyes that Sara could see from where she stood. It had just the affect that Sara hoped it would have for she craved his touch, and the way he looked at her as he made love to her.

He quickly joined her by the side of the bed and ran his hands along the silky curves of her body with a look of burning love and desire. Sara raised her arms in the air and Nathan took hold of her nightgown and pulled it off over her head, and she crawled into bed and said, "Don't take too long in joining me; it's rather chilly without your warm body on mine." She knew that this first night in their own bed as husband and wife would be one to remember.

Chapter 29

Inola and Nathan were sitting at the dining room table having their morning coffee when Sara emerged from the bedroom wearing her tight jeans, knee-high leather boots and a multi-color pullover sweater. Inola was the first to spot her from where he was sitting.

"It looks like your time traveler has finally decided to join us," he said looking at Nathan and glancing in Sara's direction.

Nathan turned to see what Inola was talking about, and a revelation hit him like a mule kick to the head. The woman he married was from the future. She would always have a different perspective and see things differently than he did. She was not what he chose to see when she was wearing Elizabeth's dress she had altered, with her petticoats and bonnet. That woman was an illusion, one that fit in nicely to his way of life. He suddenly thought he knew what was troubling Sara.

"Good morning, my love…good morning, Inola; I'll have breakfast ready for you in no time at all," she said with a smile as she tied an apron around her.

Sara still had much on her mind that she needed to work through, but she was determined not to let it show on her face or in her actions. She loved Nathan and figured the rest of her problems would work themselves out over time. Living without Nathan was not an option for her.

"What can I do to help?" Nathan asked and ignored the look he received from Inola letting him know that was woman's work.

"If you wish, you may set the table and grab one of the bottles of maple syrup from the pantry," she replied and glanced at Inola's disapproving look and a small grin came to her face.

Inola seemed to know that Nathan was going to have to walk a fine line with this woman. She was not the type to keep silent about what she thought, and she certainly was not the type to be ordered around by any man.

The three of them sat down to a cup of fresh coffee, scrambled eggs, and a stack of pancakes while they enjoyed the last conversation they would have for some time.

While Nathan was helping Inola pack his horses with the supplies he would be taking to his people at their winter camp, Sara remembered her MP3 player and went to her top dresser drawer to get it so she could enjoy some music while she cleaned up the dining area.

She had her back to the front door when she started the music and quickly cleared off the table and started to wash the dishes. She sang along with one of her favorite songs and swayed, dancing to the music when Inola stepped inside the front door to tell Sara he was leaving. Startled he quickly pulled his knife from its sheath, and stood there wide-eyed and perplexed looking all around the room trying to determine where the male voices and frenzied music was coming from. He watched as Sara danced to the rhythm of the music and joined her voice with the other voices he was hearing. He was convinced that other evil spirits had joined her in the house and bewitched her. He slowly backed out the door and quietly started to close it, still holding his knife when Nathan suddenly came up behind him.

"What's wrong Inola? You look like you've just seen a ghost," he said perplexed. Inola pointed his finger in the direction of Sara. "I told you she was an evil spirit and you would not listen! Now she is joined with other evil spirits that are chanting and dancing in your house.

Nathan looked at him like he was crazy, and started to open the door to see for himself what was going on.

"Don't go inside my friend. They will bewitch you as they have bewitched her," he warned.

He couldn't imagine what Inola had seen, but he knew it wasn't evil spirits. As he stood by the door he could hear the lively music and singing Inola had referred to and slowly opened the door wide enough until he saw Sara. He watched as she sang uninhibited and moved to the music as she washed the dishes and put them away. He had never seen a woman sway her hips and move her body the way Sara was moving to the music. He watched mesmerized as her ponytail swung back and forth and her arms, shoulders, torso and hips all swiveling as her feet glided across the floor and thought that her voice seemed more like the voice of an angel than an evil spirit. Nathan began to smile as he watched her, and the longer he watched the bigger his smile grew until Inola tugged on his arm. He slowly closed the door and turned towards him still smiling for he liked the way she moved.

"There's nothing for you to worry about Inola, and there's certainly no need to burn my house down or harm her in any way. Do you hear me? She is simply singing and dancing to music from her time. The strange music and men's voices you heard were coming from something that was invented in the future and not from some evil spirits; even though it sounded that way to you," he stated seriously. He could tell that Inola was not totally convinced, but knew him well enough to know that he would never harm Sara. "Wait out here and I'll go get Sara and bring her outside to say goodbye," Nathan stated calmly, and noticed that Inola was still wide-eyed and filled with apprehension. "Trust me, my friend, Sara is not bewitched. I've heard her sing some of those songs before, just not with the music playing. So just relax. She won't bewitch you," he said and turned to go inside and get Sara.

He warned Sara about what Inola had just witnessed and that he once again thought that she had been bewitched by evil spirits. "Shall I take my player and let him hear the music coming from it, or will that only confuse him more?" she asked.

"Go ahead and take it. I don't think this is the last time he'll hear you playing your music, but I want you to save your dancing for my eyes only," he said with a smile.

Sara went outside with Nathan and smiled calmly at Inola, who immediately spotted something in her hands. She saw his reaction when he saw it and held it in plain sight. "Inola, I'm sorry I startled you. This little object is where the music you heard comes from in my time; not from evil spirits. May I turn it on and show you? Because I dearly love to listen to my music," she stated and still noticed the apprehension in his countenance. She selected a softer, slower, love song and turned on the player, and watched as Inola's eyes widened and he took a step backwards and looked at her, then at Nathan. She turned it off several seconds later and Inola glanced at her and then at Nathan to see his reaction. Though still bewildered he realized there would be many things about Sara that he would never understand.

Inola's horse nickered and Nathan knew it was time for him to leave and stepped forward and shook his hand, "I'll see you in the spring; you take care, Inola." But Sara opened her arms and smiled. He looked at Nathan bewildered as to what to do. Nathan motioned with his head to let him know that he might as well do as Sara wanted, and Inola hesitantly stepped forward and stiffly embraced Sara's good-bye hoping his friend was right about her not being bewitched.

"Inola, I shall miss you and all the faces you make at me. You are always welcome here; you're family," she said with a smile as

Inola quickly glanced over at Nathan to see his reaction to her calling him family, and he just nodded his head in agreement.

Inola mounted his horse and turned and looked at them standing there holding hands, gave them a slight nod of his head, and urged his horse on as they watched him ride away. Now that they were alone, Nathan suggested they go sit by the fire for a while. He needed to talk to Sara and get a few things straightened out if things were going to be right between them.

He sat in his rocking chair and took Sara's hand and gently pulled her towards him. "Come sit with me," he said.

Sara sat down with him, but never expected that Nathan was choosing his words most carefully. He wanted Sara to open up, not clam up, and he had to put his house in order the only way he could see it working. The minute he said her name she knew that things were about to get serious.

"Sara...I'd like to know what is troubling you. You don't need to tell me right this minute, but I need to know what you're thinking and feeling. I'm not a mind reader. I don't want there to be any secrets between us; we're both to tell the God's honest truth no matter the cost. Can you do that for me?" he asked seriously.

Sara looked deeply into his piercing eyes and nodded. She had hoped to work things out on her own without troubling him with her confused thoughts, but it didn't look like that was the way it was going to work. She slid off his lap and dragged her rocking chair closer to his and sat there on the edge of it just looking at him for a moment while she thought.

"I'll be back in a minute. I think in order to tell you, I can best do it by showing you a few things," she said and stood up and started towards the attic.

Nathan felt a bit anxious while he waited for Sara to return. He figured the not knowing what was troubling Sara was harder on him than the knowing, so he waited patiently.

Sara came down carrying a variety of magazines she had brought with her and had planned on showing him at some point just to show him the differences between their two times. But under the circumstances, now would have to be the right time.

Sara sat on Nathan's lap once again and started turning the pages showing him everything from men and women's clothing, to appliances, to entertainment in all its many forms, to large cities, and to all sorts of vehicles and modes of transportation, and explaining in many instances how they worked. Nathan asked many questions, and he began to see why someone who had grown up with all these marvelous inventions would have trouble giving up the conveniences they provided and enjoyed.

"You would give up all these things, for me?" he asked most seriously.

She looked into his eyes and wanted so much to say "yes" without any hesitation, but he had asked her to always be truthful with him.

"My heart screams 'YES', but my flesh is having a little harder time screaming the same thing. But this I know, Nathan, I can't live without you. I won't live without you! So, I'm hoping you'll give me a little time to reconcile my heart with my flesh," Sara answered hoping he would understand.

Nathan pulled her close and wrapped his arms around her while he thought about what she said. He could now clearly see why she stared into the fire last night with such a troubled gaze. He was having a hard time comprehending how someone could love him so much that they would be willing to give up everything they had enjoyed just to be with him. This harsh reality was something that he would never forget or take lightly; her love would be cherished above all things except for his love of God.

Nathan gently rocked her on his lap and whispered softly in her ear, "You take all the time you need."

Sara felt a heavy burden lift off her shoulders. Telling Nathan the truth about what she was feeling was liberating, and she no longer felt the pressure of having to adjust to this way of life overnight. She knew that Nathan would be there to help her carry the burden until she was strong enough to enjoy the life she had chosen. Besides, she thought, until then she could always travel to her time to see her parents from time to time and bring back more supplies of the things she enjoyed.

That evening as Sara and Nathan laid on the bear skin in front of the fire that Inola had left behind, Sara asked Nathan how he and Inola had become friends. Memories, bloody and horrible, flooded his mind and none of them were good. Memories he had wished to keep buried. He told her of the fierce Indian wars that took place in that part of Tennessee and how a number of the Indian tribes usually only hunted in that part of the territory now. He continued with the fighting that took place during the War of Independence involving various Indian tribes, the militia, and the British soldiers. He paused as more memories came to mind and Sara could tell by the look on his face how painful they were to recall. He thought about how many men he had killed, both British and Indian over the years and how the memories darkened his very soul. He hesitated whether to share them all with Sara or not.

"My love, I can see how painful this is to you, and you need not go any further unless talking about it will somehow release some of the demons that torment you so," she said lovingly.

He turned his head and looked deeply into her eyes and saw only her love and concern for him. He wondered if that was what he would see after he told her the things he had done and what he was capable of doing. Then he remembered his own words to Sara that very morning, "I don't want there to be any secrets between us," and felt she had the right to know what kind of a man she married.

"No secrets, remember?" he asked and continued. "After the war when I was searching for a place to settle down I was involved in one of those battles with the Cherokee not too far from here. It was a bloody, vicious battle, most of it hand to hand once we got our first and only shot off. When the fighting was over a lot of the backwoodsmen would take scalps like the Cherokee did to them and would kill any who were left wounded so they wouldn't have to fight them again. I had my knife in my hand and held it high ready to kill one of the badly injured Cherokee, when this feeling I just couldn't kill another person came over me. I saw the look in Inola's eyes. He fully expected to die, and if the shoe were on the other foot, I would have expected the same thing. He didn't beg for mercy, but I could see something in the way he looked at me with dignity, and a pride that he was only defending his own land from invaders that stayed my hand. I bound him hand and foot and left him there until the other men retreated to their fortified camps, and then I went back. He was near death and I knew if I didn't help him he would die. I stitched up his wounds with horse hair, and gave him food and water for three days and he never said a word to me, but watched me closely with those piercing eyes of his. It was almost like he could see to my very soul. The hard part was figuring out what I was going to do with him now that he was showing signs of recovery. Did I just cut him loose and back away with my pistol drawn and ride away, or…he spoke to me before I could decide. He said pointing to himself and then to me 'life, now yours', and I cut him free. I mounted my horse and held out my hand. He took it and I swung him up on my horse and we have been together ever since. He helped me build this house and has helped protect me from any Cherokee or other tribe that wished to kill me and my family. Over the past three years I have tried to share my crops and supplies with his tribe, and in return they have left me alone."

When Nathan looked over at Sara she had tears streaming from her eyes which he gently wiped away. Sara felt like she had seen into the depths of his heart, and loved him more deeply than before. Inola now had a place deep within her heart as more than a trusted friend, as truly family.

Sara put her arm across Nathan's chest as she rested her head on his shoulder, and both laid there silent with their thoughts. She knew how one's past could shape one's future and thought she understood in some very small way why Nathan had always seemed so guarded in his speech, actions, and yes, even in his ability to let himself love someone. She could not fathom how anyone could move on with their life with the heavy burdens of their past ever before their eyes, and thought she understood why those visions from the past were why he woke so early in the morning or tossed through the night.

Nathan finally broke the silence, "Is it possible for you to love a man who has killed so many men? I'll understand if what I told you repulses you and you wish to return home," he declared with a crushed spirit.

Sara was shocked by his question and quickly raised up on her elbow and looked at him in disbelief.

"Nathan, you are the most honorable man I have ever met. From the time I entered your home I have known you to be kind, patient, gentle, protective, and most of all, capable of a deep and abiding love. You fought for the freedom of your country that you love, and every man that fought with you did the same, not because they wanted to, but because they had to. The British gave you no choice. It was kill or be killed. It wasn't murder for the sake of being evil, but doing your duty to protect those who couldn't protect themselves. I would have a problem if you killed for the enjoyment of it, but I see a man deeply regretful for what he was called upon to do. I can only pray that God will heal you from these tormented memories and give you the peace you so richly deserve. I love you more deeply than ever before, and I'm not going anywhere without you," she stated with conviction and compassion.

Nathan's eyes watered as he studied her face and still saw only love, no judgement or repulsion. At that moment he allowed the demons out that had tormented him day and night; at least a few of them.

Sara smiled at him and ran her fingers through his thick black hair and softly said, "I wish you would kiss me like you mean it," and waited for him to reach up and pull her down to his lips.

Nathan did indeed kiss her like he meant it. He wondered if Sara had ever made love lying naked on a bear skin rug in front of a roaring fire, and guessed that he would soon find out. He had never been with a woman who enjoyed sex the way that Sara did. No matter what position they were in she enjoyed every moment until they laid there exhausted and satisfied throughout the night with only a blanket to cover them until morning.

Chapter 30

Sara laid there happily watching Nathan sleep next to her. It was the first night since they were married that he did not toss and turn as if he was struggling with someone, but slept soundly and contentedly next to her. She slipped out from under the blanket and poured water that was left heating over the hearth into a basin and washed and dressed so that she could have his coffee ready. When it was almost finished brewing she poured him a fresh basin of water to wash with and laid his clothes out neatly by the fire, and then went to wake him.

Sara jostled his shoulder and before she could speak, Nathan, startled by the sudden touch roughly caught her by the wrist and looked intensely at her as if she were the enemy, and then realized what he had done.

"Sara, I'm sorry. Did I harm you?" he asked anxiously.

"No, my love, you did not harm me. I know better than to jostle someone from a deep sleep. I won't do it again," she said with a smile followed by a soft kiss; hoping to help him move past this little incident quickly. She did know better than to wake a person with PTSD, and knew that he would feel bad for treating her so roughly.

"There's warm water in the basin for you to wash with while I finish making breakfast," she softly stated, then laid her hand against his cheek and kissed him again before returning to the hearth.

By the time Nathan washed and dressed, Sara was dishing out their breakfast and went to pour him a hot cup of coffee. Nathan came up behind her and wrapped his arms around her.

"I'm sorry for grabbing you like that," he said looking tenderly into her eyes.

"There's nothing for you to be sorry about; I'm fine. Now let's eat breakfast while it's still hot and figure out what we're going to do today," she said.

"I've been thinking about that. After we feed the animals, how about going for a ride with me. I'd like to show you my favorite spot along the river, and maybe we could have lunch there. You do know how to ride a horse, don't you?" he asked.

"It's been a while, but I think I can manage. I'd love to take a ride along the river, but isn't that where the Cherokee like to hunt?" she questioned.

"There's little chance that we will encounter any of them. They're headed to their winter camps further downstream and I don't believe they will come this far East. But make sure you have your firearm with you and extra ammunition just in case," he plainly stated.

Sara was excited about their little excursion; anything to break up the daily chores she would soon be facing. It didn't take long to feed the animals and pack a lunch for their quiet little getaway. Nathan had the horses saddled while Sara was busy placing her firearm and ammunition clips on her belt.

Riding north they soon entered the forest that still had patches of trees with a small amount of fall colored leaves that slowly floated down as a cool breeze set them free when they passed by winding their way thru the steep foothills. Sara could hear the roar of the river long before she ever saw it. Nathan gave his horse a little kick and hastened the pace with Sara trying to keep up, ducking under low hanging branches along the way.

The trees were thinning out as the sound of rushing water grew louder and suddenly they were on the sandy and rocky bank and turned a little to the west and rode slowly along in single file. Sara was amazed at the beauty of the river rushing downstream over and around various size boulders, and even though most of the trees were now bare of leaves the moss and ferns along the banks were lush and green from the recent rains.

"Whoa," Nathan called. "We're here," he said with a smile turning and looking back at Sara, then swung down from his horse.

He quickly went back and helped Sara dismount and untied the basket holding their lunch. He took her by the hand as they neared the water's edge to help her keep her balance as they climbed over boulders of different sizes to reach a cluster of them in the middle of the raging river.

Nathan found a nice smooth spot big enough for the two of them to sit on, or even lay down upon. He set the basket down and held Sara's hand until she sat on the edge of the large boulder, then joined her with a heavy sigh as he gazed around at the tranquil beauty of his favorite spot along the river.

"It's breathtaking! No wonder you love to come here," she said and wrapped her arm around his as they sat there quietly taking in the beauty.

As they were enjoying lighthearted small talk as the hours passed, Nathan noticed that he no longer heard the birds singing in the trees and casually glanced around searching both banks along the river. He knew that it was unlikely that anyone would be around in this part of the woods and figured an animal or bird of prey had frightened them away, and relaxed a bit when his searching came up with nothing.

He unpacked their lunch and took a bite of his apple when suddenly his eyes caught a slight movement along the north bank fifteen feet or so back into the forest. Nathan took another bite of his apple while Sara unwrapped the sandwiches she packed and placed her apple next to her. She was still unaware that Nathan had seen anything that would concern him. His eyes studied the group of seven men on foot and determined they were Cherokee and breathed a small sigh of relief.

"Sara, is a round chambered in your firearm?" he asked looking calmly into her eyes, and she knew from her last experience not to look wildly around.

"Yes, you just have to release the safety. Indians?" she asked calmly though her heart was now pounding.

"Yes, Cherokee. They appear to be hunting and will probably pass on; we're no threat to them. Just go on with your eating," he replied and focused on the group as they moved silently closer to the bank, but had not drawn their bows.

Sara now spotted them and her breathing trembled as she exhaled. She sat there as calmly as she could taking a bite of her sandwich, but could not swallow it.

Nathan turned his head and directly looking at them called out loudly over the sound of the raging river in the Cherokee language to them. Sara had no idea what he said, but they came down to the river bank and called back to him suspiciously looking around and very curious about Sara. The conversation went back and forth and the only word that Sara understood was 'Inola', and she still could not swallow what was in her mouth and wanted desperately to reach for her firearm, but knew that was the last thing Nathan would want her to do.

She noticed that the Cherokee pointed at her several times and if she was not mistaken, she was currently at the center of their conversation. Suddenly Nathan asked Sara to stand up and pull her hair from the ponytail and let her hair fall in front of her shoulders then rest her hand on top of her handgun. She looked at him as if he had lost his mind, and yet he seemed calm and confident, and she complied without questioning. He knew they had never seen anyone quite like Sara; tall, long golden hair in the sunlight, strange clothing, and carrying a weapon that Nathan had been sure to point out.

Nathan finally called out one last time and raised his hand towards them, and they called back and slowly started up the bank and disappeared into the forest as silently as they came.

Sara finally relaxed enough to swallow the food in her mouth and took a deep breath and didn't know whether to cry or to ask him if he were out of his mind. She was still in a state of shock being put on display that way, especially after her first encounter with the Shawnee.

"Relax, darling, there's nothing to fear. Come sit back down by me," he said with a smile and then wrapped his arm around her as she snuggled up close to him.

Sara was still breathing heavily and he could tell by the questioning look in her eyes that she wanted an explanation of what had just happened.

Nathan grinned and took another bite of his apple, and as he chewed he told her about their conversation while Sara quickly finished what was left of her sandwich.

"I greeted them as a friend to the Cherokee and blood-brother to Inola. But, it was you they wanted to know about. Where you came from, what you were…"

Stunned by what they had said, she asked, "What do you mean, what I was? Wasn't it fairly obvious I was a woman?"

"Not to them it wasn't. They've never seen anyone like you and had questions about your origin, like Inola had the first time he saw you," he replied.

"So what did you tell them?" she asked curiously glancing over her shoulder for any sign of the Cherokee hunters.

"I told them that you appeared out of nowhere. Suddenly you were just standing inside my house dressed the same way they were now seeing you, and you had this weapon that fires as quickly as lightning strikes the ground. Since that seemed to impress them I told them that you were sent here to protect me and my home so I married you, so that I could surround myself with little ones just like you. After that they were more than happy to continue on with their hunting trip," he stated and grinned as he took the last bite of his apple and tossed the core into the river.

Sara was not as amused as he, and looked around once again in every direction to make sure they were alone and no one was trying to kill this strange anomaly they had seen.

"Shouldn't we be starting for home?" Sara asked still anxious.

"It's a beautiful day. Why don't we just lay back and soak up some of this wonderful sunshine while it lasts," he asked playfully and tried to get her to lay down. When he saw that Sara was truly fearful, he felt bad for making light of something that upset her so.

"You're right. As soon as we finish our lunch we should start heading for home," he said and started gathering up the food wrappings and stuffed them back into the basket.

Sara let out a sigh of relief and smiled as she quickly finished eating, then took his hand while he led her safely off the boulders they had been sitting on. Once on their horses they rode off side by side until they reached home.

Later that day when they were finished with supper, they sat in their rocking chairs by the fireplace to talk.

"Do you really think the Cherokee will leave us alone because of that wild story you told them about me?" she asked with the events of the day still on her mind.

"Inola's tribe already leaves us alone because of the food I supply to them. But, that story will spread like wildfire throughout all the tribes, and when the Shawnee pass along the story of their encounter with your firearm, I believe none of the tribes will come anywhere close to us unless they believe you have some other mystical powers," he said with a grin.

"Oh great, you had me more or less convinced until you came up with mystical powers B.S."

"B.S.?" he asked with a quizzical look.

"Bull...Shit," she replied softly and hesitantly as she spoke the last word. It sounded so much nicer the way she said it, and she never thought about it as being profanity when she used just its initials.

Nathan could see her embarrassment and laughed heartily.

"Why, Sara, I do believe you are blushing," he chuckled and then laughed again as she turned her face away.

"Come here and sit with me. I want to tell you something," he said and held open his arms.

Sara joined him and he continued, "I've laughed more since you have been here than I have in a long...long time. It's like medicine for my soul, and I can't tell you how much it means to me to have an angel like you to poke a little fun at," he said tenderly looking at her.

Sara just smiled and then laid her head against his shoulder as he sat there contentedly until it was time for bed, totally unaware that Sara's thoughts were consumed with her encounters with the two different Indian tribes.

Chapter 31

Little did Sara know that she was about to find out that settlers on the frontier had more to fear than just Shawnee attacks. There were other dangers that could be just as deadly and maybe not quite so obvious.

Some days later, Sara was greeted by a beautiful day of welcomed sunshine. It had either rained or snowed the past couple of days and she was tired of the frigid cold and the sky being various shades of grey. But now the sun was out and the rays coming through the windows were like rays from heaven and Sara's spirit was as bright as the day.

Later that day she went out on the front porch to call Nathan in for lunch, and looked out over the hills that still had patches of snow and felt the warmth of the sun upon her cheeks. As she glanced to the east she spotted four riders off in the distance headed their way at a pretty good pace. She thought it strange that they would be riding alone without wagons or family, but just four men riding abreast. Something in her spirit alerted her to possible danger and she went to the far end of the porch closest to the barn and loudly called out to Nathan, "Nathan, riders coming!"

She watched as the four men split into two groups: one group headed for the cover of their apple trees that would lead them to the north side of the barn, and the other two would ride right past their front porch. Sara swallowed hard and squinted to try to get a better look at the riders who were quickly approaching. She wondered if Nathan had heard her yell, but there was no time to yell to him again; they would hear her. She went quickly back inside the house and grabbed her firearm from off the mantle, and stuffed a couple of clips into her pockets since there wasn't enough time to put her belt on. She went to the only window on that side of the house where she could see the barn. She noticed the two riders that came through the apple trees had jumped down off their horses and ran to the side of the barn out of sight.

"Dear Lord, Nathan's walking right into an ambush," she thought and ran to the front window to see if she could spot the other two men whom she feared would try to enter the house.

Seeing neither men she crept out the front door quietly, and quickly walked against the wall along the porch until she could see the barn, and her heart sank to the bottom of her feet. Nathan had heard her and was cautiously coming out of the barn with his pistol in hand pointed at one of the two riders still mounted on their horses.

Sara could not clearly hear what Nathan was saying to the riders but the way he hesitated when he first saw them, it seemed like he knew the men. Hank was a tall thin man who wore a wide brim hat with long hair hanging loosely down his back and had his hands in the air as he spoke to Nathan. From her vantage point she could clearly see that the other rider was holding his pistol down by his side where Nathan could not see it.

"Oh dear God, what do I do? I've never fired my weapon to intentionally kill a man, just to scare them," she thought, but knew she must do something. Nathan was outnumbered, and she was sure he knew nothing about the two men on the side of the barn, and now one of them had his pistol aimed at Nathan's back.

Seeing that, Sara instinctively gripped her weapon with both hands and stepped further out on the porch and took several shots at the man dropping him to the ground. She waited a second to see if the other man would appear. Before she could even turn her head to check on Nathan the sound of a musket shot rang out, and she anxiously looked to see who had fired their pistol. It was Nathan. He had shot the thin, long haired man on his horse plummeting him to the ground, and Sara watched wide-eyed in terror as the second man raised his pistol and fired. She screamed horrified that Nathan had been shot, then realized that his pistol had misfired. Sara froze; her mind overwhelmed by everything that had happened so quickly.

Nathan had no time to reload his pistol and reached for his long blade knife as Fred came off his horse with his knife ready to fight. Nathan was much taller and stronger, but Fred was this dirty, wild hair and bearded man who moved more quickly and it seemed to be to his advantage. Sara ran off the porch towards them as Nathan yelled out, "Sara, go back inside and bolt the doors."

She stopped momentarily as she normally obeyed when Nathan gave her a direct command. But she couldn't this time. This man might kill the man she loved and she would be damned if she would let that happen.

As Nathan was engaged in the deadly knife fight, Sara caught a glimpse of the man by the side of the barn peek around the corner, but not far enough for her to get a clean shot at him. She firmly gripped her handgun and fired several times rapidly at what little of him she could see. He quickly withdrew and moments later she watched as he took off on his horse back through the apple trees.

Trembling and dazed she turned her attention to the man welding a knife and aimed and fired, but missed as both continued to avoid each other's jabs. She moved a little closer this time and fired once again, but missed her intended mark; only wounding the man in the leg and quickly reached into her pocket for another clip. She saw Nathan catch his breath as the man quickly limped back a few feet and grabbed the reins to his horse and climbed on. Fred whipped his horse repeatedly as he took off around the backside of the barn and then off into the apple orchard and out of sight.

Relieved that the two men had fled, Sara ran to Nathan expecting him to take her in his arms and tell her everything was going to be alright, but instead he quickly grabbed her by the arm and started running towards the house with her in hand.

"I thought I told you to go back inside and bolt the doors," he stated quite roughly.

"I'm sorry, but I couldn't. There was another man about to shoot you in the back. I couldn't let that happen. You know they would have come after me next," she exclaimed as Nathan pulled her inside the house. "I did the right thing, right?" she asked looking frightfully into his eyes that still had the look of combat in them.

Breathing heavily, Nathan looked at her for several seconds remembering he was not in the militia any more giving orders to the men under his command, then softened his reply, "Yes, my angel, you did the right thing. Now I want you to stay inside and bolt the door behind me. I'm going to check the two men outside and make sure they're dead. I don't want the two that got away to come back thinking they might be alive. Now I mean it, stay put!"

"Nathan, take my firearm with you," she said and ejected the empty clip and put another clip in and handed it to him.

As Nathan went out the door Sara bolted it then ran to the window facing the barn and watched as he bent down cautiously and checked the man he had shot and was satisfied that he was dead and started towards the other man lying in the dirt by the corner of the barn. He bent down and rolled the man over and looked at his back; the bullet wounds were totally different from those made by his musket. As he knelt there he looked in the direction that the two men rode away and knew what he needed to do. He slowly stood then walked back towards the house.

Sara unbolted the door as he approached and when he came through the door he stated, "They're both dead."

Sara's adrenaline rush was subsiding and suddenly the gravity of what had just transpired hit her hard. She had shot and killed a man and wounded another. Nathan could see her turn white as the color drained from her face and caught her before she hit the floor and carried her to the couch and laid her down. She came to with Nathan kneeling beside her patting her hand and calling her name. She looked up at him then burst into tears and reached up and wrapped her arms around Nathan and held on tightly.

"Shhh, it'll be alright," he whispered as she clung to his neck and sobbed. He knew what she must be feeling. He felt the same way when he killed his first man many years ago, and still had those feelings no matter how many men he had killed; this one today was no different. He sat beside her and just held her. There were not enough words in the world to take away the pain she was feeling; only time would numb it a bit if she were lucky.

When Sara finally calmed down he went to the bucket by the hearth and dipped a clean cloth into the water and wrung it out and returned to Sara and gently wiped her face and looked into her eyes and recognized the empty look.

"Do you think you can eat any of the lunch you prepared?" he asked.

Sara just shook her head. He could tell by the distant look in her eyes and her furrowed brow that she was still in a state of shock and trying to process the horrific acts that had just taken place before her eyes.

"Why don't you go lay down in bed. I'll put some more wood on the fire, and grab a quick bite to eat and then go bury those two men. You rest if you can and I'll be back in a little while," he said soothingly, and Sara just nodded and followed him into the bedroom and laid down facing the fireplace.

Nathan covered her with a blanket and added some wood to the fire and quietly closed the door behind him.

As he was digging the two graves he had time to think. He knew those men that rode up. He remembered Hank and Fred from the war. They were no good thieves that enjoyed killing men and anyone if they thought there was something to be gained of value. After the war they continued their robbing and killing as they made their way across the states and finally into the frontier for they were now wanted men with a price on their heads. The thought that troubled him most was that they had now witnessed Sara's firearm. They had not seen it, but they certainly heard how rapidly it fired and they would be curious. A weapon like that in their hands would be disastrous, and he feared that they would do anything to get their hands on it.

Now that he had finished burying the two men his thoughts turned to Sara. He hated what the men had done to her; they had robbed her of her joy and laughter that he loved so much, and they had filled her with a fear that would not soon go away. He thought of his promise to not keep secrets from each other, but that was a promise he was going to have to break.

When he entered the house Sara was still in bed, and he knew that she could not be left to dwell on what she was forced to do; it would eat at her until it destroyed her. He must get her up and her mind on other things and entered the bedroom and sat on the bed next to her. She was staring blindly into the fire and did not look up until he gently ran his fingers along the side of her face then held her hand in his.

He thought about what to say that would coax her from the bed and took a deep breath as she looked up at him with the faintest of a smile.

"I've worked up quite an appetite. I would be happy to give you a hand fixing something for supper. I thought one of those venison meat pies you make would be awfully good tonight with some apple butter and bread. What do you say? Will you join me or do I have to fix it myself?" he asked hoping for a positive response.

"That does sound good, and I would appreciate your help unless there is something else you need to be doing," she replied with a troubled tone still unable to let go of the images repeating themselves over and over again in her mind.

"There's nothing I need to be doing right now that is more important than being with you," he said, then stood up and offered her his hand.

Nathan kept her talking about anything and everything except what happened today while he helped her prepare supper, and watched as just a spark of her spirit returned and she could at least smile at him and occasionally laugh at something witty he would say.

Supper was especially good that night and Nathan was happy that he had gotten Sara to eat something and thought about what he could suggest her doing while he did what he felt he needed to do. He did not want her to just sit staring off into the fire when he left her sitting there, she needed something to keep her mind occupied. He remembered her telling him how she poured her heart out in writing her last book when her mind was troubled about loving two men at the same time, and wondered if that would help her if she were to do that now. He knew that she was already working on a novel, and would consider this idea a little more before suggesting something that might ultimately cause more harm than good.

When he couldn't think of a better idea he decided to suggest it and then find a way to tell her that he would not be spending the night inside the house with her. He needed her to believe that he would be spending the night outside close to the house to watch in case the two men decided to return, and convince her to stay inside with the doors bolted until he returned in the morning.

It was now or never to suggest his idea or he would not have the time to do what he felt needed to be done. "Sara, why don't you write in your novel tonight? I plan on keeping watch outside and need you to stay inside with the doors bolted until I return. I don't want any arguments from you, but it is important that you stay busy until you think you can fall asleep. I'll put logs on both fires so you can decide where you would like to lie down when you do get sleepy, but I want you to rest assured that we will both be safe tonight," he said as he put on his heavy overcoat and buttoned it up.

Sara knew there was no sense in arguing with him when he was this resolute about something, but wished he would not leave her alone in the house tonight. She wanted him there with his arms around her if he wanted her to sleep.

"Take my firearm with you outside tonight," she offered and went to stand up to get it when Nathan stopped her.

"No, I want you to keep that with you. I'll be just fine with my pistol and rifle; I'm more accustomed to using them if I have to," he replied calmly and assuredly not wanting her to be the least bit suspicious that he had any plans other than the ones he had told her about.

She handed him a couple of heavy blankets to take with him and then bolted the door behind him and went and sat by the fire to think. Nathan was right. She felt like she needed to be doing something other than just sitting there and dwelling on what had happened and decided that pouring herself into her book when her mind was troubled was the best thing she could do, and went and got her paper and pen.

Chapter 32

As Sara began to write, Nathan was quietly leading his horse from the barn into the apple orchard. When he had mounted he stowed his rifle and pistol and headed in the direction the men had gone and quickly picked up the horse's pace as he headed east towards the forest. He had a general idea where the men would be headed and kept his eyes and ears opened to every sound and movement. The full moon helped light his way through the cold dark forest and he stopped often to listen carefully and sniff the air for smoke. He knew they would have a camp fire even if it was a small one and looked for any sign of smoke rising above the trees in the moon light. He knew they would be like finding a needle in a haystack but he also knew what kind of shelter the men would be looking for and where they might find it.

He had been gone for a couple of hours when he caught his first whiff of smoke and stopped to listen and thought he heard the sound of a horse up ahead. He dismounted and tied his horse to a tree and continue on by foot with his pistol stuck through his belt and his rifle in his hand.

Nathan tried not to make a sound as he followed the smell of smoke and the sound of their horses, and soon could see a slight glow in the woods up ahead. He paused and looked at the ground in front of him because every step of his would be important if he wished to remain undetected. He slowly and carefully made his way towards them and picked a spot that had a clear line of fire to both men and squatted down behind a large pine tree to hear what they were saying.

"Give me that bottle of whiskey. I need it more than you do," Fred growled.

"Stop your bellyaching, that musket went clean through your leg," his comrade gruffly replied. Nathan studied his face by the glow of the camp fire, but did not recognize the man. But that did not matter; he was dangerous and had to be dealt with.

"Did you ever in all the war see a musket wound like this? I don't know what that crazy woman was shooting but it wasn't a musket, and I mean to find out what it was. You heard how quickly she got those shots off," Fred stated and took another gulp of the whiskey.

"Yeah, and it sounded nothing like a flint lock pistol being shot, but what could it be?" the other man asked.

"How the hell would I know? That's why we have to go back as soon as my leg heals up enough to ride," Fred snapped back at him.

Nathan had heard enough. He could not be looking over his shoulder waiting for these two men to return, and slowly and quietly cocked the hammers back on both of his weapons. He had no choice but to shoot Fred in the back with his rifle and when the second man stood he would fire his pistol and pray that he had killed them both with only a single shot from each of his weapons.

He took a deep breath and asked God to forgive him for what he was about to do and quietly stood up, took aim, and fired his rifle. He watched Fred, the man that Sara had wounded fall over, but he had not counted on the other man seeing the flash from his rifle. Nathan pulled the pistol from his belt but before he could take aim and fire the man stood and turned towards where he had seen the flash and fired.

A split second later Nathan clutched his shoulder. It was a mistake to give his enemy such a clean line of fire. He felt the musket ball rip through the outer flesh of his shoulder and he knew he had to fight through the pain and take careful aim and fire before this man came charging at him with his knife. He took one deep breath, held it, then aimed and fired, and watched as the man staggered towards him and fell face down feet away from him.

His heart was pounding as he let out a sigh of relief and clutched his shoulder that was throbbing and bloody. *"Damn, I knew better than to stand in the open; now how am I going to explain this to Sara? Tell her another lie? I can't do that. I've got time to think about that on my way home. Right now I have to take care of my shoulder and get these guys buried,"* he said to himself.

As Nathan removed his overcoat he went and sat down by the fire to dress his wound. He had been lucky the musket ball had only grazed his shoulder leaving a gash across it. Finding the whiskey bottle the men had been drinking from he poured what remained over his wound and winced; it stung like hell. He ripped the sleeve from his shirt and tied it with difficulty tightly around his upper arm and debated whether to bury the two men or not. It depended he decided on whether either of the two men had a shovel tucked away in their saddle bags and went to look.

As he searched he thought of Sara. Once again he was reminded of how she must be feeling and felt guilty leaving her alone on the one night she needed him most. He had killed so many men he had lost count and it still sickened him especially the way he had to kill these two men for there was no honor in it. But, even if it cost him his soul he had to protect Sara. Without her life just wasn't worth living. He felt like he had been a dead man walking after he lost his wife and daughter, and now that he had Sara he felt alive again; able to love, and laugh, and find a little bit of heaven in her arms, and peace for his troubled mind.

"Damn," he said as he came across a short handled shovel and knew what he had to do and quickly got to it. He pulled the saddles from the horses and set them free for he couldn't take them back with him; they would slow him down and he would never make it back before morning. He worked hard and winced or swore with each shovel full of dirt as he dug two shallow graves this time and buried them. Their gear he left behind and did not bother going through it. He wanted nothing of their stolen things, he just wanted to get home before morning.

Their fire was almost out so he left it burning too tired to even kick dirt over it, and carefully put his overcoat back on for it was extremely cold. The coat only showed a tear where the musket ball tore through and hoped that Sara would not notice it, or the little bit of blood that had soaked through until he had time to explain things to her. Exhausted, he slowly headed back in the direction of his horse. It would be close to morning when he returned and spurred his horse on in the hopes of getting back inside the barn without being seen.

After digging four graves in the hard packed ground that day he was dead on his feet by the time he stood at the door with one blanket in hand and the other wrapped around his shoulders to hide his injury and called for Sara to unbolt it and let him in.

She had a big smile on her face when she opened the door fully expecting him to smile and take her in his arms, but her smile quickly faded. Nathan looked haggard almost to the point of collapsing, and Sara now looked at him bewildered and stunned as he came through the door.

"I have breakfast ready and you look like you could use a hot cup of coffee," she anxiously stated still puzzled by his appearance.

"Thanks," he replied wearily and gave her a soft kiss on the cheek and continued, "But, I think I'm going to go lay down for a bit. I'll eat later," he said and started for the bedroom.

Sara just stood there dazed and watched him close the door behind him. *"He's never passed up a meal, and was that whiskey I smelled on him,"* she said to herself and slowly walked over to her rocking chair and sat by the fire to think.

Their normal lunch time came and went and Nathan still had not left his room. Sara's mind was running wild by now and knew something was seriously wrong for him to miss two meals in a row and wanted desperately to open the door and check on him. She knew better than to even gently shake him awake, but maybe she could just go in quietly and see if he was okay, she thought.

As she neared the bed she saw that he was still asleep and went to pull the blanket back over his shoulder as the fire had now gone out and the room was cold. She gently pulled the blanket up and when she laid it down she lightly rested her hand on it and he winced and opened his eyes.

She was startled by his reaction and drew back wide-eyed and gasped not knowing what to say to him.

Nathan saw the fearful look on her face and felt badly for adding to the stress she was already under. "It's okay, angel. I need to be getting up anyway. Are there any leftovers from breakfast or lunch?" he asked softly with a smile.

"Yes, I'll go fix you something right away," she said, but still had a confused look on her face as she turned to leave the room.

Nathan groaned as he sat up; his shoulder ached something terrible, and he knew he was going to have to tell Sara what happened. She was going to find out anyway when he asked her to check the wound and change the dressing on it. *"If only I had shot from cover I would never have to tell Sara anything,"* he said to himself as he stood up and started towards the dining area holding his injured arm close to his body.

By the time he sat down, Sara had his food on the table and was pouring him a cup of hot coffee. She sat down across from him and just looked at him anxiously hoping he would offer her some explanation for his strange behavior. She couldn't help but wonder how a poor night's sleep could cause such exhaustion and pain in his shoulder.

As Nathan ate he saw that Sara had noticed the tear in his overcoat and glanced between looking at it and looking at him, and was a bit surprised that she did not question him about it. When he had finished eating he knew that now was as good a time as any to tell her about what he was really doing last night.

Pushing his plate aside he started his confession. "Sara, I didn't want you to worry last night about me. You had enough to deal with and I feel badly that I wasn't here for you." Sara went to speak, but Nathan gestured for her to wait and calmly continued, "But, there was something I had to do that couldn't wait. I knew those men who rode up yesterday; well at least two of them. They weren't the type of men you want to be looking over your shoulder waiting for them to return. I assure you they would return to get their hands on your weapon, and they wouldn't have given it a second thought murdering the both of us. I tracked them down last night to their camp site and even heard them talking about returning for whatever you were using to shoot at them. They left me no choice but to kill them. In doing that, one of them got a shot off and it grazed my shoulder. I'd appreciate it if you would take a look at it and see what you can do and put a clean dressing on it."

The whole time Nathan spoke, Sara sat there breathing shallowly with a blank, hard to read, gaze on her face. Without asking any questions, or saying anything, she started towards the attic to retrieve some of the medical supplies she had brought back through time with her. Nathan poured another cup of coffee while he waited and gently removed his overcoat and tossed it on an empty chair and took his seat.

Nathan loved Sara more dearly than anything in the world, but now thought about what his love had subjected her too: Shawnee attacks, murdering raiders, laborious chores, and now the burden of having killed a man. He pondered whether he was being selfish in asking her to stay with him in his time. He wondered if it wouldn't be better for her to return to her own time; back to her family that could support her after what she had been through, back to the luxuries she was accustomed too, and back to a more civilized time. His heart was heavy as he pondered these things, and questioned his ability to live without her.

Sara came around the corner carrying an armload full of medical supplies not knowing what she was actually going to need. She saw his troubled gaze off into space, and realized that he was just as troubled and hurt as she was, and understood that if they were going to get through this difficult time they were going to have to do it together.

"There's no way I can leave this man I love, hurting the way he is. Our love is all we have to save us with God's help," she thought as she approached the table.

"Does it hurt awful badly?" she asked.

"It hurts, but you go ahead and do what you need to. I'll be okay," he said looking up tenderly at her.

She untied the shirt sleeve he had tightly tied around the gash in his shoulder and grimaced as she pulled it away from the bloody wound it was stuck to. She went and got a basin and filled it with clean warm water and grabbed a cloth to wash away the dried blood.

When she had gently cleaned it, the sight of his opened flesh made her feel faint and thought that the wound should have stitches, but knew that she would never be able to sew it up.

"I don't know if I can do this," she said and steadied herself holding onto the table.

"Sara, look at me…you can do this because I need you to do this. It really doesn't hurt that badly now that you have cleaned it," he said trying to easy her anxiety even though the pain was severe.

Nathan took another look at it once it was cleaned and thought that the gash was not deep enough to require stitches and it was too wide to stitch up anyway. "Sara, just put some of that ointment you used on my ankle and dress it. I think that will be good enough," he assured her.

Sara took a couple of deep breaths and reached for the triple anti-bacterial ointment and put a generous amount on her finger and trembled as she spread it gently across his gash and felt lightheaded again. It bled only a little and she prayed that if he kept it still enough for a few days it might not need stitches but perhaps would just scab over.

Nathan clinched his jaw and made a fist under the table where Sara couldn't see in an effort to hide the pain. He looked at her and said encouragingly, "All you have to do now is wrap a fresh dressing around it, and come sit by the fire with me."

Sara finished wrapping his shoulder with a roll of gauze and handed him four ibuprofen to swallow for the pain and exhaled deeply, happy that she didn't have to try to stitch up such a wide gash before smiling at him. Sara excused herself and went to the chest in the bedroom that held Elizabeth's clothing and took out one of her shawls to use as a sling to keep Nathan from moving his arm around while it healed.

They each took a seat in their own rocking chairs and an uneasy silence between them filled the room as they stared into the fire. Both were harboring fears they were unable to express, and yet so desperately wanted to. The silence and tension were unbearable as Sara turned and looked at Nathan. He saw her and briefly closed his eyes and swallowed hard – expressing his fears and feelings did not come easy to him. These burdens they were carrying if not shared could destroy them, and if shared, could possibly do the same.

"I still have one good arm to hold you with," he said in his deep, smooth tones and held out his arm towards her.

His voice was always soothing to her, and she quickly went and sat on his lap and laid her head against his shoulder and could feel the pounding of his heart. She could tell that his thoughts were troubled like hers, and wondered what fears he was afraid to share with her. But how could she ask him to open up when she herself was afraid to do the same thing.

After a few moments, Sara dug deep to find the resolve needed to tell Nathan of what frightened her. "My love, if we don't talk I'm afraid it will only get harder the longer we wait, and I'm afraid I might lose you forever. I'm afraid if you find me crying or withdrawn working through the fact that I killed a man, you might find me wearisome and want me to return to my own time, or draw back and not want to be intimate with me. I couldn't bare that. I need you to love me, and hold me in your arms and kiss me no matter what trials we go through. Without your love my life wouldn't be worth living," she exclaimed with tears rolling down her cheeks, and eyes filled with pain and fear.

Nathan's eyes pooled with tears as she spoke from the heart and he admired her strength and courage, and her capacity to love even after all she had been through; a love that was strong and resilient.

"You are truly an angel sent from heaven. I was afraid after all you've been through and the hardships you've had to face because I asked you to stay with me, that you would want to return to your own more gentle time. And what I fear most is that I would not be strong enough to tell you that I would understand if you wanted to return to your own time. There you would not be attacked by Indians or depraved men and forced to possibly have to kill again," he painfully uttered, as the tears that had once only pooled in his eyes now ran down his cheeks.

Sara took both her hands and gently wiped the tears from his face and gazed into his troubled eyes. "Don't be afraid, my love, I'm not going anywhere. My time would only serve to be a prison for my heart, soul, and mind, for you would be in every thought with no way to ever be set free," Sara said tenderly.

She rested her head back against his good shoulder and Nathan wrapped his one arm tightly around her as they sat there quietly; happy that they had faced their fears.

Chapter 33

Several days later, Nathan found Sara in the attic frantically going through her backpack.

"What are you looking for?" he asked standing at the top of the stairs.

"I'm looking for my wrist watch," she replied.

"Your wrist watch?" he asked perplexed.

"Yeah, a clock, or maybe you call it a timepiece," she replied.

"I know what a watch is. But why do you need it?" he asked.

"Well, my watch also tells me what date it is along with the time of day," she replied still looking anxiously for it.

"Okay. May I ask why you need to know what date it is?" he asked curiously.

"I have to know what day it is in November so I can prepare for Thanksgiving," she replied enthusiastically. "Ah, I found it! And the battery is still working," she said with a smile and joined him at the top of the stairs with a big hug of excitement.

As they walked down the stairs together Sara put the watch on her wrist and announced, "I have exactly six days to prepare our Thanksgiving feast."

"What's this Thanksgiving feast you're talking about?" he asked by the time they reached their rocking chairs.

Stunned, she looked at him and asked, "What, you don't celebrate Thanksgiving?"

"We have days set aside for thanksgiving; they are days for prayer and fasting. I've never heard about a thanksgiving feast, so why don't you tell me about it," he asked curiously.

"When the pilgrims first came to America they were really struggling and the Indians helped them plant crops and hunt, and when it was harvest time they all gathered together and gave thanks and shared a meal, and it has become a tradition in my time at least. We celebrate it the fourth Thursday of every November and families and friends come together to give thanks to God and have a special meal together. It's a really big holiday. Most people don't even have to go to work on that day," she exclaimed excitedly.

Nathan was amused watching her happily telling him about a holiday he had never heard about celebrated that way, especially if this holiday would keep her busy and her mind off of recent events. The trauma of having killed a man was causing nightmares. She woke screaming out, and often cried herself to sleep in his arms.

"So what do you normally eat on your Thanksgiving holiday?" he asked.

"Well my family usually has: turkey with stuffing, cranberry sauce, mashed potatoes, green bean casserole with onion rings, corn, carrots, steamed mashed turnips sometimes, pumpkin pie, and sparkling grape juice or iced tea to drink. Oh, and if you have guests over they usually bring a dish of something special they like," she replied picturing each dish in her mind.

"And you eat all that food at one meal?" he asked in amazement.

"Uh-huh, and then most men sit down and watch football while the women clean up all the dishes and put all the leftover food away. It usually takes us two or three days just to eat all the leftover food. Doesn't that sound like fun?" she asked excitedly.

Nathan was trying to imagine all that food at one table, and was afraid to ask what football was, but figured it was some kind of sport.

"Are there wild turkeys around here?" she asked as she helped him take his shirt off then unraveled the gauze from around his shoulder.

"I come across some every now and then, why?" he asked.

"We'll need one for our Thanksgiving meal and then I'll have to figure out how to cook it," she said staring off into space.

"Hey, would you mind concentrating on what you're doing. That hurts!" he declared.

Sara quickly looked down at his shoulder and noticed that the gauze had been stuck to the wound that was still fresh and sensitive, "Oh Nathan, I'm sorry. Please forgive me," she said aghast.

He saw how upset she was that she might have hurt him and could have kicked himself. She had been truly happy for the first time since the incident with the four men, and he robbed her of it over something that barely hurt.

He gently took her by the arm and pulled her down on his lap. "There's nothing to forgive; it barely hurt at all. I'm the one that needs forgiving for making a fuss over nothing. Will you forgive me?" he asked repentantly.

"I already have, my love. But I am sorry for being careless. Now let me take a look at your shoulder," she replied.

Sara looked carefully at the wound and didn't see any signs of infection, and it was beginning to heal over. She applied another coating of ointment and a fresh gauze bandage and no longer thought about the turkey. He rarely had his shirt off at this time of year and his broad shoulders and muscular chest and arms caught her undivided attention. She sat back down on his lap and gently ran the fingers of her hand through the hair on his firm broad chest and smiled.

"I shall never get tired of doing this," she said emphatically.

He placed his hand over hers and looking into her eyes said, "And I will never get tired of the way you look at me while you're doing it."

Sara reluctantly pulled her hand back. "I'd better help you get your shirt back on or we'll be here the rest of the day," she said with a mischievous smile.

She went to the front window and looked out at the snow that was covering the ground and watched the tree branches in the distance swaying in the breeze and wished that it had been a nicer day outside; she would have loved to go for a ride.

As she stood looking out the window she asked, "Do you think Inola would be able to join us for Thanksgiving?"

"He's at their winter camp right now, and their chief is not fond of the white man showing up uninvited and unannounced," he stated as he joined her at the window.

"That's a shame. I would have enjoyed having him as our guest," she said with a sigh.

Chapter 34

The wind had stopped blowing overnight and the sun was shining brightly that next morning and both Nathan and Sara had a touch of cabin fever.

"Why don't you put on your skirt and blouse and heavy coat so we can take a ride and get out of the house for a while? I don't want to take a chance that anyone might see you in the clothes you wear around the house. Just put your firearm in your skirt pocket. If you feed the chickens while I go check my traps for some game we can get out of here pretty soon," he announced with a smile.

"That would be wonderful. Maybe we will even come across a flock of wild turkeys!" she stated smiling back at him.

"Maybe. I'll be back soon and meet you out at the barn," he said and took his hat off the peg and started for the barn to get their horses saddled and check his traps.

Even though Sara hated wearing a dress with all the petticoats and stockings she quickly dressed; happy to get out of the house and took a small bucket full of feed to the barn. As she was feeding the chickens and gathering their eggs she heard a horse outside and thought that Nathan had returned and set the basket down on a bale of hay and went to turn around.

"I'll put the eggs in the house when we return," she said as she turned expecting to see Nathan.

Instead, there stood a man in his forties that reeked from filth; wearing tanned animal skins for britches and knee-high moccasins and a dirty shirt with a heavy fir lined coat and broad-brimmed hat. He was staring at her in a way that made her skin crawl as he scratched his long thick beard with his filthy hand.

"Well, looky what we have here. Aren't you a pretty little thing? Where's your old man?" he asked and spit tobacco on the ground and moved closer to her.

About that time his partner entered the barn. "No one's at the house, Marty. What do ye want to do?" he asked before he ever caught a glimpse of Sara.

Sara's heart was racing as she backed up against the bales of hay trembling and reached into the pocket of her skirt and prayed desperately that Nathan would return. This man had surprised her and was already too close to pull a gun on him. He could have easily taken hold of it before she had a chance to shoot him.

"Maybe she doesn't have an old man. Maybe she's here all alone and in need of a little company. How about it? There's some nice straw here, and I'll even take my time if you like," he said with a tobacco stained smile and a few missing teeth. "Jack, why don't you watch outside and when I'm finished you can have a poke at her."

Sara's fear turned to anger that consumed her and she yelled, "Get out of here...NOW! If my husband catches you he'll kill you both!" Marty took a step towards her and she swung her fist as hard as she could hoping to catch him in the throat, but he managed to roughly grab hold of it and twist it behind her back. "You're a feisty one. I like that," he said and moved even closer and ran his dirty hand along her cheek as he smiled wickedly then lowered it to raise her skirt.

"I don't think he'll be wanting to sell ye anything if ye mess with his woman," Jack anxiously stated.

"Just do what I told you. We'll take what we need when I'm finished. Now get!" Marty said as his hand ran along her now tense thigh. Sara kneed him hard in the groin, and when he went to stand up straight, his face contorted with pain and anger and he snarled, "You shouldn't have done that bitch," and raised his hand slapping her hard across the mouth.

Meanwhile Nathan was approaching through the apple orchard and noticed the horses and mule tied outside his house and pulled his pistol from his belt and cocked the hammer as he gave his horse a quick kick in the side.

Jack stepped outside the barn and hollered at Marty, "Rider coming in fast. Ye better get out here."

Before Jack could finish warning his partner, Nathan halted his horse just short of Jack, slid off and held his pistol to the man's forehead all in a fluid motion.

"Howdy friend, there's no need to be pointing a pistol," Jack said nervously.

"I'm not your friend. Is there anyone else inside the barn?" he asked pushing the pistol a little harder against his forehead.

"Marty, come on out so we can buy some whiskey and be on our way," Jack called out nervously.

"Come out with your hands up," Nathan yelled out as he backed the man up so he could see in the barn still holding the pistol to the man's head.

Sara gasped in relief when she saw Nathan and exhaled trembling while leaning against the bales of hay relieved that her terror would soon be over.

"Sara are you alright?" he called out looking beyond the man held at gunpoint.

Sara nodded then replied, "Yes, I'm alright," then rubbed her cheek and hoped that the slap had not left a red mark on her face.

"Stay where you are until Marty comes outside." Nathan firmly directed.

"Mister, can't ye lower your pistol? We was just hopen to buy some whiskey from ye before we headed up into them mountains, and maybe some grub if ye can spare it," Jack meekly stated and swallowed hard as he held his hands in the air.

Nathan reached and jerked Jack's pistol from his belt and cocked it and took a step back where he could aim at both men. Marty looked into her eyes with disdain and released his grip on her wrist and slowly turned and started walking out of the barn with his hands up in the air.

"Sara, you can come out now," he called.

Sara shook violently, unable to relax and catch her breath before joining Nathan outside. She was afraid of what he might do to the men if he found out that one of them had touched her and intended to rape her. There had been enough killing already and she was not eager to see more bloodshed on their land and had to decide quickly what she would tell Nathan when he asked what happened.

Nathan noticed immediately that she was still trembling when she passed by the men and hurried to stand behind him.

He burned with anger as he grit his teeth and asked her, "Did these men so much as lay a finger on you?"

"We were only asking to buy whiskey..." Jack tried to explain.

"Shut up! I wasn't talking to you," he yelled then continued, "Sara, did these men touch you?" he asked glaring disdainfully at the two men.

She had seen that piercing stare of his and his tightly clinched jaw and it always lead to the death of someone. She just wanted the men to go and never see them again. She swallowed hard for the lump in her throat seemed as big as a ripe apple.

"No, they just caught me off guard and startled me when I turned and saw them standing behind me. I thought it was your horse I heard and expected to see you when I turned around. I was just frightened being alone with them," she said hoping that he would believe her and not press the issue.

He glanced at her still trembling and knew there was more to the story than what she was telling him and glanced at the man's pants to see if anything was out of order.

"Let me make this clear to both of you. There is not a drop of whiskey here and we have just enough food to get us through the winter. You both look like able bodied men quite capable of trapping your own food so I suggest you get to it before I change my mind and blow your heads off. If I so much as ever see your face again anywhere close to here I will kill you. Do I make myself clear?" he disdainfully snarled.

"You're not very charitable are you?" Marty stated with a sneer, and Nathan struck him hard across his face with his pistol knocking him to the ground. Marty stood up spitting out blood and wiped his mouth on his dirty shirt sleeve as he glared at Nathan.

"I should think you would find me very charitable. I didn't blow your head off for assaulting my wife, now start moving towards your horses," he said motioning with the pistols.

The two men finally mounted and rode off through the apple orchard headed for the mountains, and Sara stood with her arms tightly wrapped around Nathan until she saw them ride out of sight.

Nathan could tell by the way Sara was still trembling that she had not told him everything. If there was one thing he understood it was the character of men, and especially men such as these that had not been around women for some time. He knew one as beautiful as Sara would have been too much of a temptation to pass up. This incident was the last straw. He made up his mind to send Sara back to her time, even though he knew that his heart, mind, and soul would never recover. It angered him that this was the choice he was forced to make. Men would always want Sara. What was he going to do kill every man he saw, and what about those that got past him like the men today?

He stood there and held her tightly as he thought, and when he had decided on what he was going to do he led her back into the house and sat with her on the couch until her trembling stopped.

He gave her a kiss on the forehead and calmly stated as he stood, "I'm going to go take care of the horses and then I'll be back and we can talk."

As Nathan closed the door Sara wondered what he wanted to talk about – was it about the incident, or whether they had seen her firearm, or just talk in general, or was this the last straw and he wanted her to return to her own time? In the blink of an eye fear suddenly gripped her mind and heart, and she dreaded his return and stared at the fire totally shutting down all thought and emotion.

Meanwhile, Nathan was in the barn unsaddling the horses already having second thoughts about his decision to ask Sara to return to her own time. He sat on a bale of hay and stared in the direction of the house as the battle raged in his mind. In the short amount of time that she had been with him she was attacked by Indians, shot and killed a man, and now he suspected that Marty had attempted to rape her. If he truly loved her then he would have to pay the ultimate sacrifice and return her to where she would be safe. In time she would move on with her life just like she did when her first husband died; at least that is what he told himself.

He figured he would hold off until tomorrow to tell her of his decision. Today he would hold her in his arms, and feel the softness of her skin and the smell of her hair, and lock them tightly in his mind for that was all he would have left was memories of her, and they would have to last him a life time. He slowly walked back to the house and took a deep breath before he opened the door.

Sara did not even turn around when he entered the room but continued to stare mindlessly at the fire. Nathan reached down and took her by the hand and lovingly said, "Come sit with me."

Sara went with him and sat on his lap and Nathan just held her as he rocked in the chair. As she laid against him and rested her head on his shoulder he could feel her body relax and she seemed to be at peace, and once again questioned his decision. They sat there together like that for over an hour and Sara was still wondering what he had wanted to talk to her about. But maybe it was nothing special because he hadn't said a word and her fears subsided.

"Sara, I need to go skin those rabbits if we're going to have them for supper. Do you want me to roast them or would you prefer making a stew?"

"I'll make a stew. I'll get things ready while you're gone," she said and allowed herself to smile thinking things would be fine between them.

Later that night when they were undressing for bed, Nathan came up behind her and wrapped his arms around her.

"Let's not dress tonight for bed. The fire will last until morning," he said as he gazed at her with hungry eyes and watched for the goose bumps.

Sara smiled as she crawled into bed and knew that they would not be falling asleep anytime soon. Nathan took his time wanting to remember the smell of her hair, the softness of her skin, the desire in her eyes, as his hands and mouth vigorously caressed over her body. She moaned in pleasure as her own hands and mouth felt the firmness of his muscular body. He took his time as their bodies entwined pacing himself to make it last as long as possible knowing this could be the last time he ever made love to her.

Chapter 35

There was a smile on Sara's face when she opened her eyes in the morning, content that everything was fine between them. As she watched Nathan dress she could only think of her love for him and how special she wanted to make Thanksgiving and Christmas for him.

Seeing how happy she was, Nathan decided to have his talk with her after they had breakfast and went to start the fire in the hearth while Sara washed and dressed. Before Sara emerged from the room Nathan came up with a compromise plan to ask her to return to her own time. He figured if he suggested she return for a visit she would see how much she was giving up and her parents would convince her to stay once they found out all that she had been through. He just couldn't bring himself to tell her that he wanted her to return and stay for her own good, especially not after the night he had just spent with her. He thought himself selfish and cowardly for wanting to keep Sara for himself which bothered him greatly, because he was anything but cowardly in the war. He fought for five years against the British and battles with the Indians. But with Sara it was different. He knew that her leaving would be the end of him. How could he be in a house where he no longer heard the sound of her laughter, or in his bed without her warm body next to him, and how could he sit by a fire and not see the glow on her face? Yes, he was a coward, afraid of what he would become without her, for how does someone live without their soul mate?

After breakfast Nathan noticed that the sun was shining brightly again that day and suggested they sit out on the porch with their coffee. Sara put her coat on and refilled their coffee cups as Nathan grabbed his hat and coat and opened the door for her. It took him several minutes to get up the nerve to mention returning to her own time because he was somewhat unsure how she would respond to it.

"Sara, I was thinking that it might be nice for you to go visit your family and that way you could bring back with you the things you still wanted. You might enjoy the peace and quiet of your time. You have to admit it would be a pleasant change from what you've been through lately," he anxiously suggested.

Sara could not believe what she was hearing and she seemed to just stop breathing. Was this his way of getting rid of her, she questioned as fear crept into her mind. Was she too much trouble having around? She knew he loved her as much as she loved him, but never in her wildest dreams did she ever think that he would ask her to return to her own time. The thought of returning to her time had crossed her mind in order to do just the things he had suggested, but thought that he would never allow it, or at least put up a good fight about it.

Nathan could see the wheels of her mind turning as she eyed him suspiciously. He thought she would have jumped at the suggestion to return home for a visit, but what he was seeing was resistance and suspicion.

"What would make you suggest this? I thought it was already clear that I had chosen to be with you. Remember, we just got through promising to never forsake each other as long as we both shall live. And besides, you know I left on terrible terms with my parents, and now you want me to return?" she asked still eyeing him suspiciously.

"It was just a suggestion. I thought you would be happy about it," he replied as calmly as he could.

She knew he was not being honest about his intentions; there was more to this than he was letting on. There was only one way to find out – press the issue and tell him she didn't want to go.

"Well, I'm not happy about it and I don't want to go," she said forcefully.

Nathan did not know what to think. Should he press the issue or not? Sara could be very strong-willed and stubborn when she wanted to be. This was not an issue about what he wanted to do, but about what was best for her – he would press the issue.

"Sara you're being irrational. I think at this time it's best for you to return to what is familiar to you and take the time to sort out your thoughts and feelings. You've been through a lot, and after you've had time to think things through and you still want to return, I'll welcome you back with open arms."

"I'm not going and that's final, and you can't make me! And you know you can't make me. It's my choice whether I leave through your attic," she yelled in a rage that was driven by fear that he no longer wanted her.

Nathan was now worked up and she could see fire in his eyes, and she knew he could make it hard on her if he chose to do so.

"I thought you loved me! That you couldn't live without me! Was that a lie just so you could sleep with me?" she asked knowing that it was a mistake before the words had finished leaving her mouth.

"You are one crazy woman! Do as you please," he said and stormed off the porch and headed for the barn.

Sara sat down and cried out of anger, frustration and fear. All she wanted to hear from him was that he loved her and didn't want her to go, but thought that just a short visit might be good for her and set a time for when he wanted her to return. A few minutes later she saw Nathan ride away at a gallop and threw her full cup of coffee off the porch and went inside and slammed the door.

She was furious as she sat by the fire. Her argument with Nathan played over and over again in her mind. She remembered how he had begged her to choose him and his time when she had returned looking for her necklace, and now he was suggesting that she return to her own time. The longer she thought about it her anger slowly changed to having her feelings hurt and her tears now were ones of broken heartedness instead of anger. She went and stood looking out the window that faced the barn in the hopes that Nathan would soon return and he could explain his reasons for wanting her to return to her time more fully to her. Better yet, she thought, he could beg her to stay with him once more. If she left to return home for a visit she wanted it to be her idea for she knew she would always return to him.

Sara finally decided that it would probably take Nathan hours to cool down, and had probably gone to his favorite spot along the river. If he was going to be gone for hours she saw no reason why she shouldn't take a walk along the little stream that ran not too far from their house. She had dressed in her skirt and blouse today thinking they might go for a ride together and didn't feel like changing back into her own comfortable clothing, and just put her firearm in her skirt pocket and headed out the back door. The stream was only about a half mile from the back of their apple orchard and it didn't take her long to get there. The sun felt good coming through the bare branches of the trees and she looked upstream and saw a pretty spot where she could sit down and do a little cooling off herself.

Sara loved to watch the clear water splash and tumble over the rocks as she walked along the bank of the stream. Not paying attention to the uneven ground she tripped over a rock jetting up through the soil and landed hard upon her hands and knees; half in and half out of the water and struggled to stand up under the weight of her wet skirt and petticoats.

"Great, just great. Now I have to sit in wet clothes. What else can go wrong today?" she cried out loud to herself.

She looked back behind her and considered returning to the house to change her clothes, but decided she had come this far and would press on to the spot where she had wanted to sit. She spread her skirt out on the dry rocks in the hope they would dry more quickly and leaned back against her extended arms and lifted her face to the sun. Her only thoughts now were about how she was going to make up with Nathan; this had been their first fight and she hoped their last.

Chapter 36

She hadn't been sitting there very long when she heard a horse nicker behind her and thought that Nathan had come looking for her. Before she could turn around she was aware that there was more than one horse she heard and quickly reached for her loaded handgun. Sara sat there stunned after reaching into her skirt pocket and couldn't find her weapon, and realized that it must have fallen from her pocket when she fell into the stream. She quickly turned her head to see who was coming up behind her and immediately started screaming out Nathan's name in shear panic.

She was terrified to see a line of Shawnee hunters with their painted faces and horses stopped along the bank just staring at her until she screamed. She watched as they looked around to see if anyone would come in response to her calls for help, and then two of them quickly charged towards her on horseback. Lifting her skirt far enough to where she wouldn't trip over the hem she jumped from the rock she was sitting on and started running along the bank screaming for Nathan. She could hear the horse's hooves splashing in the water close to her and the sound of their panting as they moved even closer. But, she never heard their riders slide off their horses, and before she could scream again she was grabbed from behind. As she struggled to be free she felt his hand tightly cover her mouth while the other one tied her hands in front of her and slipped a leather rope around it.

Her eyes were wide with terror as she stared into the painted face of her captor as he put a leather strap in her mouth and tied it behind her head so that she could no longer scream and went to retrieve their horses. She shook as she watched him walk towards her leading the horses in his moccasins, deerskin loincloth, leggings, and fringed tunic and realized she would never see Nathan again. Sure that he would think she had returned to her own time, she regretted not having left him a note saying that she had decided to take a walk by the stream. Now, all hope was gone that he would ever come to this very spot looking for her.

There were seven Shawnee in the hunting party and two of them had a deer slung over their horses and quickly rode ahead of the one pulling Sara behind his horse with the leather rope tied around her wrists as she struggled to keep up. She lost her balance on the uneven and slippery stones and fell face forward into the icy water gasping for air and choked up water as they crossed the stream and headed north towards the mountains whose peaks were covered in snow. Sara was panting heavily as they moved higher up the mountain range and fell repeatedly cutting and bruising herself as she climbed the steep and often rocky slopes in her wet and heavy clothing, and feared she would die before nightfall from exhaustion and hypothermia.

She tried to keep her wits about her and intentionally broke branches along the way hoping against all odds that Nathan would come searching for her. She dug her boots deep in the soil when her captors would stop occasionally to let her get her footing and hoped that the boot prints wouldn't be washed away by the rains or melting snow. As they continued to climb ever higher, Sara's muscles trembled from fatigue and her only dress was torn, dirty, and wet, and she was chilled to the bone.

Meanwhile Nathan had time to cool down and came riding through the apple orchid anxious to make things right with Sara. He headed straight for the barn to unsaddle his horse and give it feed and wondered if Sara had had enough time to calm down to where he could explain his reasoning behind suggesting she return to her own time. He thought about what he would say to her as he walked towards the house. He hated to admit that Sara was right; he had just made a promise to never leave her as long as he was alive. He hesitated just before opening the door for swallowing his pride never came easy to him.

As he crossed the threshold he hung his hat on the peg and called out, "Sara," as he glanced around the room. When she didn't answer he opened the bedroom door and called her name again and his brow quickly furrowed as he darted up the steps to the attic and glanced around and found nothing missing from the supplies she had brought back with her; even her backpack was there. His heart was pounding as he ran down the stairs and checked every table and the fireplace mantle looking for a note she might have left, and finding none he started to panic as fear crept into his mind. He hurried out the back door and cupped his hands around his mouth and called her name repeatedly with all his might in every direction, and listened intently for any distant response.

He was breathing heavily now and fought to keep the thoughts that she had actually been angry enough to return to her own time out of his mind, and regretted the things he had said to her in his anger. He had no choice but to sit and wait for her to return. As the daylight was fading he went and stood by the front window looking out over the hill in front of his house and wondered if Sara had crossed over and was just sitting on the hillside thinking. He prayed she would decide to come home before it was dark – surely she couldn't have been that angry with him.

Nathan was beside himself now with worry and knew that there could only be one explanation for why she didn't come home – Sara had chosen to return to her own time. He had pushed too hard, and once again had failed to tell her how he truly felt and the reasons why he suggested she return for her own safety.

As he sat by the fire he was overwhelmed with the feeling of loss, and a deep depression swept over him as he was faced with a life without Sara. He knew that his memories of her would only torment and remind him of what he had given up instead of comforting him. He broke a promise that he made to himself after the war that he would never drink again, and went to the pantry and found his only bottle of whiskey that was stashed out of sight in the far back corner. Nathan grabbed it and headed back to his rocking chair determined to rid himself, if only for a night, of his pain that was now agonizing.

As he sat by the warmth of the fire he drank his whiskey from the bottle until his mind was numb and he passed out in the comfort of his chair; while Sara was sitting on the cold hard ground tied to a tree exhausted from being pulled and sometimes dragged behind a horse for hours. She was numb from sitting in wet clothes in the cold and her mind thought of only one thing; this was all her fault. If only she hadn't provoked Nathan to anger, but had talked to him calmly about why he wanted her to return to her time he never would have ridden off, and she never would have gone down to the stream. She asked herself what would have happened if she hadn't screamed out for Nathan and just sat there quietly and still. Would they have just passed by; they were only hunting for food. Had they taken her only to keep her quiet and not draw attention to themselves? These thoughts tormented her as she watched her captors make camp for the night. When they were not looking at her, she watched as they sat by the warm fire eating their jerky, and longed for the warmth they were now enjoying.

She shifted her legs to the side of her and slowly raised her torn skirt up to her knees and wanted to cry out in pain as she looked at her dirty, bruised, cut and bleeding legs, but refused to let them see her cry. She would not give them that satisfaction no matter how much she hurt, or how hungry and cold she was – she refused to let them break her.

Sara noticed one of them seemed to be their leader, because when he spoke they listened and did what he said. She glanced at him often until she saw him look at her, then lowered her head and looked at the ground. She heard this man being called Tecumseh and wondered what it meant, but knew that it was important to stay on this Shawnee's good side.

When Tecumseh was through eating he stood and walked briskly over to her and knelt down on one knee and placed his hand under her chin and raised her head and held it there until Sara looked up at him. He studied her face after brushing her wet hair aside and looked into her eyes that were filled with anger and disdain for what seemed like the longest time, then reached behind her head and untied the gag that was in her mouth. He waited a few seconds to see what she would do, and when she sat there silently lowering her gaze to the ground he untied her from the tree and took her by her upper arm and stood her to her feet. He held her arm tightly and led her limping to their fire and said something sternly to the men sitting there. Sara watched as two of them quickly moved and made room for her to sit next to him.

She closed her eyes as she felt the warmth of the fire, and in her mind she thought of a popsicle melting on a hot summer day, for that was the way she now felt. She didn't open her eyes until she was roughly nudged and offered a piece of jerky which she quickly took with her hands still tied together, and took a mouthful and pulled hard to tear a piece free and chewed it savoring every bite for she had not eaten since morning.

When the men laid down for the night, Tecumseh went and pulled a blanket from his horse and stood over Sara and uttered a few strange words to her. She looked up at him trying not to show her disdain. He stood there looking down at her intently, and it seemed like she could read his mind – I'll give you this blanket, but if you try to run it will be the last time I do so. Sara nodded her head and gratefully took the blanket and laid down where she had been sitting and was asleep almost before her head hit the ground.

Nathan had a pounding headache when he woke and groaned as he sat up from his slumped over position. His stomach burned like fire from the whiskey he drank on an empty stomach last night, and he sat there lifeless not wanting to move, not even for food, for his mind and heart felt as sick as his stomach.

Eventually he went and sat on the front porch wishing he had more whiskey to deaden the pain as he stared at the hill in front of him. Why had he been so foolish to suggest she return to her time? This was all his fault; he had everything his heart had ever desired. Sara came willingly, and then he let her go in a fit of anger. If only he could cross through time he would search for Sara and beg for her forgiveness and promise he would never let her out of his arms again.

In the following days after his mundane chores of feeding the animals, chopping the wood, and preparing his food, he would sit entrenched in dark depression on the front porch staring at the hill in front of him. When it turned dark he hung his head as his heartache grew a little deeper for he knew she wouldn't be coming home – not in the dark. He neither shaved nor washed himself or his clothes for he had no reason to do so in his current state of mind. The memories of Sara that he thought he would cherish if he knew she was safe and happy were ever in his thoughts, but they were torments to him instead of comfort. Nights were always worse as he sat alone in silence by the fire, and chose to sleep in his chair because it was unbearable to sleep in his bed without Sara lying next to him.

After many long days of being pulled behind Tecumseh's horse she finally caught site of the Shawnee village ahead and it was nothing like she thought it would be. She had seen too many westerns on TV where the different tribes lived in Teepees, but the

Shawnees lived in wigwams made of wooden frames wrapped in birch bark and tied down with strips of wood.

Tecumseh rode arrogantly into the village pulling Sara behind his horse as the villagers came out to welcome their hunters back home with their horses laden with deer, and wild turkeys. She felt humiliated being paraded through the village like a dirty, torn ragdoll; being stared at as they hurled angry words at her. She was uncertain what awaited her when Tecumseh led her into his wigwam; she only knew that it wouldn't be pleasant.

He spoke harshly and motioned with his hand that she was to stay inside and then quickly turned and left. It wasn't long before two older women entered the wigwam and each grabbed an arm and pulled her roughly outside and took her to the sweathouse and poured water over the hot rocks. At first it felt wonderful to feel warm after being so cold, but soon the steam seemed insufferable in her skirt and heavy petticoats and she felt lightheaded from dehydration and became frantic to leave the place. They took her from there straight to the river and after removing her dirty and torn clothing they made her bathe in the icy river water as they stood on the shore and laughed as she gasped in pain for it felt like a thousand knives stabbing her. Other women joined and stood around her as she quickly waded humiliated from the water naked and shivering and watched as she dressed in a long shirt, moccasins, and poncho all made from deerskins. When she was finished dressing one of the older women shoved her, yelling harshly at her and pointed in the direction of Tecumseh's lodge. She was more than happy to return to it, for it meant that she could warm herself by the fire and escape the stares and laughter of the women who gleefully taunted her.

Sara sat shaking next to the fire, not from the cold but from fear of what kind of life lie before her, and anger at herself for being so foolish in the way she spoke to Nathan. Hours later, Tecumseh entered the dwelling and sat by the fire looking at Sara curiously and glanced away as a young woman came in and prepared his meal and left enough for Sara to eat after he was finished. She kept her eyes lowered while he ate and wished that he would hurry, because she was starving and would happily eat anything put in front of her. When she was finished, Tecumseh motioned for Sara to stand up. He stood before her and looked into her rebellious eyes as if he was sizing up what kind of a woman she was, and then slowly looked her over in a way that made her uncomfortable. She had seen that look in many a man's eyes and knew exactly what he was thinking, and then he ran his fingers through her long blonde hair and felt its soft texture and looked once again into her eyes. When he was finished looking her over he spoke arrogantly to her and pointed to a few blankets where she could sleep for the night. He watched as Sara laid down trying to muffle her groans of pain while she turned her back to him, then returned to his own blanket and animal skins. As Sara laid there she wondered why he had not forced himself upon her; there was nothing she could have done to stop him. She would later learn from one of the other captive women that Tecumseh was in mourning for his wife, and tribal law would forbid him to take her as his wife until the set grieving period was over.

The next morning before it was even light outside a woman came in and shook her shoulder and motioned for her to come with her and quickly led her outside. She handed Sara a large woven basket and led her to a large pile of wood and gestured for her to fill the basket. She pulled her roughly by her arm to the first wigwam, and motioned for her to place some of the wood by the door. When she bent over with the heavy basket several pieces of wood fell out making noise, and the woman quickly snatched her by the hair and jerked her head back as she put her finger to her lips, and then pushed her in the direction of the next dwelling. Sara caught on quickly what she was supposed to do, and pulled her arm away from the woman before she could grab it again. She made many trips back to the woodpile until every dwelling had wood stacked outside their door. It was light out when Sara was finally able to return to Tecumseh's lodging and found some cold stew in a small wooden bowl and quickly ate it with her fingers, and wondered what she would be forced to do next.

Chapter 37

Nathan was on his front porch when he heard the braying of a mule and got up to see who was headed his way. It was a trapper passing through and probably wanted to trade some hides for food or whiskey.

"Howdy," the old man said with a smile as he got down from his horse and stretched.

"Howdy, what can I do for you?" Nathan asked.

"Got any whiskey?" he replied scratching his beard.

"Nope. Drank the last of it a couple of weeks ago."

"Well, how about any tobacco?"

"Yeah, I have a little tobacco out in the barn," Nathan said and looked curiously at what was in the man's belt that was partially covered by his coat.

"What's that in your belt?" he curiously asked.

"Oh, I found this by the stream when I went to water my animals. Thought it looked somewhat like a firearm with the trigger and barrel, and all, but there's no place to put any gun powder. I just kept it because I've never seen anything like it," he said as he scratched his beard once again.

"Can I take a look at it?" Nathan asked holding out his hand.

"Sure," the man said and handed it to him.

Nathan's heart started to race and he found it hard to swallow as he looked down at Sara's firearm in his hand.

"Where did you say you found this?" he asked anxiously.

"Oh, I would say it was about a mile or so upstream from here. You act like you might have seen it before. I don't suppose you would like to trade some tobacco for it and maybe a slab of bacon?" the man asked hoping to make a trade.

"Sure, I'll trade, but only if you show me exactly where you found this."

"Well, I hate to have to backtrack, but I suppose if you give me the tobacco and bacon now I could head out that way."

"You've got yourself a deal. I'll be right back with both," Nathan said and took off running to the barn for the tobacco and his horse and then quickly fetched the bacon he had promised the man.

Nathan packed Sara's firearm in his saddlebag and mounted quickly. "Okay, now lead the way," he said and dared to allow hope to fill his mind and heart.

The old trapper climbed back up on his horse and called for "Old Sally" his mule to come along and started off in the direction of the stream.

When they reached the spot where he found Sara's weapon they dismounted and the old trapper showed him exactly where it lay when he found it. Nathan thanked him and when the man mounted his horse, he told Nathan that he hoped he'd find what he was looking for and started across the stream headed for the mountains.

Nathan squatted down and looked for signs that Sara had been there and noticed what he believed was a partial hand print in the muddy bank. He walked upstream a bit and found a few footprints here and there and a couple of spots that looked like something was drug across the bank; maybe her skirt he thought.

He felt a sudden tightening of his stomach and chest as he comprehended that Sara had not crossed back over to her time but had come to the stream for some reason; maybe to cool off as he had done. But what happened to her? He spotted the rocks up ahead and remembered how she loved to sit on the rocks to watch the stream rushing by and headed for them. Before he reached the spot he saw horse tracks and partial footprints along the bank and then they disappeared heading across the stream. Nathan felt lightheaded as the blood rushed from his head and he dropped to one knee as he realized Sara had been captured, but by whom? He swallowed hard and made himself look at the horse tracks and found that the ponies had not been shod that took Sara away; they belonged to Indians, but which ones.

Nathan's heart sank for he knew what that would mean for her, and fear now consumed his mind as she had already been gone for weeks. He mounted his horse and crossed the stream and looked up and down the bank until he found the place where the horses came out of the water and followed them looking for any sign that Sara was indeed with them. He stopped and dismounted while he followed the tracks on foot until he came to a spot where he found Sara's footprints mixed in with the horse tracks and knew that she was being led away on foot. From the direction the tracks were leading, Nathan thought it might have been a Shawnee hunting party that came across her sitting there on the rocks and had taken her back to their village.

When his mind cleared enough to think straight, his first thought was that he needed Inola to help him follow the tracks and to find out what the Shawnee might be willing to trade for her. He would give them anything they asked for, and would move heaven and hell to get her back. But he feared what Sara would be like when he found her.

Nathan returned home and packed supplies for his trip to the Cherokee's winter camp and prayed that Inola would be there when he arrived unannounced. It took him two days to find their camp and when he rode in the children ran to their huts as the men just stood and watched him ride by knowing he was a friend of Inola's.

"Inola" Nathan hollered out and looked around for him and called out a second time.

Inola soon emerged from his dwelling and Nathan rode up to him and quickly dismounted.

"Inola, Sara's been captured by the Shawnee," he said franticly.

"Come inside my friend," Inola said and led the way.

As they entered a young maiden was placing wood by the fire and quickly went to leave before they were seated. Nathan noticed that Inola smiled as she passed by and said in Cherokee, "She's very pretty and I can tell that you think so as well."

"Her name is Adsila – Blossom, and I will marry her when she is of age this spring," he said and gestured for Nathan to sit down.

When they were seated Inola announced, "A couple of weeks ago one of our hunting parties saw some Shawnee headed up into the mountains north of you and they were pulling someone behind them. They did not get close enough to see if it was a man or woman. They kept their distance and let them go their way for it was none of their business. Is this why you smell, my friend, and have not shaven?"

Nathan leaned his head close to his arm and stated, "It is pretty bad, isn't it?" he said making a face and continued. "Inola, will you help me find Sara? And do you think they would be willing to trade her for?" he asked anxiously.

"I think you would be dead before you could find that out. Shawnee not like white man in their villages nor the Cherokee," Inola replied.

"Who could I get to make the trade for me?" he asked desperately.

Inola looked away while he thought. "There is a young man in camp that came to us from the Shawnee when we found him alone in the hills after his parents were killed. I don't know how much of the Shawnee tongue he remembers, but we can ask."

"Would you see if he would be willing to go with us?" Nathan asked anxiously.

"Stay here, and I will bring boy here," Inola said and went outside to find him.

Minutes later Inola returned with the young man, now about fifteen years old. Inola sat next to Nathan on the floor and explained the situation to the young man as he stared at Nathan while Inola spoke.

Since Nathan understood the Cherokee language he learned that the young man remembered many of the Shawnee words, but had not spoken them in many years. He was hesitant to go with them because he now dressed and looked like a Cherokee and knew that he would not be readily accepted by the Shawnee unless he could speak their language fluently.

Nathan persuaded the young man to go with them to make the trade for Sara by giving him a horse of his own; Sara's horse, for that was the only other horse he owned. After packing a few things, Inola mounted his horse and gave Adohi, (which means "woods" because that is where the Cherokee found him) a hand up to ride with him back to Nathan's house for supplies while they were searching for Sara.

Two days later they arrived early in the morning and Inola took Adohi into the barn and threw a blanket over Sara's horse and put a leather bit and reins on it for their journey while Nathan was packing supplies into every saddlebag he had. When he was finished packing he thought about how remote his chances were of ever getting Sara back, and the fact that he had nothing the Shawnee would except in trade weighed heavy on his mind. He took all the money he received for his pelts and put it in his money belt in the hopes he could buy what he needed for the trade, but knew that his chances of meeting anyone this far out in the wilderness was slim to none; but still he needed to be prepared for anything.

He went and stood by the fireplace and looked at Sara's empty rocking chair, and in his despair he dropped to his knees and turned to God.

"Dear God, I know that I am a sinful man and I deserve nothing from you, but I have no one else I can turn to, or that can help me. You alone can help me get my Sara back, so I ask you merciful God to supply what I am lacking, and guide me on this journey by your mercy and grace and fill me with your wisdom so that my efforts will succeed. Please God, please help me," he cried.

Inola entered the house through the back door wondering what was taking Nathan so long and saw him on his knees, and said nothing but waited for Nathan to stand up before he spoke.

"Adohi and I have left an ample supply of food for your animals, and we are ready to ride," Inola plainly stated.

Nathan wiped the tears from his eyes before he turned around. "I'm ready. Will you give me a hand with the saddlebags?"

They each threw one over their shoulder and carried them out to the horses and Nathan returned for the last one and took one last look across the room, and it seemed so empty and lifeless without Sara and closed the door behind him.

Nathan led them to where he had picked up the Shawnee's trail up the mountain and then Inola took the lead. The tracks were fairly easy to follow at first, but as they entered the steeper slopes of the forest the tracks were harder to follow. They often dismounted and searched the area separately until they heard someone call out, then quickly continued looking for the next sign of where to go. Adohi was good at spotting broken branches along the way and they continued on until they lost their light of day and made camp.

When they had finished eating and talking around the camp fire, Nathan spread out his bedroll and laid down staring up at the stars. He remembered his first night with Sara under the stars before they were married and closed his eyes and imagined her huddled close to him to keep warm. He could smell the scent of her hair and feel the curves of her body as he wrapped his arm across her, and for a few brief moments his mind found peace. But when he opened his eyes and looked back up at the stars, he wondered who was looking at them with her tonight, and he pulled his blanket up around him and tried to go to sleep.

The sky looked stormy in the morning and you could hear the rumbling of thunder in the distance as they quickly broke camp hoping to pick up the Shawnee's tracks once again before the rain or snow made it impossible. Nathan kept an eye on which direction the storm was heading and prayed that it would pass by them before the heavens released its downpour. They were fortunate that Adohi picked up the Shawnee trail so quickly and they followed the broken branches along the single file of horse tracks and rare footprints Sara had dug into the ground.

As the days passed Nathan grew more anxious about having nothing to trade for Sara and asked God to remember him and his prayer. They had already climbed one mountain in their search and were now in a valley letting their horses drink from a stream and eat a little grass while they grabbed some jerky to eat.

Nathan was discouraged as he stood by the stream wondering if he would ever find Sara, when suddenly he heard the sound of a horse nickering in the distance.

"Inola, did you hear that?" Nathan anxiously questioned.

"Yes, wait here. I will go," he replied and mounted his horse and rode in the direction of the sound they both heard.

Nathan was anxious waiting for Inola to return and asked Adohi if they should go check on him.

"No. Inola clever; he will return," Adohi assured him.

Nathan took a deep breath and decided to wait a little longer and continuously scanned the valley watching for him. It wasn't long before he saw Inola riding hard in their direction, and wondered what he had found, or who was chasing him.

Inola brought his horse to an abrupt stop in front of Nathan and excitedly stated, "Your God has heard you, come and see," he said with a smile.

Nathan smiled joyfully, and he and Adohi followed Inola a short distance through the valley and there just ahead was a wagon with two horses grazing on sparse patches of grass. Drawing nearer to the wagon Nathan saw its owner laying awkwardly on the seat and quickly dismounted and climbed into the wagon. There was no need to check on him, he had obviously been dead for days, and seeing no wounds Nathan assumed the man had suffered a heart attack.

"If we're going to take his wagon and team the least we can do is bury him," Nathan said and noticed the man's wide-brimmed hat lying on the floor of the wagon and picked it up. "I hope you don't mind if I take your hat as well," he said and jumped down from the wagon.

Inola and Adohi were untying the tarp that covered the back half of the wagon and when they pulled back the tarp Nathan's eyes widened in disbelief as he gazed upon a barrel of whiskey, blankets, pots and pans, tobacco, and sacks of corn seed. God had provided everything Nathan would need to get his precious Sara back from the Shawnee, if she was still alive.

By the time they buried the man it was too late in the day to continue their search and they made camp for the night by the stream. After starting a fire, Inola looked at Nathan and boldly stated, "My friend, don't you think it's time to take a bath and wash your clothes. We can hardly stand you. How do you think Sara will feel when she gets a good whiff of you and your dirty clothing?"

Nathan just smiled at him and headed for the stream with a blanket and a bar of soap and jumped in clothes and all. When he had finished washing himself and his clothes he wrapped his blanket around him and hung his clothes over a make-shift clothesline close to the fire to dry.

He sat wet and shivering next to the fire as they ate their jerky and a few apples, then refilled their coffee cups as they discussed how they were going to continue their search. It would be difficult and slow to drive the wagon through the forest and mountains looking for the village, so it was decided that Nathan would stay with the wagon in the valley while Inola and Adohi continued the search, and when they located the village they would return for him.

That night when Nathan's clothes were finally dry he dressed and laid down on his bedroll looking at the stars and thanked God for answering his prayer. He was sorry that a man had died, but was grateful just the same that everything he needed was provided, and hoped that the Shawnee would be willing to trade with them. He rolled onto his side and stared into the fire and thought about Sara and what she must be going through. His heart ached thinking about how frightened she must be, and wondered if she had been strong enough to endure the cold and hunger, and being forced to walk all that distance along the steep and treacherous trail to their village. It was very late when he uttered one last prayer for Sara and finally closed his eyes.

Chapter 38

Right after a quick breakfast Inola and Adohi headed out to search for the Shawnee village. They were gone for two days before they heard the sound of dogs barking in the distance and knew that they were close to finding the village. They quietly jumped down from their horses and led them cautiously in the direction of the barking and kept alert knowing that guards could be posted around the edge of the village. A short time later they tied their horses to a tree and continued on foot until they saw the smoke rising from their lodgings in the valley below.

As they slowly moved closer they stood behind a large Pine tree on a small hill overlooking part of the village. Inola pulled the spyglass Nathan had given him from his belt and searched below to see if he could spot Sara while Adohi kept watch for Shawnee patrols. Unhappy with his limited vantage point they moved slowly, close to the ground using the brush as cover until they found a place where they could see the open areas of the village more clearly. He watched for hours until he saw a blonde haired woman carrying water and knew from her height that it was Sara; she was alive. He tapped Adohi on the shoulder and motioned for him to follow him and they carefully made their way back to their horses.

Once safely away from any Shawnee patrols, they rode hard hoping to join up with Nathan by morning. They were forced to stop for the night and give their horses some rest and made a small fire while they ate their jerky, then laid down to get a few hours of sleep.

They were up and riding before dawn anxious to give Nathan the good news. Reaching the valley they looked for the smoke from Nathan's campfire and gave their horses a kick in the side and arrived just has he was pouring his morning coffee.

Nathan quickly stood and anxiously asked them, "Did you find her?"

"Yes, my friend, we have found her! We can be there by afternoon if we leave soon," Inola said with a huge smile.

Nathan was beside himself with joy and relief, and took a deep breath and looked to the heavens trying to find the words to thank God, but was unable to say anything other than "Thank you God, thank you." He grabbed Inola and hugged him patting him solidly on the back, grinning ear to ear. Adohi unaccustomed to such behavior slowly stepped back a few feet and subtly smiled as he watched his friends rejoice.

"It's okay, my friend. Drink your coffee, you can eat as you ride," Inola cheerfully told him.

Nathan raised his cup and gulped his coffee down in one breath and kicked dirt over the fire. After he threw his bedroll in the back of the wagon and climbed in, he excitedly declared, "Let's go get my Sara back," and told the horses to 'walk on'.

Inola and Adohi had found the shortest route the wagon could take to get to the winter camp of the Shawnee and led the way. As Nathan rode along he reasoned that if God had amply supplied everything he would need to make the trade, He would also have made a way to get Sara back safely; all he had to do was not mess things up.

They stopped only briefly to water their horses and let them eat a little grass as they stretched their legs and Adohi practiced speaking the Shawnee language out loud as he continued to remember the words. It would be several more hours before they neared the Shawnee village, and Inola rode alongside the wagon and explained what Nathan was supposed to do while Adohi did the talking.

"You must not say anything while Adohi is speaking, and you cannot react to how he is treated at first. Sit there, my friend, stone-faced and follow Adohi's lead. If you are taken before the Chief do not speak directly to him or show emotion if you see Sara. You must remain calm. Adohi knows to only offer the goods in the back of the wagon at first. Only if the Chief does not accept the offer are you to offer the wagon and horses. You are only to speak to Adohi, do you understand?" Inola asked looking at him seriously.

"Yes, I understand," he replied thoughtfully.

Nathan was starting to get a little anxious as to how this trade would work itself out, and knew that it would be hard for him to sit still and remain calm no matter what took place before his eyes. He was a man of action; that was how he stayed alive through the wars with the British and the different Indian tribes.

They were finally at a point where Inola could go no further with them, but would have to wait in the woods for their return.

"May your God go with you, my friend," Inola stated boldly.

Nathan nodded, "Thanks for everything…hope to see you soon."

"Walk on," Nathan said and followed Adohi to the edge of the village, aware for some time that they had been followed just out of pistol range by the Shawnee.

Their warriors moved in around them as they entered the village, and the people came from all over to see who had entered uninvited. Adohi held up his hand and Nathan pulled back on the reins and brought the wagon to a stop and sat there stone-faced as Inola had told him to do.

Adohi addressed them in their native tongue and they listened quietly until Tecumseh broke through the crowd and pulled him from his horse and struck him to the ground speaking loudly and belligerently to him for remaining on his horse; a sign of disrespect in remaining higher than they stood. Tecumseh then turned his attention towards Nathan and was suspicious of him; instantly taking a dislike to him. Nathan looked acutely at him but said nothing and waited for Adohi to stand up and continue speaking even though he understood nothing of what he said.

Adohi turned towards Nathan and told him in English that they were being taken before the Chief to decide whether a trade would be made or not. He walked leading his horse as Nathan slowly drove the team through the village hoping to see Sara in the crowd as more Shawnee gathered around. They finally came to a stop in front of the Chief's lodging.

The Chief came out and took his seat on a crude log bench with a blanket thrown across it. He looked at Nathan, a tall broad-shouldered man with a heavy dark beard that sat there emotionless, and surmised that he was a man with disciplined self-control – a former soldier perhaps. He turned his attention to Adohi, a young man chosen because he could speak the Shawnee language and called upon Adohi to speak. He spoke briefly to the Chief and then turned to Nathan and told him to pull the cover back on the wagon and stand inside it and show the Chief what they had brought to trade before he ever told him what it was they wanted to trade for.

The Shawnee watched eagerly as Nathan held up the whiskey barrel and then the tobacco, the blankets, the pots and pans, the silver trinkets, and finally corn seed for planting. He listened to their enthusiastic chatter while all the time longing to see Sara, and wondered why she was not there in the crowd.

The Chief nodded with pleasure at the goods offered in trade and asked Adohi what they wanted in exchange. Nathan's heart was pounding as he listened and watched Adohi's gesturing to the

Chief that the only thing they wanted in exchange was a captive white woman with long golden hair. Tecumseh protested loudly and stirred up a lot of the men in support of him because he was a mighty warrior among his people. He told the Chief that the woman was to be his wife at the end of his grieving period, and asked him to agree to give them another white woman.

Nathan did not understand a word that had been said, but he understood Tecumseh's reaction and the look on Adohi's face. He knew that unless he offered more to the Chief the trade would not be made out of respect for Tecumseh's wishes.

The Chief offered Adohi another captive woman in exchange for the goods, but Adohi was adamant that they were only interested in the one white woman they had asked for. Tecumseh went to speak out again and the Chief held up his hand to stop him and looked at the wagon filled with goods and then at his people.

Nathan could tell that the Chief was conflicted and jumped down from the wagon and whispered in Adohi's ear. "Offer the wagon and team to the Chief, but only if we get Sara in the trade," Nathan said and watched the Chief's face as Adohi spoke to him. The Chief looked at Nathan and wondered what the connection was between this stone-faced man and the woman he would risk his life to get back. He then looked at Adohi and nodded his head; for he had to think of the needs of his people and not the wishes of just one man. The Chief gave instructions to bring the woman to him and Tecumseh went into a rage, mounted his horse and rode away, and Nathan knew they had not seen the last of him. It was all he could do to remain calm in appearance, but inside he was ready to take on Tecumseh and the whole tribe if necessary to get Sara back.

Minutes later two men returned holding onto Sara tightly as she struggled and told them loudly to let go of her. She had seen the wagon pass by as she was grinding corn with some of the women and paid little attention to it, figuring it was just another trader passing through and she had nothing to trade. When she was brought in front of the Chief she feared that she would be given to the trader and taken even further away from Nathan. But what did it matter, he wasn't coming for her anyway, but still she hated the thought of being passed around as some man's property. She turned to look at the tall man with a floppy wide-brimmed hat who would be taking her away. At first she did not recognize him with a heavy beard and his face partially covered by his hat. But, when he turned and looked at her with piercing eyes and those broad shoulders she inhaled deeply and put her hand over her mouth in disbelief and shock, and just stared wide-eyed at him. It couldn't possibly be him. She was seeing things! She was sure Nathan thought she had returned home. At their Chief's command the men restraining her let go and gave her a push in the traders direction. Tears ran down her cheeks as she dared to believe it was Nathan and slowly walked towards him studying every aspect of him and put her hand against his bearded cheek and looked into his eyes that were filled with love, then threw her arms around his neck and kissed him. Nathan could restrain himself no longer and wrapped his arms around her and kissed her long and deeply, and the Chief had his answer.

He ordered that Nathan's horse be untied from the back of the wagon and given to him, and guaranteed safe passage to them and Adohi as the Shawnee women descended on the wagon carrying off the goods to be distributed throughout the tribe. Nathan mounted his horse and gave Sara a hand up and she held on tightly as he and Adohi wasted no time leaving the village.

As they rode hastily away Nathan could feel the tightness of Sara's trembling grip around him, and heard her continuous sobs and wanted badly to stop and comfort her, but first he needed to get her to safety. When they reached the place where Inola had been waiting for them he lowered Sara to the ground and dismounted. Immediately he took Sara in his arms and just held her as she continued to cry; not knowing how to deal with the overwhelming feelings not only hitting her, but himself all at once. She was afraid to let go of him in fear that he might disappear and all of this had just been an illusion made up in her desperate mind. Inola and Adohi told Nathan that they would wait for them at the stream and rode off knowing that the two of them needed to be alone for a while.

It broke Nathan's heart to hear Sara sobbing for he knew it meant that she had gone through hell without any hope of being rescued, and now she would have to struggle through the process of putting her fears behind her if she ever hoped to return to the confident, carefree person she once was.

"It's alright now. I'll never leave you alone again. Can you ever forgive me for what I put you through? I never should have left you alone that day," he said remorsefully as he continued to hold her tightly in his arms.

She looked up at him lovingly with a red, tear stained face and replied, "I already have. I forgave you the day you suggested I return to my own time."

Nathan shook as he tried to hold back his tears and softly cradled his hands tenderly along the sides of her face as he looked deeply into her loving eyes wanting so badly to tell her how much he loved her, but just couldn't find any words that would express the depth of his love for her.

Sara searched into his eyes and felt like she could see to his very soul, and found all the words he was searching for and softly said, "I heard every word, and I love you just as deeply."

He happily kissed her then proceeded kissing her along her neck until she giggled and pushed slightly back from him. He looked at her quizzically and she timidly said, "Your beard, it tickles."

Nathan stroked his beard up and down, "I'll shave it off first chance I get," he said.

"I don't know. You look ruggedly handsome with it and…so not Shawnee," she said and he knew exactly what she had meant.

"We best be going, Inola and Adohi are waiting," he said and pulled her close once again, gave her a kiss, then helped her up onto his horse.

The sun was setting and it would be dark soon and they looked for a place to make camp for the night. The temperature was dropping quickly as they gathered wood for their fire and placed their bedding close to it as they ate their supper and drank some hot coffee. Everyone's thoughts ran deep that night and there was very little talk around the campfire, and Nathan thought it best to turn in for the night. He held his blanket up and waited for Sara to lay down beside him and then looked up at the stars as he pulled Sara close to him and could feel her body slightly tighten as she had resisted lying close to any man for months. He thanked God because he knew that He had looked down from heaven and prepared every step of the way for Sara's return. And now prayed that Sara would get past her fears and want his love as she once had.

"Sara, do you remember the first night we spent together under the stars?" he asked softly.

"Of course I do. But, I choose to think about the first night we spent together under the stars when we were first married. Those memories are what got me through each and every night without you," she reflectively replied.

Nathan swallowed hard and wondered how she could love him after all she had been put through, and hoped that he could find a way to make it up to her. It didn't take her long to fall asleep in his arms but woke him suddenly in the night when he found her wildly fighting the air and repeatedly groaning "No".

He wrapped his arms around her as she fought, "Sara, it's alright, it's just a dream," he said when she looked at him terrified, then buried her face against him and cried.

The commotion woke Inola whose back had been turned to them. He turned his head towards them imagining what had caused the nightmare, then turned his head back; distressed by what his friend had been through, and tried to go back to sleep.

In the morning Sara was disoriented and frantically looked around in every direction as she laid covered up on Nathan's bedroll until she saw Inola, and quickly lowered her eyes as she had been taught to do. Inola was troubled by this change in her, for they had become close friends and he had been treated like family, and now all she appeared to see was an Indian.

When Sara looked up she saw Nathan returning from the stream with a pot of water to make coffee and sighed sharply; relieved and happy that she had not imagined Nathan rescuing her and holding her in his arms last night.

As she stood to help Nathan fix breakfast, Inola stated, "Not all Indians bad. I'm family, remember?"

Sara quickly looked over at him and saw the concern for her in his eyes and tried to choke back her tears before she replied, "Yes, Inola, I remember. Please forgive me and be patient with me."

She wanted to say more but Nathan had returned and looked curiously at the two of them and wondered what had transpired that had caused Sara to tear up so quickly, but did not ask any questions. He bent down and put the coffee in the pot and set it over the fire.

"May I help you fix breakfast," Sara timidly asked as he stood up.

"Good morning," he said and lifted her chin and gave her a soft kiss on the lips and continued, "I'd love your help. Let me see what provisions we still have."

He went to one of his saddlebags and looked through it and asked, "How about some pancakes, we still have a little flour and fixings?"

"That sounds wonderful. Let me give you a hand," and went to help him carry things over by the fire. "I never thought I would eat pancakes again," she said and lowered her eyes. He felt bad that she had become accustomed to lowering her eyes when she spoke to a man and wanted to say something, but remained silent knowing that it would take time for her to move past the way she had been forced to live.

She was pouring the first spoonful of batter into the frying pan when Adohi came riding into camp calling out in Cherokee that he had caught some groundhogs for supper. Sara was startled when she looked up and saw him riding towards her and lunged backward to the ground too terrified to speak, for in her mind she saw visions of Tecumseh coming for her by the stream.

Nathan quickly went to her sitting there on the ground and calmly said, "It's alright, it's only Adohi. You remember him; he's the one that helped me get you back yesterday."

"Of course. I'm sorry Adohi, you just startled me that's all," Sara said embarrassed by her seemingly cowardly reaction, and took a deep breath and subtly smiled as her heart continued to pound away. She knew she had lied; she had not been startled, she had been terrified and still was.

She went back to making pancakes and handed a plate full to each of them.

"Where's yours?" Nathan asked.

"Oh…I'm fixing mine now," she replied and returned to the fire.

Nathan and Inola looked at each other knowing that was the Shawnee way; servants ate what was left over after everyone had been served. Both were concerned by what they had seen already in Sara's changed behavior, and knew that it was going to take some time for her to recover from the trauma she had been through. Nathan missed the confident, passionate, and sometimes

- 330 -

feisty woman he had married and hoped that woman would come back to him in time.

Chapter 39

They broke camp after breakfast knowing they still had three to four days of hard riding before they reached home. Plus, their supplies were running low after being gone so long. The three men kept an eye out for Tecumseh and some of his loyal warriors, afraid that he would try to get Sara back as a matter of pride.

They were rapidly approaching a river and Sara had flashbacks of being dragged through the rivers struggling to get her footing, and catch her breath in the icy cold waters. She remembered the bruises on her legs and hips as they hit the rocks and the heaviness of her cold wet skirt and petticoats, and she no longer enjoyed being anywhere close to the streams or rivers she once loved to sit by.

There were several more streams they had to cross on their way home and Nathan noticed that each time they crossed one, Sara clung to him tightly with her face pressed against his back. Her legs were drawn up trying to keep them out of the water, and he wondered if she had closed her eyes trying to drive the haunting memories from her mind.

She was still coping with nightmares, and Nathan tried singing to her softly as they rode along for it seemed to soothe her thoughts. Sara began to smile more often as they traveled the next couple of days, but still rarely spoke unless spoken to, and never let Nathan out of her site unless Inola was right there by her, and even that made her uneasy.

On the fourth day as they were coming over the last rise Sara caught a glimpse of their home's rooftop and the apple orchard, and was excited for the first time since her rescue.

"Oh, Nathan, we're almost home!" she said excitedly.

Nathan patted her arms that were tightly wrapped around him and smiled hoping that being back home would be just the thing to help her recover quickly from the living nightmare she had endured over the past couple of months.

Inola and Adohi rode up alongside of Nathan and Sara as they approached the apple orchard and Nathan said, "If you will drop the saddlebags off by the back door and check on the animals, I'll let Sara off at the house and join you at the barn."

They gave their horses a kick and quickly rode off eager to get back to their people, and since Nathan's horse was no longer carrying a saddlebag he brought Sara to the front porch and let her off there and waited for her to enter the house.

She slowly walked across the porch and rested her hand on the latch and hesitated, looking back at Nathan. "It's alright. I'll join you in just a bit," he said and waited for her to go inside.

She opened the door and stood just inside the threshold and looked around at a room she never thought she would see again. It was cold and seemed dark inside like the wigwam she had been forced to live in, and found it hard to breathe. *"Go on, do what you need to do. You don't want to become wearisome do you?"* she said to herself and started towards the wood pile. As she picked up the first piece of wood she had a flashback of loading wood each cold morning into a basket and carrying it to each lodge before she could eat breakfast. She closed her eyes and took a deep breath then filled the fireplace and hearth with wood and started the fires burning. She felt the need for more lighting and lit every candle in the room, and finally she felt like she was home. Sara stood by the fireplace and looked down at the bear skin lying on the floor and burst into tears. The memories were overpowering and she dropped to her knees and folded her hands on the seat of her rocking chair. She poured her heart out to God thanking Him for his mercy and grace in bringing her back home safely to Nathan, and asking for His healing of her mind and thoughts for she could not seem to find herself. She was lost in a nightmare of bad memories.

Nathan entered the back door carrying supplies to be put away when he saw Sara on her knees crying with her hands still folded. He looked around the room at all the candles lit and quietly backed out the door with his hands still full. He decided she was just where she needed to be and sat down on the back steps.

Inola and Adohi joined him carrying a string of rainbow trout that had been prepared for roasting and wondered why Nathan was just sitting there.

"Sara needs just a moment alone. I'd be grateful if you both would stay for supper and spend the night here."

They agreed, but Inola made it clear that he was eager to get back to Adsila and his village. Nathan quietly opened the back door and softly walked around the corner just as Sara was standing up. He waited for her to finish drying her eyes before he spoke.

"Inola and Adohi will be joining us tonight," he said and watched for her reaction before inviting them inside.

Sara turned and looked at him, "Good, I'm glad they're staying. I want to get out of these clothes and then I'll be back to get supper going."

She went into the bedroom and shut the door and latched it and undressed as quickly as she could. She wanted to rid herself of these clothes that conjured up so many bad memories and get back into her own clothes. As she stepped into her jeans and pulled her sweater over her head she realized that her comfortable boots had been ruined while she was dragged through the water and walked for weeks over rough rocks and through the mud and sometimes snow as the Shawnee continued hunting. All she had at the moment were the comfortable moccasins she was wearing. She tugged them up over her jeans and sat in front of the mirror and unbraided her hair and brushed it vigorously, then pulled it back into a ponytail. As she sat there and stared into the mirror she wondered who it was that was staring back at her; for she hardly recognized her anymore. She wondered how long it would be before she saw the face of the woman she once knew.

Sara folded the shirt and poncho and took them with her when she left the room to go prepare supper, hoping that Inola would give the clothes to someone at his winter camp.

As the men sat around the table talking after supper, Sara sat there and stared off into space. She was thinking about Tecumseh; how the men thought he might come for her, but she knew him well and knew that he would come sooner or later for her – his pride was hurt. As the night wore on Nathan noticed that Sara hadn't said a word and wondered what had captured her thoughts. He invited his friends to sleep inside tonight and said goodnight as he took Sara by the hand and led her into the bedroom.

He was at a loss as to what to do. He had waited a long time to take her in his arms and make love to her, but wondered if she would want any man to touch her right now. He watched her carefully as he sat on the bed and pulled off his boots to see what she would do. Sara could feel his eyes upon her and wondered whether he wanted her after she had been with Tecumseh even though he never touched her. But, he didn't know that. She longed for him to take her in his arms and make love to her, but she had spent the last two months fighting to keep any man from touching her, and she had mixed feelings as to what she should do.

Nathan could see the desire in her eyes, but seemed unable to fully give herself to him. That was all he needed to see. He stood before her and lifted her chin and briefly looked into her eyes then gently kissed her. "Why don't you change into one of your fancy pajamas you brought back with you and come to bed? I'm sure you're tired after the long day."

She smiled gently and nodded her head knowing that he loved her enough to give her time to adjust being home with him, and quickly dressed and crawled under the blanket and waited for him to wrap his arms around her.

It was early in the morning as Nathan laid there looking at Sara. She looked so peaceful at the moment that he didn't want to wake her just to put a pot of coffee on the fire. He knew from experience that you don't get over trauma in one day; it could possibly take years for Sara to put behind her all that had happened to her over the past few months. He vowed that he would be there for her every step of the way. He still felt responsible and guilty for everything that she had been through, for he was the one who begged her to stay with him in a time that was dangerous and sometimes ruthless.

He dressed as quietly as he could and slipped out the bedroom door only to find that Inola and Adohi were not in the house and had probably been up for hours. They had already put wood on the fire so all he had to do was make the coffee and wait for them to return; Sara should be up and dressed by then.

Inola and Adohi came in the back door and were talking quietly with Nathan by the hearth when Sara emerged from the bedroom and wondered what they were talking about so quietly in Cherokee.

"Good morning, has anyone had breakfast yet?" she asked as she approached them.

"No, I was just about to pour a cup of coffee for everyone until you could join us," he told her.

"Then I'd better use up some of those eggs that were gathered yesterday and make some pancakes, too," she replied tying an apron around her while avoiding eye contact.

Sara made a big breakfast knowing that Inola and Adohi would be leaving right afterwards to head back to their winter camp. She would be sorry to see them go because she knew they could use the extra pair of eyes to watch for Tecumseh; for he would come for her. While eating Sara had trouble looking directly at Inola and Adohi even though she loved them like family. The problem was they were Indians; it did not matter whether they were Cherokee or Shawnee. Right now that meant they conjured up bad memories by just looking at them. She knew that Inola would probably expect a hug good-bye since that is what she did the last time he left and the fact that he had reminded her that he was family. She knew that her thoughts were not rational at the moment, and determined she would hug Inola so there wouldn't be any hurt feelings. Besides, it was the right thing to do and maybe it would be good therapy.

When they were finished with breakfast, Nathan gave them enough supplies for their journey and walked with them to the barn to pack and bring their horses up to the front porch. They came back inside to say good-bye to Sara, and Inola knew what to expect when she hugged him good-bye, but Adohi was wide-eyed and almost rigid as she hugged him. "I shall miss you both, and never be able to thank you enough for risking your lives to find me. Please come back as often as you can," she said choking back her tears.

Nathan put his arm around her as they watched them ride off towards their winter camp. Sara looked anxiously around before returning to the house, and when she and Nathan were sitting by the fire in his rocking chair Sara directly stated, "I thought we weren't going to keep secrets from each other."

"Yes, that is what we agreed too," Nathan replied quizzically, not knowing what she might be referring too.

"What were you three talking about when I entered the room this morning?" she asked afraid of sounding paranoid.

Nathan looked at her thoughtfully before answering. "For one thing, we were just trying to be quiet, we didn't know if you were up yet or not. Secondly, they let me know that they searched the perimeter of our property and found no fresh signs that anyone has passed by here," he replied.

"Thank you for being patient with me. I'm not trying to be difficult. It's just that I can't seem to get a grip on my nerves or thoughts. I would rather know what is going on so I could at least try to cope with it, then to have you keep things from me. It keeps my mind in a turmoil," she stated in great distress.

"While we're on the subject of being open with one another, is there anything you would like to share with me?" he asked with a tenderness to his voice.

"I have no secrets. I'm sure Adohi has already told you everything that was said in the Shawnee camp. I want you to know that although I was treated brutally on the way to their village, Tecumseh made sure that no one touched me, and that I was at least given food and a blanket at night and allowed to sleep by the fire. I'm not ready to talk about my treatment in the village; let's just say that it was…unpleasant…and leave it at that," she expressed painfully and managed not to cry.

"Well, when you are ready to talk, I'm here for you," he stated and wrapped his arms around her as she laid her head against him, and he rocked his chair slowly.

Chapter 40

Sara's fear and anxiety over Tecumseh returning for her grew in leaps and bounds as the next few days passed by. She only left the house if Nathan was with her, and when he went out to the fields and barn, she always made sure that he carried her weapon with him and then watched out the different windows scanning the forest and apple orchard until he returned safely knowing that one day Tecumseh would show up.

One morning after breakfast Nathan noticed that it was a beautiful day to take a ride for he was starting to get cabin fever. Sara had not wanted to venture far from the house since she had returned, and her fear of Tecumseh was becoming an obsession. Nathan could see her slipping further and further into a dark place where peace and joy no longer existed. He wanted to take her away if only for a day to see her happy and free from the anxiety that had her tightly bound.

"Let's take a ride today and pack a picnic lunch. What do you say?" he asked optimistically.

Sara could hardly breathe as he spoke those words and looked at him as if he were crazy. "You know he will be watching," she replied anxiously.

"We'll head south this time. He can't be everywhere at one time, you know. Besides, we can't stay inside this house forever. Don't you trust me to protect you?" he asked seriously.

"Of course I trust you," she said tenderly, but had wanted to add "it's him I don't trust and you don't know how many men he might have brought with him".

"Well then, you pack a lunch and I'll go saddle the horse."

Sara watched out the window until Nathan was safely in the barn and then quickly packed a lunch and got out her winter coat and was ready when he returned.

She reluctantly handed him their lunch basket which he stowed in a saddlebag that hung in front of his saddle and extended his hand for Sara to take hold of so he could swing her up behind him. Once seated she wrapped her arms around him and closed her eyes thinking, "That which I cannot see cannot harm me," but knew in her heart that was not true. It wasn't until they were almost half way up the hill in front of their house and into the trees for cover that she opened her eyes. As they finally made their way to the valley below, Sara glanced in the direction where her company's cabin would be 200 years from now and remembered it fondly. She had never been attacked there by Indians, or renegades, or trappers; only a few deer had startled her one morning and that she could handle.

She started to relax as they headed further south for about an hour and she no longer imagined Tecumseh's prying eyes watching their every move. Finding a sunny spot in the middle of a grassy field where you could see in every direction Nathan spread out their blanket and stretched out and smiled up at Sara.

"Come join me. It's nice and soft and we can relax in peace and quiet, or perhaps work up an appetite for lunch if you so wish," he said with his usual mischievous smile.

"Dare to dream, my love, dare to dream. It might be sunny and bright but it's still cold," she said as she pulled her heavy overcoat around her and laid down beside him and snuggled up close. She closed her eyes and breathed in deeply the scent of the fresh pine trees that stood a few yards behind them. The only sound she heard was the sound of birds singing and she was at peace as Nathan ran his fingers through her hair and kissed her softly down the side of her neck just to watch the goose bumps appear.

Nathan was content just to hold her relaxed body close to him and kiss her knowing that she enjoyed it; and was happy just to be with him. They had enjoyed their leisurely lunch and their quiet time together but it was time to pack up and start for home. He wanted to get back while it was still daylight.

Sara held on tight as the horse started to climb the hill in front of the house and wished every day could be as wonderful as this day had been. When they reached the top and started down she rested her head against Nathan's back until he pulled his pistol from his belt and cocked it.

"What's wrong?" she asked anxiously and immediately started to tremble.

"I'm not sure. Just stay behind me and keep your head down. I'm going to drop you off at the porch and I want you to wait for me there. Will you do that?" he asked while cautiously looking around.

"Yes," she replied. Sara was in full panic mode now, and Nathan could already feel her start to tremble as she held on to him and her breathing become labored. He knew that she was bound to see what had taken place while they were gone. There wasn't any way to hide it from her.

He gave her a hand getting down off the horse and as she started to climb the steps of the porch she glanced at the barn and froze in mid-step.

"Oh my God...oh my God, he's here!" she cried out hysterically.

Nathan had planned to go to the barn to remove the dead chicken that had been impaled with an arrow to the barn door before Sara could see it, but he decided he didn't want Sara to enter the house unless he had checked it out to make sure no one was inside. He swung down from his horse and took hold of her firmly and pulled her across the porch and made her stand by the door.

"Give me your weapon. Stand here until I come back out for you," he said looking into her terrified eyes as she shook violently knowing what Tecumseh was capable of.

Nathan cautiously opened the front door, looked around and then entered checking each room before he went back for Sara. "Stay inside and latch and bolt the door. Don't open it for any reason until I get back. I mean it, stay inside," he demanded and went out the front door and waited until he heard her latch it behind him.

He peeked around the side of the porch closest to the barn then ran quickly to it wanting to make it as hard as possible to hit a moving target. He pulled the arrow out of the barn door and let the chicken fall to the ground and went inside to check on the other animals. He breathed a sigh of relief to find the other chickens and animals safe in their stalls and pens. The dead chicken impaled to the door was only to let them know that he was out there somewhere. He knew well this manner of man; he was toying with them. His only purpose was to strike fear in them until he was tired of playing his game, and then he would try to take Sara back, preferably over his dead body.

Nathan grabbed the chicken and ran back to the house and called to Sara to open the door. "He's gone for now, but he will be back," he said as he took the chicken to the kitchen; it would make a fine supper.

He saw Sara standing by the fireplace shivering as if she was cold. Everything he had tried to accomplish today to bring some joy and life back to Sara was gone in a moment's time and he was frustrated and angry. He went and put his arms around her and held her tight as he wished to himself that Inola and Adohi were here to help him. He wondered how many men Tecumseh had brought with him so he could plan some type of strategy to defeat them. In his past battles with the warring Indian parties he had not been alone and they had taken place in the forest not out in the open like on his farm.

Sara was quiet as he held her, but he knew that in her mind she was thinking about every horrible thing she could imagine that Tecumseh would do to get her back to save face with his people.

He lifted her chin and looked into her troubled eyes. "I'm sorry...but I will never let him take you," he said determinedly, and she could see the solider in him emerge with piercing eyes and a clinched jaw with only one thought on his mind – killing Tecumseh or any man that tried to take her. "I know you're worried, but fight hard not to withdraw so deeply that I cannot reach you...talk to me...can you do that for me?" he asked lovingly.

"I'll try. I could bear to live with the Shawnee, but I couldn't bear for any harm to come to you because of me," she said then laid her head against his shoulder.

"Will you come sit by the hearth with me while I pluck that chicken for supper? It would taste mighty fine if you were to fry it," he said hoping to restore some form of normalcy to their lives.

That evening the only light in the house came from the fireplace even though Nathan knew attacks rarely happened at night, but first light was a different matter and he would need to stay alert. Sara managed to relax a bit as Nathan held her and gently stroked his hand through her hair as they laid in bed. When she had fallen asleep he quietly got up and looked out all the windows just to ease his mind before he tried to get any sleep.

He was up before dawn and stood looking out the different windows before he ever lit a fire in the hearth. He saw no one, but knew they were out there and thought about how he was going to feed his animals. Anger burned within him and he would be damned if he was going to let them stop him from leaving his house. Once the fire was going in the hearth he put a pot of coffee on to brew and went and looked out the windows again as Sara was still sleeping after having a restless night. He was tired of looking out of windows; he took Sara's firearm and walked out the backdoor to go feed the animals. He was determined not to run or show any sign of fear; if they wanted him they would have to come out in the open for their arrows would not reach him from the cover of the orchard or forest.

He did what he had to do and returned to the house before Sara was even up. When the coffee was ready he went into the bedroom to check on her and sat beside her on the bed. He gently laid his hand on her shoulder and asked God to protect her and to bring peace to her troubled mind, and strength to deal with whatever came their way. He never dreamed when he asked her to stay with him that she would have to endure so much hardship, and wondered if they were ever going to be given a chance to live a quiet and peaceful life.

He gently stroked her arm until she opened her eyes then asked, "Will you join me for some coffee while I fry up some bacon and scramble some eggs?"

She looked at him and marveled how he could look so calm and assured of his ability to protect her and smiled at him. "I would love to join you for a cup of coffee," she said and waited for him to stand up so she could put her robe and slippers on.

She had made up her mind not to look out the windows, but to just sit and enjoy breakfast with him. He had enough on his mind without her always being so stressed out around him that he had no one to talk to or lean on for a little support. She was raised to be strong and she must find that part of her for the sake of the man she loved; for he would have his hands full until he had defeated Tecumseh and his warriors.

She thoroughly enjoyed the breakfast Nathan had prepared, and after they had cleaned up the few dishes, went and sat by the fire. They continued their conversation about their next trip into Knoxville to buy another horse for Sara when Nathan heard the sound of horses and then a Shawnee cry out as they did before an attack.

He jumped to his feet and ran to the window overlooking the barn and yelled out, "Damn them!" and stuck his pistol through his belt and ran out the back door.

Sara ran to the window and saw him running towards the barn and froze in terror when she saw the flaming arrows that had been shot into their bales of hay. They were back. Her mind became muddled and her heart was pounding as she looked towards the orchard and could see the Shawnee moving closer to the edge of the trees with their bows drawn. Fear overpowered her, and she stood their quaking unable to move. Her mind stirred up visions of Tecumseh coming towards her with his painted face and a leather strap to gag her so she couldn't scream out. She looked at Nathan and knew they would kill him if she didn't do something, and then glanced at the Shawnee prepared to launch their arrows and couldn't bear to watch any longer. She quickly turned and looked at the stairs leading to the attic. Her mind told her to run to the attic where she would be safe for everything would change – Nathan was away from the house - but her heart told her to do whatever she could to save him.

Nathan had quickly climbed to the top of the bales and began shoving them off to the ground one by one as he saw the Shawnee begin to leave the cover of the orchard. He was determined to pull the flaming arrows out and drag the bales of hay away before it destroyed the whole stack that was to feed their animals through winter and the barn with it.

With hands trembling she picked up her handgun and two ammunition clips off the hearth's mantle and stepped outside the back door just in time to see arrows fly towards Nathan and could not bear to see where they landed. She held her weapon in both hands trying to stop them from violently shaking for she knew she would never be able to hit anything but air. She started pulling the trigger as quickly as she could, shooting wildly in their direction and fumbled trying to change out the empty clip.

The arrows had failed to reach Nathan and the Shawnee withdrew in confusion back into the orchard when they heard the sound of gun shots. Nathan continued to topple bales until he reached the ones that were burning and pushed them to the ground as the flames leaped up around him. Sara kept aimlessly shooting hoping to keep the Shawnee from returning while Nathan struggled to drag the burning bales far enough away to prevent them from catching anything else on fire.

As he started running for the house he saw Sara standing by the back door pulling the trigger repeatedly to her empty weapon and pulled her back inside. He pried the gun from her hands as she stood there blindly staring into the air; her mind watching Tecumseh pulling her behind his horse, and he wrapped his arms around her.

"It's alright, Sara. They're gone for now. I'm sure they're confused about where all the shots came from, and I doubt whether they'll come out in the open like that again," he said and seriously doubted whether she heard a word he said.

She had totally shut down and he was afraid to leave her in that condition; afraid that she would go to a dark place and not be able to find her way back.

While he thought, he placed his hand that was burned by the bales on fire into a bucket of cold water to ease the pain. As he stood there an idea came to mind. He wasn't happy with it, but he couldn't at the moment think of anything else to do, and dipped a coffee cup that was sitting on the table into the bucket and threw the cold water into her face. She gasped and quickly looked at him stunned by what he had done, but it had worked – she was now crying.

Nathan put his arms around her, "Go ahead and cry. Let it all out. It's not good to keep those feelings all bottled up inside. Come, come sit with me."

He walked with her to his chair and when she was resting comfortably on his lap he said, "I want you to know that I thought it was very brave of you to step outside in the open to save my life."

"Brave?" she questioned sitting up and looking at him in amazement. "I was terrified…I didn't even hit a single one of them," she stated and burst into tears again.

Nathan grinned and pulled her close again and rocked his chair. "That's why you were brave, because you did it even though you were terrified. Who knows, maybe you winged a couple of them. All I know is that you didn't let them kill me."

"Oh Nathan, I'm a mess. My thoughts are all over the place, and I keep having the same thoughts or visions play over and over again in my mind and I can't stop them. I'm jumpy and cry at the least thing. How can you even bear to be with me right now?" she asked despondently.

"I can bear it because I love you more than anything in the world. It's normal for you to be this way. Most men who have fought in a war feel exactly the same way you do right now; they just hide it a little better with a lot of whiskey. I still have nightmares after all these years and probably will for some time to come. You're strong, and with God's help you'll come through this even stronger," he stated assuredly.

"I hope you're right, for your sake as well as mine. Do you think the Shawnee will ever give up and just go back home?"

"I don't know, but I don't think we've seen the last of them yet. Tecumseh doesn't seem to be the type of man to give up easily. You're a tough act to follow and I don't blame him for wanting you as his wife," he said.

"How are we ever going to be able to stop them? There's nothing to keep them from shooting flaming arrows into our house or killing all of our livestock," she said looking up at him.

Nathan exhaled strongly as he thought quietly. "I guess we'll stop them with a lot of prayer and bullets," he replied and then quietly just rocked his chair with Sara on his lap.

Even though Sara had probably not hit anyone in her shower of bullets fired, she had given the Shawnee something to think about and that would buy him some time. They could no longer charge the house across open ground in the daylight; their attacks would either have to come in the night or just before dawn. However, there was no way that he and Sara could be looking out their windows day and night watching for them. If only Inola and Adohi had not left they might have had a chance to pick them off one at a time, but they were not there and Nathan turned to God once again for help.

Chapter 41

A couple of days went by without any sign of the Shawnee. Sara watched out the windows with her weapon in hand as Nathan fed the animals and brought fresh water and firewood into the house. He still did not have a plan for how he was going to stop Tecumseh from taking his wife. He was only one man against a small party of determined Shawnee. But he was right about one thing; Sara's use of her weapon had given them something to think about, and they too had to come up with a plan to get close to the house.

Nathan and Sara took turns taking short naps during the day when things were quiet, for it was at night they felt the attacks might come. Then one night Nathan spotted the glow of a campfire up on the ridge behind their house and cracked the backdoor open and listened. He stood there for some time and then thought he heard the faint chanting of the Shawnee around their campfire and knew they were preparing for something, but what?

Late that night as Sara lay in bed unable to fall asleep she thought she heard a noise outside. She looked over at Nathan who had dozed off out of sheer exhaustion and did not want to wake him over nothing, so she listened attentively for any further sounds. After several minutes of hearing nothing further she decided it was not anything and went back to her thoughts. Then once again she could have sworn she heard another sound; different than the one before. There it was again! It sounded like the faint squeaking of floorboards, but the sounds came too far apart to be anyone walking about, or so she thought. She laid there breathing shallowly and afraid to move, and was still afraid to wake Nathan over nothing and continued to listen. The sounds continued infrequently over a short period of time. Sara wondered if it was only the natural sound of wood expanding and shrinking and she just hadn't paid any attention to it before, or if all the sounds were just in her vivid imagination. Anyway, they were gone now and she was happy she hadn't woken Nathan and eventually drifted off to sleep.

Before dawn Nathan got up to put more wood on the glowing embers in the fireplace and then started towards the hearth with another armload of wood. He stopped abruptly and stood there looking around the room, then quietly set the firewood on the floor and pulled his pistol from his belt. He took several quiet steps towards the dining area and noticed light shining on the floor and fury surged through his veins. He quickly moved in that direction and found the backdoor ajar and knew that someone in the night had entered his home. He examined the latch and observed that it had slowly been worked open with a knife and slammed the door shut and latched it. He was fit to be tied and wondered what their purpose was in entering his house if it wasn't to kill him and take Sara.

He was looking around the room when Sara came out of the bedroom after hearing the backdoor slammed shut. "What's going on?" she asked as she walked towards him.

She could now see that he was shaking with anger as he continued to look around the room. Fear gripped her as she took her eyes off of him and looked around the room as well, and then she saw it. It was not her imagination running wild last night. She had in fact heard someone walking around in their home late last night and there on the mantle to the fireplace was a beaded belt curled up, and Sara turned white as a ghost. Nathan noticed where she was staring and quickly went and found the belt and violently threw it across the room swearing vehemently.

She did not know what frightened her more; that someone had been roaming around in their home last night, or Nathan swearing in a rage, for he had never acted like that in her presence before. She stood there silently, wide-eyed, staring at him afraid to say anything until he had calmed down.

He still had fire in his eyes when he looked at Sara, and then abruptly put his pistol back in his belt and grabbed his rifle by the door.

"Where are you going?" Sara asked terrified.

"I'm going to kill that son of a bitch!" he raged furiously.

Sara ran and grabbed his arm and pulled on him begging him not to go outside. "Nathan you can't go outside. That's what they want you to do. They will kill you, and they might as well kill me for I can't live without you. You promised you would never leave me alone, remember? Please stay inside. Please!" she begged crying hysterically.

Nathan looked at her and went to pull away from her, but knew that he couldn't leave her in this condition, she would come after him. He set his rifle down and put his arms around her, still inhaling deeply as his anger simmered inside him.

"I have to do something, Sara. We can't go on like this," he adamantly declared.

"I have an idea. Come sit by the fire with me and let me tell you what I have in mind," she pleaded.

Nathan exhaled loudly and took his seat by the fire. "What do you have in mind?" he questioned.

"Nathan, if you are determined to go after them by yourself, you are going to need something to put the odds in your favor, or at least give you a fighting chance," she stated directly.

"Like what?" he asked curiously.

"Give me just one day. I can go back to my time and buy you a weapon that will allow you at least a fighting chance to take on the whole Shawnee party," she said desperately.

"No. I don't want you stepping foot outside that door. The last thing I want is for you to go running out of here and getting hurt. Too many things can go wrong and you might not ever be able to return to me," he replied.

"I am going! Before you can make it off the porch I'll be up in the attic and there won't be anything you can do about it! I'm right about this and you know it!" she boldly exclaimed in spite of her fear of his temper when aroused.

She could see his anger return; he didn't like threats made to him by anyone.

"You certainly have a short memory. Don't you remember what happened the last time you wandered off? Look at the mess we're in now!" he angrily replied.

Sara hung her head and cried bitterly.

Nathan knew instantly that those words should have never left his lips; they were spoken out of anger and frustration. "I'm sorry, Sara. I didn't mean it. Please forgive me, none of this is your fault," he stated and put his arms around her.

When she had stopped crying, Nathan lifted her chin and wiped her tears from her face. "Tell me again about your plan," he calmly asked.

Sara took a deep breath, "If I leave right now, I can make it back to my publisher's cabin and ask to borrow their phone to call my father. He has connections in the firearm's business and can come pick me up and take me to where I can purchase a weapon and ammunition with no questions asked. By the time we do all that it will be getting dark so we will have to wait until morning for him to drive me out to your house, and drop me off practically at our front door. You just need to stay inside and I will return to you through the attic. What do you say? Will you let me go and wait here until I return?" she begged.

Nathan took a deep breath, strongly exhaled, then stared at the floor while he thought. He had to admit, that what he had planned would have surely gotten him killed; this at least had a chance of working. Reluctantly he replied, "I don't see where I have a choice. I certainly don't have a better plan. Promise me you'll be careful, and I want you to take your weapon with you."

"I won't need it; there won't be any Shawnee when I step through your door. Please, I want you to keep it; you need more than two bullets against so many. I'll bring down all the ammunition I brought with me so you can reload if necessary. I promise you I will be careful and in no danger. My dad will be with me and make sure I return to you," she stated with great confidence.

"I thought your parents were trying to stop you from coming here. They thought you had made all of this up," he questioned.

"They did feel that way. But I left them a message and I'm sure after hearing it they will no longer have any objections to helping me. Please trust me," she begged once again.

This was the most rational he had seen her since her captivity, and knew when she was thinking clearly she was strong and resilient. "Okay, but I had better see you coming down those stairs tomorrow morning. Do you hear me?" he asked under great stress.

"I hear you. I'll be back as quickly as I can, and you'd better be here when I come down those stairs," she replied.

He took her in his arms and kissed her more deeply than he had ever before. "Go before I change my mind," he said with tears welling in his eyes, still fearful that something could go wrong and she wouldn't be able to return to him.

Sara turned and ran up the stairs and pulled on the cord leading to the attic and quickly found her stash of ammunition and took it to Nathan. Neither of them said a word, but their eyes said it all as they looked at each other one last time before she turned and headed back to the attic.

Sara found her backpack and put everything inside that she thought she would need and came across the letter she had hastily stuffed in her purse some time ago, and decided she would wait to read it when she was waiting for her father to pick her up.

Suddenly the attic changed before her eyes and Sara knew that Nathan had remembered that he needed to be outside the house before she could leave. She carefully ran down the rickety stairs and out of the house so Nathan could safely return inside.

Chapter 42

Sara ran as fast as she could through the forest of trees to the base of the hill and quickly caught her breath. She glanced behind her for only a second then continued making her way up the hill through the brush in as straight a line as she could and caught her breath once again at the top. She started making her descent a little more carefully as the ground had a dusting of snow and was icy in places and knew she couldn't afford to have an accident.

As she made her way across the field she saw that there was a vehicle parked in front of the cabin and knew that a different writer had taken her place. She hoped that whoever was staying there would be agreeable to her using their phone or she would have to walk much further wasting precious time.

Sara stood at the door and took a deep breath for she was still breathing heavily after her two mile hike and thought about what she would say to the new users of the cabin. She knocked loudly on the door and heard a man's voice call out, "I'm coming."

A man in his forties answered the door and asked, "May I help you?"

"I'm sorry to bother you, sir, but my phone is not working and I need to call my father. It's most urgent that I reach him…may I use your phone?" she asked breathing heavily.

The man looked around from his doorway to make sure this was not a setup and then looked into her troubled eyes and said,

"Come on in," and led her to his landline and handed her the phone. He stood at a distance studying her while she made her phone call for she looked familiar and couldn't quite place where he had seen her face before.

Sara dialed her father's cell number and closed her eyes as it rang and wondered what her dad's reaction would be when he heard her voice.

"Hello."

"Hello, Dad…its Sara."

"Sara, where are you?" he asked anxiously.

"I'm at the cabin. I need your help Dad. Can you come get me right away…it's important," she cried, and wondered what the man must be thinking about her.

"Of course I'll come. It will take me about an hour, you know," he replied.

"I know, Dad. Please hurry, I'll be waiting outside for you."

Seeing that she was finished making her call the man approached her and seeing her cry he asked, "Can I help you in any way?"

"You're most kind, but my father is on his way. Thank you for allowing me to use your phone," she replied drying her eyes.

"I'm sorry for staring, but you look familiar. Have we ever met before?" he asked.

"I don't believe so. You might have seen my face on a book cover, I'm Sara Chambers, I mean Sara Mathews," she stated.

"Of course! I read your last book and it was fabulous; I couldn't put it down. What an imagination you have. I hope I can be half the writer you are," he sincerely replied.

"You're most kind," she humbly responded.

"Why don't you wait inside for your dad, and may I offer you something to drink while you wait?" he asked.

"A glass of water would be great, thank you," Sara said anxiously, impatient for her father to arrive.

As the man handed her the glass of water he asked, "Are those real moccasins you have on? They look so authentic and are quite beautiful."

"Yes, they are authentic and very comfortable," she stated feeling a bit awkward, but they were the only shoes she had suitable for hiking and wondered what her father would think about them.

"I want to thank you again for the use of your phone and for the water, but I should be going now. I think I'll head up the hill a way and meet my dad there," she gratefully said as she handed him back the empty glass.

"Well, you are most welcome, and I look forward to your next book," he said as he opened the door for her.

Sara could not stand idly by waiting for her father. She needed to be doing something to help pass the time and walking up the winding road would help her burn some more of her nervous energy. She pulled the unopened letter from her backpack and read it as she walked. "Dear Sara, your mother and I are sorry for not believing you and for the way things ended when you left. We have read your books written so long ago and are deeply concerned for your safety. We can only assume that you are writing about things that have actually happened. We hope that you will find and read this letter before some of those things happen. Sara, you need to return home and buy weapons that can protect you both from the dangers you will be facing, and we will do all we can to help you. Please give us another chance. Love, Mom and Dad."

"Well I'll be darned," Sara said as she shook her head wishing she had read their letter the day she stuffed it in her purse; perhaps they wouldn't find themselves in the mess they were now in. She couldn't help but think about Nathan and wondered if he was waiting for her inside the house like he promised he would do, or whether he was forced to leave by another Indian attack. Her stomach was in knots and her mind in turmoil when she finally saw her father's truck speeding towards her.

She opened the door to his truck and climbed in throwing her arms around her father's neck and cried, "Thank you Dad for coming. I've missed you so much."

"What's going on Sara, you sounded desperate? Is it the Shawnee?" he asked while turning his truck around.

"How did you know?" she asked bewildered.

"I've read your books; all but one that is. We're having a hard time tracking it down," he said and looked over at her.

"I can't tell you how happy I am that you and mom now believe me," she said feeling a bit awkward for not having read their letter sooner.

"How could we not? The published dates and the dedications were all the proof we needed. By the way, where are we going?" he asked curiously.

"Dad I need you to take me to that gun shop in Knoxville. I need a weapon for Nathan by tomorrow morning. If I had just read your letter sooner maybe we could have avoided the trouble we're in," she said.

"It's that serious, huh? Your mother and I were afraid you were writing about your experiences and not just exciting things you dreamed up to sell a book," her dad stated deeply concerned.

"I'm afraid it is serious," she replied and feared that he would try to convince her not to return.

"Do you think you can talk the man into letting us have the gun today and about ten boxes of ammunition?" she asked hesitantly knowing that any father would have trouble allowing their daughter to return to such a dangerous situation.

"You love him that much, huh?" he asked somberly.

"Yes, Dad, I do. I have to return or they will kill him, and I shall never recover," she said and cried bitterly with no ability to control her frayed nerves.

Her father let her cry knowing she needed to let it all out. Besides, he knew that he would be fighting a losing battle trying to convince her to stay, and telling her "I told you so" would just be wrong and accomplish nothing.

The hour seemed to pass quickly as they pulled into the parking lot of the gun shop and both hopped out of the truck and started for the door.

"What type of firearm do you have in mind? You know that these weapons won't be around for hundreds of years and you can't let them fall into the wrong hands," he exclaimed. Sara bit her tongue and did not respond to her father's last comment; he was not telling her something she didn't already know. All she cared about right now was keeping Nathan alive at any cost.

They entered the shop and heard the owner call out that he would be right with them and started looking in the cases at the different types of firearms. "Nathan needs something with stopping power and has at least seven shots. I don't want anything semiautomatic or too modern, just a really good revolver would be nice," she said as the owner was on his way to join them.

They greeted the owner, Jeff Miller, and then asked, "Jeff, we're looking for a revolver today, will you show us what you have?"

Jeff led them to a different case that housed revolvers and handed him a snubbed-nosed .38 revolver to look at. Sara shook her head and her dad handed the firearm back to him and continued to look.

"Jeff, can I see that stainless steel, six inch barrel .357 magnum with the wood handles?" Don asked.

"It's a beauty," Jeff said and removed it from the case and handed it to him.

He swung the cylinder open and stated, "It's a seven shot, huh? That's good. Sara what do you think?"

Sara took the firearm and double checked that it wasn't loaded and gripped it with both hands and pulled the trigger rapidly and suddenly there in her mind were Shawnee shooting arrows towards Nathan and she gasped and quickly shook the vision from her mind. "I like the feel of it. It has a nice pull to the trigger," she said breathing a little heavily and then looked at the fine wood grain of the handle. "I like this one, Dad. What do you think?" she asked.

"Well, it sure has the stopping power you're looking for. Jeff, can we see the holsters you have for this firearm?" he asked.

Sara looked them over carefully and found a black leather one that would hold extra ammunition for easy access, and it reminded her of the holsters she used to see in all the westerns she watched as a child.

"I like this one," she said and smiled at her dad.

"Jeff, I guess we'll take the .357 magnum, this holster and ten boxes of ammunition," her dad said and pulled out his credit card.

"Ten boxes, huh. You planning on starting a revolution?" he asked with a grin.

Her father just smiled and asked, "Any problem with us taking this with us today?"

"For you, no problem at all. I'll take care of it," he said as Don swiped his card and was given the receipt.

Driving to her parent's home Sara wished there had been enough time to return to Nathan that night, but knew that she and her father would never be able to find the outcrop of rocks that would lead them right to Nathan's door. She was deeply distressed not knowing what was happening with Nathan, and her stomach was still in knots as they pulled up in front of her parents' house.

Sara's mom rushed out to meet them and hugged Sara until her father broke it up. "Let the poor girl inside for heaven's sake," he said and opened the front door for her.

Her mom started right in with a multitude of questions that started with, "How long can you stay?"

Sara tried patiently to answer her questions, but had a few of her own that she needed her father to answer.

"Dad, I hate to ask this favor, but do you think your truck could take driving through the valley and over an outcrop of rocks to the other side of the hill and back? It would take me a couple of hours to hike back to the house and maybe longer carrying all that we bought today."

"For you, anything," her dad replied and continued, "How bad of a situation is it with the Shawnee?"

He watched as tears immediately filled Sara's eyes and she closed them and bit her bottom lip unable to answer as her tears made their way down her cheeks and dripped off her chin. Her dad shook his head and sighed heavily, distressed to see his only daughter in such agony of heart.

When she was able to speak she replied, "Its bad, Dad," and went on to tell them the story of her capture and rescue, and how Tecumseh had brought a party of Shawnee with him to reclaim her as his soon to be wife.

Sara saw her parents look at each other numerous times as she told her story and knew that they would stop her from returning to Nathan if they could. But she also knew they wouldn't try for it would be a waste of time; she would return to Nathan and hopefully survive to write yet another book.

Sara went to lay down while her mom fixed an early dinner, and her dad cleaned and oiled Nathan's new weapon and loaded it and placed it in the holster then back in her backpack.

Very little was said at dinner time for each of them were lost in their own thoughts and worries. But after dinner Sara shared some of the wonderful times she had enjoyed with Nathan and showed them her wedding ring before she went to her room for the night.

Her parents were awakened in the middle of the night by Sara screaming out Nathan's name and they sat straight up in bed. Both were alarmed and Becky started to swing her legs over the side of the bed when Don took her gently by the arm and told her to wait just a minute. He listened and heard Sara crying and said with a heavy heart, "Let her be, it's just a nightmare and she'll cry herself back to sleep."

"How can we let her go back when she's obviously terrified and in so much danger?" Becky asked.

"Wouldn't you go back if I needed your help?" he asked.

"Of course," she responded quickly, and then everything became clear to her and she hesitantly laid back down and stared up at the ceiling until Sara stopped her crying.

Sara's eyes were already open about four in the morning and she started thinking about the best way to get back to Nathan quickly. She remembered the last time she returned after getting the antibiotics for Nathan. She had driven her car almost to the base of the hill in front of Nathan's house before her car broke down. She reasoned that her father's truck would be able to take the punishment and make it all the way to the base of the hill, then all she would have to do was cross over the hill and she would be home.

She turned on her light and promptly dressed and quietly went downstairs and put on a pot of coffee. Nathan now consumed her every thought and every nerve in her body was on edge. Not knowing if he was alright made her pace anxiously waiting for her dad to get up, and finally she could wait no longer and went upstairs and gently knocked on their bedroom door.

"Dad, are you awake," she called out softly.

Moments later her dad opened the door, "I am now. What time is it?" he asked.

"I'm sorry to wake you; it's 4:30 AM. I can't sleep, and I have to get back to Nathan before it's too late. Can we go after we have a cup of coffee?" she asked so distressed that her dad whispered,

"I'll be right down. Why don't you fill the thermos and we can take it with us."

"Thanks Dad," she replied and hurried downstairs and had the thermos ready to go when he came down the stairs with her mother.

"I hope you don't mind, but I would like to come along. I don't know when I will get to see you again."

Sara hugged her mom and softly said, "I'll be back to see you again. I promise."

They each grabbed a coffee cup and her mom took the last of the banana bread she made the day before and they all piled into the truck and started for the cabin. Sara was restless and kept squirming in her seat as she exhaled loudly over and over. When her mother could take it no longer she poured Sara a cup of coffee and cut her a piece of bread and told her to eat up, she would need her strength to climb the hill. Although her stomach was in knots she knew her mother was right and quickly ate what her mother had given her and went back to her restless fidgeting.

As they approached her company's cabin her father slowed down and asked Sara for directions.

"Dad, it would be easier if you would let me drive. I've decided to take a short cut; it'll take about an hour off our driving time," she told him.

Her dad stopped the truck and looked at her unsure whether he wanted to turn the wheel over to her. "What if we get stuck or break down out there? Are you sure you know what you're doing?"

"Dad, I almost made it to the bottom of the hill in my vehicle. I need to do this, and I've crossed this ground by foot many times and I promise to drive as carefully and safely as possible. If your truck breaks down the cabin isn't very far away and I'm sure you can call for a tow truck from there. The man staying there seemed very nice; just tell him you're my dad and I'm sure he will help you," she anxiously stated eager to get home.

"All right, let's switch places. Hold on Mom, this could get real bumpy," he said as Sara climbed into the driver's seat and put the truck in four-wheel drive.

Sara turned on the high beams and stepped on the gas following the same path she took before, but this time the truck fish-tailed several times over the icy, muddy ground and she slowed down slightly as she cautiously approached the base of the hill.

Sara left the engine running after putting the truck in the proper gear and quickly climbed out. She took her backpack out of the back seat and struggled putting it on, for it was very heavy. By this time her parents were standing out in the cold waiting to give her the last hug and kiss she would possibly ever get from them.

"Thank you for your help Dad," she said as she wrapped her arms around him and just held him for a few moments and continued, "I couldn't have done any of this without you. I love you more than you will ever know."

She turned her attention to her mom who was already crying and opened her arms. "Come here Mom. I love you so much, and I promise to come visit if I'm able, please don't cry," she said as she held her mom.

When their good-byes were said Sara turned and took a few steps up the slope of the hill and looked back at her parents standing there, then quickly started trudging up the hill with her heavy backpack. The adrenaline was pumping as she maneuvered thru the brush and did not stop to catch her breath until she reached the top. She bent over placing her hands on her knees as she took several deep breaths before she started down the other side and looked in the early morning light to see if the house was still standing. Sara thanked God that the Shawnee hadn't burnt it to the ground during the night, and quickly started down the hill slipping occasionally on the muddy patches until she reached the bottom and ran thru the woods to their front porch. Gasping heavily now, she pushed hard on the door and when she got it open, ran and climbed the stairs leading to the attic and pulled the staircase down. She hesitated just a moment afraid of what she might find, and closed her eyes still breathing heavily and found the nerve to enter the attic.

Chapter 43

With her first step onto its floor she was quick to smell the scent of pine and quickly turned around and when the stairs changed before her eyes she loudly called out Nathan's name as she hurriedly ran down them. By the time she reached the top of the stairs leading to the living area Nathan was there with open arms and she quickly lowered her backpack to the floor and ran into his arms and wrapped hers around his waist as he pulled her body tightly against his.

"That was the longest day of my life; I was sick with worry that something might happen to you," he lamented and held her face in both hands and kissed her long and passionately, relieved that she was safely home. When he was finally able to release her, he picked up her backpack and carried it downstairs and set it on the couch.

"What do you have in here, lead?" he asked surprised by the weight of it.

"Yes, and lots of it," she said with a smile and quickly opened her backpack and pulled out his holstered .357 magnum and set it on the couch and removed his revolver and handed it to him.

His eyes were wide with disbelief as he held it and turned it over in his hands, and then stared at her speechless.

"Do you like it?" she asked.

"I've never seen anything like it; it's magnificent," he said looking down at the wood grained handle and shiny stainless steel barrel, and slipped his finger around the trigger.

"Careful, it's loaded," she declared quickly not wanting him to discharge it accidentally.

"What's it made of?" he asked still studying the revolver.

"It's called stainless steel. Why don't you let me take the bullets out and then you can get a feel for it."

Nathan handed it to her and watched how she swung open the cylinder and emptied the bullets into her hand and closed the cylinder back into place.

"It's pretty simple to use, you just point and shoot," she said pleased with her choice of handguns.

Nathan took the revolver in his hand and felt the weight of it and held it up and pulled the trigger and smiled.

"Let's see if the holster fits you. I just guessed at the right size," she said and wrapped it around his hips and buckled it.

Nathan tugged on it a little bit and returned the revolver to its place and then quickly drew it out and adjusted the height of the belt until he drew his weapon in a fluid motion.

"Nathan, this revolver is considered to have incredible stopping power. It will knock a man clean off his feet no matter where you shoot him. It might not kill him depending on where you shoot him, but it will stop him. When do you plan to go after Tecumseh?" she asked remembering why she bought the weapon in the first place.

His whole countenance changed when he looked at her; the hardened soldier and Indian fighter had returned and he replied in a calm, cold tone, "Tonight."

Sara swallowed hard and could feel the blood rush from her head as she looked into his piercing angry eyes. She turned away and went and sat by the fire; unfamiliar with this side of him and she pitied any man that stood in his way.

Nathan came out of his temporary trance and saw how frightened Sara was and quickly went to her and knelt by her side. "I'm sorry. I didn't mean to frighten you. I'm not proud of the man I become when I'm faced with battle, but I've learned that a man who hesitates to do what needs to be done is a dead man, and I have much to live for."

Sara simply nodded looking into his eyes that didn't have the same degree of fire in them and tried to put herself in his position of fighting for his life, his soul mate, and his home, and realized she would never understand what it took to go up against such odds.

She watched as he returned to practicing using his revolver, and hesitated to mention or show him how people in her time held their weapons when prepared to fire them. She feared that he might find it insulting so she refrained from saying anything at that moment.

Since he was consumed with his new weapon Sara went to the kitchen to start preparing something for supper, and stopped and stared out the window overlooking the barn and part of the apple orchard. All seemed quiet at the moment so she went about her business and just glanced at Nathan now and then and was fascinated by the way he became one with his weapon. As the day wore on she noticed that he would close his eyes and load and unload the bullets from his revolver using the bullets from his holster. He fumbled at first dropping some of them on the floor, but by early evening he did it with ease.

Nathan was still in fight mode while they ate their venison stew and biscuits, and very little was said. Sara still hadn't noticed him using his revolver with both hands and made up her mind to find some way of showing him without risking insulting him.

After they were finished eating Sara asked, "Would you mind if I hold your revolver? I really didn't get a chance when I was at the store. My dad picked it out and bought it, cleaned it, and packed it away for me."

"No, please try it out, it's loaded so please be careful."

Sara took the revolver and stood with her legs slightly apart, one back and a little out from the other, and raised the revolver with both hands; the one supporting and steadying the other and aimed it in the direction of the front door. She noticed that Nathan had watched her closely and she could tell that he was thinking about the way she handled the weapon.

"Does everyone in your time hold a weapon the way you do?" he asked seriously.

"Yes, pretty much anyone who is familiar with this handgun holds it that way because it has a pretty good kick to it. I know our police officers do and anyone I've seen shooting at the shooting range holds it that way. But you do what is comfortable for you," she said hoping to not be perceived as being pushy or a know it all.

Nathan got up from the table and walked over to Sara. "It's my turn," he said with a smile and took his revolver from her. He imitated her stance and the way she held his revolver and went through those motions several times and Sara could tell that he was not comfortable with it. It seemed unnatural after so many years of firing his flint locked pistol and tonight he could not be trying out something new.

He turned to Sara and said, "I'll be back in a few minutes. It's time for me to change clothes."

She went and stood by the back window and her eyes carefully searched the forest behind their house, but saw nothing of the Shawnee that Nathan would soon be tracking out in the forest at night. It suddenly hit her like a bolt of lightning what was about to happen and the hairs on the back of her neck stood up and she could feel the blood rushing from her head. She panicked as she realized what Nathan was up against; six battle-hardened warriors against one battle-hardened soldier, and only one side could win.

Sara wondered if one revolver could change the odds against so many coming against him on a dark, cold night and thought there must be another way to defeat them.

Nathan soon emerged from the bedroom in black breeches and knee high boots and wearing a long sleeve deerskin tunic that came almost to his knees. As he strapped his holster around his hips and tucked his sheathed knife under his belt he glanced at Sara often as he watched her grow pale and saw the fear in her eyes but never said a word to her.

She was shaking as she approached him and saw the resolve in his eyes; he was determined to end this tonight.

"Nathan, please don't go tonight. There must be another way. How can I bear it if something happens to you? I shall never overcome it as long as I live. Please, think of another way," she desperately cried and wiped her nose on her sleeve.

Nathan acted like he didn't even hear her. His mind was walking through every step and every move he would make tonight and he would not be distracted by Sara's pleas.

"I'll be back before morning. Keep the doors latched and bolted and keep your firearm with you at all times." He looked at her tear stained face and pulled her close and kissed her, but there was no emotion behind it, no tenderness, or passion; it seemed lifeless almost mechanical and she pulled back and looked at him in bewilderment as he quietly turned and went out the front door and closed it. The last words Sara heard were, "Sara, bolt the door."

Chapter 44

Nathan lost focus when he heard Sara cry out to God to protect the man she loved, and to bring him back safely to her. He had lingered a moment too long at the door, and allowed his feelings to interrupt his concentration and focus, and hurried to the far, east corner of the porch where he could no longer hear Sara's crying. He closed his eyes and took several deep breaths of the cold night air and tried to clear his mind of Sara and regain his focus and mindset that was crucial before battle; for a battle was largely won or lost in the mind.

When his strategy was firmly established, he peeked around the corner of the house and quickly slid over the railing of the porch and headed for the forest. A cloud drifted over the moon and he was grateful for the cover it provided as he entered the forest and headed towards the last place he had seen them. He walked cautiously from the cover of one tree to another and stopped often to listen and scan the ground for clues.

As he continued up the rocky slope of the mountain with its patches of snow, he mapped out every standing and fallen tree as possible cover should he come upon their camp unexpectedly. He stopped to catch his breath that turned to clouds of vapors in the cold night air and keenly listened once again for the sound of their horses, and the crackling of their campfire. He inhaled deeply in the hopes of detecting the slightest scent of smoke from their fire and then quietly moved on.

He was getting close to where he had last seen their campfire from his attic window and moved a little slower with his hand now resting on the handle to his revolver. He had never heard them fire a pistol or rifle, but that didn't mean they didn't have one. He assumed that they would come at him with arrows, knives and tomahawks in hand-to-hand battle if he gave them that chance. He knew he had a steady hand and a cool head in battle, and usually hit whatever he shot at. But the odds were still in their favor; he would have to surprise them and take a couple of them out of the action quickly if he was going to have any chance at all. He wished he would have had the opportunity to fire his new revolver, for it was never a good idea to go into battle with an untested weapon.

He moved to his next position behind a large pine tree and rested against its hard rough bark and listened carefully for several minutes, and finally heard the faint nickering of one of their horses and continued to listen until he was sure in which direction to proceed.

Nathan moved slowly and quietly from one oak or pine tree to another not wanting to make any of their horses uneasy and alert them that something or someone was close by. He finally caught a whiff of their campfire and stood still, clearing his mind and focusing on what his next move would be. His hands were cold and almost numb of feeling when he removed his revolver from its holster and held it up tight against his shoulder as he stepped out from behind a large oak tree and slowly moved again from one tree to another keeping a sharp watch for anyone posted to watch their camp.

He finally caught a glimpse of their campfire and looked around for a good place to take cover before he moved on. Up ahead he noticed an old large fallen oak tree about forty feet away from their camp and several large pines that had grown up close to it. That is where he would make his play. He now ducked down and moved silently, purposefully planting each foot so as to not break any branches or twigs on the ground, and used every brush he could find as cover leading to the fallen tree. His eyes darted back and forth between the horses, the Shawnee around the campfire, and the pitch dark forest that now concealed Tecumseh as he moved ever closer.

One more move and he would be behind the large fallen oak where he could kneel and not be seen. As he peered over the moss covered top he could see five horses tied to a line and five Shawnee sitting around the campfire and listened carefully to their voices as he studied their faces and build. He could clearly see that the two facing him were not Tecumseh, they were too young, and he was pretty sure that the one sitting sideways to him was not him either, but the two with their backs to him he couldn't tell. He was patient and waited for them to turn their heads and when they did he slumped down and sat on the ground.

"Damn it!" he uttered softly; Tecumseh was not among them. It was important to cut the head of a snake off or it would return to bite you sooner or later; and wondered where he was. His anger boiled up; if he failed to get Tecumseh this whole undertaking was for nothing. He could not see or think clearly until he got his anger under control and sat there breathing deeply until his rage and disappointment subsided.

He cautiously peered over the log again and picked out his first two targets; the two facing him would be the wise choice to take out first. The two with their backs to him would have to turn around or try to scramble away giving him a slight opportunity to take both of them out as well. His position would allow him time to reload if necessary, because only wounding them was not an option; he must kill them first before looking for Tecumseh.

While he was planning his strategy Sara was anxiously pacing the floor for over two hours and the silence was driving her crazy as her imagination ran wild. She went to the windows often and peered out into the darkness, and then fear would overtake her and she would move away afraid that someone would see her alone in the house.

Meanwhile Tecumseh had moved down the mountain and was watering his horse at the stream planning on returning to their barn and taking their only horse leaving Nathan with no way of going for help to his friends the Cherokee. What he didn't know was that Nathan had his eyes trained on his first of five targets; for that is how he viewed them and nothing more. He raised his revolver bracing his arms on top of the log, took a deep breath and held it as he aimed for the man's chest and slowly squeezed the trigger and watched as the Shawnee was violently knocked backwards to the cold hard ground. Nathan quickly took aim at the second man that was facing him and when he stood to run he fired, instantly dropping him where he stood.

Sara heard the shots ring out and echo through the mountains and ran to the window knowing that Nathan had found the Shawnee he was searching for. The shots fired proved that he was still alive. Her anxiousness grew as she listened for the next shot to ring out for there were still at least four Shawnee she knew of that he would have to kill before he would return home to her. Tecumseh also heard the shots echo through the mountains and quickly mounted his horse and started back to his camp.

As Nathan had anticipated, the two Shawnee with their backs to him dove for cover and quickly made their way behind trees that were close by. His eyes searched relentlessly for the last Shawnee and found him trying to mount one of the restless horses trying to pull free of their rope. He stood patiently waiting for him to finally mount then took careful aim and squeezed off another shot and watched as his third victim fell from his horse. The element of surprise helped him with the first three, but these last two would prove to be a challenge. He knew that he needed to change his position and withdrew back through the trees and to slightly higher ground where he could watch for them to make their move. He no longer had the benefit of the glow from their campfire for it was pitch black with the moon once again tucked behind the clouds. He would have to wait until they were practically upon him before he had a chance to use his revolver again. Removing his knife from his belt he cut brush and placed it about ten feet out in a semicircle around the back of the tree he was using as cover, for his ears would be his best defense now.

He waited and watched, but he saw and heard nothing move and became anxious knowing that Tecumseh had heard the shots and was on his way. Nathan knew that he could not take on all three Shawnee at one time and needed to quickly draw these two out of hiding if he was going to have any chance of killing them before he had to face Tecumseh. Aware of the chances he was taking, Nathan moved from his position closer to their campsite. He leaned out quickly, then back, from behind each tree just far enough for them to see him and figure thy might have a chance to pick him off with a lucky shot from their bow and arrows, or perhaps get close enough to make it impossible for him to get a shot off before they attacked with their knives or tomahawks.

He took a deep breath of the frigid air that burned inside his lungs, looked around, and then stepped out from behind a tree and listened, then moved a little closer. The clouds moved past the moon making it a little easier for Nathan to see any movement and quickly leaned out and back a couple of times from behind a tree and then stepped out once again with his revolver at the level of his hip ready to fire. As he approached the next tree he heard a twig snap behind him, and turned sharply just in time to see a Shawnee poised ready to throw his tomahawk and fired twice. Both bullets hit the warrior in the stomach and he watched as he dropped his weapon and fell to the ground.

Nathan knew in those few seconds since he fired and watched the warrior fall he had left himself open to an attack from the other one that was now stalking him. Before he could turn or take cover an arrow came whizzing inches past him and stuck into a tree and he quickly knelt down and looked behind him. He knew the last Shawnee was close by the force in which the arrow struck the tree and his eyes darted between a few trees that had been directly behind him. Still kneeling with one knee on the ground he saw the tip of an arrow jet out slightly by the side of an oak tree. Nathan was now desperate for he heard the panting sound of a horse being pushed hard coming up the slope towards camp and knew that he needed to move quickly. With great determination and eyes now focused on his opponent's position, he took a deep breath with his revolver ready and in one fluid motion he stood and quickly moved in the only direction that would force his opponent to move away from the tree to take his shot. When he did, Nathan fired missing with the first shot but dropping him with the second.

Sara was counting the shots fired and knew that Nathan would have to reload soon and wondered if he had killed them all and continued her pacing as she prayed ardently waiting for him to return to her.

Nathan rapidly emptied the cylinder of bullet casings and reached for replacements from his belt, but it was too late. Tecumseh's horse came running through camp but Tecumseh was not on it. He quickly put his revolver back in its holster and grabbed his knife, knowing that Tecumseh would be upon him any moment and looked hurriedly around him.

Suddenly, bursting out of the darkness he saw Tecumseh with his painted face rushing towards him with a knife in one hand and a tomahawk in the other and in a split second he knew what he must do. There was both fire and hatred in Tecumseh's eyes as Nathan grabbed his raised forearm holding the tomahawk and he dropped to the ground flipping him over his head to slow him down, then quickly stood to his feet with his knife ready to fight. Tecumseh came at him slower this time swinging both weapons which Nathan agilely dodged jumping backwards and taking a swing himself. He had never faced a warrior of Tecumseh's caliber in all his previous battles, and wondered whether he was outmatched this time.

Tecumseh was swinging and jabbing like a wild man, filled with too much hatred and anger, and Nathan prayed that this would be his downfall; that he would make a mistake which he could take advantage of. Tecumseh kept coming at him wielding his knife with his tomahawk poised to strike as Nathan swallowed hard and kept backing up and nimbly avoiding each swing.

He quickly looked behind him not wanting to back into a tree preventing him from dodging Tecumseh's attack. That was the second Tecumseh needed for his knife to rip across Nathan's tunic cutting through the deerskin hide and grazing the skin of his stomach. Nathan grabbed his wrist and fell backwards with Tecumseh not far behind. He firmly gripped his knife and held it upward and when Tecumseh landed on top of him the knife stuck deep inside his belly and Nathan quickly pushed him off, pulled his knife out, and raised it above his head. Tecumseh watched wide-eyed as Nathan said disdainfully, "Sara's mine," and drove the knife into his chest and turned it. Nathan watched as the life drained out of Tecumseh then fell over sitting on the ground breathing heavily as his breaths turned into clouds of mist. It was over. He had defeated his enemies and could go home to Sara, but would not go home empty handed. He roughly pulled Tecumseh's necklace of bear claws and earthen beads off his dead body, a symbol of his status within the tribe and put it around his neck.

When he had caught his breath, he reloaded his revolver though he could barely feel his fingers and went to check each Shawnee to make sure they were dead and not just wounded. He did not want any of them to be able to return to their village and tell them what he had done; what had happened would die with them there.

Nathan left their bodies where they lay and gathered up their horses and rode back on Tecumseh's horse leading a string of them behind him. It had been over an hour since Sara heard the last gunshot and was anxiously looking out the back window for his return when she heard the sound of horse hooves and neighing before she ever saw them in the darkness and strained to see if it was Nathan or the Shawnee coming for her. Once she caught sight of Nathan she excitedly yelled out his name and ran from the house and reached him just as he had closed the door to the barn and threw her arms around him and kissed him exuberantly as she cried overwhelmed with joy.

Nathan could scarcely hold on to her from shear exhaustion, both physically and mentally drained, but managed to smile at her exuberant joy at seeing him. After tenderly kissing her he wearily stated, "It's over now, you don't ever have to worry about seeing his face again. What do you say we go inside? I'm mighty tired," and put his arm around her shoulder and slowly walked back to the house.

Sara could feel his weight upon her shoulders as they climbed the few steps to the porch and was anxious to get him to his chair by the fire. His face was like ice when she had kissed him, and tried not to think about his last kiss for it seemed cold with no tenderness to it at all. That was not the only thing she tried not to think about; she was all too familiar with the bear claw necklace and there were only horrid memories attached to it that she never wanted to think about again.

The warm air from the fireplace greeted them as they came through the door and Sara was glad to be out of the dark and back inside with the glow of the fire and candles. As she turned to him to ask if he would like a nice hot cup of coffee her eyes were drawn to his tunic. They grew wide as she stared at the tear across it soaked in blood and looked up at him and frightfully declared, "You've been hurt! Why didn't you say something? Let me help you off with your tunic so I can bandage it."

"It's only a scratch. It can wait until after I lay down for a bit and then you can take a look at it. You wouldn't mind holding off fixing breakfast for me for about an hour or so, would you?" he asked while unfastening his belt and laying his revolver on a table close to him.

She looked into his tired gaze and quickly at his torn tunic and noticed that the blood did seem to be more dried than fresh. She hesitantly nodded and said, "Go lay down. I'll tend to it later," and lightly kissed him on the cheek and stepped aside to let him by.

As he closed the door to the bedroom he pulled the bear claw necklace from around his neck and studied it and could not remember why it was so important for him to take it; but he had. Before laying down he placed it in the bottom dresser drawer under his clothing and went and laid down on the bed facing towards the fire. As he watched the flames dance he fell into deep thought, disturbed not by the fact that he had just killed six men, but how easily killing came to him; he was good at it. He knew that the Shawnee had given him no choice but to come after them, but the way he did it made him wonder what kind of a man he truly was. He had been so consumed in his plans to kill them that he had totally ignored Sara's pleas and gave no consideration to the brutal trauma she had just been through and was dealing with. His own thoughts had been more important to him at the time. As he continued to stare into the fire he had a flashback to the way he had killed Tecumseh with such anger, or was it hatred when he plunged his knife into his chest and told him "Sara's mine". Though physically and emotionally drained his mind would not let him sleep. He had to search his soul for the truth about himself and wondered if it were even possible to be that honest with one's self. He knew he loved God, and he knew he loved Sara, and he tried to live in such way to please both of them. But when he was pushed, something inside his mind snapped; a line had been crossed from which there was no turning back. He thought about King David; he was a man of war, and he loved God and was considered to be a man after God's own heart. Nathan wondered if it bothered him how many men he had killed and how he felt after he did it.

His thoughts were interrupted when Sara entered the room, for almost two hours had passed and she wondered if he was ready for breakfast. He buried the thoughts that had troubled his mind and responded, "Yes, and I'm hungry enough to eat a horse," and forced a smile.

Sara set a hardy breakfast before him and took her seat across from him able to better enjoy watching him for she was overjoyed to have him back home safe and pretty much unharmed. As she gazed at him while he ate she thought she would see a look of relief or joy to be home, but instead he seemed to have a distant look as if he were a million miles away. Sara thought about saying, "A penny for your thoughts," but after further consideration she decided not to. After all he had just been through, she knew from experience he just needed a little time to sort things out in his mind. She also knew from previous conversations how much it bothered him to have to kill again. He had hoped to put that part of his life behind him when he moved to the frontier for a little piece and quiet.

Sara started thinking about the short time she had been with Nathan; his life seemed to be in constant turmoil, not that she was to blame for the unsavory characters who had passed by their way and stirred up trouble. But nevertheless, Nathan had never found the peace he was looking for and wondered how she could help him find it.

He was just licking his fingers clean when Sara came up behind him and gently laid her arms down against his chest and softly whispered in his ear, "I have some hot water for your bath so

I can bandage your wound when you're through and thought you might enjoy me washing your hair for you. Then, if you like, you can stretch out on the bearskin rug with your head in my lap and let me brush your hair while you relax. Would you like that?" she asked tenderly.

Nathan placed his hands over hers and said looking up at her, "I would love it."

He carried the pot of hot water to the bedroom while Sara got the soap, washcloth and towels and followed him to the tub in front of their fireplace. As she helped lift the tunic over his head she noticed fresh blood around the cut across his stomach and knew that she would have to bandage it soon, but first he would have to finish undressing so she could pour the warm water over his head. She could see his body relax as she poured several pitchers of the warm water over him then soaped up the washcloth and simultaneously washed and massaged his back then handed him the cloth to finish washing while she washed and rinsed his hair. She brought him a towel to dry off with while she went to get a box of butterfly band aides and ointment. She knelt beside him on the bearskin rug and pulled the towel just below his naval and gently spread the ointment over his wound and put a series of bandages across the cut. When she was finished she sat down and Nathan closed his eyes as he rested his head in her lap and she stroked the brush gently through his hair while she sang softly to him in the hope he would relax. As she brushed his hair she felt his body go limp and was content to sit there with his head on her lap while he slept.

Chapter 45

A week had passed since Nathan's encounter with the Shawnee. His wound was healing nicely, though he still had that distant look from time to time as his troubled thoughts about the way he killed Tecumseh still haunted him.

He had just finished his early morning chores in the barn and was headed back to the house to get another cup of coffee. He suddenly stood still and looked towards the mountains where the vultures had been circling for days, then lowered his head and continued to stand there. Sara happened to be looking out the kitchen window and noticed his peculiar behavior and wiped her hands on her apron and met him as he was coming up the steps to the porch.

"Is everything alright?" she asked, and then heard the distant sound of wood being chopped up in the mountains and looked at him bewilderedly.

"You heard it too, huh?" he said with a scowl and sat down.

"Who would be up there chopping wood?" Sara asked as she took her seat next to him on the porch.

Nathan sighed heavily then replied, "The sound seems to be coming from where I had my encounter with the Shawnee."

Sara had never brought up the subject about what happened that night and figured that he would tell her about it when he was ready.

"But why would someone be chopping wood in that particular area?"

Nathan had that distant look in his eyes again, then finally responded. "My guess would be that the Shawnee have come to take their bodies back to be buried and they're chopping wood to make sleds to carry them on," he said in a downcast tone as the events of that night played in his mind.

Sara's heart sank and anxiously thought about what this would mean for them. She had fought hard to put the events with the Shawnee behind her, and had hoped that their dealings with them were over. "Will they come here?" she asked looking fearfully at him.

"I honestly don't know," he replied.

The chopping sound continued for hours, and Nathan went inside and picked up his revolver for the first time since that cold and dark night. He cleaned his weapon thoroughly and fastened the holster around his hips and sat silently in his rocker by the fire. Sara brought him a cup of coffee and picked up her sewing and sat down trying to keep busy in the hopes that it would keep her from dwelling on the unknown plans of the Shawnee. Once again peace became a fleeting dream as the day wore on.

All was quiet that night, but early the next morning as Nathan was drinking his coffee looking out the back window he saw a single file of seven horses winding their way down the side of the mountain. They formed a straight line at the edge of his property and just sat there.

Sara came up behind him and wrapped her arms around him and said, "Breakfast is ready," then looked over his shoulder and squeezed him tightly.

Nathan placed his arm over hers, "Try not to worry, it doesn't look like they mean to attack…They want something…I just don't know what, but I'm sure they will let us know sooner or later."

Nathan turned towards Sara and held her in his arms and kissed her tenderly several times and looked into her eyes that were counting on him to once again protect her.

"Let's eat before it gets cold," he said with a gentle smile and a calmness that puzzled her.

When they were finished eating Sara passed by the window while she was cleaning up the kitchen and called for Nathan to join her.

"Nathan, they've left," she said with a puzzled look.

He stared out the window and replied, "They'll be back."

The day passed with no further sign of the Shawnee and Sara and Nathan cautiously went about their business, but frequently stared into the forest wondering what the Shawnee wanted from them.

That night as Nathan and Sara were sitting by the fire, Nathan happened to glance down at the bear skin rug and it suddenly came to him what the Shawnee wanted, and knew they wouldn't leave until they had it. She could tell that he was deep in thought as he stared back up into the fire, but still couldn't bring herself to ask him what happened that night.

"I know what they want," Nathan suddenly blurted out. Sara looked intently at him and waited for him to continue.

"They want Tecumseh's necklace. I took it from him right after I killed him. Their chief will give it to the next warrior who will become their war chief; it is a symbol of his status and authority within the tribe."

Sara didn't respond, but rest her head back against her chair. She remembered the necklace, for Tecumseh was never without it, and visions of him played over and over again in her mind. It made her feel weak and insecure and she no longer felt confident like she once had and it made her angry.

Sara sat up and looked at Nathan full of angry emotions and determinedly said, "I'm tired of being afraid, and I've had enough of these troubled thoughts that make me feel weak and helpless. I refuse to give into them any longer; I'm stronger than that! I want my life back. I want to feel the passion I once felt!"

Sara got up and sat on Nathan's lap and looked longingly into his eyes and kissed him in a way she hadn't kissed him since her capture. He had waited patiently for Sara to feel this way again, and now highly aroused he looked at her with intense desire as he felt his body start to throb. He lowered her to the bearskin rug and they quickly undressed and came together with overwhelming passion that would not easily be quenched. He took her hard and fast the first time, and as she laid there breathing heavily he kissed her, then looked at her with a smile that told her to hold on he would soon be ready for another round. He started down her neck with hot, open mouth kisses to the rest of her body until he was ready, then took his time as she moaned in pleasure with every thrust and touch of his hands and mouth upon her body and never once thought about the Shawnee.

Both Nathan and Sara were up before dawn the next day. While Sara was preparing breakfast Nathan stood looking out the back window with a hot cup of coffee in his hand watching for the line of Shawnee warriors winding their way down the mountain, for he knew they would be back for the necklace.

"They're coming," Nathan said and Sara joined him by the window and watched as they lined up at the edge of their property and six of them were pulling sleds carrying the bodies of the dead warriors. One of them rode halfway to the house and stuck his spear into the ground and sat there by it waiting for Nathan to come out.

Nathan set his coffee cup down and removed his coat then strapped his holstered revolver around his hips and stuck his knife under his belt. He wanted them to see his weapons for he was aware that they viewed him as a mighty warrior. They had all seen the six bodies from their tribe lying in the forest and knew that he had been able to kill each of them in the dark of the night. They respected him for the way he faced Tecumseh in hand to hand combat for Tecumseh was fierce and had the experience of killing many a man and the scalps to prove it.

Sara was extremely anxious as she watched him prepare to face the Shawnee alone, and was amazed that he showed no sign of fear, but was calm and focused as he went to the bedroom to get Tecumseh's necklace.

Nathan could see Sara's anxiousness written all over her face and in her body language, and went to her and held her face in his hands and looked calmly into her eyes. "Sara, there's no need for you to worry, all they want is the necklace. In their eyes I'm the big, white, war chief and they respect that. I want you to stay inside and let me handle this. The last thing I need is for you to come outside pointing your firearm at them. Okay?" he stated calmly.

"Yes, I understand. I'll stay inside, but I will have my handgun ready," she quickly replied.

He couldn't help but smile at her tenacity in wanting to protect him even though she was anxious and trembling. He kissed her tenderly and opened the back door and calmly walked out carrying Tecumseh's necklace in his left hand.

Nathan could feel every eye on him and the strange weapon he was wearing on his hip as he walked straight out to the warrior waiting for him in the middle of the yard, and looked him in the eyes.

"I believe you came for this," he said boldly and held up Tecumseh's necklace.

The warrior looked down at him curiously then bent over and took the necklace from him and Nathan had the feeling that he understood what he had said.

"Tecumseh was a mighty war chief and I did not want to kill him, but he gave me no choice. He went against your chief's decision to return my wife to me in a fair trade. I hope you will go in peace. I have no quarrel with the Shawnee people," Nathan boldly stated.

"We will go in peace Waba Mkwa – White Bear," he replied in English, and abruptly turned his horse and joined his party that had turned to go back into the forest and return their dead to be buried.

Sara was there to greet Nathan when he entered the house and wrapped her arms around his waist and looking into his eyes with a big smile boldly stated, "I'm so proud of you! You were so brave the way you faced them; so calm and cool and confident!"

It pleased Nathan to hear her say those things. "I'm glad you think so. Maybe now we can finally enjoy a little peace and quiet around here," he said with a grin and went to finish his coffee.

Chapter 46

While Sara and Nathan were busy building a corral to keep the Shawnee's horses in until they could take them to Knoxville to sell, Inola was busy tracking an unidentified hunting party who had captured Adsila and two other women.

The women had been downstream from their village washing clothes in the river when they were surprised by another tribe returning home from a hunting trip. They were gagged and taken away before they could cry out for help. When the women did not return when expected, one of their sons was sent on horseback to check on them.

Inola heard him yelling as he rode back into camp and went outside to see what all the fuss was about.

"The women are gone! The clothes are lying on rocks in the river, and there is no sign of them; just horse tracks leading up to the river and then on the other side heading south," the young man declared out of breath.

Inola's anger flared up instantly when he heard that Adsila had been taken and he ran into his lodge and gathered his weapons then mounted his horse followed by a dozen or more braves from the village yelling a war cry as they raced to the river to pick up their trail. Their horses sent water splashing high into the air as they charged across the river and Inola quickly spotted the tracks leading away in single file.

Inola's party followed the tracks for two days until they lost them in a rocky area, and the men he was with no longer wanted to pursue them and turned back. Inola knew he would never be able to rescue the women alone and turned back with them just to get Adohi and head to Nathan's place for help.

They rode hard knowing that each day their enemy's lead increased and their trail would be harder to follow. By mid-afternoon the following day they could see Nathan's house in the distance and pushed their horses a little harder. Nathan and Sara were just finishing up attaching the gate to the corral when Nathan saw dust being kicked up in the air and knew that riders were headed their way. He pulled his revolver from the holster and checked to make sure it was fully loaded and kept his eye on the trail of dust.

"Who do you think it can be?" Sara asked anxiously.

"I don't know, but they sure are in a hurry," Nathan replied as he shaded his eyes and squinted.

"Why don't you wait inside until I see who it is?"

Sara turned to leave when he reached out and caught her arm. "Wait, that's Inola's horse; he must be in trouble if he's riding like that."

Within minutes Inola and Adohi pulled up on the reins and jumped down from their horses tired and thirsty.

"Sara would you mind tending to their horses?" Sara nodded and took their reins and led them into the barn to feed and water them.

"Why don't you two come inside and tell me what's going on," he stated with concern.

Inola was passionate in his anger as he spoke loudly telling Nathan about what had happened. He listened silently as his own rage grew for he knew exactly what Inola was going through and had already made up his mind that he would do whatever he could to help his friend.

Sara came to the back door when she was through with the horses and could hear the anger and desperation in Inola's voice and hesitated before opening the door. She knew something was terribly wrong for she had never heard Inola so outraged. They were still speaking in Cherokee when she finally went inside and stood next to Nathan sitting at the table. He looked up at her with piercing eyes and a clinched jaw as he reached over and wrapped his one arm around her and pulled her close as she stood by his side. He was silent as he gazed at her thinking pragmatically how he was going to help his friend, and wondered if Sara could handle the stress and rigors of such an excursion, or whether she should remain home with Adohi to look after her.

"What's happened, Nathan?" she asked seriously.

"Adsila and two other women have been taken captive, and Inola's village has called off the search for them," he stated and carefully watched for her reaction.

Sara looked at Inola horrified. "We must help him find her. Inola is family," she declared frantically.

Inola looked at Nathan quizzically, thinking Nathan would never consider taking Sara along after all that she had been through and questioned Nathan in Cherokee.

"English, please," Sara said looking at Nathan.

"Inola questions the wisdom in taking you along after what you've been through."

"Well I'm certainly not going to remain here. Where you go, I go." she stated emphatically.

Nathan looked at Inola thoughtfully and said, "I know you don't think it is a good idea to take Sara along, but she could be very useful to us, and she's quite good with a handgun. Besides, I've promised to never leave her alone again."

"Adohi will be here. He will protect her," Inola quickly retorted.

Nathan looked at Sara intently. "Are you sure you're up for this? We can't be worrying about you and do what we have to do at the same time. If you come, you will have to do exactly what we tell you to do, when we tell you to do it."

Nathan could see the resolve in Sara's face and said to Inola, "I guess she's coming. Let's get packed and head out, we still have at least five hours of daylight."

Preparations were made rapidly but thoroughly, taking only what was necessary for they needed to travel light and quickly if they were ever going to find Adsila.

They only took one extra horse along to carry their supplies and started out after saying good-bye to Adohi and thanking him for watching over their place while they were gone.

They headed southwest over the rolling hills in the direction Inola had last seen the tracks and lost them over the rocky terrain. The sun had almost set before they stopped for the night and made a small campfire. Inola was still not convinced that Sara would not crack under the pressure, but respected her for her willingness to help him.

As Nathan spread out their buffalo hides on the cold ground he watched Sara as she was brewing a pot of coffee. He was proud of her. She never complained about the cold or long hours in the saddle and was cheerfully eager to do whatever needed to be done.

As they sat around the fire eating jerky and drinking coffee Inola told them about Adsila, and Sara could see how much he loved her and prayed that they would be able to find her unharmed. They all turned in shortly after supper wanting to get an early start in the morning for whomever took Adsila had a four day head-start on them.

By late morning the next day they had arrived at the place where Inola had last seen the tracks. He went to the right and Nathan and Sara to the left of the rocky area and rode back and forth over the next couple hundred yards out until Nathan whistled loudly several times. Inola gave his horse a quick kick and took off in the direction of the whistle he heard. Nathan spotted him and whistled again for Inola was slightly off course and immediately wheeled his horse around and headed straight to them.

"Tell me what you think," Nathan said knowing that Inola was the expert in identifying tracks. He dismounted and squatted down and closely looked at the ground and moved on for about twenty feet checking the ground and bushes close by. Inola looked back at them and smiled, then raised his head in the air and loudly whooped out in pure delight; Nathan had found their tracks.

Sara was beaming with joy as she looked at Nathan, kissed him, and said, "Good job," as she mounted her horse. He was pleased that he had brought her with them; she seemed to be the happy, confident woman he fell in love with, and she brought with her a certain kind of balance that was greatly needed to keep them focused but not driven by vengeance or hatred that never ended well.

Inola took the lead, and stopped frequently to check the tracks and try to determine which tribe had taken Adsila and the other women. He finally came across a campsite they had used and they all dismounted and stretched as they carefully looked around for anything that might have been left behind.

They decided this would be a good place to rest while they ate some jerky and gave their horses some water. Not wanting to sit any longer, Sara walked a short distance from the fire pit rubbing her backside when she spotted something that looked like writing in the dirt.

"Inola, take a look at this," she said and waited for him to join her and then pointed to what she saw.

He quickly knelt down and looked where Sara had pointed and immediately looked up at her in amazement. Nathan joined them curious about what Sara had seen that so amazed Inola.

"Well I'll be damned," he said with a smile.

"What is it? What does it mean?" Sara asked bewildered.

Inola pointed to the markings on the ground and replied, "This is symbol for blossom and this one for fox," he said and smiled; Adsila had left a sign for them to follow.

"Good job," Nathan smirked trying to be humorous. Sara caught on to his humor right away and shook her head. "Copy Cat," she teased and mounted her horse to catch up with Inola who was eager to get started again.

They continued on for days following the tracks that never strayed too far from the river that ran south. Inola could tell by their campsites and the way their horses were tied at night that there were at least a dozen men in their party but still wasn't sure which tribe they were following.

Then one day when they were watering their horses at the river, Inola spotted something white by the water's edge and curious he walked over and picked it up.

Nathan asked, "Did you find something, Inola?"

Inola stood up and walked over to Nathan with a smile. "Chickasaw. We track Chickasaw."

"How do you know that?" Nathan asked.

"Chickasaw wear white arrow in hair before they have proven themselves a warrior."

Sara went walking downstream a little distance to have some privacy and when she was headed back she came upon the remains of a butchered deer. When she rejoined the men she asked, "Can you tell anything by the remains of a butchered deer?"

Nathan and Inola looked directly at each other as if she had spotted a pot of gold.

"Show us where you found it," Nathan said, and she led them to the spot and pinched her nose and looked away, for it not only stunk but it had maggots crawling all over it.

"I'd say it was butchered no more than two days ago. What do you think?" he asked turning towards Inola.

Inola nodded, "Two days," then looked intently downstream and Sara wondered what he was thinking.

There was still several hours of daylight and Inola was eager to press on hoping they would catch up to them in little over a day, maybe two, if they kept moving. Their spirits were high when they finally stopped for the night for they now knew who they were tracking and that they were gaining ground on them. Inola surmised they had slowed down to do some hunting and became careless thinking that the Cherokee had given up tracking them.

That night as they laid down, Nathan held Sara in his arms under their buffalo hide for it was extremely cold that night as they gazed at the stars and spoke quietly.

"I think Inola is going to try to make a tracker out of you yet."

"Really?" Sara mused.

"Yeah, you've got a keen eye, and an amazing analytical mind. It must be all that writing you do. You know I questioned whether it was a good idea to bring you with us or not, but I'm glad I did. I didn't know if you would be strong enough to handle another encounter of this nature. But I've seen a side to you these last few days that fills my heart with pride and joy, and a deeper love than I ever thought possible."

Sara raised her head and looked at him perplexed. "I'm not quite sure what you mean."

"I don't want to hurt your feelings, but I thought after seeing all the inventions and luxuries in the future, that people in your time would be weak, self-centered, and dependent on things to make them happy, but you have proven to be strong and resilient even after all you've been through. Yet, you've remained caring, thoughtful, and gentle, with a spirit as strong as I have ever seen in anyone. You're an amazing woman, Sara Chambers."

"You talk too much. Kiss her and go to sleep," Inola said grinning to himself and turned over on his side pulling his buffalo hide over him.

"You heard the man," Nathan said smiling and bent over and kissed her good and long, then kissed her again before lying down next to her.

The next morning as soon as it was light enough to follow the Chickasaw's tracks they started out. The trail was easy to follow at first because of the recent snow and light rain that had left deep hoof prints single file through the wooded areas along the river and they traveled along at a good pace. When they came upon a rocky area Inola would dismount and search on foot until he picked up their trail again. He often called Sara to join him so he could show her what to look for and Nathan was pleased to watch them together for Sara seemed to have a natural talent for tracking and she enjoyed it. The three of them pushed hard that day convinced that by tomorrow they would spot their camp. Late that afternoon when they had stopped to water their horses Inola walked a little further following the tracks and bent down by a pile of horse dung to see how old it was.

"Sara," he called and gestured with his hand for her to join him. Sara handed Nathan the reins to her horse and went to where Inola was squatting down. He picked up a piece of dung and broke it apart and said, "Texture of dung can tell you how long ago they passed by. Feel this. You can tell that it was left this morning," and raised his hand for her to take it.

"No thanks, Inola, I'll take your word for it."

Nathan laughed heartily at Sara's refusal, but Inola looked at her disappointedly and said, "You never be good tracker unless you willing to get hands dirty," and tried again to get her to take it.

Sara didn't know what bothered her more, Nathan laughing or Inola trying to get her to handle horse dung. She closed her eyes and sighed, then looked at Nathan who was still chuckling, then Inola, and held out her hand. When she took it and broke it apart Inola looked proudly at her, but Nathan laughed so hard she thought he would fall over.

"Very funny," she said to Nathan as she washed her hands in the river and then stood and dried them on the front of his shirt, looking him straight in the eyes.

Nathan ate that kind of attention right up and went to grab her arm and pull her close when he realized he was about to do the one thing he swore he couldn't do – lose focus. They had traveled this far for one purpose and one purpose only, to get Adsila and the other women back alive.

"Let's mount up, we still have a couple of hours before we make camp for the night," he said matter-of-factly and quickly mounted.

Sara was a little surprised by his sudden change in behavior but quickly dismissed it and mounted her horse and followed close behind as they continued following the tracks. She noticed that they were steadily climbing in elevation and looked ahead and saw that they would be approaching a heavily forested region with huge boulders and outcrops of rocks by the time they made camp for the night.

When they finally stopped Sara started to gather wood for the fire and when she had an armload she stood still and gazed at the beautiful sunset that would be gone in minutes. Nathan came up behind her and wrapped his arms around her and whispered softly in her ear, "It's beautiful isn't it?"

Sara turned her face and looked at him and replied, "Yes, it is," and stood watching until the sun disappeared behind the mountains then finally returned to camp to start the fire.

It was obvious that Inola was anxious about tomorrow and found it difficult to sit still and relax by the fire. He was sure that they would come across the Chickasaw camp site sometime tomorrow morning. Sara could see the same concentration in Inola that Nathan had had the night he went searching for the Shawnee and did not disturb him.

After they were finished eating, Nathan picked up one of the buffalo hides and wrapped it around Sara and himself as they sat by the fire drinking a hot cup of coffee, for it was frigidly cold again that night. Little was said as they listened to the coyotes yipping at the moon in the distance, both thinking about how everything would play out tomorrow.

Chapter 47

In the morning you could feel the tension in the air as they quickly broke camp and Inola took the lead through the forest. A couple of hours later they saw a large cluster of boulders surrounded by trees about a quarter mile up ahead and dismounted and tied their horses where they wouldn't easily be seen. The three of them took off on foot and walked around the boulders and found a narrow entrance that led between them that could easily hide the four women from sight.

"You and Sara wait here while I find their camp, and then I will come for you," Inola stated with intense focus of mind.

Nathan nodded and they watched Inola take off cautiously on foot through the forest headed towards the river. He noticed the anxiousness and concern Sara was experiencing and wondered if she would be able to hold up under the stress that was soon to come, or if she would be overcome with fear.

"Are you alright?" he asked worriedly as he pulled her close and wrapped his heavy overcoat around her as they waited in the cold and misty air.

"Yes, I'm fine. Just a little anxious," she replied and looked for a spot to sit down while they waited.

Nathan sat down with her at the base of the boulders and calmly stated, "Remember, you're to do exactly as we tell you, our lives depend upon it. Take a good look around at your surroundings, because if this turns out to be a good place to hide when we join up with Inola, you will have to be able to lead the women here by yourself until it is safe for us to join you."

"I understand," replied Sara swallowing hard and pulling his coat up tightly around her as a cold breeze suddenly passed by.

Nathan was suddenly alerted when he heard the faint sound of a branch snapping. He watched vigilantly for any movement and was relieved when he spotted Inola returning, and Sara quickly returned his overcoat to him.

"I found them. It looks like they won't be breaking camp today. There's a dozen men in camp and one of them is watching the women dress a deer close to the river; he's armed with a musket. We will need to go on foot from here and be very careful not to be seen for the odds are not in our favor." Turning towards Nathan he continued, "We will have good cover up to about fifteen feet from them and then it will be open ground leading down to the river. I will try to draw their guard closer to the trees where I will not be easily seen when I kill him. Nathan, if you can work your way closer to the women, just out of sight, then wait for my signal and get their attention and gesture for them to come to you. We might have a slim chance to get away undetected." Inola then looked directly at Sara and continued. "Sara wait in forest until you see the women headed your way, and bring them back here. Are we ready?" he asked looking at each one of them most seriously.

Sara nodded though her heart was pounding and felt herself trembling inside, but was determined not to let them down. Nathan just responded, "Let's move."

Sara followed their lead and moved from tree to tree looking carefully around before slowly moving to the next. Inola stopped and put his finger to his lips and looking directly at Sara put up his hand to let her know to stop there. Next he signaled Nathan to work his way closer to the edge of the trees by the river, while he moved in closer himself.

When they both were in position Inola picked up a small pebble and after carefully looking around threw it low and side-armed hitting Adsila in the leg as she knelt dressing the deer beside the other women. He watched as she stopped her work and slowly turned her head and gazed around for only a few seconds. She then went back to work unsure about what was going to happen, but knew that she needed to be prepared to act.

Inola silently and slowly changed positions to where he would be behind their guard. He tossed a rock where he had been standing to make just enough noise to make the guard move closer to check out the sound he heard. Adsila slowly looked over her shoulder having heard the sound just inside the tree line. She waited until their guard was close to the edge of the trees and loudly snapped at the woman next to her. "Move over," she purposely said distracting the guard.

That was the opportunity Inola had been waiting for. With partial cover from the rest of the Chickasaw party he quickly left the cover of the trees and grabbed the guard's mouth from behind and simultaneously cut his throat and dragged him into the woods and dropped his body.

Meanwhile, Nathan leaned away from the tree he was behind and placed his finger over his lips and motioned to Adsila to move quietly and slowly to him. When she was on her way he motioned to the other women to do the same, and when Adsila reached him he pointed in Sara's direction and told her to follow his wife, she was waiting for her just up the hill a ways.

Sara was watching from a safe distance and saw Inola backing into the woods with the guard's musket and Adsila heading her way.

Before the last woman entered the woods a Chickasaw warrior saw her and yelled out alerting the camp that the women were escaping into the woods. Two of them came running towards them not knowing that two men were lying in wait for them, and both

Inola and Nathan had their weapons ready to fire as soon as they were close enough.

Sara stepped out from behind the tree where she had been hiding when she heard the commotion from the Chickasaw camp, and when the women drew close she started running up the hill to the outcrop of boulders.

Nathan quickly glanced over his shoulder and saw Sara leading the women back towards the safety of the boulders and quickly turned his head and fired.

Both men running towards them were hurled to the ground, but the shots had stirred the whole camp into action. Two of them swiftly mounted their horses racing to circle behind whoever was attacking them while several more were heading towards Nathan and Inola through the cover of the trees with their muskets and bow and arrows.

By this time Sara stood at the entrance between the boulders breathing heavily as clouds of vapors rose in the cold morning air. She motioned for the women to move to the back of the crevasse and be silent as they tried to catch their breaths. Sara was the last one to enter and stood between them and the entrance as she had her handgun drawn and ready to fire. The three women had heard stories about Sara and studied her with great curiosity. The early morning sunlight filtered through the mist of that cold morning casting a strange glow around Sara, and her blonde hair looked like fine spun gold, and when they had caught a glimpse of her weapon they looked at each other with apprehension, but remained silent and still as they continued to watch her closely.

As she guarded the entrance she listened to the war cries and the volleys of muskets fired, followed by the sound of Nathan's revolver echoing repeatedly through the forest and her heart raced wildly as she tried to steady her hands waiting for them to return.

Inola and Nathan were continuing their retreat back through the forest when Sara heard the sound of horses coming around the far side of the boulders. She knew it couldn't be Nathan and Inola, their horses were tied a quarter of a mile away. Her mind was now filled with a bizarre mixture of thoughts. She had been instructed to remain between the boulders until they returned, but she also thought about the marauders ready to shoot Nathan in the back, and she feared it was about to happen again. Confused, she hesitated then slowly moved to the entrance and peered out just in time to see the two warriors dismount with their musket rifles and head back towards camp hoping to catch their attackers from behind.

She closed her eyes and took a deep breath; she couldn't let them get to Nathan and Inola who were most likely facing in the opposite direction as they backed their way towards her. Determined not to let fear conquer her, she quickly turned towards the women and gestured for them to stay put. After taking another deep breath she stepped away from the entrance with unwavering resolve and stood in the open and yelled "Hey". With her heart beating out of her chest she stood there shaking and watched as they quickly turned their heads and having seen her started running towards her. Turning quickly she ran back inside the entrance to the boulders scared out of her mind, and gripping her handgun in both hands was prepared to open fire as soon as they showed their faces. Moments later a warrior cautiously peered between the boulders then stepped inside with his musket raised and slowly moved forward. Sara stood trembling waiting until she saw his face then rapidly shot twice and watched him drop at her feet. She waited as her hands shook violently for the second one to appear and when he didn't, she carefully stepped around the dead body lying on the ground and moved closer to the entrance. She listened carefully, and wondered if he was waiting for her to step outside again. She was terrified to leave the cover of the boulders but knew that she had to make sure this warrior wouldn't be a threat to Nathan or Inola. Taking a shaky deep breath, she looked quickly around the corner and pulled back. She took another deep breath and overcoming her fear stepped outside and took a couple of steps towards the end of the boulders and suddenly shrieked as she came face to face with the painted face of a Chickasaw warrior and panicking pulled the trigger repeatedly emptying the remaining five rounds into him. Her feet seemed to be glued to the ground as she stood there stunned staring at the warrior face down on the ground by her feet.

The sudden sound of something moving quickly through the forest made her look up, and saw Nathan and Inola racing towards her having heard the shots fired from her handgun. Nathan yelled out, "Get back inside and wait." Sara quickly made her way back to the entrance and grimaced as she carefully stepped around the body of the dead Chickasaw and reloaded her handgun prepared to use it again if necessary, while Nathan and Inola squatted down at the base of the boulders and watched and listened for any Chickasaw that still might be in pursuit of them. Nathan looked at the body lying close by with five bullet holes and wondered what had happened to cause Sara to leave the safety of their hiding place when she had been told to stay inside.

After waiting a short time and neither seeing or hearing anyone, they approached the entrance and found the second body lying just inside the crevasse and each of them grabbed a leg and dragged him out of the way. Nathan quietly called out, "Sara, you can come out now." She put her firearm back in the holster and motioned to the women to come with her. Inola was waiting there for Adsila and immediately embraced her bringing a sigh of relief to both Sara and Nathan.

It was Nathan who now took charge; Inola's focus was on Adsila. After quickly retrieving the Chickasaw's horses and handing the reins to the women, he ordered, "Let's move out. We need to get back to our horses."

He took Sara by one hand and held his loaded revolver in the other as they started back through the forest of mostly tall spindly saplings with Inola bringing up the rear. They had to wind their way through the trees and brush until they reached their horses that had been tied out of sight.

Sara rode with Nathan, while the rest of them mounted their horses and quickly followed the river that would lead them back home. They pushed the horses hard the first hour, then stopped to water and rest them as both Nathan and Inola watched the trail behind them to make sure they were not being followed. Nathan figured the Chickasaw would cut their losses for they had been on a hunting trip for their village and had only taken the women because they unexpectedly came upon them and didn't want to be detected crossing through Cherokee territory.

Nathan could tell from the way Sara rode behind him that she was struggling under the weight of her thoughts. To have fired five bullets at close range into a man, she must have been terrified. He was painfully aware of her changed behavior for she no longer spoke, or even held on to him the way she did when she was happy and relaxed.

When they finally stopped for the night and made camp, Sara saw that the women were content to gather the wood for the fire and prepare the food so she left them alone to do it. They still looked at her curiously because of the stories they had heard about her and the way she took charge with authority as a warrior would have done. But, what made them even more guarded and skittish was the way she handled the strange weapon she carried and they kept a watchful distance.

Sara ate very little that night and sat staring into the fire and seemed unaware of the presence of anyone around her. Nathan knew that stare, and knew her troubled thoughts were something she would have to work through, and the best way to help her was to let her do it.

Inola seemed loud and boastful to Sara as he recounted the story of their rescue. The women laughed joyfully and seemed carefree, but they were not the ones who had pulled the trigger, she was, and now their painted faces and shaved heads except for a strip of hair running down the middle with feathers tied towards the back haunted her. Sara looked up from the fire and looked at the smiling faces and listened to their laughter and turned to Nathan who was resting against his saddle on the ground. "I'm going to stretch my legs," she said with a faint smile.

"Don't go too far," he said and handed her a wrap to keep warm.

"I won't; just down by the river," she replied.

A few moments later Sara was listening to water rushing over the river stones and gazing at the moonlight shimmering across the water as her troubled thoughts continued to plague her.

Nathan was worried about her. The last few days he had seen her so happy and lighthearted, and now that lively spark he loved so well was gone, buried under a load of deep and troubling thoughts. He gave her a few moments by herself and then joined her; wrapping his arms around her.

"You didn't murder those men. There's a difference between having to kill someone to protect yourself and your loved ones, and murdering someone out of anger or for no reason at all, and God certainly knows the difference."

Sara turned her head and looked into his loving eyes and faintly smiled, then turned and faced him, resting her head upon his shoulder as he continued to hold her. "I can still see the look on their faces," she cried, and he held her tightly in his arms.

"I know...but over time those faces will fade away when you forgive yourself, though there is truly nothing to forgive; you weren't given a choice," he replied lifting her chin up so he could look into her eyes.

She knew he was right; she hadn't been given a choice, but that still did not free her from the pain of having to do it. She rested her head against his shoulder again and seemed to draw strength from his embrace, and took heart knowing that if she had not done what she did Nathan might not be holding her now.

"I just want to go home. I want to lie in your arms on our bearskin rug by our fireplace," she uttered in a melancholy tone.

"Just lie?" he asked with a grin.

Sara raised her head and looked right at him, "You know what I mean," she said and rested her head against his shoulder again.

"Well, hold on to that thought; we should be home in about a week," he said in a more conciliatory tone.

"A week? Why so long?" she asked with a pout.

"We have to see Inola and the women back home to their village, and I'm sure Inola would like us to be there for his wedding. And don't forget, it will take two days to get back home after we leave the village," he explained.

Sara did not respond. She just stood there soaking up the heat coming from Nathan's body and wished they could be alone that night.

"Come on, we'd better head back before you freeze out here. I promise to hold you tight under the buffalo hides," he assuredly offered.

"Just hold?" she asked looking over at him smartly.

Chapter 48

It did indeed take four long days of hard riding in the saddle to get back to the Cherokee village, but what a reception they received. Everyone came running from their lodgings and from whatever they were doing, and whooping and hollering could be heard everywhere. There was a great assembly gathered around the fire at the center of the village that night and both Inola and Nathan were called upon to tell their story of the rescue while Sara sat silently next to Nathan not understanding a word that was being said. Up until that night, Sara had mostly seen the serious, no nonsense side of Inola, but that night she saw the actor and comedian side emerge right before her eyes. He had the crowds' full attention as he told his story even including the part where he taught Sara how to tell the age of horse dung. He even acted out the parts when he got Adsila's attention by throwing a rock and then killing her guard and the others who had followed them into the woods. She could feel their eyes trained on her and eagerly looking to see if she were wearing her weapon while Adsila told how she led the women to safety then killed two warriors attacking from the rear. She felt anxious not knowing their language and what was being said about her, and just being in an Indian village again brought back unwanted memories.

Nathan did his best to put her at ease during their stay, and even taught her a few Cherokee words so that she could thank the people for all the gifts they brought for rescuing the women. As anticipated, Adsila's father agreed to give his daughter to Inola in marriage since he had risked his life to set her free from her captors. Their wedding would take place the following day with everyone expected to witness it, for Inola was now a hero among his people.

Sara thought the wedding ceremony was simple, yet beautiful. Adsila looked stunning in her deerskin tunic that had been painted white with blue designs painted along the neckline and down the long sleeves. There were small sea shells tied in several rows across the bodice and long fringe along the hem and down the sleeves. Inola stood tall and proud as the Chief had them join hands and spoke to them of their duties to each other, then Inola took her into his lodging with the people whooping outside his door.

The Cherokee's holy man asked Nathan if he and Sara would sit with him for a while before they returned home. While they were seated by the fire the holy man looked closely at Sara for he had seated her where the sunlight came through the roof of his lodging. He took a long drag on his pipe and handed it to Nathan. He continued to look at Sara until Nathan handed the pipe back to him after he had taken several puffs then formally introduced Sara to him. He was curious why the holy man stared at Sara the way he did and questioned him about it. The holy man told him what the women were saying about Sara, and wanted to see for himself if what they were saying was true.

Nathan glanced at Sara in the sunlight to see if there was a glow about her, for he too had heard the stories about her hair, and then responded to the holy man.

"I assure you my wife is not a spirit, but flesh and blood as we are," he stated in Cherokee. Sara whispered to Nathan hoping she was not offending the holy man by speaking and asked, "Can't you translate what you both are talking about?"

Nathan turned and asked him if it would be alright for him to relay to his wife what was being said, and the holy man nodded.

"Sara, move a little closer to him and hold out your hand. I am going to ask him to touch your hand and feel your hair, because the women have told him that you glow in the sunlight of the morning and your hair is fine spun gold," he stated.

"Is that why the women won't come anywhere close to me?" she questioned, then held out her hand.

Nathan asked him to touch her hand and hair and see for himself that what he was saying was true about his wife. He looked into Sara's eyes and then down at her hand and took it in his and squeezed it, then rubbed a strand of her hair in his fingers and looked back at Nathan and smiled.

"The women have a vivid imagination, but in their defense you have an extraordinary wife who can stand up to warriors so bravely. You and Golden Hair are welcome here; you may go in peace," he said in Cherokee.

Nathan translated what the holy man had said, then offered Sara his hand to help her stand. They were finally able to start their journey home and Nathan saw a smile come to her face for the first time since the day they rescued the women, and knew that Sara would be alright. He just needed to get her home.

Since they were getting a late start that day, they decided to take it easy and chose a campsite along the river while there was still some daylight for Nathan to trap a groundhog for supper; for there were many of them close by. They were tired of venison jerky and this would be a pleasant change. Sara was happy to finally be alone with Nathan. She was tired of being stared at from a distance and whispered about, and tired of the lack of privacy at night when she was under the stars and covers with Nathan. She longed to be intimate with him again, especially when he looked at her in the way that started her body to throb just anticipating his touch.

Sara had the fire going and the buffalo hides spread out on the ground by the time Nathan returned carrying a groundhog already skinned and ready to roast. Once it was over the fire, Nathan turned and looked at Sara in that way that drove her crazy, and she felt her body respond in impassioned anticipation as he teased her with his kisses.

"Will a buffalo hide by the fire do in place of a bearskin rug?" he asked provocatively.

"It might," she said aloofly and proceeded to crawl between the hides and began to remove her moccasins and then her clothing. She craved his love, both physically and emotionally; it was a welcomed diversion from her troubled thoughts.

He smiled as he joined her under the heavy buffalo hide where Sara eagerly helped him remove his clothes in anticipation of the pleasure that would soon overtake her and was already breathing heavily.

Nathan eased his body on top of hers and the heat from his body kept her warm as he repeatedly kissed her deeply cradling her head in his hand. She could see the overwhelming hunger in his eyes and felt his lingering kisses along her neck and body before she felt him enter her and totally surrendered to their passion that was all consuming. She no longer thought of, or felt the pain life had brought her way; she was caught away to a place where she was one with Nathan and she had no desire to leave any time soon.

The groundhog was nearly burnt by the time Nathan pulled himself away from Sara and grabbed the skewer and brought it back to their buffalo hide. Neither seemed to mind the slightly charred areas as they picked the meat from the bones, for they were content, and free from prying eyes to do whatever they wanted to do. When they were finished eating they went back under the covers.

They returned home by early evening the following day after a long day in the saddle. Adohi was happy to see them and offered to take care of their horses so they could go inside and get warm. When they entered the house they were greeted by the aroma of venison stew and cornbread cooking in the hearth, and after warming themselves they went and set the table for three and waited for Adohi to return. During supper Nathan started to tell all about their rescue of the three women and Inola's wedding, and continued the story long into the night with Adohi eager to hear all about what happened.

It was very late when they went to bed and fell asleep quickly lying on the soft mattress instead of the hard ground. Adohi slept inside by the fireplace and was the first one up in the morning, for he was eager to return home to his village after being away for so long. After breakfast Nathan gave him supplies for his journey, and thanked him for all his help. Sara and Nathan enjoyed a time of peace and quiet for the next few months, but signs of spring were in the air and Sara was longing to visit her parents.

Chapter 49

The trees were leafing out and setting buds, and there was much to do now that the temperatures were above freezing most mornings. Nathan and Sara were busy getting the ground plowed and ready for planting crops and Sara was still trying to finish her dresses to wear into town. They had little free time to just relax and enjoy each other's company, and were often too tired to even make full use of the bearskin rug by the fire.

Sara was content most of the time, but soon became restless once the crops were planted, and her wandering thoughts drifted back to her time and her parents. She tried hard to suppress these thoughts for she had made her choice to remain with Nathan and endure the hardships of frontier life. Besides, the unwanted thoughts were fleeting as long as she was by his side.

Nathan began to notice the distant stares and quiet sighs that only lasted for a few moments, but were becoming more frequent. "What are you thinking about, Sara?" he asked one morning while they were drinking coffee on the front porch.

She shook the thoughts from her mind and looked at him with a smile, "Oh, nothing really. I suppose I'm just a bit restless."

Nathan wondered if it was something more than what she was letting on to. He questioned whether she had already tired of his time and living alone on the frontier, for she was used to all the hustle and bustle of city life and all the luxuries that went along with it.

She could sense his troubled thoughts and quickly got up and sat on his lap and looked into his beautiful blue eyes. "Please don't worry about me. You know there's no place in the world I'd rather be than with you. You're like the air that I breathe," she said softly.

He searched deep within her eyes and knew that everything she had said she truly believed, but still, there was something definitely on her mind.

"Come on, why don't you go pack a lunch and we'll take a ride out to our favorite spot along the river after I feed the animals. It is too nice a day to hang around here."

"Well then, you'd better get started because it won't take me very long to get ready," she replied with a smile. Now that they both had weapons that could hold off a small army she no longer feared trips to the river as long as Nathan was there with her. He had been right, her traumatic memories were slowly fading and only manifested themselves periodically in her recurring nightmares.

It was a beautiful sunny day for a ride; the skies were clear and a deep blue, and the air was fresh and crisp as they made their way through the forest that was coming alive. Even the horses could sense it was springtime and were energetic and spry, and within an hour they reached the bank of the river and found the spot where they had sat many times before. All the melting snow higher up in the mountains had caused the river to be wildly turbulent as it rushed and tumbled rapidly over the rocks, and Sara once again enjoyed the sight of a river as she dismounted from her horse.

Nathan took her by the hand as they climbed to their favorite spot and spread out their blanket to sit and lay back on, and he was hoping to get Sara to relax enough to tell him what was really on her mind.

While Sara was sitting up taking in the beauty of the raging river and enjoying the peace and tranquility of that early spring day, Nathan laid back resting his head in his hands, and waited for Sara to join him. Looking over her shoulder at him lying there and smiling, Sara laid down next to him with her head resting on his shoulder and sighed happily.

"This was such a splendid idea coming here; my parents would love this place."

"You miss them, don't you?" he asked casually.

"Yes, I do," she thoughtfully blurted out and sat up looking at him wide-eyed. "You sneaky little rascal! You brought me here hoping I would open up, didn't you?"

He laid there grinning, "Yes, and it worked beautifully. So, why don't you go visit them? The crops are planted, and this would be the perfect time for you to take a short trip back to see them. Would two weeks give you enough time? I couldn't bear to be without you for any longer than that."

She looked at him so conflicted that she couldn't speak. The thought of leaving him even for a short time pained her to the very core of her being. But yet, she did have a desire to see her parents, and she looked away staring off into the distance.

"You don't have to go, I just wanted you to know that I understand you wanting to go for a visit. I think of my family back in Boston often, and wish that I could see them again," he said reflectively.

Sara looked back at him thoughtfully. "Two weeks, huh? I don't believe I could stay that long. I think we would drive each other crazy. My dad and I are too much alike and too opinionated. Don't get me wrong, I love them but in short bursts at my age."

"Well, you stay as long as you like. I'll be here when you get back. Now come lay back down," he said and held open his arm so she could rest her head upon his shoulder. Nathan made up his mind not to say another word about her leaving. He had told her

- 414 -

how he felt about it and now it was up to her to decide if, or when, she would leave.

A couple of days went by and Sara still had not brought up the subject of visiting her parents. She and Nathan were still enjoying the peace and tranquility they had been longing for, and she no longer felt the keen desire to return to her time. Then one day she felt a tenderness in her breast; a feeling she had never experienced before. She was hesitant to say anything to Nathan about it since it might go away by itself. A few more days passed and the tenderness was still there and she began to wonder when was the last time she remembered having her period and had totally lost track. She had her suspicions of what was causing the tenderness and only returning to her time to take a pregnancy test would confirm them.

The following morning when they were having their morning coffee Sara daringly asked, "So, you really don't mind if I visit my parents for a short time?"

"No, I don't mind. Why, have you decided to go?" he directly asked.

"Yes. When I returned to buy your revolver, I promised my parents I would return when I could stay longer, and I hate to break my promises. I was thinking about leaving tomorrow morning for at least a week. If I don't go right away I might change my mind about going," she said anxiously and watched for his reaction.

Nathan could see that she still had mixed feelings about returning to her time. "Don't you worry about me. I will miss you while you're gone, but I know you'll return. So go and have fun and I'll be right here waiting for you," he assured her.

Sara smiled and asked, "Then what would you like to do today?"

Nathan gave her that look that always either gave her goose bumps or caused her to blush and seductively said, "I know what I'd like to do all day, but it would be nice if we could bake a few loaves of bread in between so I don't get too hungry while you're away."

"I think we can manage to do that," she blushed and looked away to avoid his gaze.

Nathan laughed heartily, "Do you have any idea how much I love to watch you blush?"

"I think I do; you do it often enough," she replied still blushing.

Nathan stayed and helped her prepare the dough, but as soon as they set it aside to let it rise, he lifted her chin and looked into her eyes. After kissing her he picked her up in his arms and playfully said, "Let's go have a little fun," and carried her into the bedroom; wanting her to remember what she would be missing while she was gone.

The next morning Nathan asked, "Do you have everything packed and ready to go?"

Sara just nodded. She was still conflicted about leaving as she drank the last few drops of her coffee.

Nathan stood and opened his arms wide, "Well then, come give me a kiss good-bye; this isn't going to get any easier if you wait."

Sara immediately teared up as she stood and stepped into his waiting arms and held him tightly; unable to look up into his eyes or kiss him good-bye. He could feel her reluctance because he felt it as well, but was trying to make it as easy for her as possible to leave. He finally raised her chin and smiled as he looked into her eyes and kissed her softly.

"You'd better get going. You have a long walk ahead of you. You be careful and I'll be here waiting for you when you're ready to come home," he said with a smile though his heart was already longing for her return.

"I love you," she replied softly looking into his beautiful blue eyes, and turned slowly and started up the stairs towards the attic.

Sara only made it halfway up the staircase when out of nowhere the feeling that she might never see him again swept over her. She stopped abruptly, turned around and loudly called out, "Nathan, wait!"

He was almost to the front door when he heard her call out and stopped and waited for her. "Sara, what's wrong? You're starting to worry me; you do plan on returning, don't you?"

"Of course, my love. I just needed another kiss and to feel your arms around me one more time. I miss you already," she said and seeing his confusion reluctantly let go of him.

Nathan caught her by the hand and pulled her close and kissed her good and long, "Now get going before I change my mind."

Sara smiled contentedly and started for the attic. When she reached the floor of the attic she picked up her backpack with her purse and handgun inside, and watched as the dust and cobwebs appeared and knew Nathan had stepped away from the porch. Tears rolled down her cheeks as she turned and slowly walked down the stairs and made her way out the front door and wondered why she was acting so abnormally emotional. She didn't look back until she reached the foot of the hill and then glanced behind her to take one last look before climbing; for she had made up her mind not to look again for fear she would change her mind and stay. It took her a little more than an hour to cross over the hill and walk through the valley that was now covered in green grass and patches of wildflowers, and for the first time in a long time she thought of Richard. She remembered how she would talk to him on her walks and whispered softly, "I thought you would like to know that I've found happiness again. I think you would like him; he's a lot like you – strong, yet gentle, honorable, and was a soldier in the War for Independence. You both would have had a lot to talk about. I shall always have a special place in my heart for you...good-bye Richard."

Chapter 50

Approaching the patch of trees just east of the cabin she wondered what the current author would think when she showed up at his door asking to use the phone again. As she was rehearsing her speech she noticed the man was locking the front door, and knew she must hurry if she was going to catch him in time before he left.

Sara started running and called out when she saw him open the door to his car, "Excuse me, sir, can you wait just a minute?"

By the time she reached his car she was out of breath and the man looked at her curiously. "I know who you are. You're Sara Mathews, the author, aren't you?" Sara just nodded still out of breath. "What can I do for you?"

"Well, believe it or not, I would like to use your phone. I was going to call for a ride into town," she replied still panting just a little.

"I'd be happy to give you a ride into town. I'm Jake Scott by the way."

Sara happily accepted his ride and enjoyed listening to him tell her all about the book he was writing. He was, however, curious why she showed up at the cabin with only a backpack and no cell phone or vehicle close by.

She had to come up with a believable story quickly and replied, "Well, I get my inspiration for my books when I'm alone hiking through the woods; it just seems to awaken my imagination.

As for my vehicle, well unfortunately it broke down along the base of that ridge just a couple of miles to the east of you. That's why I need a ride into town. I need to call my dad and have him come pick me up and get a new battery installed in my vehicle for me."

Jake seemed to be satisfied with her story and dropped her off at the grocery store after letting her use his phone to call her dad.

While Sara was waiting for him to come pick her up, she bought a pregnancy test and tucked it away in her backpack and took the bottle of flavored water she bought and sat down on the bench outside the store. The hour passed quickly and her dad soon pulled up to the curb and Sara quickly hopped inside his truck.

"Hi Dad, thanks for coming," she said and gave him a kiss on the cheek and continued, "I hope you haven't given all my clothes away, because I didn't pack any to bring with me."

"They're still hanging in your closet so you will have something to wear when you come to visit. So, are you planning on staying for a while?" he asked glancing over at her.

"At least a week if you and mom don't have any plans to go somewhere," she replied.

"The only plans we have are to enjoy our daughter's company. We almost gave up hope of ever seeing you again. Your books are the only way we can keep up with what has been going on in your life," he said with a smile.

Before she knew it they were pulling into the driveway and all she could think about was: taking a shower, then her pregnancy test, and then changing into some clean clothes.

Her mother was thrilled to see her and greeted her with a big hug and asked, "Are you hungry?"

"Yes I am, but first I'd like to take a shower and change clothes; then we'll have the whole week to catch up on things," she said as she walked inside with her arm around her mother.

Sara pulled the pregnancy test from her backpack and set it on the counter while she took her shower. She had forgotten how good it felt to have a hot shower and lingered under the pulsating spray head. As she dressed she waited for the results of the pregnancy test. When the time was up she took a deep breath, picked up the tester, and soon was smiling with excitement and couldn't wait to share the news with her parents.

"I'm glad you're both sitting because I have some news to share with you that I hope will make you very happy," she joyfully declared.

Her mom had a big smile of hopeful anticipation, but her dad was less than thrilled and showed more concern than happiness.

Sara quickly picked up on both their reactions and proceeded with her announcement, "Mom, Dad, you're both going to be grandparents by the end of the year!"

Her mom let out a squeal of happiness and jumped up and hugged her all smiles, but her father just sat there and made a weak attempt to smile and look happy for her.

"Dad, you don't look very happy. Why?" she asked a little surprised.

He looked at her thoughtfully for a minute before answering. "Don't get me wrong; I'm happy I'm going to be a grandpa. But, it is hard enough to raise a child when you have doctors and parents close by, but out on the frontier with no one around, well it scares me," he said frankly.

Sara remained thoughtfully quiet as she sat on the sofa, for she had the same concerns her father had and couldn't disagree with what he had said.

"There's plenty of time to work out all the details; right now let's just be happy and celebrate this wonderful news," her mother said optimistically and continued, "Come, let's go have lunch; it's ready."

For the next several days Sara and her mother spent a good portion of their day window shopping to get ideas for what Sara would like to buy for the baby to take back with her on her next visit. The evenings were spent eating out at her favorite restaurants and having lively discussions about her life choices, especially about living all alone on the frontier. Don loved to bring up all the dangerous things she wrote about in her books because he knew they were based on actual events. He tried to push his points of view on why they should at least move back to Boston where his family lived. Becky stepped in when the discussions got a little overheated, and usually had some sweet dessert to take the place of all the contentious words. Sara had anticipated having these issues with her father, and tried hard not to say anything she would later regret because she knew that his concerns were coming from a place of love for her.

Each night as Sara laid awake in bed she longed to be home with Nathan. She closed her eyes and could almost feel his arms around her, the passion of his kisses, and look in his eyes that were always filled with desire for her, and the cares of the day would melt away.

The week was almost up when Sara was out in the kitchen with her mother preparing breakfast. They happily discussed where she would go when it was close to the time for the baby to be born, and what items she would need to stock up on that wouldn't be available in the 1700s - which was just about everything. Her father was in the living room watching the morning news when she overheard something that caught her attention.

Her father called out, "Sara, you should come listen to this."

Sara wiped her hands on a dish towel and quickly took a seat on the sofa. Her eyes grew wide as she watched a forest fire started by lightning burning out of control. When they showed a map of the area affected by the fire she moved closer to the TV and saw that it was in the forest just northwest of where her publisher's cabin was located. The fires were being driven on by high winds and the only way to reach the fires to put them out was by air.

Sara watched the news coverage closely with her parents. She saw that it was creeping ever closer in the direction of Nathan's house and was overwhelmed with fear; realizing that house was the only way back to Nathan.

"Dad, you know that everything I own is in both your names, and you are free to spend it anyway you choose should I not return," she anxiously stated.

"We know that, but why are you bringing that up now," he questioned.

"Because I need your truck Dad. I need to leave right now if I'm ever going to make it back in time," she said in a panic.

"Have you lost your mind?" her mother asked fearfully.

"Sara, stop and think. You're at least an hour away and how do you think you're going to make it back to the house; it'll be surrounded by fire by the time you get there. Are you willing to risk your life and the life of your baby to get there?" her father questioned most seriously.

"Dad, I have to go. You know what it would do to Nathan if I don't return. Besides, he needs to know that he's going to be a father. How could I raise my child without him? It would be a slow death for me every time I looked at my son or daughter and saw Nathan's likeness or characteristics. I'm going to do this. If you won't give me your truck I'm going to take my car you had repaired, and you know I probably won't make it if I do," she adamantly stated and held out her hand waiting for the keys.

Her father looked at her mother as his brow furrowed and knew he was fighting a losing battle. Reluctantly he handed Sara the keys to his truck. She hugged both her parents and looked directly, and lovingly, into their worried faces. "If I don't ever see you again, I want you both to know how much I love you," she said with a trembling voice as tears started to run down her cheeks.

She grabbed only her purse and backpack with her weapon inside and a couple bottles of water and hurriedly started out the front door to the truck. Her heart was pounding wildly in her chest as her mind tried to think of the best way to get back to the house. Her fear and anxiety so filled her mind that it pushed every rational thought out, and she found it impossible to think clearly about anything.

Sara kept changing channels on the radio trying to get information on the spread of the fire and gave no thought to the speed she was going; she must make it back in time that was all there was to it.

Almost an hour had passed when she reached the place where she had once before pulled over before attempting to drive over the steep rocky hill. She sat there by the side of the road to see if it was even possible to return to the house that way, or if she would have to try to climb over the hill on foot where she normally crossed over to the house when hiking. She had seen the fire blazing for miles while she drove and the majority of it was in the mountain range behind their house, but spreading quickly down into the valley and in some places had reached the hill she must cross over at some point. She suddenly heard fire engines racing her way and honking their horns. She knew they were going to try to stop the fire from reaching all the expensive homes in the area, and she had to decide right now which way to go before it was too late.

Sara turned the wheel sharply and started across the valley heading in the direction of the outcrop of rocks before anyone could force her to stop and turn back. She prayed that the truck would offer more protection to her if she had to drive through areas on fire and figured she would have no chance at all if she attempted it on foot. The smell of smoke already filled the air and was seeping into the truck as she approached the rocks, and could see thick dark smoke rising up from the mountains over the hill. She quickly changed gears and started over the outcrop of rocks carefully weaving her way around the trees and boulders. As she neared the top she noticed that some of the dead trees were on fire and feared what she might see as she neared the bottom of the hill.

The smoke was swirling around her truck making it difficult to see as it moved ever closer to their house, and she could feel the heat even though the air conditioner was on the highest setting. Though already coughing from the smoke seeping into the truck, she could see the glow from the fire had reached where their apple orchard stood in the past and knew that it would soon reach the house. She was panic stricken and trembling violently at the thought of having to enter the house if Nathan was not there. There would be no way of escape; she and her baby would die and prayed that it would be from the smoke and not the fire.

The flames had now reached spots along the path to the house and she altered her route just a bit to avoid the fire from blocking her way. She finally caught a glimpse of the house up ahead and it did not appear to be on fire, but it soon would be and prayed once again that Nathan would be home.

She was forced to stop the truck about fifty feet from the house and quickly poured some of the bottled water onto a shirt she found in the back seat to cover her face as she ran through the smoke. The heat from the fire burned her lungs, and her skin already felt like it had a bad sunburn as she ran towards the house coughing and barely able to see with her eyes dry and burning from the heat.

Finally reaching the front door and coughing hoarsely she pushed hard on the door and forced her way in and ran up the stairs and quickly pulled down the stairs to the attic. As she climbed them she knew she would not smell the scent of pine but hoped to see the dust disappear as she neared the top, but the smoke was already beginning to swirl down through the missing shingles on the roof obscuring her vision. When she ultimately stepped into the attic it was empty; Nathan was not home, and even worse he had no clue that Sara or his house were in serious trouble.

What was she to do? Should she pull the staircase up or leave it down? Would it be better to try to break the attic window or leave it closed? Her mind was confused as she poured more water onto the shirt and held it over her mouth and nose as she watched the smoke start to make its way up the staircase.

Sara screamed over and over for Nathan even though she knew he couldn't hear her, but she was desperate. Her eyes burned, it was hard to breathe, and her skin was turning red like from a sunburn, and she was terrified as the fire crept ever closer. Now every time she tried to scream Nathan's name she coughed and suddenly felt nauseous and wanted to vomit as she sank to the floor of the attic. She wanted to cry but her eyes were too dry and she sobbed tearlessly, terrified of being burned alive as she watched roof shingles drop to the floor of the attic one by one. Sara struggled to her feet in one last attempt to escape the fire and started down the staircase, but when she saw the flames leaping through the front door she quickly retreated back to the attic for that was where she needed to be if she was to have any hope of ever seeing Nathan again. She sat back down on the floor of the attic and closed her eyes and finally lost consciousness and fell over on the attic floor, and her last thought was of her baby.

Nathan had just ridden in from hunting and entered the house carrying a large turkey. He hung his hat on the peg and slowly turned and sniffed the air. He glanced at both the fireplace and hearth and didn't notice anything different about them, and walked further into the room and sniffed the air again. Something seemed strange to him and he laid the turkey down by the hearth and went to the base of the stairs and the smell of smoke was stronger there, and he was curious and confused by what could be causing it. As he neared the attic the smell was even stronger and he pulled the staircase down and started quickly up the steps and before he reached the top he saw Sara lying there on the floor.

He stood shocked for just a moment near the top of the stairs, then quickly called out her name as he rushed to her. The smell of smoke upon her was so strong that it nearly took his breath away as he stared stunned at the redness of her skin, and the soot around her nose and ashes lightly covering her body. He pulled her to himself terrified for he could not see or feel her breathing; she was still unconscious and he rocked back and forth with her in his arms as he rubbed her back and cried, afraid he had lost her forever.

Picking her up in his arms he looked around the attic and nothing was out of place or smelled heavily of smoke except for Sara, and quickly carried her downstairs bewildered by how she got this way. After he had laid her on the bed he felt for a pulse; it was weak but she had one and opened her mouth and breathed strongly into hers trying to fill her lungs with fresh air. He could taste the smoke in his mouth as he forced air into her lungs several more times and she coughed weakly but still did not respond as he called her name. He propped her up slightly with pillows behind her and went and brought a basin of cool water and a cloth. He wiped her face and neck for they were hot to the touch and red, and continued to bathe her in the cool water until he had removed the soot from her nostrils and her skin felt cooler to the touch, then laid the cloth across her forehead.

Nathan prayed earnestly for her, for he had no experience in treating these kinds of symptoms; all he could do now was hold her hand and pray as tears rolled down his cheeks. He had seldom known fear – not even in war - but it consumed him now.

As the hours passed he tried to give her sips of water to soothe her throat and watched as she coughed up small amounts of fluids that smelled of smoke and cried out for God's help and mercy. Nathan never left her side, not even to eat, but watched her closely for any sign that she was regaining consciousness and continued to bathe her in cool water.

In the early morning hours he raised her off the pillows and held her in his arms and gently patted her on the back causing her to choke and cough hoarsely. She suddenly gasped and Nathan pulled back and looked into her open eyes which quickly closed. He prayed that the worst had passed. Leaving her propped up he went to get something to eat and put a pot of coffee on the hearth once he got the fire going again, then returned to Sara while the coffee was brewing and bathed her in cool water once again.

As the hours passed Nathan left her side briefly to feed the animals and bring in more firewood, and then quickly took his seat by her side. It was early afternoon when she opened her eyes briefly for they were dry, painful, and blurry. She opened them again and squinted as she reached and held her head that was throbbing in pain and looked around the room confused as to where she was and why she felt so awful. Nathan could see the confusion on her face and softly called her name as he took her hand.

Sara turned towards him and quickly jerked her hand from his and stared through the blurry film that covered her eyes unable to recognize him.

"Sara, it's me, Nathan," he said worriedly.

She blinked her eyes repeatedly trying to clear the film from them hoping she could see his face, but they were too dry and painful so she closed them tightly.

"Where am I," she asked hoarsely and tried to swallow.

"You're home Sara, in your own bed," he replied deeply concerned by the confusion he saw in her face.

"What happened to me, and how did I get here?" she asked bewildered.

"I don't know what happened to you. I was hoping you could tell me," he stated anxiously.

"Who did you say you were?" she asked softly and shied away as he touched her arm.

"Sara, I'm your husband, Nathan. Don't you remember?" he asked in frightened confusion. He could see her searching her mind for lost memories; trying to piece things together.

"May I have some water?" she asked huskily.

Nathan quickly poured her a glass of water and handed it to her. After taking a few sips she said weakly, "I'm tired. I'd like to get some rest now."

Nathan sighed with a heavy heart and gently replied, "I'll be back to check on you in a little while," and went and sat in his rocking chair and stared at Sara through the open door, puzzled as to how to help her. All he knew was that she went to visit her parents and was supposed to be away for another couple of days. He hadn't the faintest idea why she returned early and in the condition he found her and wondered if he ever would find out what really happened.

While Sara was sleeping, Nathan plucked and prepared the turkey he had shot earlier for roasting and after he placed it on the skewer over the fire he went to check on Sara. He stood in the doorway to the bedroom and watched her as she slept. He was troubled by her loss of memory and hoped that it was only a temporary side effect from inhaling too much smoke.

He watched as she started to toss and turn, but when she started to thrash about waving her arms in the air and mumbling he went and sat on the side of the bed. He listened carefully and it sounded like she was calling his name, and he was hesitant to wake her if she was dreaming about what had happened to her. He wanted her to remember and was afraid if he woke her too soon she would forget everything. When she was totally frantic he gently grabbed her arms that were flailing in the air and said, "Sara, Sara…wake up darling; it was only a dream."

Sara was wide-eyed and frightened as she looked up at him, almost like she was questioning whether it was just a bad dream or if all these things she dreamed about had really happened. Her eyes darted back and forth and her brow was furrowed as she thought and then suddenly it was like everything was becoming clear to her.

She slowly looked back at him and cried, "Nathan!" She covered her mouth and cried though the tears stung her dried eyes as she looked at him with recognition. "Oh, Nathan, I was afraid I would never make it back to you!" she said and coughed hoarsely.

"Do you remember what happened?" he asked anxiously.

"I was at my parent's house helping my mom in the kitchen when my dad called me to come watch something on the television…" she said staring off into space still squinting as if searching for what happened next. "The news was on and they were showing a fire burning out of control…I remember looking at a map they showed where the fire was burning…and saw that it was in the forest behind our house and the winds were driving it closer by the minute…I told my parents I needed to leave right away or I would never make it back to you in time; our house would be gone and you would never know what happened to me. I took my father's truck and could see the fire burning mile after mile as I drove back…I made it through the valley and over that outcrop of rocks further down the ridge from us before the smoke and heat started seeping into the truck…I remember the trees being on fire as I made my way up to the house and ran the last distance through the trees and into the house praying that you would be there…I knew I had to get to the attic and by that time the house and roof had caught on fire, and I remember screaming for you…I was terrified of being burned alive," she confessed and broke down and cried holding her eyes tightly shut for they still stung. Nathan took her in his arms tightly and wept bitterly, unable to say anything. They sat there in each other's arms for the longest time before Nathan laid her back against her pillows, and gently stroked her cheek with the top of his hand still unable to find the words that might comfort her.

Out of the blue Sara looked at him with an unsettled gaze. There was something that she had been suppressing; a thought she didn't think she had the strength to deal with.

"What is it Sara? What's troubling you?" he asked not imagining anything being worse than what she had already told him. Yet whatever it was it seemed to be more painful than anything she had expressed to him so far.

She just looked at him as a deep sadness embraced her. A realization was pushed to the forefront of her mind and she had to face it no matter how painful it was. She bit her bottom lip and closed her eyes then swallowed hard. It took her a minute before she could speak and when she opened her eyes she looked at him sorrowfully. "Your house no longer exists in the future; it has been burnt to the ground and the portal to the future with it. I'll never be able to return to my time again, and I'll never see my parents again," she said disheartened as it all sunk in, and she realized the finality of it all.

Nathan hung his head, for her words had cut him to the heart and he felt that all of this was his fault. Even Inola knew that she had no business being there; she didn't fit in. He should have known better than to beg her to stay. He should have seen the difficulties she would face in this world of his and been strong enough to do the right thing for her right from the start, but he knew he needed her like the air he breathed.

She saw what her words had done to him. She might just as well taken a knife and cut his heart out. She had to make this right for she had not told him the most important thing.

"Nathan, my love, please don't feel bad. I had a choice. I could have watched as your house burned to the ground, but I chose to be with you above all else. Yes, I will miss some of the things from my time, but flames or no flames, I would risk everything to get back to you. You are the one thing in life I cherish most and couldn't live without. Don't you understand yet just how much I love you and need you? There's no place on this earth that I would rather be than in your arms, and see your smile and the way that you look at me."

Nathan choked back his tears as he listened to Sara pour her heart out to him. He saw the love in her eyes and realized she was there to stay, not because she had no choice, but because she chose to be with him even if it nearly cost her life. He took her in his arms and held her tightly; no longer would he question whether she belonged there or not. Even time knew she was destined to be his soul mate.

He looked tenderly into her eyes with a heart bursting with joy and kissed her long and lovingly before resting her back on her pillow. "Why don't you rest a little longer while I finish fixing something for dinner?" he smiled, and gently brushed her cheek with his hand before leaving.

While Nathan was busy getting supper ready to dish out, Sara slowly got dressed in clean clothes and sat on the bed to brush her hair. As she was brushing it, she remembered there was something she had wanted to tell Nathan. Pondering what it was, it suddenly came to her and she smiled – he's going to be a father!

Fear suddenly filled her mind as she placed her hand on her abdomen and wondered if all the smoke she inhaled and the fact that she had been unconscious for so long could have hurt her unborn child. She had no doctor to ask, and no internet to search for the answers to her questions. She contemplated whether she should even tell Nathan that she was pregnant for she could quite easily miscarry. She sat there on the edge of the bed looking off into space and reasoned that she was young and healthy. It was early in her pregnancy, and worrying about it wouldn't change a thing. She determined in her mind that she would have faith, and trust that God would bless them with a strong and healthy baby.

Nathan interrupted her thoughts when he entered the room to help her to the dining room for supper. He swept her up in his arms and Sara looked at him quizzically and asked, "What are you doing? I'm able to walk, you know."

He looked at her and smiled. "That's nice, but I'm still going to carry you."

Sara's strength was slowly returning and her breathing was less labored though her lungs still burned as she enjoyed a quiet supper with Nathan. He couldn't take his eyes off her or keep from smiling for he realized that she was there to stay, and how close he came to losing her forever. When they were finished eating Sara asked, "Can we go sit in your rocking chair, I have something to tell you?"

"Sure," he replied, but anxiously wondered what she wanted to tell him that was so important. He picked her up again and Sara smiled as he carried her to the chair and sat down with her on his lap and looked at her with apprehension.

"Don't look so worried. I hope you will be very happy when I tell you that you're going to be a father just before Christmas time this year," she stated looking into his anxious eyes.

He sat there silent, looking almost stunned until what she had just told him sank in. She watched as a smile grew on his face and he exclaimed, "Sara, that's wonderful! Are you sure?"

"Yes, I'm sure. When I returned home I took a pregnancy test, and God willing we'll have a healthy baby just in time for Christmas," she replied and laid her head against his shoulder.

Nathan rocked his chair as he held Sara in his arms, but the happiness he felt slowly faded as he thought about his first wife and young daughter and how he had lost them a couple of winters ago to influenza.

Sara could feel his body tighten and his breathing become shallow and raised her head and looked into his troubled eyes. She seemed to instantly know what was troubling him and tried to choose her words carefully.

Looking straight at him she calmly stated, "Nathan, I'm strong. I've always had a strong constitution ever since I was a child. In my time we have vaccinations, medicines that prevent us from getting all types of diseases. Two hundred years couldn't keep us apart; neither could marauders, trappers, Indians, or fire. I'm afraid you're stuck with me and all the children we will have for as long as we both shall live, and I'm betting that will be for a really long time."

He studied her face as she spoke, and she had such confidence in what she was saying that it was contagious and a smile soon returned to his face.

"You're right, my angel. You're absolutely right. I'd better start getting all those upstairs' rooms ready for all those kids," he announced jokingly with a smile and pulled her close and kissed her, but his heart still grieved for the daughter he had lost.

Late that night Sara noticed that Nathan was not in bed, and wondered where he was. It was not uncommon for him to have nightmares and she supposed he had gone to sit in his rocking chair so he wouldn't disturb her. Now that she was awake she decided to join him and possibly make some hot chocolate for the both of them since she still had a few packets left that she had brought back with her. When she left the bedroom she noticed immediately that Nathan was not sitting by the fireplace, and glanced up the stairs to the second floor and noticed a faint glow coming from the attic. Curiosity now had a firm grip on her and she slowly and quietly climbed the stairs and paused at the bottom of the stairs to the attic. She wondered whether it was any of her business what he was doing up there in the middle of the night. She couldn't help herself; she had to know what compelled him to go up there and slowly climbed the stairs just far enough to where she could peer into the attic, and then stopped and hung her head. Some memories you are never free from; they're just buried in shallow graves in your mind and heart. Nathan was kneeling in front of the toy chest holding the ragdoll Elizabeth had made for his daughter. As he held it he ran his fingers through the black yarn hair of the doll, and the mournful, gut-wrenching look on his face said it all. Tears came to Sara's eyes and her heart broke for him as he remembered his daughter – his first child - and now he was faced with having another child and she could only imagine what was running through his mind. She thought it best to leave him alone and slowly crept down the stairs and went back to bed and thoughtfully considered what impact this child of theirs would have upon their lives. Sometime later she heard him slip back into bed and casually asked him, "Is everything alright?" "Yes, my dear. Try to go back to sleep," he said and softly kissed her on the forehead.

Chapter 51

Eight months later – It was already the second week in December and Nathan was standing looking out the front window as it snowed heavily. It had been snowing for days and didn't show any sign of letting up and it troubled him as Sara's due date was drawing near. She joined him by the window resting one hand on her tight, well-rounded abdomen and slipped her other arm around his waist. Both were thinking about the same thing; would Inola and Adsila make it to their place in time before the baby was born. Sara was happy that Nathan had taught her the Cherokee language after she told him he was going to be a father so that she would be able to join in the conversations once they arrived.

Nathan looked over at Sara and placed his hand just below hers in time to feel the baby kick, and a fist or knee run a bump under his hand as the baby turned within her and he smiled.

"This little guy is a fighter; he can't wait to get out and raise a ruckus," he said with immense pride.

"Well he needs to just simmer down and wait for Inola and Adsila to get here, or his daddy is going to have to welcome him into the world," she said with a raised eyebrow.

Nathan tightened up and took a deep breath. "You're mom's right; you simmer down in there, because I don't know anything about birthing babies," he said bending over and speaking directly to the baby.

Sara laughed, but she was thinking that she didn't know much about it either and was anxious as she looked out the window again hoping the snowstorm would end.

"Why don't you go sit by the fire and I'll bring you a cup of hot apple cider to warm you up."

"That would be wonderful," Sara said and started for her rocking chair feeling she looked like a duck waddling along.

Her mind was consumed this last month with all kinds of worries about how she was going to take care of her baby. She had counted on being able to bring back diapers, wipes, baby bottles, formula, clothing and a million other little items from her time that would have made things so much easier. Now she had none of those things and she was scared. She tried hard to not let her fears show, because she knew Nathan had his own fears he was dealing with. Besides, every generation before hers didn't have any of the things she thought she couldn't live without, and yet managed to raise babies and lots of them over the centuries.

Nathan handed Sara her cup of hot apple cider and took his seat with a cup of hot coffee.

"I don't know how you women do it. You look mighty uncomfortable sitting in that rocking chair."

"God made us tough!" she said and winked at him before continuing. "He knew if it were up to men to have babies, Cain would have been the only baby born and that would have been the end to mankind," and wondered just how tough she would be when it came right down to it.

"I'm sure you're right about that," he confessed. "Would you like for me to bring you your drawing tablet, you seem to be spending a lot of time working on something in it."

"Yes, I would like that, but promise me you won't look inside it," she said anxiously.

"I promise," he said and left to get it for her, but wished she hadn't made him promise, because now he was curious as to what she was working on.

"Here you go. I'm going to go check on the animals and give you some time to work on whatever you're drawing," he said and kissed her on top of her head.

It was still a little over a week before the baby was due, according to Sara's calculations. But as she was drawing a picture for Nathan as part of his Christmas present she could feel some weak contractions starting and knew that her time was drawing near and prayed that nothing would delay Adsila from being by her side when the time came for her to deliver.

Nathan was stirring a pot of venison stew the following day, while Sara was mixing the ingredients for some cornbread to go with it, and noticed that the contractions, though mild, were becoming more frequent. While the bread was baking she went and stood looking out the window again and wished that it would stop snowing. The baby suddenly kicked hard diverting her attention, and she could tell from where the baby had kicked that the baby's head was down and ran her hand along her abdomen and was aware the baby was positioned much lower.

Nathan kept an eye on her as she stood thoughtfully staring out the window while he was getting things ready for supper and could sense that there was something Sara was not telling him. When things were ready he walked over to her and wrapped his arms gently around her and asked, "You seem worried, is there something that I should know about?"

Sara turned towards him and hesitated before speaking for she did not want to worry him unnecessarily. "I'm just a little anxious. The baby, I believe, has dropped into the birth canal and I'm starting to get mild contractions. I've been told that these can go on for weeks for some women, but…"

"But it could also mean that you'll go into labor sooner than you were counting on, is that right?" he asked showing great concern.

"Yes, I'm afraid so. Maybe if I sit down and keep my feet up more it will slow things down, but I just don't know if that will help or not," she said showing great apprehension.

"Sara, this is a new experience for both of us. I was here building this house when Elizabeth had our daughter in Boston staying with my parents. But, with everything we have been through together, we will get through this also with God's help. I promise, I won't let you down. I will be with you every step of the way. You're strong, my love, and I'm sure you'll surprise yourself with how well you handle everything when the time comes. Now let's go sit down and have supper, and then I want you to put your feet up for the rest of the evening, okay?"

"Okay, and thanks for not freaking out. I feel much better now that you know what's going on."

Three more days had passed and it had finally stopped snowing. Christmas was just four days away and Sara was happy that they already had their Christmas tree up and decorated, and the fresh garland spread across the fireplace mantle. It was certainly going to be very different from any Christmas she had ever experienced. There was no rushing around from store to store to find the perfect Christmas gift for everyone on her list. No decorating every nook and cranny of the house and hanging outside lights. No pressure to mail out Christmas cards and make sure you had baked enough cookies, pies and cakes, and of course had enough eggnog and hot chocolate on hand. No, this Christmas would be very different. She actually had time to reflect on the true meaning of Christmas, and with her own first baby on the way she could identify with how Mary must have felt.

Since the sun was shining and the snow was mostly melted off the front porch, Sara went out on the porch after breakfast wrapped in a heavy quilt and stared in the direction Inola and Adsila would be coming from. She scanned the horizon in the hopes she would spot them heading their way, even though she knew that was wishful thinking.

"Shouldn't you be sitting inside with your feet up?" Nathan asked as cold vapors escaped from his mouth as he joined her on the porch. He wrapped his arms around her and could feel the baby moving and stretching, and knew that he would be a father again very soon and continued, "It is too cold for you to be outside." He turned her towards him and looked at her with the morning rays of the sun shining on her. "You're so beautiful," he whispered tenderly.

"Beautiful?" she echoed amazed.

"Yes, radiantly beautiful," he smiled and kissed her long and fervently.

She seemed to melt into his arms for it seemed like forever since he had kissed her that way. She missed the passionate and intimate times they shared and wondered if it would ever be the same after the baby was born.

"I'll come inside if you'll kiss me like that again," she said smiling up at him.

Nathan took her by the hand and led her in front of the fireplace and removed the quilt she had wrapped around her and tossed it on the couch. He wrapped one arm around her and cradled the back of her head in his other hand and kissed her more ardently than he had before and continued until she felt like putty in his hands.

"Do you think you can sit on the floor? It is awful hard for us both to fit in my rocking chair anymore." he asked.

"I might need some help getting up," Sara replied and knelt awkwardly on the bearskin rug and finally sat down. Nathan sat behind her leaning against the couch and put his arms around her as she rested up against him perfectly relaxed with her legs reaching the end of the rug. He sang Christmas carols softly to her as his hands rested where he could feel the baby move and could feel her contractions getting stronger and more frequent. He continued to sing as he gently massaged her body, but his mind was praying that Inola and Adsila would hurry up and get there.

Sara could not remember the last time when she had been so happy and content just listening to him sing to her. When he finished the song he was singing she reluctantly said, "You must be tired by now sitting on the floor. If you'll help me get up I'll bring you another cup of coffee."

She rolled over onto her knees and as Nathan took her hand to help her stand, her water broke and she stood there astonished looking at him.

"Is something wrong," he asked nervously.

"My water just broke," she announced looking terrified.

Nathan returned the wide-eyed stare and then asked, "What do you need me to do?"

Sara stopped to think; this was all new to her and she tried to think back to all the articles she had read and the videos she had watched on childbirth over the years, and tried to adapt them to what was available. "Will you put a pot of water on to boil, then bring some towels, washcloths, a sharp knife, and a couple of basins to the bedroom. I'm going to clean up and change into my nightgown and lay down and pray that Adsila gets here PDQ."

Nathan looked at her confoundedly. "PDQ – pretty damn quick," Sara said with a smile and started for the bedroom.

As Sara propped up in bed trying to relax, her mind raced from one thing to another. For one thing: she wished she was now in a hospital where everyone knew what they were doing, and for another she wished that at least her mother, or Adsila, was there to help her. Her contractions quickly intensified after her water broke and she found a focal point and started to breathe like she had seen on a video – he-he-he-who, he-he-he-who until the contraction ended.

Nathan entered the room with an armload full of the things Sara asked him to bring and was baffled by what he heard. "Are you okay?" he asked with a bewildered look and set down the things he was carrying and went and sat next to her on the bed.

Sara's contraction was now over and she answered, "This is how they teach you to breathe in my time when you're having a contraction."

"And that helps?" he asked with a befuddled look.

"It seems to," she replied with a smile and immediately started with the "he-he-he-who" again until the contraction was over. Nathan sat nervously with his heart pounding and thought, *"I'd rather be fighting Tecumseh; at least I knew what I was doing,"* and Sara watched as his jaw tightened.

She placed her hand over his and smiled. She could see how anxious he was and knew that only one of them could freak out at a time. "Please try not to worry; I'm fine. Everything is going as it should, except for Inola and Adsila not being here. Why don't you check on the water to see if it is boiling - you are going to have to sterilize your knife. When you return will you bring me one of the towels and fill one of the basins with cool water; I would appreciate it," she said and started breathing through another contraction.

Nathan was anxious to leave the room and went out on the porch and scanned the horizon hoping to see Inola and Adsila headed his way, but saw no one and quickly went back inside to see if the water was boiling. It was, and he took his knife and held it in the water then placed it inside a clean cloth and returned to the bedroom and brought Sara the towel and basin she asked for.

After five hours the contractions were now a minute apart and Nathan anxiously paced the floor between them and then held her hand as she squeezed it tightly as her breathing became louder and quicker paced. She had Nathan stretch the towel out for when the baby made its grand entrance into the world and pulled up her nightgown and draped it between her knees, and desperately looked at Nathan dreading the next contraction. He soaked a cloth in cold water and wiped the perspiration from her brow and gave her a sip of water wishing there was more that he could do for her. He knew she was in great pain and marveled how she never cried out, but just panted her "he-he-he-who" a little harder, louder, and faster.

The contractions now seemed to follow one after another and Sara, breathing heavily, turned to Nathan and said, "I have to push. Will you help raise me forward until I tell you okay?"

He just nodded breathing heavily himself.

"Ahhhhhh," she cried out and started pushing as Nathan raised her up.

She pushed hard for about ten seconds then said, "Okay," and then rested against her pillow and looked at Nathan hoping to draw some kind of strength or courage from him.

"Ahhhhhh," she groaned and grabbed hold of her knees as she pushed and Nathan supported her back then abruptly cried out, "Keep pushing, Angel, I see the baby's head.

Sara strained and kept pushing for she felt some relief as the head, then shoulders, and finally the baby was lying on the towel crying loudly; then collapsed against the pillows and smiled for she had done it without the doctors, or fancy hospitals, or anything for pain.

Nathan quickly went to the baby and took his knife and severed the cord and proudly declared, "It's a boy!" and wrapped a clean towel around him and gently handed him to Sara.

She held him in her arms and took her finger and pulled the towel back just a little and peered at the most beautiful face she had ever seen and smiled at Nathan and whispered, "My very own little angel, Gabriel." She placed her knuckle to the baby's lips and when he began to suck on it Sara unbuttoned the top to her nightgown and placed Gabriel against her breast.

Nathan sat next to her on the bed relieved that it was all over and gently moved her hair away from her wet brow and kissed her forehead and said, "That's what we'll name him, Gabriel Michael Chambers. How are you feeling, my love? What can I do?"

"I'm fine, just tired," and before she could say anything else they heard horses out front.

"That's probably Inola and Adsila; better late than never I guess," he said with a smile of relief and quickly went to investigate.

Adsila entered the house alone as the men went to take care of the horses. Sara was anxious to try her first conversation in the Cherokee language and called out as she saw her standing just inside the doorway, "Welcome Adsila, I'm so glad you're here. Please come and join me."

Adsila was still a little apprehensive after her first encounter with Sara and slowly came and sat on the bed next to her and looked down at little Gabriel. "I'm sorry we did not make it in time to help, but it appears Nathan did a fine job," she said timidly.

"Oh Adsila, you're wrong. I very much need your help, there is so much I don't know about taking care of a baby," she said, but held back from saying 'during this time period' for only Nathan and Inola knew the truth about her.

Adsila smiled and meekly asked, "May I wash him for you?"

"Yes, but would you do it here by me so I can watch," and scooted over on the bed to give her more room.

Adsila went to her pouch and pulled out a cloth that was filled with a salve and placed it on the table and then went and filled the basin with warm water and picked up a fresh cloth and towel. Taking Gabriel from her arms she laid him on the bed and unwrapped the towel from his little body and Sara rolled to her side and anxiously counted his little toes and fingers for the first time and praised God that her little angel seemed perfectly healthy.

As Adsila gently washed him, Gabriel held on to Sara's finger as his little arms and legs thrashed in the air and seemed perfectly content as his eyes looked dartingly around the room. When she was finished washing him she applied a little salve to his naval and wrapped his body in swaddling cloth and a light blanket that Sara had made and handed him back to her to nurse.

Nathan and Inola finally entered the house and Sara could hear him say to Inola, "Come and meet my son," and covered her breast and had Gabriel ready to hand to Nathan.

He had a big grin on his face as he carefully took his son in his arms and offered him to Inola, who quickly shook his head "no" and held up his hand in refusal. But, Inola moved the blanket back just a little so he could get a good look at him and smiled at Nathan and said, "You have a fine son, my friend, and you did a good job helping Sara."

Inola turned his attention to Sara and she quickly held out her hand towards him which he took and moved closer to her side and said, "I'm glad to see that you are well. You have given my friend a fine son. Inola proud of you," he said with a smile which meant more to Sara than he would ever know.

"Thank you, Inola. I'm so glad you both came, and I hope you can stay with us through Christmas at least."

"We will stay as long as needed," he replied and then continued, "You rest now with little Gabriel while we fix supper, then you join us – not good to lay in bed too long."

Sara smiled and simply said, "Yes, sir," and Nathan reluctantly gave Gabriel back to Sara but not before he kissed him on his forehead.

When supper was ready, Nathan came in and sat on the bed next to Sara and lovingly asked, "Do you feel well enough to join us?"

"I think so, if I take my time. Would you mind putting Gabriel in his cradle; he's asleep," she asked in a whisper and handed Gabriel to him.

Sara stood and was surprised by how everything seemed to have shifted inside her body and took Nathan's arm after taking a couple of steps and looked anxiously at him. "Would you like for me to carry you?" he asked.

"No, Inola would not approve and think that I am weak, but thank you for your kind offer," she said and smiled as she slowly walked with him to the dining table and sat down. She spoke to them in the Cherokee language and thanked them both again for coming and for fixing supper for she was as hungry as a young grizzly bear.

Inola smiled and told Sara, "You speak the people's tongue very well for a beginner."

"I'm glad you think so, now will you pass me another piece of cornbread?" she said beaming with pride.

Nathan sat quietly at the table enjoying the company of his friends and reflecting on the events of the day. He was overwhelmed with emotions having watched his son being born, and how Sara bravely handled many hours of labor without any complaints. His heart was bursting with love for this incredible woman who would endure anything just to be with him. He would treasure this day as long as he lived.

When they were finished eating, Nathan accompanied Sara to her rocking chair and Inola asked, "Adsila, would you bring Sara her gift and show her how to use it?"

Sara was all smiles as Adsila soon returned and knelt by her chair holding a papoose and explained how it was used, as the men watched amused by their excitement.

"Now you will have no excuse for being lazy and sitting around all day with the baby; you can take the baby with you while you do your chores," Inola said with a mischievous smirk knowing that he was pushing her buttons.

Nathan laughed heartily while Sara just gave him one of those looks that let him know that paybacks can be hell, and then suddenly turned her head towards the bedroom and listened carefully.

"I think I hear Gabriel fussing. I'm going to see what my little angel is fussing about then turn in early; it has been a long and memorable day," she said as she stood up slowly. Nathan jumped to his feet and asked, "Do you need my help?"

"No, I'll be fine. You stay with your friends and catch up on all the news," she replied looking into his eyes that were filled with love. He swooped her up in his arms and turned to his friends and said, "I'll be right back. The least I can do is to carry her into the bedroom and give my son a kiss goodnight."

When Nathan finally joined her in the bedroom after making sure Inola and Adsila had settled in for the night, he put another couple of logs on the fire then crawled under the covers and noticed that Sara was still awake. She smiled and gently pulled back the blanket so Nathan could see that Gabriel was still nursing and he lightly stroked the back of his head running his fingers thru his soft, jet black hair.

"I'm hoping he'll sleep for a couple of hours so I can get some sleep," she whispered, then gently picked him up and laid him in his crib by the bed.

The next couple of days seemed to pass by quickly. Nathan and Inola went hunting for their Christmas dinner turkey while Adsila helped Sara with Gabriel and the chores around the house. Their home was filled with laughter, the company of good friends, and the aroma of apple pies baking for their Christmas dinner tomorrow.

Nathan woke early and laid there looking at Sara. He thought back to the first time he saw Sara standing in his living room wide-eyed and scared, and how he resented her complicating his life. He now thanked God for bringing this angel into his life to fill it with love, and looked forward to all the adventures they would have in the future with Gabriel and hopefully a couple more children.

He lightly brushed her hair aside and when he saw her stir he whispered, "Good morning, my love, Merry Christmas."

Sara opened her eyes and smiled looking into his loving eyes. "Merry Christmas," she softly uttered and leaned in and kissed him.

"I'm going to see if Santa came, and give Inola and Adsila a hand getting breakfast ready. Take your time getting dressed and seeing to Gabriel, and I'll come get you when breakfast is ready," he said, then quickly dressed.

When he had closed the bedroom door he noticed that Inola and Adsila had already prepared the turkey for roasting and went to give them a hand preparing breakfast. When all was ready and the candles on the Christmas tree were lit he went to get Sara and Gabriel to join them.

After a good hearty breakfast and all the gifts were opened with their friends, Sara sat silently and contentedly in her chair by the fire as she watched Nathan holding Gabriel in his arms, looking tenderly down at him with unconditional love. At that moment she no longer questioned her decision to live in the 1700s with Nathan; she knew beyond a doubt she was exactly where, in time and place, she was always meant to be.

THE END

Made in the USA
Middletown, DE
06 August 2021